PRAETORIAN OF DORN

'IT MUST BEGIN now, Mal,' said Horus, the words seeming to answer Maloghurst's silent doubts. 'The first shot must be fired now, or it will not land before the true battle begins. Sol must shake in the firmament, and its protectors bleed.'

'He can do it? *He* and his Legion are flawed weapons.'

'He can do it. This is the war they were made for, the war they have been preparing to fight since we began. It is true that he and his sons are flawed, but that is only another reason to use him for this now, while his skills are still relevant.'

Maloghurst bowed his head, his heart unsatisfied but his duty of counsel done.

'As you will it, sire,' he said.

Horus held his gaze on his equerry for a moment, and then turned away, stalking back to his throne. He settled into its embrace with a murmur of armour servos. Cold light from the viewports fell across him, pouring darkness into the recesses of his face and armour.

'We make for Terra,' said the Warmaster, 'and I would see it burning in greeting.'

THE HORUS HERESY®

Other Novels and Novellas

*Many of these titles are also available as abridged and unabridged audiobooks.
Order the full range of Horus Heresy novels and audiobooks from*
blacklibrary.com

Download the full range of Horus Heresy audio dramas from
blacklibrary.com

John French

PRAETORIAN OF DORN

Alpha to omega

BLACK LIBRARY

For Graham, Jim, Nick, Chris, Gav, Dan, Rob and Aaron,
who stood at the beginning of the Age of Darkness.
And for Liz, Laurie, Andy, Alan, Greg and Ead, who held the walls within.

A BLACK LIBRARY PUBLICATION

Hardback edition published in 2016.
This edition published in Great Britain in 2017 by
Black Library,
Games Workshop Ltd.,
Willow Road,
Nottingham,
NG7 2WS, UK.

10 9 8 7 6 5 4 3 2 1

Produced by Games Workshop in Nottingham.
Cover by Neil Roberts.

A CIP record for this book is available from the British Library.

ISBN 13: 978 1 78496 437 5

See Black Library on the internet at

blacklibrary.com

Find out more about Games Workshop
and the world of Warhammer 40,000 at

games-workshop.com

Printed and bound by CPI Group (UK) Ltd, Croydon, CR0 4YY

THE HORUS HERESY®
It is a time of legend.

The galaxy is in flames. The Emperor's glorious vision for humanity is in ruins. His favoured son, Horus, has turned from his father's light and embraced Chaos.

His armies, the mighty and redoubtable Space Marines, are locked in a brutal civil war. Once, these ultimate warriors fought side by side as brothers, protecting the galaxy and bringing mankind back into the Emperor's light.
Now they are divided.

Some remain loyal to the Emperor, whilst others have sided with the Warmaster. Pre-eminent amongst them, the leaders of their thousands-strong Legions are the primarchs. Magnificent, superhuman beings, they are the crowning achievement of the Emperor's genetic science. Thrust into battle against one another, victory is uncertain for either side.

Worlds are burning. At Isstvan V, Horus dealt a vicious blow and three loyal Legions were all but destroyed. War was begun, a conflict that will engulf all mankind in fire. Treachery and betrayal have usurped honour and nobility. Assassins lurk in every shadow. Armies are gathering.
All must choose a side or die.

Horus musters his armada, Terra itself the object of his wrath. Seated upon the Golden Throne, the Emperor waits for his wayward son to return. But his true enemy is Chaos, a primordial force that seeks to enslave mankind
to its capricious whims.

The screams of the innocent, the pleas of the righteous resound to the cruel laughter of Dark Gods. Suffering and damnation await all should the Emperor fail
and the war be lost.

The age of knowledge and enlightenment has ended.
The Age of Darkness has begun.

~ DRAMATIS PERSONAE ~

The VII Legion 'Imperial Fists'

ROGAL DORN	Primarch of the Imperial Fists, Praetorian of Terra
ARCHAMUS	Master of the Huscarls, 'The Last of the First'
SIGISMUND	Lord Castellan of the First Sphere, First Captain, Marshal of the Templars
FAFNIR RANN	Lord Seneschal, Captain of the First Assault Cadre
BOREAS	Sergeant, First Company
HALBRECHT	Lord Castellan of the Second Sphere, Fleet Master
EFFRIED	Lord Castellan of the Third Sphere, Seneschal
CAMBA DIAZ	Lord Castellan of the Fourth Sphere, Siege Master
DEMETRIUS KATAFALQUE	Captain, 344th Company
KESTROS	Sergeant, 65th Squad, 344th Company

The XX Legion 'Alpha Legion'

ALPHARIUS	Primarch of the Alpha Legion
INGO PECH	Captain

MATHIAS HERZOG	Captain
PHOCRON	Headhunter Prime
KEL SILONIUS	Headhunter
KALIX	Headhunter
HEKARON	Headhunter
MYZMADRA	Operative
ASHUL	Operative
INCARNUS	Aventian progression savant
SORK	Agent, captain of the scavenger vessel *Wealth of Kings*
OMEGON	

Imperial Personae

MALCADOR	Regent of the Imperium
SU-KASSEN	Solar Command Staff, former Admiral of the Jovian Fleets
MORHAN	Strategos, 56th Veletaris Tercio, Second Solar Auxilia Cohort (the 'Saturnyne Rams')
CHAYO	Magos, Primary Voice on the *Unbreakable Truth*
ARMINA FEL	Astropath-adjutant to Rogal Dorn
HELIOSA-78	Cult Matriarch of the Selenar
ANDROMEDA-17	Personified-scion of the Selenar

Harrowing

1. *to draw a blade across the land in preparation for seed, the first step towards a final reaping.*

2. *to cause distress, to create panic and suffering, and through such means banish calm and control.*

3. *to break apart and turn over.*

– definition from *The Ten Books of Meaning,*
pre-Unity, author unknown

PROLOGUE

The Command of Serpents

THE GHOST IMAGE collapsed into smoke. A mist of ectoplasm and ash hung in the air. The remains of the astropath lay on the deck, its flesh hissing as it dissolved into an oily foam which clung to its bones. The remains of its green robes looked like a rag pulled from a stagnant river.

Horus Lupercal, Warmaster of a divided Imperium, looked away from the space where the apparition of his brother primarch had stood. Shadows crawled in the lines of his face, and bled from his eyes.

'Will he do it?' asked Maloghurst.

Horus looked back to the collapsed heap that had been the psychic conduit for the audience.

'He will,' said Horus.

'We cannot trust him.'

Horus shook his head.

'We never have been able to trust his word. Cradled in lies, as Rogal once said. He was right about that, at least.'

Maloghurst was silent as the Warmaster looked back to where the ash had begun to settle on the deck.

'I am trusting in his nature, rather than his words,' said Horus, at last.

'He will do what is needed not because I command it, but because it is what he wants, perhaps what he has wanted since before I set the galaxy to burn.'

'He said it would take time to prepare...'

'Time we have,' said Horus quietly.

Maloghurst felt words form on his tongue but struggle to take shape.

'It must begin now, Mal,' said Horus, the words seeming to answer Maloghurst's silent doubts. 'The first shot must be fired now, or it will not land before the true battle begins. Sol must shake in the firmament, and its protectors bleed.'

'He can do it? *He* and his Legion are flawed weapons.'

'He can do it. This is the war they were made for, the war they have been preparing to fight since we began. It is true that he and his sons are flawed, but that is only another reason to use him for this now, while his skills are still relevant.'

Maloghurst bowed his head, his heart unsatisfied but his duty of counsel done.

'As you will it, sire,' he said.

Horus held his gaze on his equerry for a moment, and then turned away, stalking back to his throne. He settled into its embrace with a murmur of armour servos. Cold light from the viewports fell across him, pouring darkness into the recesses of his face and armour.

'We make for Terra,' said the Warmaster, 'and I would see it burning in greeting.'

PART ONE
TERRA

ONE

System transport vessel Primigenia
Outer Terran approaches

'BRING US ONTO the line.'

'Entering the line now.'

'Transmitting clearance.'

'Clearance acknowledged.'

'Hold steady, and make ready for pilot cadre.'

'Hold steady, aye.'

Lieutenant Maecenas V Hon-II let the voices from the bridge wash across him. He sat on the throne of the second attendant deck officer, feet on the lapis and bronze instrument console, arms crossed across the rippled blue and yellow of his uniform. His eyes were closed, and his chin rested on his chest.

All the command crew knew that this was the most likely position to find Maecenas in when he was on second attendance. They would not bother him, even though anyone else sleeping on watch would have been shackled, electro-whipped and left in the brig for the journey back to Jupiter. Not Maecenas, though; he was of the Consanguinity. Everyone else on the ship was oath or marriage bonded at best. That meant that Maecenas had the right to do as he pleased. After all, in a very real sense, the ship almost belonged to him. Had his uncle, or his first cousin, come onto the ship and told him to take his feet off the console, he would have obeyed, but the polar Shoal-city stations were a long way away in the wrong direction, and getting no closer. So the crew let him sleep through his watch. It was better than him being awake after all.

He was awake, though. He was always awake.

From behind his eyelids Maecenas watched the command crew prepare for the pilot cadre. They had all done this so many times that well-worn routine had replaced indignance. System-wrights began to power down their stations. Chromed neural cables snaked from their scalps to ducts in the floor. Their skin was almost translucent under the glow of their instruments. Wide, black eyes watched data values change on screens, and long-fingered hands made fine adjustments. All were Jovian bred, and most had never felt the pull of a planet's surface or breathed unfiltered air.

The *Primigenia* was a Jovian trading barge, a little over five kilometres from prow to stern. She had been born in the Shoal-cities above Jupiter's pole, and had swum the solar voids for twenty-eight generations. Her engines and systems were not the products of Mars, but the secrets of the void clans saved from the darkness of Old Night. In times past she had hauled plunder from the edges of the system, and traded with the warlords of Terra. Now she was one link in a chain of ships spooling through the system's inner and outer reaches. Filled with supplies she passed through controlled corridors of space until she docked at one of the Throneworld's outer void stations, and unloaded her cargo. Rogal Dorn might have barred its gates, but Terra's hunger could never be sated. So, the *Primigenia* and her sisters made their way to and from Terra again and again, like laden mules to the gates of a citadel.

'We are at dead stop. Monitor craft coming alongside,' said one of the crew.

Maecenas watched the ship's master glance at the first attendant and nod.

'Extend docking gantries,' called First Attendant Sur Nel Hon-XVII. She was Maecenas' second cousin by oath, and he made a show of holding both that connection and her rank in contempt. She hated him in return. That was good. It stopped her noticing anything else about him.

'Pilot cadre on board. Looks like a full inspection force,' Sur Nel muttered, as data scrolled across her visor.

The shipmaster let out a long breath and shook his head.

'This is not going to move quickly.'

'It never does,' replied Sur Nel.

Behind his closed eyes, Lieutenant Maecenas V Hon-II began to count the seconds, one after another.

Gobi tox-wastes

Terra

THEY RODE AHEAD of the dawn light, the crawler shaking, the smell in the crew compartment getting worse by the second. It had been eighteen hours since they had left the settlement at the edge of the tox-plateau. Eighteen hours of twelve humans sitting and sweating in a metal box while the night passed by unseen.

Most of the scavenger contingent had started the journey with jokes and attempts at conversation. That had stopped when it became clear that Myzmadra and her two colleagues were not interested in being friendly. The scavs had retreated into silence, fiddling with their weaponry and equipment. They were all big, all vat-graft muscle and crude augmetics. They had a lot of scars too: jagged craters from bullets, pale splashes from acid burns, and furrows from knife cuts. Most of them wore what armour they had over bare skin, as though daring anyone who fought them to give them a new scar. They smelt of gun oil, sump liquor and greed.

Myzmadra looked at the triangulator on her wrist, and frowned. Cogs whirled and bubbles of mercury shifted behind the crystal casing.

'What is that thing?' growled the scav sat opposite her. She looked up. He was a big one. The rest of the gang called him Grol. He had a drill hammer instead of a right arm, and a pair of machine claws bonded to his spine. His face was red chrome above his teeth, and he had slots for eyes. She looked back down at the triangulator without replying.

'It's a triangulator.' She looked up again to see who had spoken. The scav boss, who had said his name was Nis, grinned back at her. She caught the glint of the silver inlay in his ceramite teeth. His eyes were cones of focusing lenses, and his hands were spiders of brass. His grin widened. 'Clever little piece of archeotech. Lets you find somewhere even though the rad is bad out here and the signal storms are worse. Worth its weight...'

He let the word hang on the edge of his grin.

She held his gaze. The rest of her was utterly still, the fingers of her right hand poised above the triangulator. Inside her body glove she tensed muscle groups, and let the breath settle to the bottom of her lungs. She was poised, a single reflex away from movement, while outside of her skin nothing had moved.

She held Nis' gaze. He raised his brass hands.

'Just joking,' he said, grinning wider. 'After all, you pay the likes of us to come out here and dig, you got to have something worth finding, and a way to find it, right?'

She nodded, and looked back down to the spinning cogs and mercury.

Numbers had started to tick around the edge of the triangulator.

'Close,' said Ashul softly from beside her. She hadn't even realised he was awake. He had folded his hands over his chest and gone to sleep just after they had left the settlement, not moving since. 'And right on time too,' he said, pulling his rebreather mask down over his face.

She took a mask from the rack behind her, and gave the figure on the other side of her a nudge.

'I am quite awake,' said Incarnus. 'How I could be thought to be otherwise under the circumstances is to stretch imagination to its outer tolerance.' He ran his fingers over his scalp, and Myzmadra could see a skim of moisture on his skin. He blinked, grey lids flicking over iris-less eyes. She handed him the mask.

The scav gangers had noticed them getting ready and were already racking weapons, and plugging breath filters into their mouths. Those that had mouths.

She pulled her own mask on and flicked the visor's outer layer to black. Beside her, Incarnus flicked a hand at the triangulator.

'On time,' he said.

Bhab Bastion
The Imperial Palace, Terra

ARCHAMUS WOKE AND came off the stone of his bed in a single movement.

'Threat report...' The order began in his throat, and died on his tongue. His hearts were hammers inside his ribs.

The cool gloom of his chamber answered him with silence.

He looked around. The night sky looked back at him through a firing slit in the wall above him. Besides that the only light came from the candle which sat in a niche above the bed. Hours and minutes were marked as lines and numbers on the tallow. One hour remained between the flame and the midnight line. He had slept for thirty minutes. Just enough for dreams to begin, but not enough for him to remember them.

His bolter was heavy in his hands, drawn and armed even as he woke. Slowly he tried to let his muscles relax. He could feel his blood fizzing. Behind his eyes he felt the static sensation as his mind caught up with his nerves. The bionics of his right leg clicked and hissed as his weight shifted.

Thirty minutes. Thirty minutes in which the world had turned, and his eyes had been closed. His ears strained for the sound of running feet, of sirens.

Nothing.

Just the beat of blood in his hearts and the distant crackle of dust blowing into the void shields high above the bastion's walls. The machine rack holding the pieces of his armour sat silent in the space before the door. Its readout lights blinked green. His arming servitors stood at the edges of the room.

He let out a breath and lowered the gun. Aching weariness crawled back into his muscles.

Thirty minutes. It had been the most sleep he had managed in months, a necessity rather than the luxury it felt like. The catalepsean node at the back of his brain let him defer the need to sleep, but he could not outrun fatigue forever. So, he had let himself sleep fully, and tried not to think of it as weakness.

He took a step to the granite bowl of water on a shelf opposite the bed. The servos in his bionic arm clicked as he set the bolter down. A thread of cold air ran across his skin. Night stole what little heat clung to the air this high up, and the firing slit held no glass to keep it out. Ice had formed on the surface of the water in the bowl. He plunged his right hand through it, and scooped the liquid onto his face. The cold was reassuring in its sharpness. The water in the bowl settled, ripples stilling, pieces of ice knocking against the bowl's lip.

For a second he found himself looking down at fragments of his face reflected in the water. Time and service had left their marks on him, both within and without.

Old and worn, he thought, as his eyes traced the tangle of lines and scars on his cheeks. His beard had been the grey of slate for four decades, but now there was a hint of chalk at the edges. He looked at the three studs bonded to the left of the brow. All of them were jet, black as the void, each a half-century of war in an unkind age.

He scooped up another handful of water, and the reflection vanished in fresh ripples. He straightened.

'Armour,' he said.

Three servitors stepped from the edge of the room. All were hunched, their backs bent beneath haloes of mechanical arms. Brass visors with cruciform holes for eyes covered their faces. Black robes hung over what remained of their flesh. They lifted the first pieces of armour from the armature, disconnecting power feeds and slotting components together.

They clad him layer by layer, riveting each plate in place, connecting wires, sealing ports. At last they stepped back and he stood, burnished yellow gleaming in the candlelight. The star of Inwit sat on his chest, moulded from silver and gold, its rays clasped in a fist of jet. A black-and-red cloak trimmed with ice lion fur hung from his shoulder. His mono-eyed, Crusade-mark helmet was locked to his waist, leaving his face bare. He felt the usual twinge in his nerves as the connections to his bionic limbs asserted themselves fully.

He took up his weapons from the rack, locking his bolter to one thigh, his bolt pistol to the other, and fastening a broad-bladed seax to his hip. Last of all, he lifted *Oathword* in his bionic hand, metal fingers clacking on its adamantium haft. Its head was fashioned from black stone that he had mined from the dead world of Stroma, and shaped over the course of a year. The ball of the pommel was half silver and half black iron, etched with the star constellations of Inwit. It was heavy but in his machine grasp its weight was nothing. He looked at it for a second, noting the crystal flecks shimmering beneath the stone's surface. Unbreakable, almost unworkable: a stone that defied the universe by its existence. He nodded and touched the mace's head to his scalp, then he locked it to his war-plate with a snap of magnetic force.

He walked from the chamber into the gloom of the corridor outside. A gust of air ran past him and the light of the torches burning in the wall brackets billowed. He began to walk. The signals array in the collar of his armour started chiming, and vox transmissions began to fill his ears. He could hear every military signal in a sphere of space that extended ten kilometres in every direction, and up to the edge of Terra's atmosphere. His mind sifted the information, building patterns of strength and weakness. The Huscarl squad assigned to the primarch's person was in place. The second and third security cordons were spread throughout the bastion. Beyond that, forty-six Legion units moved through the Palace on carefully randomised patterns. Other forces were reporting nothing that gave him pause. Everything was as it needed to be.

His eyes moved over the stones of the passages and stairwells as he climbed towards the command chamber. It was an ugly creation, both in intent and in execution. Chisel marks cut the faces of the granite walls, and its crenellations bit the air like bared teeth. It was a brutish, unrepentant creation in Archamus' eyes. He had wondered, once, if perhaps its makers had not intended it to last, but simply to endure through the trials of some lost age. Endure it had. He could not deny that.

What will endure of what we have made? he wondered, and walked on while a palace waiting for war whispered in his ears.

Damocles Starport

Terra

INNIS NESSEGAS HATED the night, but it was all he got to see. The hours of his oversight had been allocated to his father when the old man – long dead now – had ascended to the position of third prefect of the Southern Transport Arterial Lock. There were two other prefects who watched over the system of doors, hoists and loading platforms: one of them for the day, one of them straddling the sunset. They, just like Nessegas, had inherited their positions, and their times of watch. Sometimes he wondered if either of the two envied him the night, but more often he was sure that they pitied him.

Seen at a distance, the port was a jumbled mountain of metal. Landing platforms jutted from its sides, some large enough to take a macro-lander. Shuttle craft arrived and left without cease, buzzing like bees around a hive. Nessegas never saw them. His world was far beneath the landing platforms and the layers of storage chambers. But even down at the roots of Damocles, the patterns of activity were the same. Bulk haulers and caravans of cargo-crawlers came and went at every hour. The time they spent in the Southern Transport Arterial Lock belonged to Nessegas.

Vehicles entered the lock through one set of doors – some fifty metres high – and entered its first cavern, where gangers off-loaded the cargo. Once that process was complete, the vehicles passed into a second cavern, and then out into the world again. Nessegas knew that the system was called a lock after an ancient method of allowing ships to pass between rivers of water. He did not know if the comparison was a good one. He had never seen a ship, or a river.

Fifteen hundred men, women and servitors worked to cycle the cargo to and from the vehicles. Fifty-one sub-prefects, seventy-four divisional sub-prefects and seven hundred overseers supervised those gangs, and all reported to Nessegas. From his cupola, suspended beneath the roof of the first cavern, he watched as vehicles came and went. Gangers and crew moved over and around them like insects over food. Blue data flicked across the retina of his left eye from the projector mounted on his cheekbone. His face twitched. The projector had never functioned properly and would regularly send a shock through the nerves of his face. But it was what the data was telling him that he really did not like.

He reached out and depressed a key on the brass console in front of him. Static crackled in his ears.

'Cohort thirty-three, you are five minutes and thirty-three seconds behind timetable,' he said.

'*Apologies, worthy prefect,*' replied an overseer. '*It's the inspection crews. They want to go through this whole load. They can't go any faster.*'

'That is not my problem, but it is increasingly yours. The loss margin on that freight is being deducted from the cohort's wealth-ration and will continue to be until this blockage has cleared.'

Another crackle of static. Nessegas could almost hear the invective it hid.

'*As you decree, worthy prefect.*'

He clicked the vox-link off and glanced around at the other figure in the cupola. She had heard the overseer's words just like him, but if she cared she said nothing. Her face was just as bland and controlled as ever. She wore the red-and-black uniform of the Damocles Port Militia, and the silver swords pinned to her collar said she was an Ojuk-agha First Class. She had said her name was Sucreen. He had never seen her before, but that was not unusual; the security protocols put in place by the will of the Praetorian of Terra meant that there was always an officer of the militia with him in the lock-control, and two hundred militiamen were present in the caverns at all times. They were never the same unit, and the officer who watched him had only been the same ten times in the six years since the protocols came into force. The militia watched, checked and searched cargos at random. It was worse when they had one of the Imperial Fists with them. Then all latitude disappeared, along with any hope of him meeting his quotas. Not that Nessegas said a word in objection. Not when one of the sons of Dorn was present, at least.

He glanced down to where a caravan was being dismantled under the eyes and guns of a dozen militiamen. Behind it a five-section crawler was just rolling through the doors. He recognised the heraldry of the Hysen Cartel and muttered a curse to himself. Even one of the crawler's sections would hold close to a thousand tonnes of cargo. The chances of clearing it through the lock within the time contracted to the Hysen Cartel seemed remote. The flow rate for the night traffic was already the subject of acute personal embarrassment to Nessegas. If it carried on getting worse it would become a matter of censure.

'Are you going to be searching with this degree of thoroughness from now on?' he said, turning to Sucreen.

She met his gaze, shrugged, but said nothing.

Nessegas suppressed an urge to scream. He was considering what he could say, when Sucreen frowned.

'What is that?' she asked, looking over his shoulder. He turned back to his console. A light was flickering amber amongst the dots of green. Nessegas bent over it and allowed himself another muttered oath.

'Air circulation fault,' he replied. 'Third time in the last division.'

He began keying a request in to the console, the keys clacking down on their arms as he jabbed at them. It was pointless; the red priests would not respond to his summons, and if they did it would most likely be several hours later.

'Is it severe?' asked Sucreen.

'We will still be able to breathe,' he said, and then added to himself, 'though if you were to suffocate, I would not complain.'

'What?'

'Nothing,' he said. 'It's just a cold-drain, that's all.'

Sucreen nodded. Born and raised in the starport, she had grown up with the cold-drains. They were as much a factor of life as the taste of the water and the stink of machine oil. Sometimes a ventilation sluice connecting two volumes of the starport jammed open. Air flowed up and out of the deep areas, drawn into the rest of the port structure. In a deep area – like the Southern Transport Arterial Lock – that meant that the temperature would drop to near freezing. Uncomfortable, but nothing to worry about.

Down in the cavern beneath the cupola, the Hysen Cartel crawler came to a halt. Behind it, the outer doors began to close.

The Underworld
Terra

THE DARK AT the root of the world was like no other. It pressed against the eyes and ate any light that tried to banish it. It stretched silence and made thunder of the smallest noise. It had a soul, and that soul was unkind. Of that the youth was certain.

He waited, crouched on the edge of the fissure. It was best to wait. He had learned that quickly. The others had not. They were with the dark now. He alone remained.

How long ago had that been? There were no days down here, and so perhaps there was no time. The darkness ate that too. How old was he now? He did not know that either. Certainly his father had called him young, and his father had been the last person he had spoken to, but how long ago he did not know. His father had not learned about the dark. It had taken him soon after they fled down to the root of the world.

He let out a breath, very slow, quiet enough not to disturb the dark, and slid into the fissure. It would take him some time to reach the bottom. No matter how many times he came back, this last descent got no easier. The place he was going to had only one way to reach it: a climb down a sheer drop without light or stair to guide the way.

There was endless dark piled above him, days and days of it, all the way up to the light and sky. In that realm he had touched and seen strange things: iron bridges crossing gorges without roads leading to or from them; glowing snakes swimming in lakes of water that went down and down, past drowned windows and doors. But nothing compared to what waited for him at the bottom of this climb. He had given it a name. He called the place the Revelation.

The depths held the remains of the civilisations that had failed before He had come to save mankind from itself. The underworld was a borderland between the divine and the mundane. That was why they had fled here, because in the dark they could be safe, and close to their God. And the Revelation was a door into the sacred realm. It was the dream that had kept them alive as they fled the iconoclasts: that by going down into the dark they would find light.

Light.

There was a light below him, at the bottom of the fissure.

He blinked. The light was dim, but to his eyes it was like a scream in a silent room. It was green and diffuse, as though he was only seeing its edge.

He waited, trying to control his breathing, and the sudden racing of his heart.

There had been no light before, but this meant that something else had found his secret. He knew it would happen eventually. As soon as he had made the Revelation his own, losing it became inevitable.

He thought about climbing up the fissure, and running into the dark and never coming back. He thought about it while his blood beat in his ears, and the glow beneath him filled his eyes.

The light vanished.

He waited.

It did not return.

Perhaps it had not been there at all. Perhaps he was just so afraid of losing the Revelation that he had imagined it. Perhaps it had been a ghost in his eyes.

Slowly, finger by finger, inch by inch, he began to descend again. At the bottom of the fissure he stopped. A gulf waited beneath him, just as it had the first time, just as it always did.

He jumped.

A brief rush of air, the silent scream of panic as he fell...

And then smooth stone slammed into him as he landed and rolled. He came to his feet, eyes sweeping around him. There was no light, no waiting beast.

Yes, it must have been his imagination: not a real light. He stood and edged forwards, feeling the seams in the stone floor with his feet. When he reached the wall, his hands found the missing block, and the handle within the space. A tug, a low grinding, and then the light. Not a phantom in the dark this time, but a narrow line of orange.

He knelt. His fingers were trembling as he pulled the crack wider.

He looked through.

Fragments of light fell down to him, and he had to close his eyes. The sound of dripping water filled his ears, and the smell of rust and damp filled his nose. He waited for the blindness and stinging to fade, and then opened his eyes and looked into the realm of his God.

A tangle of debris covered a stone floor on the other side of the door. Moulds covered every inch, some green, some white. Pools of liquid reflected the light that fell down the shaft above. Stairs and balconies marched up and up above him. All of those he could see were in the slow process of collapsing. Doorways opened off into other dark holes. But further up there was light – yellow, golden light.

'The God-Emperor watches,' he whispered, his eyes watering as he stared up at the light of the Revelation.

This was what his father had wanted to be close to but had never seen. This was what kept him alive in the dark. Somewhere high up above him was the heart of the Imperial Palace. Up there – beyond the light – the chosen hands of the Emperor lived, and did His will.

'The God-Emperor watches,' he said again. The tears were rolling down his face.

When he had first found the door he had thought it chance, but of course it was not. How could it be? A door from the dark into the fortress of a living god: how could such a thing exist by chance? No, this was not chance. It was a blessing, a gift to the faithful who could come this far. He had not found it. It had been given to him. He was never alone. He was never scared. He was blessed, for he could see the light of divinity.

The rest of the prayer his father had taught him came to his lips.

'The God-Emperor sees all,' he said. 'His hand lies upon all of us. The Emperor protects.'

He stopped, the rest of the words hanging on his tongue. The skin of his arms prickled. He looked behind him, at the edge of the light from the open door. Blackness looked back at him, flat and unmoving. He turned his head. The memory of the light he had thought he had seen rose in his mind. But that had not been real. It had been his fear, and he had no need to–

Hands came out of the dark, and broke his neck in a single movement.

Storage Vault 62/006-895
The Imperial Palace, Terra

THE WARRIOR WITH no name came to life, and began to drown.

Thick liquid was all around him, filling his lungs, wrapping his limbs, strangling him even as his hearts began to beat again. He could not see.

He could not move. His body was folded, legs pressed against his chest, arms over his head. He struck out. Something hard met his hands.

Questions and needs roared through his mind.

Who am I?

He needed to move.

Where am I?

He needed to breathe.

What is happening?

The questions screamed on unanswered. He did not know. He did not know anything.

He needed...

...to stop.

Calmness flooded him, blotting out every other instinct and thought. He let the stillness hold him for an instant, and then let his thoughts move again, one at a time.

He could remember nothing: not how he had come to be where he was, not why he was there, not his name.

But he knew that he needed to stay still, and calm. The truth that he needed would come.

He waited, his hearts beating so slowly that they seemed not to beat at all.

Understanding came piece by piece, appearing like the remains of a wrecked ship floating to the surface of a sea.

He had been dead. He had been curled in the dark, not breathing, not a flicker of blood, nor pulse of a nerve signal moving through him. He had been that way for a long while. Now he had woken. There was a reason for that, and for the oblivion he had slept in. He could feel the answers just out of sight but getting closer. Other information came first.

He was in a metal tank. Its sides were airtight and made of plas-teel. At its thinnest point the walls were 7.67 centimetres thick. The fluid filling the tank was the liquefied residue of bioprocessing in the nutri-factories of the Somon Prime orbital city. The tank was one of several hundred stacked together in a storage vault beneath the Imperial Palace on Terra. The Palace might be under the watch of the Custodian Guard, and the stewardship of Rogal Dorn, but the millions within its walls still needed to eat in a time of siege. The stores held by the Palace had increased tenfold in preparation. That had been his way in.

Curled inside his tank – floating in a soup of rendered flesh and biomatter – he had passed down through the transport chain from Terra's orbital docks, and through the layers of the Palace's security. Each time the biometric reader fields had passed over the tank they had detected nothing besides dead matter. No pulse, no bioelectric field, no shadow of life. Once inside the Palace, the tank had been stored. He had lain within his temporary tomb and time had passed, time that had now expired.

Slowly he flexed his fingers. Their tips brushed the mechanism welded to the inside of the tank. There was no room for him to turn or move his arms, but he did not need to; the mechanism was just where his fingers would find it.

A flex of force, and then a low clunk echoed through the liquid around him.

He went still. This was a dangerous moment, when he was at his most vulnerable. Gently he pushed upwards with his legs. They met the lid of the tank, and he felt it shift. Stillness again. A rebalancing of muscles. He pushed again, and the lid rose. As it did, he twisted over, switching the pressure on the lid between legs and arms.

Information was still coming to him from the fog of memory. The images of holo-projected plans and pict-captures were suddenly bright and sharp in his mind.

He pushed the lid to the side, and his head broke the surface of the liquid. His eyes snapped open. A vast chamber extended away before him. Columns rose from the floor to meet a vaulted roof. Pyramidal stacks of cubes sat between the columns. Stencilled numbers ran down the floor between them. There was no light source, but his eyes gathered the scraps that there were and let him see. Nothing moved. Long moments passed.

At last he let himself rise from beneath the surface.

Still nothing moved.

He let himself vomit up fluid from his lungs, then took his first breath of new life. The bio-soup in the tank smelt foul, a mixed organic and chemical reek that would cling to him for hours.

He looked around, reading angles and the numbers on the floor, tasting the temperature in the air. He suddenly knew that he had to move. There was an access door, three kilometres away. He knew each of its code-lock settings. Once he was past that, there was a stair up one level, then a diversion through an air duct. He would have to break through three gratings, but unless they were fitted with very sophisticated alarms he would not need to change his route. There were other routes, of course – forty-three of them, all mapped from multiple sources, and as clear in his mind as if he had already walked them. He had twenty-three minutes and four seconds to be at his first waypoint.

He reached back into the tank and felt the metal sides, until he found the two objects that he knew would be there. A tug, and they came free of the side of the tank. The blades were silver-black, double-edged, without grip or guard, like the shards of a broken sword. He flicked them free of slime. He understood their balance instantly. A more complex weapon would have risked detection by deep auspex scan, but the blades stuck to the inside of the tank were invisible to such methods.

He replaced the tank's lid, climbed down and began to run. He made no sound, and he moved without disturbing the gloom.

In his mind the seconds flicked past.

As he reached the door out of the chamber the answer to the first question he had asked came to him, as memory gave him a name.

Silonius, he thought. *I am Silonius.*

TWO

System transport vessel Primigenia
Outer Terran approaches

MAECENAS CAME TO his feet as the pilot cadre approached the *Primigenia*'s bridge. He had ended his show of sleep when the muster alarm sounded.

The seconds remaining in his mental count were vanishing.

First Attendant Sur Nel stared at him as he smoothed his hair and arranged his tabard. Contempt bled from her gaze. He smiled back. There was very little about what he was doing that involved anything as petty as spite, but he let himself have a second of pleasure at the thought that he would soon not have to smile at her at all.

'Attend,' the shipmaster called, as the main doors to the bridge began to open. All the bridge crew stiffened where they stood. Maecenas and Sur Nel both looked to the shipmaster. He was facing the doors, chin raised and eyes steady, the spun silver of his tabard hanging from his thin frame, the bones of his face sharp beneath his black eyes.

Maecenas' silent count flicked through one of its last seconds.

The pilot cadre marched onto the bridge, ten figures in two lines. Plasteel armour plating clad their chests, the backs of their arms and shins. Domed pressure helmets covered their heads. On their shoulders, the heraldry of the Saturnyne Rams Second Solar Auxilia Cohort sat on its white-and-blue field. Maecenas knew their reputation. These were elite troops raised to do war on ships and void stations. Much of the work of overseeing supply vessels approaching Terra had fallen to them in the last years.

A low buzz filled the air as the auxiliaries spread out across the bridge. The arc rings of their volkite chargers were glowing.

Last to enter was an officer. The rank chevrons on his shoulder proclaimed him a strategos of the elite Veletaris. He held a data-slate rather than a weapon, and the visor of his helm was hinged up, exposing a scarred but handsome face. He glanced briefly at the shipmaster.

'You are Shipmaster Hys Nen Castul Hon-XXIX,' said the strategos. 'This vessel is the *Primigenia*, bonded to the Oberon Consanguinity, and bearing mixed cargos from outer gulf station Epiphus under writ and instruction for the supply of Terra.' The strategos looked up. His eyes were pale gold. 'Can you confirm that these details are correct?'

Out of the corner of his eye Maecenas saw the shipmaster frown. The rivalry and distrust between the Saturnyne Ordo and the Jovian Void Clans was as old as the turning of the planets. Two centuries of alliance under the rule of the Emperor had reduced the rancour between the old enemies, but not removed it.

'I can confirm that the details you have related to me are correct,' said the shipmaster, with a stiff bow of his head. 'In honour and loyalty I welcome you on board.'

The strategos looked down at his data-slate. As he did his eyes flicked at Maecenas.

The mental count of seconds reached zero.

The exchange of hand signals looked like nothing.

'Good,' said the strategos. He drew and fired his pistol so fast that Maecenas did not have time to blink. The volkite beam hit the shipmaster in the chest and reduced him to ashes. Sur Nel managed to begin a shout before the beam flicked out again. The rest of the troops began firing a second later.

It was over within a minute. The communication controllers died first, before their screams had even sounded. The rest followed.

The strategos turned to Maecenas as the sound of the last shot faded. A smell of static and burning filled the air.

'We are on schedule?' asked the strategos.

'Yes,' replied Maecenas. He was already moving to the primary engine control.

'The cargo was substituted correctly?'

'Yes. It is exactly as required.'

'And the ship's course?'

Maecenas frowned as dials spun under his fingers as he worked the engine controls. Now that he was here it felt strange. He'd thought that he would feel something more, some form of exultation. But he felt nothing, just hollow, as though he were about to lose something by finally casting off his false life and beginning anew. He turned another dial, and watched as a set of brass hands clicked around to the red segment of an ivory circle set into the helm control. Beneath his feet he felt a rumble as the *Primigenia's* engines lit, and the ship began to accelerate through the void again.

'It's moving, course as before. They will notice something is wrong eventually, but by then...'

'It won't matter,' the strategos said, and nodded. 'Good,' he said, raised his pistol and fired once. Lieutenant Maecenas V Hon-II managed to open his mouth before his last words were blown to dust.

Gobi tox-wastes
Terra

THE RAD-WOLVES LEAPT into the glare. The light of the melta-torches caught the wet sharpness of their teeth. Myzmadra watched as a rad-wolf the size of a horse landed five paces away. Scales surrounded rows of red eyes running down the side of its muzzle. The rest of its pack bounded forwards behind it, hunger and instinct driving them towards the light and the smell of flesh. Myzmadra tilted her head, eyes steady, arms folded. One of the wolves snarled, muscle coiling under iridescent fur, then leapt.

The rotor cannon screamed from behind her. The rad-wolf became a spray of liquid and meat. A torrent of tracer fire panned across the pack of wolves for a few seconds. Blood lacquered the rocks where the beasts had been.

'You want to help next time?' said Nis, as he stepped up next to her. The exoskeleton, wrapped around the scav boss' torso, hissed as he moved. The barrel of his rotor cannon was still spinning down. The ammo feed leading from the hoppers on his back clinked against his legs. 'You know how to use those, right?' he said, nodding at her holstered guns.

'If I did that kind of thing myself what would I be paying you for?' she said, and turned away.

The glare of melta-torches fizzed in her sight from where the scavengers were cutting into the hardpan. The crawler was drawn up on the other side of the dig site. She could see the silhouette of a figure standing on the vehicle's roof, looking out towards the night on the other side. Like Nis, the sentry was wearing a crude exoskeleton and carrying a serious piece of weaponry. The rad-wolves had been coming at them ever since they got out of the crawler. When the scavs had started ripping into the crust layer, even more of them had come.

'It's the smell,' Nis had said, once the first two packs had been cut down. 'They can smell the dust and the burn from the torches. Makes them hungry. Makes them come looking to eat.'

She squinted at the excavation. The pit was a ragged bite into the plateau's surface, twenty metres across at its widest point, and five deep. Rock dust and powdered crystal sprayed up in the glare from the melta beams. The scavs were outlines in the haze. They knew their business, though; she had to give them that. They worked without stopping and even though they seemed to dig, drill and cut like starved beasts tearing into food, they were careful.

She looked up as Incarnus came to stand beside her. Face hidden by the visor of his breath mask, limbs coated in a dark red body glove, he seemed even more like an insect than normal. He nodded down at the scavs in the pit.

+Yes, they are more precise and careful than you would think from looking at them, aren't they?+ he said, his voice a purr in her skull.

She tensed, and felt her skin prickle against the inside of her body glove.

Get out of my head! she thought, pouring as much loathing into it as she could.

Incarnus laughed, tilting his head back and then shivering. There was something smooth and unpleasant about the movement.

+My apologies,+ he said, still in her mind, and she felt clammy heat crawl over her scalp. +Anyway, your kind are so dull. So many safeguards and mental cut-outs. I would have to do some damage to do anything really interesting.+

Get. Out, she thought, carefully. *Or do you want me to see if I can shoot you before you can stop me reaching my guns?*

He recoiled as though struck.

+You would not dare. The operation...+

You should know that there is always another way, Incarnus. Redundancy, that's how we do things. .

He raised a hand, and she heard him take a breath to say something else.

A cry rose from the pit. She turned and saw that the glare from the melta beams had dimmed. The scavs were clustering around something still hidden by the curtains of dust and vapour. She stepped forwards and jumped down into the pit. As though conjured up from the air, Ashul was at her side. Incarnus followed a pace behind. The scavs cleared a path as they crossed the bottom of the pit, casting puzzled glances at each other.

'Light,' she shouted, and a stab-beam swung over her as she bent down next to the path of bare metal they had uncovered. She brushed her hands across the dull surface, fingers searching. After a few seconds she found an edge, and then a corner. She looked up at Incarnus, ignoring the stares of the scav gangers.

'Is it them?' she said across their private vox.

'Can't say,' said Incarnus, who bent down and placed his hand on the flat metal next to hers.

'You can't say?' growled Ashul.

'If it is them, they are barely alive.' Incarnus shrugged, patting the dust from his gauntlets as he stood. 'No thoughts. No dreams. No little sparks of consciousness for me to sense.'

Myzmadra looked down at the exposed metal.

'Get this out,' she said, her voice loud on the night air. 'There should be nine more close by. Be very careful. Any of them get damaged, and you don't get paid. Any of them get destroyed, I have your boss' agreement that half of you die.'

They did as she asked.

The wolves came four more times while the scavs dug, and the rotor cannon chattered into the dark. She did not look around to watch the slaughter. Nis knew his business, and besides she found she could not look away as the metal blocks emerged from the earth. They found the other nine, one after another, and dug around them until they could lever them out.

Eventually, ten blocks of dull metal sat on the hardpan, studded with bolts and crossed by reinforcement struts. Five were cubes, a metre square. The other five were large iron caskets.

She nodded to Ashul.

'Begin,' she said. 'We are running lean on time.'

They started to work on the first block, removing covers from the sockets dotting the sides of the caskets. Incarnus attached tubes and wires to the ports and linked them to the pumps and vials they had brought in the crawler, hissing words to himself as he worked. Myzmadra and Ashul left him to it, and began to cut open the welded seams on the five metal cubes with compact lascutters.

Some of the scavs paused to watch them.

'Better hope this works as it should,' muttered Ashul, as he glanced at the gangers. 'Or we are going to have to get creative.'

Incarnus was linking fluid feeds and power to the last casket.

'It is them,' called Incarnus. 'First one is almost conscious. I can feel his thoughts firing.'

Myzmadra looked at the horizon. Pale light had crept into the corners of the sky.

'How long?' she asked.

'Five minutes,' said Incarnus, 'perhaps thirty, maybe fifty. As much of a miracle as this is, it is not... *precise*, nor without complications. Their bodies and minds have to reconstruct awareness, humours must rebalance, and nerves have to mesh with muscle. Oblivion must become waking.'

'Hope that it is fast and less poetic,' said Myzmadra, her eyes on the figure that had joined the rest of the scavengers.

'What is all this wonder from beneath the earth, then?' asked Nis, as he walked towards Myzmadra. His exoskeleton clanked with each step, the feed for the rotor cannon tapping against the frame.

'What you were paid to help us find,' she replied. 'Shouldn't you be watching for wolves?'

'They don't come when the light comes back to the sky,' said Nis. He moved to where the metal cubes and caskets lay on the ground.

'I am wondering something,' he said, his voice soft. 'These things are big. Serious heft to them. But we ain't got a crawler to haul this weight and the rest of us, and the gear.' He stopped beside one of the casket-like blocks. 'So I am guessing that the boxes are just to keep it safe. Must be real valuable to be kept so safe.' He reached out and laid his hand on the metal. Brass digits whirred as they tapped the surface lightly. 'Open it.'

'The agreement—' began Myzmadra. Incarnus was motionless next to one of the caskets. Ashul had faded away out of sight.

'Open it!' The rotor cannon spun up. Around them rock drills whined to life, and melta-torches lit as the scavs closed the circle around them.

Myzmadra nodded slowly. Inside, under her stillness, she began to tense and relax muscles in sequence. She turned her head to Incarnus and flicked a hand at the casket he stood next to. The extra movements of her fingers were unnoticeable to any who were not watching for them.

'All right,' she said, and moved towards the casket. She picked up a driver and began to pull the bolts from the top of the block. It took a few moments. Nis watched her all the while, the lenses of his eyes altering their focus as he tracked her movements. His tongue was resting between his teeth.

The last bolt came free, and she put the tool down and heaved at the lid. It did not shift. She tried again.

Nis' face twitched with impatience.

'Grol,' he said, and flicked his head at the casket. Grol came forwards, machine arms unfolding from his shoulders with a hiss of pistons. Myzmadra took a step back as Grol locked the machine arms onto the top of the block and pulled the lid free. Nis stepped forwards and looked down at what they had dug from beneath the soil of Terra.

A figure lay within. The light from the melta-torches and stab lights fell across scarred muscle and a broad face. Tubes led from sockets in its skin.

'What–' Nis had time to begin the question before the flechette round hit him in the jaw and ripped half of his face off. The needle pistol and hand cannon were in Myzmadra's hands before the gang boss hit the ground.

Grol twisted, the lid of the casket still clasped in his machine arms. She shot him three times. The first needle hit him in the cheek, the second in the throat, and the last passed between his open teeth as he began to scream. His muscles spasmed as the venom in the needles did its work. He managed to stumble forwards, swinging the casket lid like a club. Myzmadra ducked the blow, came up and put a hand cannon round through his left eye. Meat and torn chrome spun through the air as he slumped into a heap of metal and flesh. She leapt over his corpse, a gun in each hand.

The rest of the scavs were halfway between fighting and dying. She saw one with a melta-torch and a face of iron take a cluster of flechettes in the spine. He fell, body suddenly a red rag doll with cut strings. She fired as she moved, dodging jets of melta-torches and wild lunges. Her needles and bullets drummed out a steady rhythm of death in reply. Incarnus was standing beside the caskets, hands raised. Sparks coiled through the air around his arm, and there was frost on his fingers. One of the scavs swung at him with a piston hammer, froze in place and began to judder. Blood poured from under the ganger's mask. Incarnus tensed. The frost around his fingers thickened. The ganger turned, legs dragging, and sank his hammer into the chest of his nearest comrade. Blood and bones exploded from the impact.

It was over in three more heartbeats. The quiet was as sudden as a gunshot.

Myzmadra moved amongst the bodies, checking if any of the scavs were still alive. She ended any doubts with her hand cannon.

Ashul appeared from the night, his flechette rifle cradled in his arms. He looked like he had just been out for a stroll.

'Good timing on the first shot,' Myzmadra said, as she glanced at him. 'Hit a little low, though.'

'Didn't have time to get my aim set. You know I work best when I'm not rushed.'

'Well get used to not having the luxury,' she said, and moved back to the open casket. 'Get the others open,' she said. She looked down at the figure in the casket Nis had made her open. Its skin was so pale and still that she would have thought it dead, if she had not known better. She leant in, eyes tracing the old surgical scars and sculpted muscle.

A hand clamped around her neck, so fast that she did not have time to realise what was happening. Pain exploded through her. Part of her, the part that had been trained to observe and reason even when the rest of her thoughts were broken, knew that the hand on her throat could cut off air or blood with the slightest pressure. It could break her neck before she could blink. The hand pulled her face down as the figure in the casket opened his eyes.

'Code phrase,' rasped a voice. The pressure on her eased a fraction.

'Cal...' she breathed. 'Calisto.'

The hand around her neck opened. She fell backwards, steadied herself and almost vomited into her rebreather. The figure rose from the casket, snapping tubes from the sockets in his flesh. He was a demigod sculpted in imitation of humanity. Muscles flowed under his skin.

'Mission parameter?' he asked, as he moved to one of the five metal cubes and pulled its lid off.

'Orpheus,' said Myzmadra. 'The mission parameter is Orpheus.'

The demigod paused for a second, then nodded and began to retrieve objects from the cube in front of him, hands working fast. Sections of war-plate emerged and were locked over his body one at a time. Then the weapons, ammunition and equipment.

'Time until strike?' he asked.

'Two hours, twenty-three minutes.'

He glanced up to the brightening arc of light on the horizon, and nodded. The figures in the other caskets were stirring too now. Incarnus was moving between them, speaking the code phrases to each of them.

'What do I call you?' she asked the demigod.

'You will call me Phocron,' he said.

Bhab Bastion
The Imperial Palace, Terra

A SCULPTURE OF the Solar System, carved in cold light, filled Archamus' eyes as he stepped into the command chamber.

A vast holo-projection filled the centre of the room. Within a cone of light the system rotated: its planets spheres, its moons dots, and the

reefs and debris fields washes of light. The projection crackled and flickered as it turned. Tech-priests moved around the large holo-projector,
their red robes dragging on the stone floor as they made adjustments
and clicked to each other in machine cant. Smaller holo-projectors
and pict screen stacks filled the rest of the chamber, each a cluster of
quiet activity. Men and women in the uniforms of Solar Auxilia officers
talked in low voices, occasionally calling out an order and receiving
a reply. Beside them, servitors twitched in their cradles as they performed their functions. Images of orbital defences glowed in the air
above them. The room ached with static.

The chamber was the heart of the Bhab Bastion, a place of counsel
and refuge for warlords and tyrants since before the Age of Strife. Now
it had become the seat from which the last protectors of truth and
humanity looked out across their defences. Whether from here, or the
strategium on the *Phalanx*, the guardians of Terra had been watching
for the first attacker to appear on the horizon since word had come of
Horus' treachery. They had been waiting a long time.

Archamus noted the position of each of the Imperial Fists watching over the room. All of them were Huscarls, Rogal Dorn's personal
bodyguards, their duty marked by the black cloaks hanging from their
shoulders. Each was utterly still, but he knew they would have missed
no detail of movement in the chamber.

'Saturnalia,' he said into his vox. A click was the only reply to say that
he had spoken that hour's watch word correctly and so would live to
take his next step. The word changed at random every hour. It was an
old method, but effective. To those who called such measures unnec-
essary, or awkward, he gave no reply. He did not need to. He had one
duty: to protect and serve the lord who stood in an open space beneath
the turning holo ghost of the Solar System.

Rogal Dorn did not look around as Archamus approached. The pale
light of the projection stole the lustre from Dorn's armour, and had set
shadows in his eyes and the hollows of his cheeks. Quiet radiated from
the Imperial Fists' primarch, like the stillness at the heart of a storm.

Archamus bowed his head and brought his right fist to his chest. Dorn's eyes flicked to him, and then back to the display.

Whenever Dorn was not concerned with other matters, he came here. Years ago, when the war had first started, the primarch had a habit of walking the battlements, looking out as his will remade the Palace, then Terra, and then the Solar System into a fortress. That time had passed. The fortress was long complete, and Dorn no longer walked its towers and walls. There was no respite. Not for the Praetorian of Terra.

The Solar System was a battlefield within a greater war. While the galaxy burned and the warp shrieked with storms, the heart of the Imperium smouldered with conflict like a fire teetering on the edge of becoming a blaze. The old divisions in the Unity of Terra creaked under the pressure of fear and ignorance. The rebellion on Triton had been put down and its horrors kept secret, but there had been others, waves of panic sweeping through populations who had been unified for centuries, but alone for much longer.

Mars was a cauldron of war. Fire wreathed its orbits as the Imperial Fists tried to keep their fingers clamped over the wound next to their heart. The rebel forges hurled rockets and mountain-sized shells at Terra. Ships tried to break orbit, sometimes alone, sometimes in swarms that rose from the polluted skies like iron locusts. Only the efforts of Camba Diaz and his blockade fleet had kept the anger of the Red Planet's spite at bay.

Then there were the incursions on the outer sphere. They came without coordination, but without cease: wild fleets of warships, crewed by men and women who bore jagged marks on their flesh, and who screamed with madness as they went to their deaths. They had begun at the edge of the system in the early months of the war – first a few and then more and more, until they were striking the outer sphere of defences like rain ringing from a roof. But dangerous though they were, the incursions were claws scrabbling at the gate. The Solar System was a fortress waiting for its final battle.

Every night was the eve of invasion, every dawn the beginning of another cycle of waiting.

It would come. One night a new star would appear beside the old, and that star would be the light that said *Horus has come*. It was certain – the only question was when.

'*Terra is a fortress with two walls,*' Dorn had once said to Archamus. '*The Emperor, my father, stands on the inner wall that is the war of the paths beyond the golden gates. We stand on the outer wall that is the Solar System. If either wall falls, humanity falls. That is what is at stake. Not honour or rightness, but existence. If we fail for an instant, all is lost.*'

The realm of Sol burned, and bled, and waited. And between it and ruin stood the Imperial Fists, and the will of their primarch.

Archamus felt a phantom shiver run through his bionic leg and arm as he watched the fortress of the Solar System rotate in the dark. His eye went to where runes marking void battles blinked beyond the orbit of Pluto. With the time it took for signals to travel from the edge of the system to Terra, the ships represented by those splashes of light would have died hours before. Bodies would already be freezing in the void, fires cooling in the wreckage. Archamus' gaze moved to the count of hostile ships that had tried to breach the Solar System's outer sphere.

'Twenty,' said Archamus. 'Fewer than yesterday.'

'Too many,' said Dorn, softly, eyes still on the light above.

'Did any of them breach the First Sphere?'

Dorn gave the slightest shake of his head. Archamus turned his gaze back to the display.

'Move the *Tenth Eagle* and *Imperial Mercy* back from the outer sphere. Best speed for Mars. Command transfers to Camba Diaz.'

'Yes, lord,' replied one of the human officers, a veteran Jovian admiral called Su-Kassen. Scars ran up her neck, above the collar of her blue uniform. She had commanded hundreds and thousands in her time, and was used to exercising authority. She hesitated. 'First Captain Sigismund's forces in the outer sphere will be–'

'They will be adequate to his task,' said Dorn, his voice falling like a hammer on stone. Then his features shifted. When he spoke again his voice had softened. 'Another surge will come from Mars soon. It will come in the next twenty days, when the solar storm is predicted to break. Camba Diaz will need both the ships and the men, Kassen.'

'Of course, lord,' said Kassen, and saluted.

Dorn nodded, gave a last glance up at the system map, and then walked to the chamber's doors. Another duty waited for him, and even if Terra slept, its Praetorian never did. Five of the Huscarls fell in behind him. Dorn turned as he reached the door and looked back at Archamus.

'The vigil is yours, captain,' he said.

Damocles Starport
Terra

'WHAT NOW?' NESSEGAS rubbed his eyes as he keyed the vox.

'*Outer doors have jammed shut,*' came the voice of one of his sub-prefects.

The man was reliable, but at that moment Nessegas would have cheerfully seen him flogged. The temperature in the Southern Transport Arterial Lock had dropped to the point that ice frosted the crystal of his cupola. Down on the cavern floor, the militia were still searching the huge ground hauler. Behind that, the bulk of the Hysen Cartel crawler sat going nowhere. He had twenty-three loads backed up, and the flow through the lock was now eighty-six minutes behind schedule. That meant he was almost certainly facing exile, most likely to one of the Albion sink hives.

He closed his eyes and put all the control he could into his next words.

'Then... unjam them,' he said.

'*Can't, honoured prefect. Whole mechanisms have locked. Nothing is responding.*'

'Keep trying until they do respond,' he snapped, and cut the vox. He shivered. The cold was starting to get inside the cupola. He would have to try to summon the tech-priests again. His first plea had gone unanswered. Behind him Sucreen hovered, her silence and presence making it difficult to think.

He almost missed the first shots. A stutter of flat cracks sounded from the cavern floor. He frowned and leaned forwards to look down, the frost blurring his view. Another stream of cracking noises, then another, and then shouts. Behind him he heard Sucreen swear.

What was happening? He could not...

Figures were moving amongst the vehicles. He saw one of them pause, bring something up to his shoulder and...

There was blood spraying from the back of a militiaman's head as he fell. And now he could see the guns in the hands of the figures, and hear the shouts of the militia, and see the flash of las-fire.

He felt his mouth opening. Sucreen was shouting into her vox-link. He saw a masked figure drop from the open cab door of the Hysen Cartel crawler. Other figures were moving around the vehicle, working controls and turning wheels. They were wearing cartel overalls, but breather masks covered their heads.

Cracks appeared down the centre of the five cargo sections.

His eye caught a figure raising what looked like a section of pipe onto his shoulder.

Nessegas had enough time to realise what was about to happen, before the missile stuck the cupola and ripped it from the cavern roof in a ball of flame. Debris and fire fell through the freezing air. Smoke billowed up into the air vents leading to the rest of the starport.

On the cavern floor, the five sections of the Hysen Cartel crawler split open like flowers unfurling to greet the sun. Gas poured from each container, shimmering with warmth as it rose to follow the smoke up and out of the cavern.

✠ ✠ ✠

Northern Reaches
The Imperial Palace, Terra

THE INFILTRATOR MOVED up through the Palace from the door into the underworld. He moved quickly but with care, passing through the derelict layers, and then up through seldom-trod paths. He wove past patrol servitors and sensor nodes, following a route held in his mind. The eyes of patrol servitors touched him, but did not see him.

In a dank tunnel running between water cisterns, the ghost met the second of his kind. Both of them paused, weapons and eyes steady on each other.

'Calisto,' he whispered.

'Hecate,' the other replied.

The first nodded once, his weapon unwavering.

'Mission parameter?'

'Eurydice.'

The first infiltrator nodded and lowered his weapon.

The two moved together in silence, flowing up through the Palace's shadows. In a machine shaft, two became three. None of them spoke after exchanging code phrases. How each of them had entered the Palace was irrelevant. They had their mission parameter, and that was all the understanding they needed.

They flowed on like a breath of wind. Their armour hid the heat of their bodies, and the cameleoline bonded to the plates drank light and blurred colours. The armour was slight compared to the type normally worn by their kind, but their greatest protection was their skill in remaining unseen. That skill was sharp enough to see them through the Palace's lower levels at speed.

Only when they reached the middle levels did matters become more complicated. Patrols of kill-servitors increased, but they only slowed the infiltrators. The true danger would come when they were close to their target. Then they would be in the domain of the Imperial Fists, and the Custodian Guards. When they entered that realm they would have to use every ounce of skill and planning to succeed. But succeed they would. Of that there was no question.

Up and up the three Headhunters went, winding backwards and forwards through corridors of cut stone, folding into the darkness beside a statue of a forgotten tyrant, listening for the sound of foot or breath that would mean danger.

On and on, up and up. Like shadows. Like snakes coiling up the trunk of a tree.

Central Reaches
The Imperial Palace, Terra

THE LABOUR BRUTE was exactly where it was supposed to be, and died without a sound. Silonius lowered the body to the ground slowly. He had broken the brute's neck rather than using a blade; blood was noticeable and difficult to conceal quickly. He dragged the body to the shadow of a pillar. It would be found, but there was no time to hide it properly.

Crouched in the gloom next to his kill, Silonius began to strip it. He worked by touch, not taking his eyes from the corridors to his left and right. The labour brute was the same size as him, and wore an ochre robe and a black-and-white checked hood. A heavy medallion hung around its neck, showing the seal of a regional magnate within the Palace. That magnate had done just as his mission instructions had said, and sent the labour brute down to die in a passage beneath one of the Palace's main processionals.

Silonius slipped the brute's robe on. The cloth reeked. He could smell the brute's vat-broth diet, and taste the stimms it had swallowed to keep its muscles growing. The smell matched his own. Scent markers had laced the soup of biomatter in the tank he had slept in; the same reek saturated his own skin. With his shoulders hunched, and his hood up, he would look and smell like the creature he had just killed. He took the brute's ownership medallion and slipped it over his own head. Last of all he took the bundle of scrolls the brute had been carrying, and slung them over his back. He started walking, feet shuffling and slapping on the flagstones. He passed down a passage, up a flight of stairs and then out into the crowds streaming down the processional.

It was raining. Heavy drops pattered down on the granite slabs, and ran along channels into bronze grates. The clouds clinging to the inside of the roof half a kilometre above his head swirled in the microclimate's wind. The crowd moved quickly. Menial workers clustered in herds, their clothes hanging from them in sodden folds. Teams of serfs bore canopies of patterned fabric or sheet metal, sheltering men and women of higher status. Groups of servitors moved against the flow, following their functions with blind determination. There were soldiers too: warbands in personal heraldry clustered around their paymaster, marching ranks of men and women bearing the emblems of eagles, hounds, hawks and other beasts on their pennants.

Silonius took the entire scene in at a glance. His eyes found the Imperial Fists standing sentinel on the upper balconies above the main walkway beyond the veil of rain. He found the hidden watchers a second later: hunched behind their camo-cloaks in the high niches, looking down at the river of humanity through gunsights. There were no Custodians that he could detect. That was good.

He checked his mental count of time, paused for three seconds and then shouldered into the press. Rain began to soak him. Most of the crowd made way. Some called out to him as he shoved past them, but he did not respond. The labour brutes were mute for the most part, and his silence was expected. The count went on in his head, the beat of the seconds passing matching his steps.

A figure rammed into him from the left and almost fell. Hands gripped his robes.

'Cursed fool, get out of the way,' spat the figure. Silonius saw a flash of a gaunt face and dark beard, and then the figure was gone. Silonius felt the weight of the metal sphere the man had slipped into his hand.

Needles snapped out of the sphere and began to jab into his skin rhythmically. The rhythm became a pattern, the pattern information, and the information a new set of memories unlocked in his mind. He walked on, the rain drumming against his skull, the seconds ticking past.

Ten paces, and he brushed past a herald leading a pack of felids on silver chains.

A metal cylinder was now in his hand.

Another fifty-one paces, a swerve to turn around the statue of a bull, another brush of contact and another object to vanish beneath his robe.

More seconds passed, his steps following a pattern threaded through time and space as he moved through the crowd beneath the gaze of the sentinels of Terra.

At last he saw a rain canopy of golden fabric swaying above a tracked carriage ahead of him. Six labour brutes, in robes and hoods identical to his, held the awning up on long poles. Raindrops burst on its shining surface. He quickened his step. Silver mesh screens hid who rode within the carriage. No one noticed as he stepped from the crowd and took one of the poles that held up the canopy. The brute that had been carrying the pole took the bundle of scrolls from Silonius, and vanished into the crowd. It was so casual and quick that it was as though it had never happened at all.

He passed through the Unity Arch, beneath the guns of the guards and through the sweeps of auspex fields. No weapons were permitted beyond the Arch, and he watched the warbands of the Terran nobility strip their gear under the eyes of sentinels in eagle masks. A lone Knight war machine stood before the Arch, its towering bulk seeming small beneath the gilt pillars. Its cannons hung relaxed at its side, but its head moved ceaselessly – back and forth, back and forth, like a dog set to watch on a threshold. Silonius looked up at it as its gaze hovered on him for a second, and then swept past. Moments later he was through the Arch, and another step on his path was complete.

The canopy above the carriage was furled as it began to ascend the Anavros Stair. No one noticed that one of its bearers had vanished. In the gloom of a side passage, Silonius found the grating in the floor and dropped into the darkness of an air duct.

The rest of his equipment came next. He found it a piece at a time: the rounds for his boltgun in a sump pool, the firing mechanism wrapped in oiled fabric beneath a tile, the plates of his armour in a dozen different niches. Some of the items had no purpose that he knew – a cluster of metal shards, a silver sphere, a set of metal rings – but he retrieved them all the same. A different agent had planted each item over the last decade. None of them had known of more than one location, and most had been disposed of after they had performed their task. The explosives, melta charges, blind grenades and haywire detonators came last, pulled from their hiding places and settled into pouches across his chest.

By the time he reached the inner reaches of the Palace he no longer wore the robe of a serf. Plates of armour and ballistic fabric covered his flesh. His form was a blur, the substance of his outline dissolving into textures of light and dark. He moved fast, never pausing, or hesitating.

There was no sign of the Custodians, and he could not detect even the slightest hint of their recent presence. That could only mean one thing: the Emperor was absent from His seat of power. For an instant he wondered where the Master of Mankind was. He discarded the question. It meant only that his mission was simplified.

He paused when he reached the Dome of Illumination. Crouching on a ledge high above the walkway that circled the abyss beneath, he watched water fall from the mouths of the three statues which bore the kilometre-wide roof on their shoulders. The water roared as it struck the vast crucible far below. Above him, dawn light was falling through the hundred-metre-wide aperture in the vast dome.

The target was close. In fact it was a few hundred metres above his head, but layers of rockcrete and plasteel meant that he would have to take one of the doors that led from the walkway below. He knew which door he would take, but he could not take it yet. The moment was coming, but it was not here.

Not yet.

THREE

THE PRIMIGENIA SLID through the void towards Terra. Space became more crowded with every second. Ships and void stations filled the outer orbits. Even with tight control over which vessels could approach this close, there were hundreds moving to and from the planet. Many sat in void docks, regurgitating their cargos into vast stores. Then there were the orbital plates. Old before Unification, they were like cities cast from Terra and left to hang in the heavens.

Around and between them floated strings of weapon platforms. Monitor craft moved amongst stations and cargo ships in shoals. Each monitor was small for a warship, but bristled with firepower equal to warp-capable craft many times its size. Imperial Fists battle-barges and cruisers stalked amongst the other craft like lions. And larger than all of them, hanging above Terra like a second moon, was the *Phalanx*. In all the Imperium, there was no warship larger, or mightier. Even the Gloriana-class craft fell short of Rogal Dorn's fortress flagship. It held station on the edge of Terra's grasp, looking both inwards and outwards: the guardian standing over the last gate.

Past and through this throng, the *Primigenia* surged on. The monitor craft locked to its side transmitted clearance codes as it entered into Terra's outer control sphere. A last check with the pilot cadre on the *Primigenia*'s bridge confirmed that all was well. Neither the monitor nor any of the other vessels noticed the shuttle that slipped from the cargo ship's rear launch bay.

The first sign that anything was amiss came when the *Primigenia* needed to make its first turn to synchronise its course with the orbital dock. Signals passed from the dock to the *Primigenia* and its monitor craft when it failed to alter course. No response came from the pilot cadre on the *Primigenia*'s bridge. Alerts began to sound on the monitor craft. Assault troops began to run to the docking limb linked to the *Primigenia*. Five seconds after the cargo ship failed to respond to the signals, warnings began to shrill through the orbital defences.

Alarms began to sound across the orbit of Terra. Gun platforms rotated to face the *Primigenia*. Commands flashed between the nearest warships. Vessels close by began to scatter. Chains of other ships queuing for the orbital docks broke apart. Those ships closing on the outer orbits cut their speed.

Signals battered the *Primigenia*. It burned on, silent, falling towards Terra like a dagger.

Beacon tower 567-Beta
Gobi tox-wastes, Terra

THE TOWER SAT on the edge of the hill-line ahead of them, jutting up into the sunrise like a tooth. The strike team had dumped the crawler just over the horizon, and run the rest, striding through the dark as it faded to day. The pace sent breath sawing in and out of Myzmadra's lungs. The glands embedded close to her heart dumped pain suppressants into her blood.

The five Space Marines had not slowed from the moment they had dropped out of the crawler. She could no longer tell which one was Pho-cron. They moved as one, speeding over the ground like oil. Ashul had peeled off a kilometre back, found a shooting point and settled down to watch the tower. Wrapped in a cameleoline shroud, staring down his rifle sight, he was the strike team's eyes as it ran through the last of the light.

'*Five hundred metres out. No movement,*' came Ashul's voice in Myz-madra's ear. '*Large heat signatures inside. Machines most likely. Twenty human-sized signatures. None outside. If they have any sentries, they are heat-baffled.*'

'Low likelihood.' Phocron's voice cut into the vox, growling with the echoes from the inside of his helm.

Myzmadra ran on, feet dancing over the dust and broken rock at the bottom of the dry river bed. The five armoured warriors were thirty metres ahead of her. She could hear the low whir and buzz of their armour. Behind her Incarnus was loping along, long arms swinging as he fought to keep up.

'*One hundred metres out,*' said Ashul. '*There are three on the roof now. They are lighting up lho-sticks. Nice.*'

The course cut by the dry river bed curved away to the right. On her left, Myzmadra saw the tower rise from the ground just set back from the river bank. A cliff of loose soil and rock marked the outside of the bend. Phocron and the other four warriors took it in a single bound.

'*The three on the roof still haven't seen you,*' said Ashul.

She could see the tower clearly now. She had seen it before of course, its shape and details familiar from pict-captures. It was neither large nor impressive, just a square block of rockcrete and plasteel rising from the hills at the edge of the tox-plateau. Gun barrels jutted from firing loops in its flanks. Crenellations ran around its top, and a sin-gle door was set in its side. It was just what it seemed: a worn and half-forgotten marker at the edge of desolation. Worthless by almost all estimation. Almost all.

Myzmadra scrambled up the bank. The five warriors were sprinting towards the door at the tower's base.

'*They've heard you!*' called Ashul. Myzmadra heard a cry from the tower top. Her pistols were in her hands. Incarnus was just cresting the river bank behind her.

'*Execute,*' said Phocron. He was not even breathing hard.

A sound like the flutter of wings rippled through the air above her. The cries from the top of the tower vanished.

One of the five warriors fired. A white-hot line punched from his weapon's muzzle and struck the tower's door. The air screamed with heat. The door became a spray of molten metal. The warrior with the meltagun ran through the breach. The rest were just behind him.

Myzmadra triggered the glands next to her heart with a single thought. Stimms dumped into her blood as she sprinted towards the glowing wound of the door. Gunfire boomed within, rolling on and on like thunder. She came into the first chamber. Chunks of meat and ashes covered the floors and walls. Explosions flashed down the spiral staircase bolted to the wall.

She was not looking at the corpses, or listening to the brief screams from above. Everyone in the tower needed to be dead within ten seconds. Any more than that and there was a chance of them sending a distress signal. That would not be happening, though.

Her eyes scanned the walls and floor. The plans had not been specific on where the hatch would be.

'There,' said Incarnus, panting as he came to a halt beside her. Her eyes followed the direction he was pointing and saw it. A square hatch sat flush with the floor, half covered by a canvas sleeping cot. She kicked the cot away, and bent down. The lock was hidden behind a thin access panel. The cogs-skull emblem of the Priests of Mars looked up at her from intermeshed wheels and gears.

She swore. Incarnus looked over her shoulder, saw the lock and added his own choice words.

'Melta charge?' she asked. He moved past her, shaking his head as he crouched next to the lock.

'That would do too much damage to the conduit,' he replied, eyes flicking over the exposed lock. 'The intel didn't include the key to this.' He shook his head. 'I can crack it, but it's going to take thirteen minutes.'

'Too long,' growled Phocron, as he stepped down the spiral stairs. He had pulled his helmet off and his armour was flecked with drying blood. 'We have to be active in nine minutes.'

Incarnus shrank back as the warrior loomed above him.

'It's five centimetres of plasteel and ceramite, the only way through–'

Phocron punched down into the lock mechanism, closed his fist and wrenched the hatch out of its setting. Chips of rockcrete fell from its frame as he tossed it aside.

'Proceed,' growled Phocron. Incarnus uncurled from where he had crouched, glanced up at the warrior's impassive face, then back at the ragged hole in the floor. He nodded, and dropped into the space below. Myzmadra followed, unfastening the pouch that had sat across her back for the journey across the plateau.

The shaft under the hatch dropped straight down into dust and darkness. She lit a stab light and swept the beam through the dark. Incarnus winced and cursed as the light found his face. She saw his pupils shrink from the size of coins to pinpricks.

'Cut the light!' he hissed.

'I need to see,' she said, panning the beam away from him.

'Not as much as I do,' he muttered, but dropped his hands.

They were crouched in a rockcrete-lined tube. Bunches of cables ran along the walls, which stretched beyond the reach of the light. Brass-cased machine blocks were bolted to the tunnel walls just below the access shaft. Strips of parchment hung from them, stirring in the sudden flow of air. Incarnus already had a bundle of tools out and was breaking the wax seals on the casings. Seconds later he had the machine blocks open. Pulsing lights and whirring clockwork filled each of them. Incarnus paused, eyes scanning the contents, fingers tapping on his chin.

'Yes,' he said after a moment, and held out an open hand without looking around. Myzmadra placed the objects from her pack on his palm. There were three of them, each no larger than a bolt shell. In form they resembled crustaceans made from polished chrome. Tendrils of silver cable hung from them, making them look like the fresh catch from a sea of quicksilver. Incarnus slid them into the exposed mechanisms, fingers snapping the toothed ends of each tendril onto a different cluster of wires. The silver objects shivered and then pulled themselves into the mechanisms. Myzmadra watched them squirm into the cogs and wiring, wondering briefly what they were and who had made them.

'They are something complicated made to do something simple,' said Incarnus, looking up at her. She felt the tingle of static on her scalp and snarled. He raised his hands placatingly. 'Sorry, your mind was almost shouting your question. Difficult to miss.'

She composed her face and looked down at the device on her wrist.

'They are ready to transmit?'

Incarnus nodded.

'Of course.'

'Good,' she said, and looked up the shaft. Phocron was standing above the opening. He looked down at her as the stab-beam touched his armour. Its hue was black in the direct light, but for a second she had seen scales sketched in blue and green across the plating. 'Ready and standing by,' she said.

Phocron nodded, face expressionless.

'Go,' he said.

Bhab Bastion
The Imperial Palace, Terra

'IT IS HOLDING course for surface impact,' Admiral Su-Kassen called across the command chamber.

'Distance from the nearest vessel?' said Archamus. Above him the holo-projection showed the *Primigenia* trailing fire as its engines pushed it deeper into Terra's orbit.

'Two thousand and fourteen kilometres,' said a human officer.

He nodded. Calculations sped through his thoughts.

'Still too close,' he said. 'Get them clear.'

The quiet of the chamber had vanished. Amber light flashed. Distances and velocities spun through the holo-displays. Ships, stations and shuttle craft blinked back at him in cold light. Every officer in the room was speaking, calling information and orders over each other. The servitors were rocking and rattling in their cradles, fingers dancing over systems. The tech-priests stood amongst them, twitching as they and the machines flooded their synapses with data. And above them the image of the *Primigenia* fell down and down through the dark.

'*Reason of Truth* confirms it has range and lock on the target...'

'Orbital rotation bringing it above the horizon in thirty-five seconds.'

'Gannemus defences have firing solution.'

'I have request for order to fire...'

'Minimum safe distance.'

'A reactor of that size...'

'Target three seconds away from the medial orbital layer.'

'Still no reply signal from the bridge...'

It had been forty-one seconds since they had come to full alert. But in the compressed instant of Archamus' awareness it felt like the blink of an eye. He could hear each voice in the chamber, and his eyes and mind were reading data from the displays faster than the tech-priests and humans could process it. He saw and understood it all.

The *Primigenia* might have suffered a catastrophic accident. Its crew might have overcome the pilot cadre, and set the ship to crash into Terra's surface. There were dozens of possibilities, and none of them mattered. The ship would die, before it touched Terra's atmosphere. Its reactors and fuel would stain the sky for a few moments. Those other ships close by might suffer superficial damage, but no more. That was the cruelty of necessity, and, to the praetorians of Terra, acceptable.

'Signal the *Reason of Truth*,' he said. The sound dimmed for an instant, and then a vox-link crackled into life.

'*The* Reason of Truth *stands ready*,' came a voice like a growl of thunder.

'This is Archamus. I speak with the Praetorian's voice.'

'*We hear and obey, Archamus. What is your order?*'

'Last vessel is approaching outer edge of target ship's reactor explosion radius,' buzzed one of the tech-priests.

Archamus blinked, watching the *Primigenia* fall.

'Fire,' he said.

There was a pause as the signal reached up to the *Reason of Truth*. And then the warship fired. It was a battle cruiser and its weapons could break star fortresses, but for this execution it used a fraction of that strength. A pulse of turbo laser fire struck the *Primigenia*'s engines an instant before macro shells ripped into its hull. The unstable plasma cylinders and explosive compounds hidden within the crates packed into its holds detonated.

And fire ripped across the heavens like the burning laughter of a cruel god.

Damocles Starport
Terra

THE GAS FLOWED up though the branches of Damocles Starport's ventilation system. Colourless and odourless, it poured through every duct and trunk.

The first to breathe the gas in was a man in one of the labour pens. He straightened from where he crouched over his workbench, and tried to shake the pain in his neck. It was not good. His father had suffered pain in the same place before he had begun to waste from the inside. It might not mean the same thing, but the man knew it did. He was sure. He just didn't know what to do about it.

He took a breath. He coughed. Those nearby did not look around from their workbenches. They never did. Others had died at their stations, and no one even turned a head. Not their business how each other lived or died, as long as they did not interfere with each other's work.

The man coughed again. Something was tickling in his throat. Another cough. The pain in his neck was suddenly much worse. He brought his hand up to rub at it.

And froze.

Something was moving under his skin. Something with legs.

He yelped and brought his hand away. The skin of his arm was bulging as he looked at it. He shrieked. Shapes flowed up the limb. Some of the others turned to look. The skin of his fingers split before his eyes. Feelers and legs reached out from beneath. He shrieked again and ran, tearing at his flesh. The bugs were everywhere, running over the floor. More poured from the mouths and eyes of those who turned to look at him. Their skin was coming off, peeling back from a mass of brown, clicking bodies. His hand found a metal bar, and he swung and swung.

As the first blow landed another person's world exploded into nightmare, then another and another.

And so it went, on and on, with each poisoned breath of air, as fears and desires buried down beneath sanity and obedience rose up and became real.

Within ten minutes half of the population was screaming. Within twenty, the starport was howling as it tore itself apart.

Down in the cavern where the cargo crawler had dumped its payload into the air, the masked figures worked quickly. The communication systems for the port were beyond their abilities to subvert or damage, but the speaker horns mounted throughout the structure were a different matter. As the gas flooded through the levels above, the speakers began to proclaim a single message again and again.

'We have come for you...'

✠ ✠ ✠

Northern Circuit
The Imperial Palace, Terra

THE THREE INFILTRATORS broke cover as the siren sounded and began to sprint up the tunnel towards the distant daylight at the top of the ramp. There was no way of avoiding this moment. For all their stealth in coming this far, they could only take this last step in the open. A gun-servitor barred their path. Its heavy bolters armed as targeting beams reached from its eyes. The first stalker round punched through its targeting lens and blew out the back of its skull. A second and third round tore chunks out of the exposed flesh of its neck. The trio of infiltrators were already past the servitor as it fell. A blast door began to drop across the passage. They rolled beneath, came up and kept running. Another servitor shrugged free of its niche in the passage wall. They put a cluster of rounds into it and vaulted over its body as it collapsed.

Sirens boomed through the air. They could see the daylight was getting closer. The walls shivered as armoured doors slammed down across openings to either side. Lights cut out. Their visors switched the darkness to monochrome twilight. They had five seconds before the scanning beams flooded the passage. Their feet rang on the stones beneath their feet. The Palace's guardians would know they were here within minutes. As long as those defenders were not busy elsewhere, of course.

Dome of Illumination
The Imperial Palace, Terra

THE IMPERIAL FISTS squad swept into the Dome of Illumination. There were twelve of them. Their left shoulder pads were bare iron. Black lightning bolts marked their chests.

Veterans, thought Silonius as he watched them.

They were good, very good in fact. The squad split, trios of warriors running in different directions, vanishing through doors to other parts of the Palace. Now there were just three on the walkway. One of them had a portable auspex in his hand. Silonius could almost feel the sensor waves reaching for him, itching across his skin. They moved as one, firing arcs overlapping seamlessly as they ran along the walkway, eyes and boltguns sweeping the vast chamber. They had not seen Silonius, but they would. It was only a matter of time, unless...

Light flashed through the opening in the dome above.

Brilliant white. Blinding. Strobing.

The Imperial Fists looked up, and then froze, staring at the fire pouring from Terra's sky. The siren screamed louder, and shifted in tone.

Silonius triggered the charges he had attached to the underside of the walkway. Stone and metal became smoke and flame. One of the Imperial Fists vanished in the explosion. A section of the walkway broke away from the chamber wall. Another yellow-armoured warrior went with it, spinning end over end down into the dark. The last of the squad was blasted backwards off his feet, hit the walkway floor and rolled. Silonius swung down from the ledge above, and stabbed with a shard blade as the warrior came to his feet. It was a good blow, a killing blow, smooth and precise.

But the Imperial Fists legionary was fast and was not used to dying. The point of Silonius' blade glanced across yellow armour, and the warrior was up and ramming his gun into Silonius' chest. Force shuddered through Silonius' ribs and flesh. They were so close that he could see his reflection in the green lenses of the warrior's helm. He twisted aside as the gun roared. A cone of flame skimmed his side. He cut as he moved, once, twice, three times. Blood sheeted down. The warrior's left arm sagged. Blood was pouring from the inside of the elbow and wrist.

And suddenly Silonius found that he was smiling.

The sirens were a drum beat. Everything was a blur, but everything was also so clear. The Imperial Fist stepped back. Silonius moved with him, blade flicking out and more blood gushed as the blade opened joins in wrist, elbow and knee. The boltgun fell from the legionary's hands. Silonius wondered for an instant what it must be like for such a warrior to feel strength flee him, what it was like to feel one's inferiority. It had always been like that for those who thought themselves strong or gifted when the Legion laid them low. The worst moment was not dying, but realising that there were others who were better.

The legionary came forwards, shedding blood.

Silonius lunged once. The point of his shard dagger took the warrior in the throat. The body twitched once, hands grasping nothing. Silonius let the dying warrior hang for a second and then kicked him off over the edge of the walkway.

He flicked his blade clean, and felt a stab of pain in his left leg. He looked down. He was bleeding. A long splinter of stone had pierced his thigh. He looked at it, frowning at the fact he had not felt it before. He pulled it out. Blood pulsed briefly in the wound then began to clot. He dropped the splinter, glanced around and found the doorway he needed.

He began to run. There was no need for stealth now. Chaos was his cloak, and all that mattered was speed.

FOUR

Terran orbit

THE PRIMIGENIA'S DEATH light spread across the night skies of Terra. Seen from the walls of the Imperial Palace it was a blinding flash that pulsed on and on, stuttering like a corrupted pict image. It sent shadows dancing in the smoke pits of Atlantia. On the heights of Himalazia the cyber-nomads woke and saw the light writhing behind the clouds, and whispered the old legends of the sky dragons that had eaten the sun. On Luna the last of the gene-wrights saw it as a jagged star cut into the face of the mother planet.

And the explosion did not fade, but rolled out and out through high and low orbit. Gannemus dock vanished. Hundred-metre-long chunks of debris spun out, struck smaller space stations nearby and tore them apart. Blisters of fresh fire flashed into being. The clouds of debris cascaded though the sphere of Terra. Ships twisted and burned, trying to outrun the blast wave. Hundreds failed. Clouds of shrapnel tore into the armour of warships and system monitors. Gas and fire bled into the void. Wreckage began to spin down to the world beneath, burning as it fell.

✠ ✠ ✠

Beacon tower 567-Beta
Gobi tox-wastes, Terra

'What was that?' asked Incarnus. His bald head twitched up as light flickered down the shaft above them.

'Something that is not our concern,' said Myzmadra. She nodded back at the silver objects embedded in the mass of cogs and wires. Smoke had begun to peel off the connections. 'Is it working?'

Incarnus glanced at her, lip curling.

'It's working. If you were in the Imperial Palace you would not be able to move for the panic.'

She frowned, still looking at the box of techno-arcanery.

'Strange isn't it? That they left a main trunk into their alert system all the way out here, with practically nothing to guard it? Very accommodating.'

Incarnus shrugged.

'What is that the Legion says? What you assume is strength is weakness. Get access to this and there is not much anyone could do, except bring everything up to maximum alert. What kind of attacker would want to warn their enemy of an attack?'

He showed her his teeth. The gesture reminded her of the grin of the blind fish in the cave pools of her home world.

'There are others out there, aren't there?' he asked, nodding up at the light pulsing from above. 'Other cells setting their own little fires of mayhem? How many do you think the Legion activated for this?'

'I don't know.' Myzmadra shrugged. 'Enough to achieve the objective.'

'And that is?'

'Time has expired,' came Phocron's voice from above. 'Send the second stage, and be ready to move.'

Incarnus blinked and shuffled closer to the open junction boxes. He peeled the glove off his right hand, reached out and stroked each of the chrome objects clinging to the cogs and wires. A high vibrating note filled the air. Myzmadra could feel it in her teeth.

'Done?' she asked.

Incarnus nodded, pulling his glove back on. She noticed that he had no fingernails and the smallest finger looked as though it had an extra joint. She pulled herself up the shaft. Phocron and his brothers were all there. She looked at him. Up to this point she knew the plan in precise detail, but from here she was in an unmapped future.

'Demolitions?' she asked, glancing up at the blood-splattered walls of the tower.

Phocron shook his head.

'We leave it.'

Myzmadra looked at him sharply.

The legionnaire tilted his head, face utterly still. His scalp was a smooth dome of bare skin. The only mark on it was a line of scales running from his right tear duct down his cheek. He looked exactly like dozens of the others she had met. She still found it disconcerting.

'They will be able to discover a lot about us if we just leave,' she said.

'That is the intent,' said Phocron, and turned, snapping his helmet on over his head.

Myzmadra blinked and then pulled her own mask back on. One of the warriors was at the door, scanning the horizon. The others gave swift checks to weapons. Behind her, Incarnus hoisted himself up from the hole in the floor and brushed dust from his body glove.

Phocron glanced around at them all, nodded and led them out into the wastes of Terra. Fire scarred the dawn sky above him. Behind them, beneath the floor of the tower, the chrome devices screamed a single word over and over, battering it into Terra's vox-traffic like the blows of a fist.

'Lupercal! Lupercal! Lupercal!' they shouted without end.

Arcus orbital plate
Lower Terran orbit

THE SIRENS RANG out across Terra. They blared from the spires of hive towers and echoed through the City of Sight. Hands froze in their tasks.

Billions of eyes looked to the skies. Troops and militia scrambled for weapons as officers shouted deployment orders. Those who could see the sky saw lights falling like stars. Defence batteries woke and began to track the skies for targets. Enforcers and civil-marshals surged into the avenues, tunnels and streets of the great conurbations to meet the panicking crowds that shouted of the Warmaster's coming.

The Arcus orbital plate crested the skies above the Europan zone as Terra began to scream. Kestros ran for the launch decks through the pulse of alert lights. His squad was with him. The blast door slammed open in front of him. Three gunships lay ahead. The yellow of their hulls was black in the beat oι ᵖd light. Fuel cables were breaking free of their flanks even as he crossed the distance to them. His eye caught Nestor of the 65th squad swinging into the compartment of the second gunship. The junior sergeant spared a second to nod. Then the darkness of the gunship's interior was around Kestros, and a mag-harness locked over him. The ramp was closing as the last of his squad vaulted on.

The scream of engines rose. The display inside his helm shone with mission data. It was a full alert, maximum threat level, surface and orbital. It was not just the three gunships and squads in his reaction force. The whole company was dropping straight down into the lower atmosphere. That made Kestros stop for a second. His strike force was one of two hundred stationed on the Arcus plate. Over seven hundred Imperial Fists would be diving down to the face of Terra like a cast of falcons. And he was first, the tip of the arrow.

Despite himself Kestros smiled. He was going back to the planet that had birthed him, and he was going to war again.

The ramp closed, and he felt the gunship lurch as the launch cradles gripped its sides. The doors in the floor beneath it broke open. The night side of Terra skidded past beneath. Across the underbelly of the Arcus plate dozens of other launch doors opened. Engines lit. Burning cones roared up into the hangar bays. The launch cradle holding

Kestros' gunship tensed. Force slammed through it. Pistons clenched. The cradle snapped open, and the gunship dropped and cut down through cloud and night.

Bhab Bastion
The Imperial Palace, Terra

Is this how it begins? thought Archamus, and that thought brought quiet to the cacophony. It could be the first blow to fall in the battle to end the war. These moments of sound and shock could be the true and final end of everything that had been. The possibility sank through him, heavy and cold.

The sound of sirens beat the air. The holo-projections were spinning with tactical and strategic data. Above it all, the rogue signal saturating the vox-link shouted its triumph.

'Lupercal! Lupercal! Lupercal!'

It could not be...

Archamus could feel himself calling out orders, slicing the crisis up into portions, ringing each with the logic and experience of sixteen decades, reducing disaster to grains of action.

Could it be?

'Lupercal! Lupercal!'

The *Primigenia* had exploded two and a half minutes ago, but in that slice of time chaos had fallen on them like a tidal wave. The ship had detonated not with the strength of a solitary reactor, but with the force of a dozen nova shells. Half of the heavens were burning. Ships rolled in confusion in the clutter of Terra's orbits. There had already been twenty-five catastrophic collisions.

'We have no word from the...'

'...they expected us to fire on the ship...'

'...Damocles is reporting rioting on all levels, casualties...'

'*...Lupercal!*'

He shut out the whirl of noise and turned to Halik. The old seneschal's face was a mask of control as he looked up at Archamus.

'The Three Hundred and Fourth Company are in the air?' he asked, and received a nod of confirmation. 'They go to Damocles. Immediate deployment, maximum speed.'

'Force discretion?' asked Halik.

'Contain and cleanse,' said Archamus, and turned back to the blur of the unfolding moment. The sight of the holo-display caught his eyes.

'Riots under way in Corona Hive Conurbation...'

'The Ionian Basin is burning...'

'Macro plasma detonations across Atlantian population zones...'

It could be. He felt his skin prickle inside his armour, and the words he was about to speak catch in a dry throat. *The invasion is starting now. Here. From within.*

Alarm signals were flooding in from across the eastern face of the planet.

'The primary vox trunk is jammed!'

'*We have come for you...*'

'...Eighth Legion methodology...'

'They are using Fourth Legion signal base...'

But if the enemy was coming, then what he was seeing was just the fire set within the walls, the arrows falling from the night to send the screams and flames rising while out beyond the gate and parapet...

'What is the status of the Outer Sphere defences?' he called, but he could see the answer blinking on the edge of the projection of the Solar System.

'Last report was that they were engaging intruder ships, but signal delay is currently two hundred and forty-six minutes.'

Over four hours. Four hours in which an armada could have begun to drop from the warp and hit their defences.

'Mistress,' he called, pacing forwards, eyes dancing across the tactical information. 'Have the warnings come from the rest of the system?'

Armina Fel, astropath-adjutant to Rogal Dorn, followed him, stick-thin limbs shivering beneath the green silk of her robes as she moved.

'No,' she said. 'There is no word.'

The first axiom of defence, he thought, *is to understand what you defend against.*

'...Lupercal!'

'Security alarms sounding in northern levels of the Palace.'

'Damocles Starport is not responding...'

Archamus saw the lines of defence Dorn had placed around Terra, the fixed points of strength around the planets and moons, the shoals of ancient debris and fields of mines. He saw the Imperial Fists, spilt into five forces spread from Terra, through Mars, Jupiter and Neptune to Pluto. Each force was ready to move to counter an enemy as they fought into the system. Unless they were looking somewhere else.

'Mistress,' he said, pitching his voice so that only the astropath could hear him. 'Send word to Lord Castellans Camba Diaz, Effried and Halbrecht, and First Captain Sigismund.'

'Lord?' said Armina Fel, and her voice pulled his gaze from the shrunken sphere of the Solar System. She was looking at him, empty eyes wide holes within a mask of control. He had never seen such an expression on her face. 'Lord,' she said again, 'the signal?'

He breathed out.

'Fire on the mountain heights,' he said, and paused.

She bowed her head, and then looked back up at him.

'Truly? Is this it?' she asked, and for a second he thought he saw a tremor pass under the skin of her cheeks. 'Is this the invasion?'

Archamus stared at her, an answer failing to form on his tongue.

'No, mistress, not this day.' The voice cut through the sound of the room. Archamus turned, and every eye in the chamber turned with him. Rogal Dorn swept forwards, his steps swift, his face set.

'There will be no signal,' said the primarch. He looked at where Admiral Su-Kassen stood. 'Send word to Hector on the *Reason of Truth*. He has orbital command. Bring the Terran fleet to full inward and outer

alignment. His guns cover outer system approaches and surface targets. After that clear every other ship that is intact out of the debris
zone. No shots fired unless necessary. If a ship does not respond, take
it with the blade rather than shoot it from the void.'

Dorn looked up at where the vox-horns shouted.

'*Lupercal! Lupercal! Lupercal!*'

'Magos Crusix,' he said, without looking at the senior tech-priest,
'silence that.'

A second later the vox cut out.

'This is a dark moment, but this is not the coming of the Warmaster. Be strong in yourselves and unstinting in your duties, and this
shall pass.'

The silence that had fallen with his words became a heated murmur
of exchanged orders.

Archamus came to stand by his lord, mind still parsing through the
last few moments and the scraps of information still filtering in. He
had been wrong, and he would review the reasons for that later. But for
now it was irrelevant. Even if the invasion was not beginning, they were
still in the middle of a crisis. And there was something else happening,
something hiding under the surface of the noise and destruction. He
pulled a data-slate from a tactical cogitator and spun the dials on its
case. Signal and security data spun across the screen. His instinct had
been right; he had just been looking in the wrong direction.

'The First Axiom, Archamus,' said Dorn softly, and Archamus glanced
up to see his lord looking down at him. 'You were right. What we
are defending against here is not an attack by ships or troops. We are
fighting...'

'Anarchy,' said Archamus.

Dorn nodded once.

Archamus' eyes were scattering across the surface of the data-slate in
his hand. 'Everything that has happened, the ship breaking the cordon,
the orbital cascade, whatever is happening to Damocles, the explosions, the riots, the triggering of our defence alarms, the saturation of

our communications, it means nothing. There is nothing to take strategic advantage of. Except–'

'Except for the fact that it makes us blind,' finished Dorn. The primarch was looking at the chamber around him with almost casual control. The panic had drained from the chamber and been replaced by a tense focus. It had happened the moment Dorn had spoken, radiating from him like cold from ice. It was like a cloak that he could fold over the world around him.

'Polar orbital batteries request permission to fire,' called one of the officers, twisting to look at Su-Kassen and the primarch.

'When there is something for them to fire at I will let them know,' said Dorn, the ghost of a smile softening his face. The officer bowed his head, and Archamus could almost feel another layer of fear peel from the chamber. Dorn turned his head fractionally and continued in the same soft tone as before, so that what he was saying was said to Archamus alone. 'The question is, what are we not supposed to see?'

Archamus was skimming though the torrent of alerts crowding in. What was he discounting or not considering? There was so much. Panic was seeping into the major population sinks as warning sirens rang out. Military garrisons across the planet were scrambling to full alert. Damocles was tearing itself apart. *We have come for you* – the murder cry of the Night Lords – was echoing over its screams. What did that mean? He felt the tug of the question and then discounted it. This was not about what he could see. It was about what he was not letting himself see.

He stopped. His skin prickled cold inside his armour. He looked back at the flow of confusion and saw. There it was, buried amongst the vox-logs scrolling across a bank of pict screens. Every check and confirmation from every military unit under the Praetorian's control passed across those screens. There were hundreds of thousands of signals from the last few minutes alone. But he knew what he was looking for: an absence, a missed part of a pattern.

He saw it. The cold on his skin pinched deeper.

'Lord,' he said, keeping his voice low and controlled. 'Squad Labrys, deployed to the Dome of Illumination at first alert, and then split to cover the approaches to the Northern Circuit. The element left in the Dome should have checked in one hundred and eighty-eight seconds ago. They did not. Sensors registered vibration and sound elevation. They also registered a low-grade explosion in the approach tunnels of the Investiary five hundred and three seconds ago.'

Dorn's face was utterly still, and then he was turning and striding for the door, cloak spilling behind him. The chamber doors opened at a gesture.

'With me,' he called, pace quickening.

'Lord–'

'Now.'

Archamus followed, locking his helmet in place as he moved. His bionics hissed and clacked as they synchronised with his stride. The five other Huscarls in the room were with him, weapons ready. Ahead of him, Dorn was already a golden blur. The wail of the sirens echoed the sound of their feet as they ran.

Questions poured through Archamus even as he pulled *Oathword* from his waist.

How had this happened so quickly? How was it possible? What were they facing?

But louder than the questions was a memory, its image and sound as alive as the pounding of blood in his ears.

'Do you know the old Terran riddle of the tower?' Dorn had asked all those decades ago, as the wind had shivered off a frost-desert. Archamus had shaken his head, and Dorn had smiled grimly. 'The riddle goes – Stand on the tower and see far. Raise the tower higher and see all the land. High or low, what does the far looking eye see not?' Dorn had laughed, the humour brief and bright in his face. 'Not very good as word play, but the point is sound, do you not think?'

Archamus had nodded, and answered.

'If you are on a tower looking out then the one thing you cannot see is what is beneath your feet. You cannot see the tower itself.'

Archamus remembered the words, and ran on through the Imperial Palace. The wail of the sirens followed him like the laughter of old nightmares come to the waking world.

The Investiary
The Imperial Palace, Terra

SILONIUS FOLDED INTO the shadows at the edge of the Investiary. The blush of dawn was pulling at the black dome of the sky, and the falling embers of the fire above were pulling streaks of flame across the gaps between the clouds of pollution. A cold wind blew across the open circle of the Investiary, slicing the sound of the sirens. He could smell dust, and dew turning to frost. He looked up.

Vast figures loomed against the night sky above him. Shadows clung to the recesses of their faces, and the growing light caught the edges of weapons. There were eighteen of them, standing in a circle around the outer edge of the Investiary. Shrouds covered nine of them, but the white marble of the other nine stood pale and proud in the growing light.

Silonius looked at the nearest statue. A pair of furled wings hung from its back, and a sword rested point down in its hand.

Sanguinius, he thought. *The Father of Angels.*

He shifted his gaze to the statue furthest from him. The face of Lion El'Jonson stared back from across the open kilometre of stone. This place had once been the heart of the Great Crusade. Oaths made here had forged the greatest empire mankind had ever seen. That empire now burned, and the ideals that had raised these statues were ashes. Yet the statues of the eighteen primarchs still stood, as though somehow the circle that Horus had broken could be whole again.

It almost made him laugh.

He froze, tingles running up and down his skin.

There were others with him in the wide emptiness. He could not see them, but he was certain they were there. He could smell them as a slight scent in the air, and hear them in the sounds hidden by the wind and the noise of distant sirens.

He paused, and then slid across the shadows until he was at the base of Sanguinius' statue. He stopped, cocked his head and listened. Slowly he began to move around the base.

'Be very still,' came the voice from above and behind him. He obeyed, holding himself perfectly immobile. 'Good,' said the voice. The speaker was six metres above him and two back. A good position, he reflected, difficult to reach before being shot to pieces. 'Speak the word.'

He hesitated. So far the memories that had come back to him had been precise and clear, but now he felt others begin to surface from the murk. A new understanding settled into his thoughts.

'Calisto,' he said at last, and paused. 'And you? What word do you have for me?'

'Hecate,' said the voice, and he heard the soft noise of several figures moving close by.

The figure that had dropped from the statue's base seemed to blur into the gloom. Silonius could make out the hints of compact recon armour, infra-sight visors and weapons. He was looking at himself, he realised; not a reflection but a shadow cast by the same outline.

'Mission parameter?' he asked.

'Eurydice,' said the shadowed figure.

Silonius felt a pause in his thoughts as the word brought a strand of action into focus.

'Confirmed,' he said. 'What is our strength and status?'

'Seven now,' said the shadow. 'You are the last. Three others converged with us two hundred and ten seconds ago. If there are any others coming, they fall outside the parameter. The Fists will be here soon.'

'Then we had better be done before they arrive,' said Silonius, and began to unharness the explosives from his back.

FIVE

THEY RAN THROUGH the Dome of Illumination. Doors opened before Rogal Dorn, slamming back into their mountings. Archamus sprinted in his lord's wake, muscle and piston surging in time. Ten Huscarls were with him.

'Isolate the northern zones,' shouted Archamus into his vox. The nearest Imperial Fists force was half a kilometre away and five levels down. They could not reach the Investiary in time, but the whole area was now a ground of battle.

The remains of a collapsed walkway barred their path, but Dorn took the gap in a bound. Archamus followed, rolling as he landed. His eyes caught the smears of blood on the floor, and the bolt casings lying amongst the rubble.

One of us died here, he thought, the realisation cutting into his mind. *A legionary of the Imperial Fists fell within the Palace.*

A wide passage sloped up towards a distant archway. Dead servitors littered the floor. Oil and blood was slick on the pale stone of the steps. Dorn was already a third of the way up. The blast doors had been melted open. A wisp of smoke was rising from the cooling metal. His eyes caught a line of red in the smoke. Dorn was ten strides ahead of him.

'Mine charges,' Archamus shouted. Dorn unclamped his bolter from his thigh and fired without pause. Bolts punched into the frame of the ruined door. The charges concealed in the frame detonated. Shrapnel blasted out. The shock wave spilled back down the tunnel, picked Archamus up and threw him down. He spun to his feet. Red markers flashed at the edge of his vision. His chest and face were numb. Smoke and dust filled the world around him. Green markers picked out the other Huscarls as they got to their feet and ran on. There was no sign of the primarch.

SILONIUS LOOKED UP as the crack of the detonations rolled around the Investiary. A cloud of dust billowed up and out, enveloping the shrouded statue of Magnus the Red. For a second the world seemed to slow. He could see the chips of stone and metal spinning in the blast wave. He noticed the thin light catch the edge of the dust, and break into a halo of yellow and red.

We have run out of time, he realised. The other six infiltrators were still scattered amongst the statues. The last charges were in place, but they would not all have time to get clear.

That did not matter, though. In fact it made things much easier.

'Here it comes,' he muttered to himself.

A figure broke from the cloud of debris. Dust matted the gold of its armour, but there was no mistaking what it was. Who it was.

Rogal Dorn fired as he ran. On the opposite side of the Investiary one of the other infiltrators fell from the plinth of Ferrus Manus. Bright red blood stained white marble. Silonius was already swinging down from where he had been crouched beneath the shroud of the twentieth primarch.

A spray of bolter fire reached out from between the feet of great Sanguinius. Explosions burst across Dorn's armour. He did not even slow down. He fired again, and another figure was falling in a shower of splintered skull and chunks of brain.

ARCHAMUS HEARD THE sound of gunfire and ran towards it. The dust cloud was all around him. His helmet display flickered as it tried to lock on to targets. He was bleeding. He could feel it now, could feel the muscles in his legs squeezing around the pieces of shrapnel that had found the soft seals between armour plates. It was not pain yet, but it would be. He broke through the dust.

An echoing quiet greeted him. Two of his brother Huscarls ran with him. Dorn was ahead of them, moving into the centre of the Investiary's circle. Archamus signalled the other Huscarls and they formed an arrowhead with their primarch at the tip. A volley of bolts exploded in front of them. Shards of stone chimed as they struck Archamus' armour.

Dorn paused, aimed and fired once. The incoming fire cut off.

Silence had slid back into place across the Investiary. The wind pulled at the smoke.

Dorn shook his head.

'This is not as it should be,' he said.

'Lord?' asked Archamus. The adrenaline was still burning in his veins. His eyes were scanning for targets, but none moved in his sight.

'They mined the entrance, but nowhere else,' said Dorn. 'If they had time to do that they could have wired traps into the ground. They have not.'

'They might have, but the charges failed,' replied Archamus.

'They have not,' repeated Dorn, turning again. 'They are still here. Five are dead, but others remain. Two at least.'

Archamus reached up and pulled his helmet off. The buzz of static from his damaged vox vanished. The quiet wrapped around him. He could sense nothing, and the reek of explosives and dust filled his nose.

'We should seal the entrances and bring the gunships over.'

Dorn glanced at Archamus, and a spark, hard and bright, seemed to catch at the edge of his eye. He shook his head, and Archamus recognised something in the expression that he had not seen in his lord for a long time.

Rage.

'No, Archamus. No one comes to the heart of this fortress and forces me back into a hole. We go forwards. We find them.' He paused, and Archamus watched a muscle move and settle in Dorn's jaw. 'We take the last of them alive.'

Archamus nodded, but Dorn was already moving forwards. Above them, the graven faces of the primarchs looked down on them like a court of gods standing in judgement on the living.

SILONIUS LAY UTTERLY still beneath the shroud. His armour and body suit had shifted to the white grey of the marble he clung to. He could hear the Imperial Fists moving across the Investiary. He stilled his breath.

Four of the others had died in as many seconds when Dorn had stepped from the dust cloud.

Silonius could almost feel the primarch's presence, like the edge of a sword held just above the skin. He turned his head, unfolding the muscles a fraction at a time, until he was looking at the small charges attached to the shroud tethers. The last one still needed to be armed. Once he did that, his lifespan was measured in seconds. Dorn would hear the noise and a bolt would pluck away Silonius' life before he heard the gunshot. That was a problem. Dying was not part of the mission parameter. But neither was failure.

He reached out for the charge, and snapped the arming mechanism closed.

Gunfire whipped out towards Silonius, but he was already dropping from the shrouded statue. He yanked the blind grenades from his harness as he fell, landed, and pulled the arming pins as he rolled. He came to his feet running, tossing the grenades behind and in front of him. A cloud of white mist burst from the first grenade as he broke from cover. The world beyond the cloud vanished.

The clatter and roar of bolter fire echoed from the stone as shots cut the air around him. He swerved, breaking the rhythm of his run as the other two grenades triggered. Fresh clouds of blank white gas filled the air. He was running down a corridor of clear air between expanding clouds. The sounds of gunfire distorted.

A bolt-round flicked out of the cloud and exploded at his feet. Shrapnel ripped through the fabric over his thighs. Blood pumped from the wound as he ran.

He pulled the detonator from his belt. It was a black cylinder as long as his hand was wide. Dials etched with numbers capped one end, a simple switch was at the other. Any other surviving infiltrators would be doing the same, and all would be making for their escape routes.

He reached the wall running along the edge of the amphitheatre, and ran along it until he found the drainage grate. It was raw plasteel, plated in bronze and welded in place. He locked a melta bomb onto it, and ducked aside as the metal became vapour. He looked up. The statues of the primarchs loomed above the dust and smoke. Gunfire rattled in the murk. He did not know which escape routes the others were making for. It did not matter. He turned the dial on the bottom of the detonator wand.

The figure came out of the fog at a run.

Silonius jerked sideways. His bolter was in his hand, finger pulling the trigger.

He froze.

The other infiltrator stared back, gun aimed at Silonius. Dark recon armour covered his torso, shoulders and shins. Dark green-and-blue fabric swathed his head. Blood was clotting in tears in the fabric over his arms. He was breathing hard from traumatic shock.

'The charges are... set...' coughed the other infiltrator, and swayed.

Silonius nodded slowly.

'Good,' he said, and shot him.

The warrior fell where he stood, his skull scattered in red fragments across the stone floor. Silonius stepped towards the drainage grating and looked up one last time. He had a clear route from here out of the Palace, and to the next element of his mission. He had not replied in kind when the other infiltrator had given the mission parameter as Eurydice. Even though his mind was still locked behind blank doors, one of the first things that had come back to him was the reason he was here. He had a mission, the end of which he could not see, but which he would follow, and the parameter of that mission was not Eurydice, it was Orpheus.

He keyed the detonator and dropped into darkness, as above him the roof of the Imperium shook.

THE FIRST EXPLOSION cut through the sound of gunfire like an axe blow through flesh. Archamus turned in its direction. The statue of Lion El'Jonson trembled where it stood. Cracks raced over the contours of armour. The face of the First Primarch split, and the cracks raced through the blade he held to his chest. Then a second explosion ripped through the base of the statue.

It fell.

Carved fabric and flesh broke apart. Shards exploded as they hit the floor. A wave of dust spilled through the air.

Another explosion, and another, and the Khan was a shattered ruin on the stone floor, and Russ was toppling, and the sound rose up to greet the rising sun. Detonations raced around the circle of statues, ripping them from their plinths and shattering them as they fell. Archamus just had time to clamp his helmet in place before the blast waves enveloped him.

The world was dust again. The ground shivered beneath his feet, and the thunder of explosions rolled on, growing and growing, until at last it faded.

Pieces of marble rang on his helm like heavy rain.

'Lord?' he shouted. His helmet display had cut out completely.

'I am here,' said Dorn from close by.

The dust drained slowly from the air. The sight of the sky returned first, the light breaking into coloured rays as it fell through the cloud.

Then other shapes appeared: the high tiers of the Investiary's bowl, the high towers of the Palace, the top of the Pillar of Unity.

Then, one at a time, the shapes of the two remaining statues emerged.

Eight traitors had fallen. The wind stirred the tatters of their shrouds amongst the rubble they had become. Here and there a recognisable fragment remained: the reaching claws of Curze, the single eye of Magnus set in his proud face, the hand of Horus resting on the pommel of his sword.

Of the nine brothers still loyal to the Emperor, one remained unbroken amid the devastation. Rogal Dorn, Primarch of the VII Legion, Praetorian of Terra, stood against the sky, his eyes set on the rising sun.

Dorn stared at the carved image of himself, and then turned to look at the only other statue that now stood unshrouded and unbroken.

Fabric had hidden its features for years, but a series of small charges had cut the ropes holding the covering in place. The shroud now lay at its feet, shed like a snake's skin. Archamus almost thought he saw a grim smile flicker on his lord's face as he looked up, as though a suspicion had become a certainty.

Above the Investiary – face hidden behind a crested helm, weight leaning on a spear, the tip of which pierced the throat of a two-headed serpent at his feet – stood Alpharius.

Dorn stood looking up, his face unreadable, his eyes hard and dark.

'No one enters here, besides my Huscarls. Not the Custodians, not others from the Legion, not the vassals of the Regent.'

'The Regent himself?'

'No one,' said Dorn, then gestured at the settling dust. 'Bring servitors in to sift the rubble. Every scrap of evidence left by the enemy will be found.'

'Lord...' began Archamus, looking down at where the carved feather of an angel's wing lay amongst a jumble of broken marble. It was Pendelikon marble, threaded with fine grey veins and shaped with such skill that it seemed as though feathers had been transmuted into stone rather than carved, exquisite even in ruin. 'What...' The words stopped in his throat. He looked up and met his primarch's eyes. 'What was this, lord?'

Rogal Dorn was still for a long second, and then he looked up at the statue of Alpharius, then to where his own carved image stood amongst the rubble.

'It was a message,' he said, and then strode away through the settling dust.

SIX

Damocles Starport
Terra

THE CHAINSWORD CYCLED down to silence. Kestros kept his eyes on the entrances of the lift shaft. He pulled the empty magazine free of his bolt pistol and snapped a fresh one in place. The ammo counter chimed, and a rune flashed green in the corner of his helmet display. The empty magazine clanged off the support girders and walls of the shaft as it dropped down into the dark. Blood splatter covered half his view, but with infra-sight he could see straight through it. The rest of his squad were yellow silhouettes of armour above and below him. The drying blood coating the lift shaft was a cooling green against the cold black of the metal. A body, wedged in the nearest door, was still orange with warmth.

'Nothing showing on auspex,' said one of his squad over the vox. 'Levels of hallucinogen are dropping.'

'Very well. We are dropping in ten seconds. Stand by.' He gunned the chainsword once. Clotting blood and scraps of skin sprayed free of the teeth.

It had been twenty hours since the company had dropped onto

Damocles Starport. He had been fighting without cease from the moment he had leapt from the gunship's assault ramp. A wave of cargo-loaders and menials had met them in a frenzied wave, and from that point he and his brothers had been hacking and shooting without respite. They had held the landing pads until heavier gunships had dropped prefab defence lines and more warriors. Then they had begun to drive inwards, into the guts of the starport. Screams had filled its corridors. Bodies had strewn its floors, and blood daubed its walls. They found no one sane. Hordes of humans would break from tearing at each other and charge onto the Imperial Fists' guns. They did not respond to threats, or words, and after a while the order went out to engage without hesitation. The retaking of the starport had become a purge. That bloody task was still under way.

This is not war, he thought. *This is butchery.*

Kestros closed his eyes for a second, and flexed his fingers on the grips of his weapons.

'Drop on my lead,' he said, and fixed his gaze on the abyss below. 'Drop.'

He stepped off the ledge into the darkness of the shaft. Gravity yanked him down. Girders and doorways rushed past. The black pit beneath him grew. Voices roared around him, booming from vox-horns in the open mouths of passing corridors. He saw light from an open door shining across the floor at the bottom of the shaft.

He triggered his jump pack for an instant. Flames lit the dark, and force snapped through him as his speed vanished. Light flared above him as his brothers triggered their own packs. He landed on the rockcrete floor at the bottom of the lift shaft, and came up firing. The doors vanished in a wall of detonations. Kestros bounded through. His visor lit with target runes. He fired, recoil hammering back into his hand. The first figure came out of the smoke. Its body was a red blur of heat, the chain in its hands cold blue. He let the swing come, stepped into it and brought the chainsword up in a cut that split the attacker from groin to crown. He ran on, taking another two figures as they came at him. His squad were already through the door, their guns finding targets, hammering shells into bodies.

The sounds of madness and slaughter reached up and filled the chamber's high roof. He blinked his visor to full-sight. Through the gun smoke he could see the shapes of macro haulers lined up across the space. A mass of debris lay across the back of three of them, and twisted remains of girders hung from the roof above. Bodies carpeted the floor. The air was vibrating with the distorted shout of the vox-horns. Movement twitched at the edge of his sight.

'Take the gantries,' he called, his voice a rasp, as he hacked through another flailing figure. Four of the squad triggered their jump packs and boosted through the air. They landed on the network of gantries high above and began to fire downwards.

'Brother-sergeant,' called one of them, 'there is–'

He heard the thump of the missile launching, and twisted to look up, in time to see the ceiling explode. Two more missiles struck, a blink between each of them. The gantries fell. Kestros leapt to the side, struck the ground, rolled and fired his jump pack as he came up. The wreckage hit the floor. A fuel cell in one of the haulers ruptured, and a fist of fire thumped into the air.

The blast batted Kestros aside. Damage runes flashed in his eyes. Gunfire rattled into the air, hard rounds loosed in bursts. His head was spinning as he tumbled through the air, thrusters still firing.

The purge had been bloody, and they had faced humans prepared to kill anything they found, in any way they could. But this was different. This was not madness.

He cut the jump pack and tucked into a ball as he fell. He hit the side of a macro hauler, and the impact ripped through the skin of its cargo container. His armour screamed. His left pauldron tore away, servos burned out as they tried to absorb the impact. He felt bones break.

He uncurled and leapt up through the hole he had ripped into the hauler. There was another percussive boom, and a missile struck the cargo container where he had fallen. Shrapnel clattered off his armour.

The runes of his squad brothers were distorted yellow in his visor. He could see the enemy now, a cluster of figures moving behind cover. His eyes took in their breath masks, weapons and movements.

Trained, he thought. *Dangerous, for humans*. He shot two of them before they could raise their weapons. At his back, three of his squad landed and fell into an arrow behind him. They ran forwards, clearing debris, bodies and crates in fluid bounds. He felt the drum beat of hard rounds clattering against his armour.

He saw the real threat almost too late.

Two figures crouched behind a mound of crates, their missile launchers levelled at him as he came from the clouds of smoke and dust. He fired again, and jinked to the side a second later. The shell hit the launcher as the missile's propellant ignited in the tube. A wave of shrapnel ripped the second shooter apart just as the missile roared into the air. The explosion burst above his head.

The silence was sudden, as though the noise had been sliced away with a knife. The haze of Kestros' helmet display showed only the rolling clouds of smoke. Nothing else moved. Targeting runes searched for threats and found none. Kestros blinked back to infra-sight, but cooling greens and blues painted the world. The heat from the fires rippled in red, but besides his brothers no warm blood beat in the chamber.

He walked over to the nearest enemy, or what remained of them. They were simple human stock, fit but unexceptional. What was exceptional was that in all the hundreds they had butchered as they descended through the starport, these were the only ones who had not acted from madness.

Slowly, he reached down and pulled the breath mask off the corpse. The face beneath was slack. Terran trade cartel brands covered the neck and lower lip, he noticed. He recognised the geometric design of the Hysen Cartel seal.

The noise coming from the vox-horns finally fell silent.

'Sergeant,' came a voice from behind him.

He rose and turned. His squad brother's armour was dented and dotted with impact marks.

'Yes, brother?' he said.

'Area is clear. We have three casualties, no fatalities.'

Kestros nodded. He breathed out.

'Make ready to withdraw,' he said, looking back down to the corpse at his feet. 'We are done here.'

'A holding force–' began the other warrior, but Kestros cut the question off.

'They can send auxilia or militia to deal with this slaughterhouse.' He paused and looked at his left vambrace. A thick coat of drying blood hid the yellow ceramite. On the ground further away, he saw a severed arm, still wrapped in the tattered uniform of the starport's militia. 'Our duty here is done.'

He gave a small shake of his head, but if his brother noticed he said nothing.

He glanced at the corpse with the cartel tattoos on its neck and dropped the rebreather beside it.

Bhab Bastion
The Imperial Palace, Terra

THE CORPSES LAY in darkness. Archamus crossed the vault slowly, his bionics clicking and hissing. Ghost pain ran up and down the pistons that had once been muscle. It had been constant since the encounter in the Investiary. Flesh that had never had a chance to grow old ached as he moved. It was not tiredness, even though he had not rested since the night of the attack. No, it was something else: an echo of a thought escaping the control of his will.

He had not seen the primarch since the attack. The sun had turned through the sky, but the orders from the Praetorian had come via others. Where Dorn was and what he was doing remained unknown to the master of his bodyguard. That did not concern Archamus, though; the primarch often was concerned with affairs that Archamus knew nothing about. No, what worried Archamus was that Dorn had now called for him, and him alone. That was what itched at the back of his skull as he walked towards the dead.

Stasis fields enclosed the granite blocks that the corpses lay on. As Archamus approached he could see the remains under the layers of cold light: a charred hand, its fingers curled into a claw; a bare torso, the ragged edges of its meat weeping frozen beads of blood; an exploded skull laid out in wet fragments. Armour plates and weapons lay beside them, arranged like grave goods beside warriors from a less enlightened age.

Do we truly live in an age of enlightenment any more? he wondered, as he stepped into the cold glow around the stasis fields.

He looked down at the nearest slab. A collection of limbs and lumps of burned flesh lay in the rough shape of a corpse. Three bolt shells had hit it in the chest, one after another, in a neat line from gut to neck. The rest of the damage had come from the corpse being in the blast radius of a demolition charge. Even torn to shreds, it was clear what the corpse had been when it lived. It was a Space Marine.

'What do you see?' Dorn's voice came from the dark beyond the glow of the stasis fields. Archamus moved on, not answering straight away, knowing that while a reply was required, it was also expected that his response be a considered one.

Archamus frowned at the remains nearest him, and then glanced at the others.

'These are the dead we took from the Investiary. An infiltration and sabotage team. Six members in all. Light armaments and armour,' he said.

'But what else do you see?' asked Dorn, closer but still not within the circle of light.

Archamus leaned closer to the corpse that had caused his frown. All that was left of it was the torso, which sat on the granite like a butchered portion of meat.

'This one has signs of slight muscle atrophy,' he said, leaning his head to change the angle of his view. 'If the others were intact I am guessing they would show the same. In our kind that might be the result of a bio-weapon, or some malfunction of gene-seed. But that is not likely.' He straightened up. 'The damage was from long-term hibernation in a sus-an coma. They were asleep here on Terra. They were woken for this... *task.*'

'And...' said Dorn stepping closer, the pale light catching the sharp edges of his face, and the eagle heads carved into his armour. 'Beyond *that* what do you see?'

'This was planned a long time ago. The routes in, the layout of the Palace, the coordination of different assets to enact multiple operations at the same time. This is not something that was thrown together. This was laid down years ago. Before the war even began, perhaps.'

Dorn stepped up next to the slab. In the cold light his armour seemed silver, his hair the white of frost.

'They had time,' said Dorn, softly. 'They had all the time they would need to prepare, to gather information, to plan.'

'In the time before the Massacre at Isstvan,' said Archamus, 'while they wore the cloak of loyalty.'

Dorn shook his head, eyes still fixed on the flesh and bone on the slab.

'Before that. This is a treachery older than Isstvan.'

'But before Horus turned, what reason would the Alpha Legion have to plan an attack here on Terra?'

'Every reason you can imagine,' said Dorn, and turned away.

Archamus watched him for the moment, but the primarch did not add to his words. He looked back at the remains, a frown forming as he took in the details of grenade and ammunition harnesses.

'What were they hoping to achieve?' asked Archamus at last. Dorn turned. Archamus gestured across each of the slabs. 'The damage to our orbital defences will be repaired. The Damocles Starport will be repopulated and return to functionality. The riots will be quelled. The attack on the vox-network served only to mask the other attacks, and if anything has alerted us to a weakness. What purpose was there in any of this?'

'The purpose was to show that they could,' growled Dorn.

Archamus shook his head.

'There must be something else, something they have gained by doing this?'

Dorn glanced sharply at Archamus, and then pointed at one of the bodies on the slabs. Of all of them it was the most complete. Only its head was missing. Pieces of skull lay above the ragged stump of its neck. A piece of jaw and cheekbone hung from a shred of skin.

'Have you noted this one?'

Archamus looked at it.

'Killed by an excellent shot,' he said.

Dorn nodded, but his face remained fixed.

'A shot I did not make,' said Dorn. 'I know where each of the others took their targets, and how they fell. This kill was not mine.'

'A lucky shot by one of us through the blind grenade fog?'

Dorn shook his head.

'This was a clean and deliberate kill.'

Archamus looked at the corpse again, his eyes moving across the shards of skull laid out where the head should have been. He blinked, allowing his eyes to find details. After a minute he nodded, and let out a long breath.

'The shell was not explosive.'

'Quicksilver,' agreed Dorn.

'And it entered just above the jaw, and blew out the crown of the skull with the initial impact.' He turned to one of the other plinths and gestured at it. Servitor eyes saw the movement from where they watched at the chamber's edge, and the stasis field vanished. Blood began to ooze across the stone from the chunks of flesh. Archamus picked up the bolter that lay on the slab beside the remains. He gestured again, and the field blinked back into being. He turned the bolter over, snapped the clip out and clicked the topmost shell free. 'Stalker rounds,' he said, holding one up.

'Neither I nor the Huscarls were using such ammunition during the battle,' said Dorn.

'So this one,' Archamus nodded at the headless corpse, 'was killed by one of his own.'

Dorn gave a single nod.

'That means that not all of them died in the Investiary,' said Archamus, looking down at the shell in his hand. The brass casing and polished tip gleamed in the cold light. 'One of them escaped, and killed his brother in the process.'

'Brotherhood is a term that does not apply to the Twentieth Legion,' growled Dorn.

Archamus was still looking at the shell.

'This was not panic. This was an execution. Whoever did this is here, on Terra, and they killed their own to ensure that they went alone.'

He looked up at Dorn.

'Why?' asked Archamus. For a second he thought he saw a glimmer of sorrow in the primarch's face.

Dorn reached out and took both bolter and shell gently from Archamus. He slid the shell back into the magazine, loaded the weapon, gestured and replaced it beneath a stasis field.

'What is going to happen is not going to be easy,' said Dorn. 'I am sorry that it must be you. You are the last of my first sons, and I would have preferred that another take the burden that you must carry.' He paused, and breathed out slowly. 'There is something I must ask you to do for me, my friend.'

'Of course, lord. Your will is my–'

'There is no need for formalities here, not now. Not with what I am going to ask of you.'

'Request or order, they are the same to me, lord.'

Dorn gave him a long look, and then nodded slowly.

'You are right. This is the beginning of something. There are greater wheels turning the fate of this war, but I cannot ignore what has happened. Neither can I fight it as I would like.' He paused. 'I need you to defend the Legion, and Terra. I need you to be a praetorian to praetorians.'

'Have I not always been that, lord?' replied Archamus.

✠ ✠ ✠

Southern refuse sprawl
Terra

THE AIR THAT touched Silonius' face was cold, and smelt of burning refuse and rotting waste. He stood for a moment and breathed deeply, letting the scents fill his nose, and the cold his lungs. Heaps of smouldering rubbish loomed above him. Smoke coiled from their sides, and the daylight falling through the pollution layer was yellow and rotten. The crevasse behind him led down through a maze of rock into the collapsed strata of Terra's history.

It had taken him two days to make his way down through the Palace to the forgotten door. He had moved quickly at first, relying on speed and the chaos of the moment to protect him. Later, as the shock of the attack had drained away, he had moved more slowly, creeping and sliding through the edges of the security net that was clamping tight over the Palace. Then he had gone into the underworld, and begun his journey up through the crushed cities and caves. He had needed to kill four times. Nothing challenging, but necessary if he was to reach his rendezvous on time. He had kept his armour, but shed the spent demolition equipment piece by piece. Some lay in the Palace, some in the dark of the world beneath.

He took another breath. He was somewhere in the midden heaps south of the parapets of the Dhawalagiri Prospect. Not his preferred surfacing point, but acceptable. He would be able to reach his primary rendezvous if he made good time.

He pulled out the labour brute's robe that he had worn to move through the Palace, and pulled it on over his armour. Within half a kilometre it would be so daubed with ash and refuse slime that he would seem like one of the scrap hunters. He checked the direction of the light and then began to lope across the burning ground.

✠ ✠ ✠

Bhab Bastion
The Imperial Palace, Terra

THE WIND CUT across the roof of the world. On the parapet of the Bhab Bastion, Archamus watched as the glow of the sun began to sink behind a thick layer of cloud. There was ice in the air, and the taste of snow. He thought of Inwit, and the winds driving the snow from the night. Dorn stood beside him, hands on the stone of the parapet. Both of them were armoured, and their cloaks rippled and furled in the wind. The tower top was deserted apart from them, and neither had spoken since they had left the vaults far beneath.

'You must do this alone,' said Dorn without looking away from the line of light on the horizon. 'You may claim whatever resources you need with my authority, but the knowledge of whom and what you hunt will remain with you, and only you.'

Archamus was silent.

'Speak your thoughts,' said Dorn.

'That will make it difficult to discover what the Alpha Legion intend. Knowledge defeats secrecy. We should cut the ground away from under them. There should be no place for them to hide. Every door they try should be barred, every weakness made strong.'

'A good way, but for this it cannot serve.' Dorn paused and looked down at where his hand rested on the stone of the parapet. 'Tell me, what did you feel when this began?'

'When the *Primigenia* exploded...' Archamus felt his words catch as an echo of that instant shuddered through him. 'When the alarms sounded there was a moment... a moment when I thought that it might be real. That we might have lost before we even began to fight.'

Dorn gave a short, bitter laugh.

'Clever is it not? Clever and vile.' Archamus saw the lines of his lord's jaw harden. '"Such are we that in this art of war are like unto serpents, to lie out of sight, to strike swift, to carry such poison in our mouths that men fear to tread where we may lie." My father once quoted those words to me when I asked Him of the Twentieth Legion's ways of war. The true threat is not what they plan, or what they will do, but what the questions will do to us.'

'I understand,' said Archamus. He felt suddenly cold, as though a ball of ice were growing in his guts.

Dorn watched him for a second, and nodded.

'Remember what you felt when the attack began. Remember the shock. Remember the way that your instincts, good instincts, pulled you to act, to see threats that were not there. That is Alpharius' way, and the way of his Legion. They are the shadow of a monster thrown on a wall, made greater by fear. As soon as you know they are there, you begin to look for them, to wonder what they might be doing, what their end might be. You see shadows and believe them real. And then you begin to doubt your eyes and ears, and then the true threat appears, and it is too late.'

'And so none can know they were here, or are here still,' said Archamus carefully. Phantom shivers ran up and down his bionic limbs.

'My brother was cradled in lies,' said Dorn. 'Begin to think about what he is doing and you hand him his greatest weapon. This is his doing, even if others strike for him. His sons are the same. They have many heads, but all carrying the same venom.' Dorn was still watching him. 'But I cannot allow the threat to pass. Clever and vile indeed. Find whatever forces the Alpha Legion have left in the system. Uncover what they intend, and keep their poison from crippling us. That is what I ask of you, Archamus.'

'You speak of poison. Do you trust me not to succumb to it?'

Dorn put a hand on Archamus' shoulder.

'There is no other that it would have pained me more to see take this burden, and no other that I would trust more to see it done.'

Archamus bowed his head. He suddenly felt very tired.

'I will do this duty for you, lord.'

'Thank you, old friend. This is not the war I raised you to.'

'But I cannot do this alone. I am a warrior and architect, not a hunter of shadows, and I have grown old as both. I will need help.'

'Do what you need to do,' said Dorn, then fell into a silence.

The daylight was a molten red-and-yellow blaze beyond the tops of the mountains and the towers of the Palace.

Archamus shook his head slowly. Dorn glanced up at the movement, eyebrow raised in question.

'Why did they do it this way?' asked Archamus. 'Why show their hand? They could have pursued whatever comes next and remained completely undetected. Instead they have shown their presence. It is almost as though they want us to face them, as though they wish the contest.'

'Because this is not about winning,' said Dorn, his voice suddenly tired. He blinked and ran his fingers across his eyes. 'It is not about winning, and it never was. It is about pride.'

Southern refuse sprawl
Terra

'WE WILL HAVE to go soon,' grumbled Incarnus. Myzmadra shot him a look, but the savant was staring up at the sky. Around them the cargo lighter buzzed as its engines grumbled in low register.

'We are still within the window,' said Phocron from the bottom of the ramp. 'We wait until the allotted time has passed.'

Incarnus flinched, but did not reply.

One of the five legionnaires had split off from the team just after they had moved out from the signal tower. None of the others had said anything to him or questioned why he was going, accepting that the lone warrior's mission was now different from theirs. And just as one of their number left, now they waited for another to join them.

Myzmadra let out a breath and went back to watching the horizon. The light was draining from the sky, and the layers of pollution were turning the last of it into a molten glow that caught in the tops of the spoil heaps. The skies of Terra were bare. Aircraft and trans-atmospheric shuttles normally sliced the air into shards with the wash from their wings, but now only a few circled in the lower reaches like sullen carrion over a wounded beast. Most of them would be war planes of the Imperial Fists, and its auxilia. Perhaps even the Fire Condors of the Legio Custodes were abroad, watching for prey, ready to strike.

'Whoever it is, they missed the first rendezvous,' hissed Ashul from the lighter's cockpit. 'Got to put their chances at low.'

'There could be any number of reasons for them missing the primary rendezvous,' replied Myzmadra, watching Phocron carefully. He crouched in the shadow of the lighter's fuselage, weapon ready, eyes fixed on the folds of the land around them.

Heaps of refuse extended away in every direction, rising as high as hills, oozing steam into the dusk air. Streams of fouled liquid ran at the bottom of valleys. Crags of wreckage protruded from the peaks. In the distance the tips of the Himalazia loomed like teeth. The rest of Phocron's team were scattered across the refuse piles around the lighter, still shapes in the growing gloom.

'Some poor souls live here,' said Myzmadra, as much to herself as anyone else.

'What?' asked Incarnus, glancing at her, puzzlement creasing his face.

'There are tribes of people who live out here, thousands of them. Children are born, and grow and die, and believe that the whole universe looks like this.' She paused. 'That there is nothing better.'

'And?' Incarnus arched a hairless eyebrow. She ignored it and did not elaborate. After a minute he rolled his neck, stretched and turned his eyes from her, back to the darkening land.

'Whoever we are waiting for – they aren't coming,' he muttered again, and then flinched as the sonic boom of an aircraft rolled over the land. Myzmadra tensed, but the echoes of the jet's passing faded.

Flakes of ash and debris stirred in the downdraught as Ashul briefly cycled the engines up. They had picked the lighter up fifty kilometres east of the tower they had attacked. Hidden at the bottom of a gorge, it looked to be made of rust, but it flew just fine. Part of her wondered how long it had been there: months, years, more? She thought of the boxes buried under the surface of the top wastes, but then cut the thoughts off. There was a point at which questions led nowhere useful, or safe. She had learnt that lesson many times over since she had begun her service to the Legion.

'Time's almost up,' said Incarnus beside her. 'Were they mission-critical?'

She shook her head, and was about to say something when Incarnus straightened, eyes fixed on the dark gathering at the bases of the refuse hills.

'Something is out there,' he said. 'I can sense it.'

Phocron raised his boltgun, the muzzle aimed.

Myzmadra squinted, but could see nothing. Then she saw something moving across a slope. It was hunched, and walked with a loping gait that reminded her of a maimed dog.

She glanced at Incarnus, but his eyes were fixed on the thing coming towards them. The pupils had almost vanished in his eyes. A pearl of frost gathered at the corner of his left eye as he reached out with his mind.

'It's not human,' he said, his voice a rasp.

As though in answer to his words, Phocron's brothers rose, their guns levelled at the figure.

The figure paused, its head cocked to one side under the fabric of its hood.

'What word do you bring?' called Phocron.

Another pause.

'Eurydice,' said a voice. 'And you?'

'Calisto,' replied Phocron. And then the warriors were running back across the slopes. The shrouded figure came with them, but now it was not limping, but moving with the same fluid strength as the rest. They reached the lighter and vaulted on board one by one, collapsing their watch on the hills until only Phocron remained, and then he was jumping onto the ramp and the lighter was lifting from the ground in a scream of released power.

The figure that had joined them stank of ash and foul water. He was a giant, as tall as Phocron, but the newcomer wore only a ragged shroud over form-fitting recon armour. He slipped the hood from his head. His features were the smooth sculpture of strength that many of the Legion bore in direct echo of their primarch.

'I am Silonius,' said the newcomer. The ground was racing past beneath them now, the air roaring through the hatch as it shut. Phocron pulled the helm from his head.

'You will call me Phocron,' came the reply.

Beside her, Myzmadra felt Incarnus staring at the two warriors.

'Don't worry, you get used to half of them looking exactly the same,' she said.

The lighter lurched, and Terra dropped away beneath them.

Battle-barge Alpha
The interstellar gulf, beyond the light of Sol

THE WARSHIPS TUMBLED through the dark, spinning end over end with the momentum of the last thrust of their engines. No light shone within or without their hulls, and they had toppled through the void for long enough that ice clung to their bones. There were hundreds of them, some only half a kilometre from prow to stern, others vast cities of armour plating and weaponry. Seen from close enough that they were visible, but far enough that their shapes were hidden, they would have appeared as a cloud of debris, the remains of some ancient explosion, or collision of moons. From a distance at which their nature started to emerge, they became the corpses left by a storm or battle. The eye which moved close enough that it was weaving a path through the spinning hulls would have noticed that most were whole, and unmarked. But even then, neither eye nor sensor would have seen anything but cold, dead metal.

The largest ship was called the *Alpha*, and it was a metal mountain range studded with weaponry. In a chamber deep within her hull core, a stasis field blinked out of being. The field's generator had been sipping power for a year, draining its tiny reserve second by second, until nothing was left. The amount of power in the reserve, and the rate of drain from the stasis field, had been calculated so that it would fail at that exact moment.

The figure who had stood within the field completed the blink he had begun a year before. The chamber around him was suddenly empty and dark. A moment before it had been filled with tech-priests and servitors, and the air had buzzed with static and the click of machine code. Now his senses reached into blackness and found nothing.

A blue rune lit in his helmet display.

Cold. Fatal levels of cold.

He stepped off the stasis plinth.

The sound of his steps rippled back to him as echoes. He paused, and let his mind adjust to a present that was utterly different from the past he had just left. He had entered the stasis field in the last phases of the fleet's preparation, but even at that stage the battle-barge had been filled with noise and movement. Now there was nothing besides the sound of his own breathing, and the glow of his helmet display.

He began to walk, his steps echoes. There was no need to rush; he had all the time that he could want. The door out of the chamber had been left open for him. Without power the pistons and locks would have held them shut to all but a melta-blast. It was the same for each of the other hatchways and arches he moved through. He passed a servitor after an hour. It had frozen solid midway through some task that it had tried to pursue even as the dark and cold had closed around it. White frost crystals clogged its eyes and covered the exposed patches of its skin. He left it to its never-to-be-finished task and walked on.

The hoists and lifts were inactive, so he ascended by stairs and ladders, rung by rung, metre by metre. The chamber in which he had woken was far from the ship's bridge. They had kept the bulkheads sealed, and so his path was through a labyrinth of vents. Dealing with counter-incursion traps also added time. There had been a minimal chance that anything would have been able to detect the systems running the stasis field, but they did not have to tolerate that possibility, and so they had buried him deep. It took him another hour to reach the command level.

At last he dropped onto the bridge. It was utterly dark. Armoured shutters blocked the view of the stars beyond. The ghosts of data-stacks loomed in the silence. Rows of machine-wrapped servitors hung motionless on the walls of deep trenches running across the deck into the unclear distance. The empty command throne sat above him, skinned in ice, glinting in the light from his eye-lenses.

He moved across the chamber, finding the console he needed easily even in the dark. It was powered down and cold, but its initial operation was physical. The crank handle filled the dark with the rattle of chains and gears. He kept turning until the machine resisted, and then turned a series of dials set into the console. Somewhere beneath the deck a power reserve woke and began to siphon life into a very small number of systems.

Lights flickered down in the machine-canyons, and a trio of servitors twitched as fresh, warm blood was pumped into their flesh. Out on the hull, a single communication array began to sift the emptiness for signals. It would not find any yet, but it was not expected to; it just needed to be awake and listening when the signals did come.

The figure ascended the steps to the command throne, and sat. It would be a long wait, but as he had just passed a year in the blink of an eye, a few weeks more were nothing. Besides, he would not be alone for all of that; there was a Legion and armada to wake for war.

But, for now, the hollow silence and darkness would be his, and his alone.

GIFT OF THE FATHER

835.M30

One hundred and seventy years before the betrayal at Isstvan III

I

THE BOY WAITED in the dark. The only light was the brief glare of a hatch opening when they brought him food. The light was bright, and he could not look at it without being blinded. After the hatch shut, he found the food by smell and ate it by touch. The light and the food were all he had to mark the passage of time in the cell. He kept count of both in his head. He had eaten one hundred and four times, and seen the light one hundred and eight times. The four times that the hatch had opened and no food had appeared had served no purpose that he could be certain of. Perhaps eyes had looked in at him. Perhaps it had some other meaning. Perhaps it had no meaning at all.

He waited, slept and explored the edges of the dark. The floor, walls and ceiling were metal. Lines of rivets marked the seams between the slabs on the floor. There were twelve thousand, six hundred and seventy-eight rivets. He had counted them all by touch. None of them were loose. The door had hinges only on the outside. The narrow hatch at its base was without crack or seam. The cell itself was a cube, twice the length of his body on each side. Two small grates were set into the ceiling. A slow stream of air came from one, heavy with the smell of oil and machine fumes. The other covered a light, or at least he guessed that it did. These details never changed.

The only thing that changed was the song of the walls. Sometimes the song was a low rumble, like the pulse of a machine. Sometimes the walls were silent. Sometimes they shook like the case of a chain gun as it fired. Each song came and went, sometimes lasting for an age, sometimes rising and falling away quickly. The first time the song came he had beaten on the door and shouted. No one had come, and at last he had collapsed to the floor. When he woke next the song had changed. He listened to it and waited. By the time he had eaten one hundred and four times, the songs of the walls were almost all that he lived for, but they had gone silent now, and the hatch had opened twelve times since they had last sung.

His latest bowl of food eaten, he fell asleep in the silence.

When he woke he was not alone.

A man sat against the opposite wall. A battered metal bowl and a candle sat at his feet. A broken morsel of bread lay in the bowl. He was thin, his skin pocked by scars where smelting sparks had burned it. Black hair hung to his neck. There were patches of grey in the stubble that covered his face. He looked tired, but tough, like an old knife that was still sharp despite the notches in its blade. He looked like some of the gangers who the boy had grown up with. He looked like the home he had been taken from.

'You are not afraid,' said the man, his voice rasping with pollution damage. The boy shook his head, not sure if the man had been asking a question. The man brought up a hand and rubbed his right eye. Strands of tattooed feathers criss-crossed his fingers. 'Quite a thing, to not be afraid. Fear can be good – keeps you alive, keeps you sharp. But knowing what you are really afraid of, well... That is strength.'

The boy looked at the man, taking in the marks which said to him that he was looking at someone who came from the Agate Vault. A gang boss too, with both blood and power to his name.

'Why are you here?' said the boy at last.

The man shrugged.

'Why are you?'

The boy did not answer.

The man picked up the bowl and held it out. The boy shook his head. The man shrugged again and put the bowl back down.

'You were in a gang, right?'

The boy hesitated and then shook his head.

'No?' The man raised an eyebrow, and the movement sent inked feathers ruffling across his skin. 'You look like you were to me.'

The boy shook his head again, suddenly cold. He felt his fists tense. The man watched him for a second.

'Ah,' said the man. 'Yes. You're right. There's a difference, isn't there? Even if you ran with them, even if you took the marks and killed with them, if you kept something back then you were not one of them.'

The boy shifted, suddenly aware of the mottled burn scars on his hands and arms. The memories were suddenly bright in his head. The roar of shot-cannons; the weight of knife and pistol, heavy in his hands. The gang warriors had called him Kye. He had accepted the name, just like he had accepted the food, and later the kill brands on his right hand and forearm. Those had not been marks of defeat, though; they were just the price for survival.

The man gave a small smile and shook his head.

'Living and not surrendering, even if those around you thought they had won. Live quick and sharp. That's right, isn't it? Give just enough and no more, and never let the pain break you.' The man nodded, his gaze steady. 'Fast, and quick, and not afraid. What did you dream of? Never dreamed of dying? No, that would be surrender, wouldn't it? But maybe a dream of getting out of the dark and living without a knife as your pillow? Yes, that is an old dream, old and false. Or maybe you thought that one day you could escape by being the one in charge. A few cuts here, some quick footwork there, and...' The man smiled, and suddenly looked very old. Creases cut across the tattoos around his eyes. 'And maybe you would have made it too – a gang of your own, a clan even. But no one holds power forever. A bullet or a knife would have found you, and that would have been that.'

They held each other's gaze, and Kye for a second felt very sorry for whoever the man was. There was a feeling of weight in his silence, like the pressure of unspoken moments piled up just before the present. The light of the candle somehow made the walls seem closer, but the ceiling further away, as though the walls just went up and up to the dark.

If the man was a gang boss from Agate Vault, then he could have been taken at the same time as the boy. He had not seen the giants in iron take anyone else. They had just swept through the sub levels killing as they went. The boy had outrun them for ten days, until there was nowhere left to run to. He had tried to fight them. It had not worked, but they had not killed him. A blow from one of the giants had sent him down into the dark of this cell.

The boy shook his head slowly, licked his lips and spoke.

'You're not really from the same place as me, are you?' he said to the man. 'You look like you are, you talk like you are, but you're here for whoever took me.' He looked up at the man, eyes hard in the flame light. 'I'm right, aren't I?'

The man gave a small smile.

'Sharp and quick,' he said, and let out a breath. 'But no one put me in here, and I have been to where you came from even if I was not born there. I have seen the turf wars down under the smelting levels. I have been there when a bullet takes someone in the eye, because they were too slow, or too bold, or just unlucky.' The man's eyes darkened as he spoke.

'You are a liar,' said the boy carefully.

The man laughed, and the sound ricocheted around the cell.

'In a sense,' he said. 'In a sense that is exactly what I am.'

'What do they want? Why am I here? Why did they send you?'

'They want you to become something that you cannot imagine,' said the man softly. 'And I already said that no one sent me. I am here because I wanted to be sure my choice was right.' He looked at the boy and nodded. 'Still not afraid?'

'No,' said the boy, and for the first time there was an edge of defiance in his voice.

'Everyone is afraid of something,' said the man.

'I won't submit,' growled the boy. The man smiled. A tattoo of a hound snarled on his temple as the skin folded.

'That is why I chose you, Kye,' said the man.

The boy froze at the sound of his name. Needles of cold ran up his skin.

'How...?' He began to ask, but the cell door swung open with a clank of releasing bolts. Light poured in. The boy flinched back, hands covering his eyes. Heavy steps shook the floor, and a teeth aching-purr of machine power filled the air. The boy called Kye tried to blink away the sudden blindness in his eyes.

'Stand,' said a voice. He looked up, eyes stinging, moisture running down his cheeks. A golden giant stood above him, a bladed pole in one hand and a crimson cloak falling from its back to the floor. 'Stand and follow,' said the giant. The boy could feel his heart hammering in his chest.

What are you afraid of?

Kye looked down, past the golden figure to the other side of the cell where the man had sat. The space was empty.

What are you really afraid of?

He stood. His head barely came up to the golden giant's midriff.

'What is going to happen?' he asked, his voice strong and clear.

The giant placed a hand on his shoulder. The fingers were warm, like metal left out in the sun. Kye felt the power in the giant as he was turned and guided towards the open cell door.

'You are going to meet your lord,' said the giant as they walked out of the cell and into the light beyond.

✠ ✠ ✠

II

'KNEEL,' GROWLED THE golden giant from behind him.

Kye did not move.

'Kneel,' came the command again. Still he did not move.

He could not. He stood in a chamber of stone and black steel. It was as large as the largest vaults that he had seen beneath the smelting levels of his home. Glow-globes hung from the beams that ran across the ceiling. Each shadow glinted with polished metal and shaped stone. It was the most incredible structure Kye had ever seen, but it was not the room that froze him in place.

A figure looked up from a stone table at the room's centre. He was tall, taller even than the golden giant, but with a bulk that was perfectly proportioned to his size. Power flowed through his smallest movement. He wore black robes edged with white fur. Dark eyes glittered in an unsmiling face of hard edges beneath a shock of white-blond hair. Strength spread from his gaze like furnace heat. Kye had never felt anything like it before: not running into the gunfire of rival gangs, not in the time he had strayed into the grounds of the rust-cats, or leapt a crevasse.

'What...' began Kye, the question catching on his tongue. 'What are you?'

The golden giant began to growl a rebuke, but a glance from the figure silenced the words.

'What I am is a matter that I am still coming to understand, but who I am is a question I can answer. My name is Rogal, of the House of Dorn.'

Kye blinked. Every part of his being was telling him to kneel, to swear allegiance and undying loyalty to the figure who stood before him. But he did not.

He brought his palm up to his mouth and bit down. The tips of his teeth opened his own skin. His blood was a brief taste of iron on his tongue. He held his hand out, squeezing it into a fist. Red ran between the knuckles. Rogal Dorn watched the blood patter onto the stone floor. His expression did not change.

'You offer your blood for what?' he said, and his voice was cold. 'As surrender? As oath?'

Kye shook his head, though every fibre of his being said to run.

'As defiance,' said Kye, the words thin in his dry mouth.

The drops of blood from his hand were slowing, and the pain from the bite was fading into a warm numbness. Rogal Dorn's eyes were fixed, unblinking and fathomless.

'You are right not to kneel,' said Dorn, and he turned away.

Kye felt something cold in his chest. His arm and bloody fist dropped slowly to his side. He blinked, suddenly unsure what had happened or what he felt.

Rogal Dorn stepped back to the table at the centre of the room and leant on it, eyes fixed on what lay on its surface. Golden armour lay on the black stone. Each section gleamed like the flicker of candle flames. Winged creatures, similar to those on the armoured giant who still stood at his shoulder, covered its plates. Kye could see talons picked out in silver. Red gems gleamed from eyes set above sharp beaks. Rogal Dorn looked at the armour for a long moment and then picked up a gauntlet. He turned it over in his hands.

'Do you know what this is?' asked Dorn, his eyes watching the light flow over the gauntlet. He looked at Kye, who shook his head. 'It is a gift. A gift from a father to a lost son. It is also a symbol, of unity, of purpose, of change.' He put the gauntlet down on the table exactly where it had been. 'I am the son, and the father, whom I did not know until now, is the Master of all Mankind.'

Kye frowned. He did not know exactly what Rogal Dorn was talking about. He had always known that there were places above and beyond the hive's smelting strata and the warrens beneath, but he had never seen them. He wondered again where he was, and how far he had come from those familiar places.

'Gifts such as these have meaning,' said Dorn, staring at the armour, and then at Kye. 'I was an emperor. I ruled chains of stars, but now I am to be something else. Now I am not to rule, but to conquer so that my father can rule. That is what this gift means.' He turned to Kye. 'You are also a gift. You were marked and taken when the Emperor conquered your world. You would have gone on to serve Him, but now are marked to be among the first of a generation of warriors raised under my command. You are intended to be a symbol of a new age.'

Kye looked up into Rogal Dorn's eyes. They were as cold and unyielding as the stone beneath their feet.

'Are you going to refuse your father?' asked Kye.

Dorn shook his head.

'No. I gave him my oath when we first met,' said Rogal Dorn, and then paused.

Kye looked at his bloody hand. The blood had started to clot and bind his fingers together. He looked up.

'You should have refused,' said Kye. He could feel his limbs shaking and fought to control them.

A frown passed over Rogal Dorn's brows.

'Why?'

'Because defiance is all that life is.'

Dorn's silence stretched on, and then he seemed to shiver.

'There is more to life than surviving,' said Dorn.

Kye began to shake his head.

'I met my father, and I knew that I was no emperor. I knew what my oath to Him meant.' Dorn pointed to Kye's bloody hand. 'I said that you should not have knelt. I said that because you do not know what I am. You do not understand what you would help create.' Dorn turned and began to walk across the chamber. 'There is something for you to see.'

Kye hesitated for an instant and then followed. Behind him the silent giant in gold followed too, the haft of his spear tapping on the floor. They came to a halt beneath the centre of the vaulted ceiling. Dorn looked up and gestured with a nod. Kye followed his gaze. The engraved patterns on the bronze ceiling looked back. A low rumble filled the room, and then, one by one, the panels of the ceiling slid down into the walls.

Kye stared.

Light, endless points of light scattered like frozen sparks. Swirls of colour like patches of rust on black iron.

He fell to his knees, mouth open, unable to stop staring. In part of his mind the old stories of sky and stars came back to him, and he knew that he was not looking at a myth, or dream, but truth.

'This will be the domain of mankind,' said Rogal Dorn. 'This will be my father's gift to humanity.' He looked down at Kye. 'That is the purpose I was made for, and why I gave my father my oath to serve Him.' Kye felt weak, as though the ground had fallen away beneath him and he was falling without moving. 'You will join me on that path if you wish, Kye.'

He pulled his gaze away from the field of stars, swallowed and tasted the echo of his own blood in his mouth. All that mattered was that you never broke, never gave in, never let anyone take the only thing you could ever own away from you.

'And if I won't?' he breathed.

'I am not asking if you will give me your oath. You have a path to walk before that choice.'

III

THEY BEGAN WITH pain. Deluges of pain, pain that ate into his bones. There was no edge to it, just a sea of agony that went beyond the horizon. On and on it went, swallowing time. Seconds bled to hours. Hours collapsed to minutes. The past and future dissolved into a present that stretched and stretched. Red clouds billowed through the grey of his mind. The pain changed shape again and again, one second shrill as the edge of razors, the next wrapping him in fire. He could not hear. The pain had severed every other sensation from him. There was nothing left of him, just the core of torment rolling over and over through eternity.

He was supposed to break. They wanted him to submit, to surrender, to let himself rise from the red ocean, clean and blank and broken. He could not remember even who *they* were, but that did not matter. All that mattered was that he would not let go. He would not give in. And so the pain went on. And so did he.

And then it ended.

He screamed at the shock. Cold blankness flooded into him, and he was flying through a void, tumbling end over end.

This is death, he thought. It was not pain. It was the end of pain. It was nothing.

And into the nothing came the voices. Hundreds of voices, whispering as he slid on through the void, just beyond hearing. Then colour replaced darkness. Shapes compressed, folded and expanded. Every colour he had ever seen was there, sliced into sharp slivers. Sometimes he thought he could see a pattern or recognise a shape, as though he were looking at a scene through rippling water, but then the patterns would splinter and he would pass back into the whirlpool.

Light struck his eyes. He tried to blink, but could not. The sphere of colours and shapes vanished as abruptly as the pain. The light was white, simple and bright. It stung. His eyes were watering. There were shapes moving behind the blur in front of him. Something cool touched the skin under his eyes. His sight began to clear. He tried to blink again.

'Do not do that,' said a voice from just to his side. 'Your eyelids are pinned open. Try to blink too hard and you will rip them.' The speaker stepped into sight. He looked like a man, but a man if he had been shaped to a grander scale. White robes covered hard muscle. A starburst tattoo covered his bare scalp and face, and his eyes were grey and steady.

Apothecary, Kye thought, though he did not know how he knew. *Legiones Astartes. Solar privateer tattoo from pre-recruitment culture.*

'We will leave the pins in,' said the Apothecary. 'You will have another dose after the first implantation, and you will need your eyes open for that.' He paused, mouth closing briefly. Kye felt the grey eyes flicking across his face. 'And then another dose once you are past that.'

Hands came up, and Kye felt a pressure he had been ignoring release from his skull. The device that the Apothecary lowered past Kye's view looked like a helm. A mass of cables and bulbous machinery clung to its dome. Dozens of lenses sat in chromed wheels above where the visor would fit over the eyes. The Apothecary stood back and pressed a switch on a block of yellow plastek. The bindings holding Kye upright released, and he pitched forwards onto the floor. He lay there for a second, breathing hard. He pushed himself up onto his knees.

'What's...' he began to ask, but his throat and lungs were raw. 'What's your name?'

The Apothecary paused, looking down at him, the starburst tattoo on his face creasing.

'My name is my own, and not for you.'

Kye tried to spit, but his mouth was dry.

'Most ask me why this is happening,' said the Apothecary.

Kye shook his head and forced words out of his throat. 'I know why.'

The Apothecary raised an eyebrow.

'You want to break me,' sneered Kye.

The Apothecary shook his head, hesitated and then pulled him to his feet.

'No,' he said, and gestured at the rest of the chamber. Rows of metal racks stretched away under a vaulted roof of frosted crystal. A human figure stood at the heart of each rack, naked, bound by loops of plasteel. Helmets, like the one the Apothecary had taken from Kye's head, hid their faces. Their bodies twitched as lights flickered around the edges of their visors. Tubes linked to their arms and chests. Kye could see the veins standing out under the skin next to where the needles went in. He rubbed his own arm and felt the puncture wounds. Many of the figures in the racks hung slack against the restraints. Blood streaked their bare skin. Servitors in red robes and one-eyed masks moved down the rows of racks, pulling limp bodies from the restraints and dumping them onto carts.

One in a hundred survives the first phase. The ratio rose in his mind from the same place where his recognition of the Apothecary and the servitors had come from.

The Apothecary pointed at a figure who fell from the rack as the bindings were undone. The youth was still alive, but barely. Blood ran from his mouth, and his eyes were rolling. His arms and legs thrashed wildy as he tried to stand, and then struck at the servitors. One of them put a thick tube to the back of the youth's head. There was a dull thunk of pneumatic force and punctured bone. The youth collapsed, blood leaking from a neat hole in his skull.

'That is what breaking looks like,' said the Apothecary. 'We don't want you to break. We want you to be unbreakable.'

'I won't submit,' growled Kye.

The Apothecary looked down at him, and there was a glimmer in his grey eyes.

'Good,' he said.

IV

THEY CUT HIM. He was awake for most of it, and numb for some. They scooped out chunks of flesh and nested fresh organs in their place. A second heart began to beat next to the first. His blood began to change, began to thicken the faster he bled.

When they had finished, the pain came back slowly until it was like a ball of barbed wire in his chest. He showed none of that pain. He knew something they did not, something that the cuts and new flesh and hypno-immersion could not touch.

'You take this well, boy,' said the grey-eyed Apothecary, as he examined the staples running down the centre of Kye's chest. 'Some die from this even after coming so far.'

'Most,' said Kye. The Apothecary looked up at him, grey eyes steady. Kye stared back, unblinking. 'Most die before the end of what you are doing to us.'

'Yes, they do,' said the Apothecary.

The architecture of his thoughts changed. He could feel it. Information and experience became cleaner. The gap between thought and action shrank. Pieces of emotion withered and fell away. His memories of what had happened before drifted into the distance. He could still see them, but they felt like something that was not really part of him any more. All the while, new memories filled his head, some sharp, some blurred and smudged. He knew more than he had before, but did not know how. The machines they clamped to his head were doing this, he knew, pouring change into his mind like metal into a mould.

The pain got worse, but so did his capacity for it. The pain of surgery and hypno-saturation became islands in a wide and deep ocean.

Time lost meaning. Life became the passing of different agonies.

He saw no one alive except pain-fogged glimpses of Apothecaries. The only words he heard were the droning commands of servitors to move his limbs as they arranged him for the next phase of alteration.

He did not refuse. He knew what they were doing. That was one of the first things they gave to him: the knowledge of what they were trying to make him. He let them. Death would be the only way to halt the process, but death was not victory.

V

THEY CHAINED HIM to two others before they tried to kill him the first time. He had seen neither of the two other aspirants before. One was taller than Kye, and lean, with skin the colour of rust. The other was shorter, but with brands criss-crossing his corded muscle. Both had surgical scars that matched his own. Staples marched across the base of their necks and down their chests, like chromed parasites feeding on their flesh. They all had plugs in their arms now.

The chains linked them to each other by the manacles around their necks. Each chain was long enough that they could stand at arm's length from each other, but no further. The first thing that Kye had done once the servitors had finished was to test the chains. They were still warm from the welding, but did not yield. The other two watched him as he tried each link in turn.

'They will not break,' said the taller of the two, his voice a low purr. His eyes were half shut as though he were sleeping while standing. 'You should know that by now.'

Kye ignored the words. He was examining the walls of the space in which they all stood. Piles of debris dotted the metal floor. A rusting forest of girders reached up to a ceiling high above them. Now that the servitors had gone, the only light was the orange glow of heat vents in the ceiling. The air was thick and hot. He knew this kind of ground. He had grown, and lived, and learned to kill in places that looked just like this.

He gave the chain a gentle tug. He was on one end of the chained trio. The tall one was on the other end, and the one with the brand marks between them. He squinted at the manacles on the necks of the others, and explored his own with his fingers.

A clank echoed from the distance, then another, and another. The other two tensed, exchanged a look and slammed their shoulders together. The chains yanked Kye forwards, and he almost lost his balance. He recovered and yanked back on the chain. Something was coming. He had to get free and get moving. The other two staggered and swore.

'What are you doing?' shouted the taller one. Something howled in the dark, and more cries answered, rolling around the red gloom. Kye looked around. He needed a weapon. If he killed the middle one, then he could cut the manacle off, but then there was the tall one. He would have to kill them both and quickly. His eyes found a length of pipe on the edge of a heap of debris just a pace away. He just needed...

The chain snapped taut and yanked him off his feet. He twisted as he fell, ready to lash out. An elbow met his face as his nose exploded into a red spray. He staggered and lashed out, but not fast enough. A hand spun him around, and he was on the floor, a foot at the base of his neck, the manacle digging into his throat.

'Blood and night, he is from a fresh cohort,' growled a voice from above him. The foot stamped down on Kye's neck, snapping his face down into the floor. He did not recognise the voice, and that meant both the voice, and the foot on his neck, belonged to the branded aspirant. 'You hear that, slime? That's a pack coming for us, and you are dead weight on the chain.'

'Let him up. There is no time,' snapped the tall one. The pressure did not ease on Kye's neck or throat. 'Let him up, or we are all dead anyway!'

The foot came off his neck, and he was pulled upright. The howls came again, closer, rolling through the gloom and echoing from the roof. The other two were not looking at him. They were looking out at the dark, at where the howls were rising. The tall one turned his head sharply, and his hand suddenly had Kye by the throat. It was fast. Kye had seen fast before, but this was something else, like the flinch of a spider.

'You want to get through this? Then you are with us,' he said.

The other two were shoulder to shoulder, facing out. They had pulled metal bars out of the debris and were holding them in both hands.

'Get in formation,' yelled the branded aspirant, and tossed Kye a metal bar. Kye hesitated. His face was still aching. The howls were rising. 'Now!'

A creature of blades and muscle bounded out of the dark. Kye had time to see a hunched body, and loose skin hanging over ribs and legs. Then it was on them, steel fangs bright in a wide mouth.

'Back!' shouted the tall one, as he leapt away from the creature. Kye was slower and almost fell again. The creature landed in the space where they had been. It looked like a hairless cat. Skin hung in folds over whipcord sinew. Rusted metal scales covered its head, and its teeth and claws were shining blades. It snarled in frustration, tensed and pounced. A length of metal bar slammed into its open mouth. Steel teeth and blood flew into the air. The beast skidded backwards, two paces in front of Kye.

'Kill it!' roared a voice next to Kye's ear. The beast was rising, metal claws scrabbling at the floor. Kye lunged forwards, swinging the bar above his head with both hands. The beast looked up, yellow eyes set in scales of rusted metal. Kye slammed the bar down, once then twice more, the impact thudding up his arm. Blood flicked across his face. The beast was a mashed ruin at his feet. He found himself suddenly aware that he was not even breathing hard.

'Eyes up. Here they come!'

Kye's gaze snapped upwards, as a ripple of howls cut through the air. The other two aspirants were with him, one shoulder of each pressed against his, so that they were an unbroken triangle.

Then the beasts were on them, bounding out of the dark, and the world became a whirl of jaws and the reek of rotting-meat breath. He swung and battered, thumping the bar into everything that moved in front of him. The beasts did not stop; they poured forwards as though driven by starvation or agony. He could feel the other two striking, but they never broke contact with him.

He slammed the tip of his bar into an open mouth, and kicked the body away. A brief space appeared around him, and he glanced upwards. A forest of girders was ten paces away.

'We need to get up into the girders,' he shouted. 'If we stay down here we will die.'

The words felt strange even as they left his mouth. He had been a razor in the gangs, a loner, shunned and used for his quickness. He had been marked and answered to others, but he had never been one of them; he had never had his survival depend on anything other than his own wits and reflexes. Now, by the fact of the chains around his neck, he could only live if those standing beside him lived as well.

'You lead,' called the taller one.

Just like that, thought Kye, *no questioning.* Minutes before they had been fighting him; now they were following his word without question.

A pair of beasts bounded over the body of their kin and leapt at him. He shifted his feet, feeling the blood on the floor under his toes. One of the creatures reached for him with its claws. He pivoted, and slammed the bar into the side of its skull with the full force of momentum and muscle. The beast dropped, the side of its skull a crumpled mass of metal, bone and blood. Kye leapt into the space where it had been. The other two aspirants came with him, and they battered their way into the oncoming tide.

The forest of girders loomed above them. Kye was reading the best way to make the climb, when a grunt of pain came from behind him. The chain yanked at his neck, and he stumbled. A beast's claws flicked out. Pain exploded across his thigh. Blood sheeted down his leg. He twisted and struck the beast with a back-handed blow. The creature snarled and retreated. Kye looked over his shoulder, muscles bunching in his neck as the manacle bit deep.

The tall aspirant was lying on the floor, a wide gash open down the left side of his chest. He was shaking, blood pumping in time with ragged breaths.

'Get him up!' shouted the one with the brand scars. The chain linking him to the bleeding figure had pulled him to his knees, and he was whirling his metal bar over his head. The beasts were a wall around him, eyes and jaws pressing close.

Kye hesitated. They needed to climb, and quickly. Dragging a dying body would be almost impossible.

'He's–'

'Move!'

Kye moved, dropping the metal bar. He gripped the wounded aspirant under the arms, lifting him onto his shoulders. The movement was strangely easy. He began to move. The branded youth was just behind him, swinging his bar in a circle. They had a second before the beasts realised they were vulnerable. Kye was at the base of a girder that met the ground at a sharp angle. He gripped the metal with one hand and used the other to steady the body across his shoulders. He could hear breath bubbling. Blood was flowing down his skin. His own wound was a dull throb at the edge of thought. He braced his feet and began to climb.

He felt a brief tension in the chain, and then the other aspirant leapt from the floor and gripped the girder. The chains linking them clanged against the rusted iron. Beneath them the beasts howled and leapt up, claws dragging sparks across the girder.

Kye breathed hard. The beat of his old and new hearts rose. Blood was spattering down into the jaws of the creatures. He hauled himself up, shifting his grip and feet until he reached a crossbeam. It was narrow and rough with rust, but as its coolness touched his skin, he thought that he had never felt anything more perfect in his life.

The aspirant with the branded face hoisted himself up next to Kye a second later. He was bleeding from a dozen gashes in his chest and shoulders. He looked at Kye, bloodied chest rising and falling as he sucked air.

'That was quick thinking, and better climbing.'

'Where I was from you learnt things like that fast.'

A smile spilt the branded face.

'We all came from somewhere like that,' said the aspirant with the brand marks. 'I am Archamus.' He gestured at the figure who was half slumped on the girder across Kye's back. 'And he–'

'Is still alive enough to give his own name.' The figure stirred and rolled off Kye's back. His movements were weak, but the wound in his chest had sealed. Hard nodules of congealed blood gleamed in the low light. Kye glanced down at the cut in his own leg. It too had closed, and the blood begun to clot. 'I am Yonnad,' said the wounded aspirant, his voice low and solemn. 'Thank you. Thank you for my life. May I know your name?'

Kye paused. He felt strange, as though he had moved into a different world without moving.

'I am called Kye,' he said.

Archamus grinned again and spat a thick gobbet of blood from between his teeth. Down below, the beasts bayed louder.

'Get up, Kye,' said Archamus, and began to pull himself along the girder. 'We have a long way to go if we are going to reach the exit.' He moved around Kye and helped Yonnad into a crouch. Kye shook his head, but Archamus spoke before he could. 'You have carried him enough for now, Kye. And besides, you should lead.'

Kye looked at him for an instant, and then began to climb. Behind him the beasts howled, and the chains linking him to the other two clinked.

VI

'I WILL NOT submit,' Kye shouted, as the saw pulled back. The blood was bright on his teeth as it spun down. 'I. Will. Not!' He forced the words out, one after another. Machine limbs reached down, and he heard the crack as they pulled his ribcage open.

Above him the grey eyes of the Apothecary looked down from behind the mechanical arms.

'Why?' said the Apothecary, his voice echoing from a speaker in his collar.

Kye could feel the pain coming again. He was always awake when they operated now. Always awake, and never numb. Needles twitched in his arms and neck. He could feel his body fighting to suppress the pain and staunch the flow of blood. But there was too much pain, and too much blood. Too much, but not enough that it would release him from its hold.

'I asked you a question, aspirant,' said the Apothecary.

'Kye,' he hissed. 'My name is Kye.'

'Is that why you will not submit, for pride?'

Another set of machine arms swung into view above him. A tubular lump of grey flesh hung from the machine's chrome fingers. A web of blood vessels hung from it.

'Can you remember why you resist?'

'I...' began Kye, and reached for the memories and feelings that lived behind his defiance...

He would not submit. He would not break. He would not bow. He would not.

...and found nothing. He did not know why he would resist, only that he would.

'I do not remember,' he said, eyes snapping back into focus to see the arms lowering the grey lump of flesh into his chest.

'Strength does not require reasons,' said the Apothecary.

VII

KYE HUNG IN silence and dreamed the dreams of two worlds.

In one world his mind was asleep, his thoughts tumbling down through echoes of compressed memories.

In the other world his eyes watched the corridor junction, his thoughts moving with the same, slow beat as his blood. His eyes were open, and they twitched as though seeing things move in front of him. But there was nothing in front of him, just three long, dark corridors. He had been like this for fifty-six hours, half of them fully awake, the other half split between the waking and sleep that he could now enter at will.

'*Kye?*' Yonnad's voice fizzed inside his ear. '*Kye, respond if you can hear.*'

His eyes stopped twitching, and he blinked rapidly. He had to bite down on the instinct to vomit as his dreams meshed with a waking world that he could already see. The pressure of the void suit was a sudden sensation on his skin, and he felt his hearts begin to thump faster.

'I hear you,' he said.

'*Confirm status,*' said Yonnad.

'Steady at intersection twenty-one. No movement. Just like before.'

'*They are out there*,' said Archamus, his voice a growl over the vox-link. '*They are coming. Did that rust pit of a hive you were born in not teach you patience?*'

'Oh, it did, but somehow it failed to make me enjoy floating in the vacuum, waiting for an unknown enemy to appear,' said Kye.

Archamus laughed, the sound a quick bark that settled back into quiet.

'They might not be coming,' said Kye at last. The thought had been itching away at him every time he came out of a split-sleep cycle.

'*That is not the way things are done*,' came Yonnad's measured tones. '*If we are here, then so is the enemy.*'

'What if that is not the lesson?' asked Kye, shifting to stare down one of the three passages. Cables dangled from crumpled inspection hatches, and pipes hung from ducts like severed blood vessels. They were in a damaged region of a transport barque which had been left open to the void. There were other trios of aspirants scattered throughout the structure. Each had a different mission, but none knew where the other trios were, or the details of their missions. Kye, Archamus and Yonnad were watching a cluster of dead passages. All of them were skinned in armoured void suits, and armed with shot-cannons and chainblades.

'*What do you mean?*' growled Archamus. Kye took a careful breath before answering. The Inwit-born youth could switch in temperament from jovial to abrupt to anger in the space of a heartbeat. The alterations being made to his mind and body had not dulled that quality; if anything his temper had become more marked.

'What if waiting is the wrong thing to do? What if there is no threat, and the only thing holding us here is that we think there is a threat?'

'*No, Kye*,' said Yonnad, speaking before Archamus could. '*We have a task, and we will see it done.*'

'But what is the mission?' asked Kye. He turned to look down the second passage. The movement spun him over, and he had to grab hold of the tether attaching him to the wall to steady himself. The second corridor was empty, just like the first. 'What if we have not understood it correctly?'

'Kye...' began Yonnad, but Archamus cut in.

'What do you mean?'

'I mean there might be no enemy here. They might be somewhere else, somewhere that is struggling because we are held here by fear.'

'This is duty, not fear,' said Yonnad.

'Is it?' snapped Kye, before he could stop himself. He regretted the words as soon as they were out of his mouth. He had noticed that happening more and more recently; emotions and impatience would bubble up out of nowhere. It was like another person was living in his thoughts, someone with cold edges and hot bile. He had no idea why. 'I am sorry...' he began to say.

'Enough,' said Yonnad. 'We are brothers, you need say nothing more. Just never say such a thing again.'

Kye swallowed and nodded even though no one could see him do it.

Brother. The word was still as strange an addition to his world as the organs stitched into his flesh.

'Perhaps he is right,' said Archamus. 'We have not heard anything, and the command channel is static. We are too scattered. Even if that was the ordered formation, we are exposed. We could link up with each other and form a trio. If it is clear up to the core bulkhead, we can form a core defence.'

'No,' said Yonnad, his voice hard. 'We stay. If we start second guessing...'

'Kye,' said Archamus. 'I am going to move towards you. Try not to shoot me when you see me.'

Yonnad hissed something in the language of his birth world. Kye didn't understand the words, but he didn't need to.

'Detaching tether, and moving now,' called Archamus.

Kye turned so that the passage Archamus would come down was at the edge of his sight. He kept focused on the others. After a few moments, a light flickered in the far darkness of the passage.

'Nothing here,' said Archamus. 'Unsurprising.'

'*I do not like this,*' hissed Yonnad. Kye could hear the tension in the words. He was suddenly not sure that he should have voiced his thoughts about changing the battle plan.

'*Victory comes from suffering,*' said Archamus, the edge of laughter back in his voice now. '*I can see your suit lights, Kye. Closing on your position.*'

'Confirmed,' said Kye, and glanced back up the tunnel to where the light was bobbing closer. 'I can see yours too.'

'*I do not have my lights on,*' said Archamus.

Kye heard the words and felt them slide cold over his skin. He turned. The light closing towards him was accelerating. He brought his shot-cannon up.

Blinding light flicked down the passage towards him. He pulled the trigger. The cannon roared. The gun's recoil spun him over in the weightless dark. And saved his life. A bolt of energy skimmed his upper arm. Fabric and rubber flashed to vapour. Flakes of burning material peeled away. The tether connecting him to the wall snapped tight, and he was tumbling over and over. Pain burned in his right arm. Air vented from the hole in his suit. A pressure-loss alert began to ring in his ears. The wall slammed into him, and he caught it before he rebounded. His shot-cannon was still in his left hand. The pain in his right shoulder exploded as he pulled himself against the metal plates. Bolts of energy flashed past him.

He could see the light now. It was not one light but four, closely bunched, moving in jumps through the black. He had an impression of bronze plating and steel limbs. He fired again. The cannon flashed. Force slammed though him, but this time he was braced for it. The lead light went out. Air was streaming out of his suit. He could hear it, a low hiss in the silence.

A line of energy burned into the wall next to him. He fired again, and again, switching the angle of fire to send the scatter shot ricocheting off the walls. Another light went out. Something flashed at the edge of his eye, and he glanced to his side where the other corridors led off into the dark. Lights were moving towards him down both passages.

'Brothers!' he shouted the word, as he fired a scatter shell down each passage. The recoil almost sent him spinning again.

'*I am almost with you,*' yelled Archamus.

'*I am moving,*' said Yonnad.

Kye fired again, rebounding from shot to shot. He could see the servitors now. They crawled over the walls like spiders. Articulated metal limbs moved in place of arms and legs, and their heads bent upwards on necks of ribbed steel. Weapon pods projected from their spines like scorpion stings. And there were dozens of them.

'*I see you,*' came Archamus' voice. '*I have clear targets.*'

The flare of gunfire lit the distant passage, blinking as shrapnel tore through the vacuum. Kye grinned, sudden joy blotting out the pain of his arm. He had felt it before, and knew it. This was the warrior's song singing in his veins, the joy of feeling death reach for him and shouting back into its face.

He braced and fired again. Three shots. Four explosions of flesh and metal. He glanced over his shoulder. Archamus was ten metres away, wedged between the wall and a block of machinery. He was firing at the servitors closest to Kye.

'Well,' shouted Archamus over the vox. 'At least we found the enemy.'

Kye laughed, and turned to fire again.

A flash of energy burned out of the dark. And the world ripped away like a banner blown into the night sky.

VIII

HE WOKE TO cold light. Numbness held his body.

'You are persistent,' said a voice from just out of sight. 'I will give you that.' The grey-eyed Apothecary stepped into view. 'Lucky even. An aspirant with your injuries would normally be allowed to die, or be made into a servitor. But it seems that fortune is on your side.'

Kye took a breath and felt fluid rasp in his throat.

'Archamus...' he hissed. 'Yonnad...'

'The other two in your trio? One dead. One alive.'

The words sank through him, cold in the sea of his numbness. The Apothecary watched him, unblinking.

'Which one?' asked Kye at last. The Apothecary raised an eyebrow. 'Which one died?'

'The one who was closest to you when you were hit. I do not know the name. He was caught out of position and overwhelmed.'

Archamus, thought Kye.

'It is not just the weak in body that we winnow out,' said the Apothecary. 'It is those who are flawed in thought. He was not strong enough to become what he needed to be, and so he fell.'

'It was me,' said Kye. 'He should have been in position. It was me that wanted to alter it.'

'Then he died for your weakness,' said the Apothecary, and moved away, leaving Kye with the words echoing in his thoughts.

IX

HE LAY IN the dark and felt the ghosts of his lost limbs. Shivers of pain rain down his right arm from shoulder to fingertip. He could feel his right leg ache when he lay still. The energy blast had vaporised his arm from just above the elbow, and scooped a chunk of bone and flesh from his torso. A second blast had struck his knee. To simplify the fitting of the bionics they had removed the remaining flesh and bone up to his shoulder and hip.

When they had first fitted the bionics, he would stare at the bronzed pistons and wires of his new limbs, and feel another set of fingers and muscle twitch somewhere within the unmoving metal. Now he lay in the dark of his cell and waited, clenching his right fist, one digit at a time.

What are you afraid of? The words came again, along with the face of the man who he had seen in his cell. *What are you really afraid of? He will ask you.*

The darkness did not answer.

The door to his cell opened. Light fell across him, bright and golden. His eyes adapted instantly to the change in illumination.

'It is time,' said the figure by the door. He did not recognise the voice, but the size and the purr of active power armour told him enough. Once he would have thought the figure a giant, but as he stood their eyes were on a level. The plugs in his spine still itched, but he no longer even thought of the hard, black carapace under his skin, or the beat of his second heart, or the channels that his thoughts flowed down. Only the question – asked by a man who had not been there, to a boy who was no longer there – tugged at his calm.

What are you afraid of?

He stepped towards the door. The warrior came into focus. He wore yellow-and-black battleplate, draped with a white surcoat. A sheathed sword hung at his waist, and his face was as cold and unmoving as carved ice.

The warrior gestured for Kye to go in front of him, and they began to walk down the long corridor. The doors of the cells on either side remained closed.

It took them an hour to reach the arming chamber. There the serfs gave him his final skin. His nerves buzzed as the armour activated. He remained silent, and the yellow-and-black-armoured warrior watched him without blinking. When it was done, they put his bolter in his hands. The ready-lights on the casing lit as his fingers curled around the grip.

Fully loaded, he noted. *Now I truly am the weapon they have made me.* A tremor of ghost pain flared in his right arm, and he had to clamp down on it. He looked at the other warrior.

'I am ready,' he said. The warrior nodded and led him onwards.

✠ ✠ ✠

X

THERE WERE TWENTY of them. Twenty in burnished yellow armour, their boltguns held across their chests, their heads bare. Kye saw Yonnad as he fell into position. Their gazes touched, and slid away from each other. They had trained together since Archamus had fallen, but had only talked in abrupt bites of tactical information. Kye understood why. What was there to say?

An open archway waited before the twenty. Two warriors stood to either side of the doorway, drawn swords resting point down at their feet. Both warriors wore white surcoats crossed with black. Coals burned in iron braziers clamped to the door's pillars, but the chamber beyond was dark, as though the door led to oblivion.

They waited.

And a light appeared in the dark beyond the door. A flame flickered to life, grew and reached upwards. From where Kye stood, the fire seemed to hang in the dark.

'Approach and enter,' said one of the warriors by the door. The twenty walked forwards and crossed into the blackness beyond. The chamber grew in the light of the fire at its centre. Black granite pillars rose to a shadowed height, the light strong enough to give only an impression of a domed ceiling. The walls were bare, the stone smooth and unblemished. Black iron poles jutted from the upper reaches of the walls. The whole space felt empty, as though it were waiting.

The twenty formed a broken circle around the flames, which burned in a wide bowl set on a frame of brushed copper. They all watched the yellow tongues as they reached up into the air.

'Welcome.' The voice rolled through the air, echoing off the bare stone. Kye recognised it though it had been a long time since he had last heard it. Rogal Dorn stepped from the dark. He looked around the circle of twenty, his eyes catching the light of the fire.

'One day, the names of every warrior of the Legion will line these walls, and the banners of victory will hang above the heads of those who stand where you stand now.' He paused, turning his gaze to meet that of the twenty. 'But you will be the first. You have brothers already scattered across the stars, tens of thousands of warriors who fight the war that you will join. In time all of them will come here and make their oaths. But you are the first. The first to become warriors of my flesh and blood since I took a place at my father's side. Twenty. Twenty from thousands. Twenty with the strength to reach this point.' He nodded carefully. 'I know you all, every detail of your path here. I have watched you. I have seen your strength and will. But...'

He paused, and Kye felt as though Dorn's words and presence were wrapping around him alone, as though he were the focus of a lens, as though his skin were charring under the light of a sun.

'You will need greater strength, and greater will than that which has brought you this far. You are warriors in a war to change existence. Our Great Crusade does not serve vanity, or pride. It serves mankind. Illumination, the light of reason, and freedom from the dark – that is what we bring. That is my father's gift to the galaxy. We exist to see mankind fulfil a destiny where the savagery that we were raised from is lost to memory.

Humanity has a destiny. We are not that destiny, but we will be its creators. There is no higher purpose, no greater meaning to our lives than this task. If it demands our suffering, we will bear that pain. If it demands our lives, then we will go to our deaths knowing that we die for the future. If victory demands eternity from us, then we will give it. We will do all this and never flinch from the path, never doubt, never turn away from the truth, or from each other.'

Dorn stared into the fire, and, for a second, Kye thought he could feel the heat of it reflecting from the primarch's gaze.

'The oaths you make today are to me, and through me to the Emperor, and through the Emperor to the future of all humanity. Remember them. Carry them in your breath and blood. They are everything.'

Dorn stepped up to the fire and raised his right arm. The gauntlet snapped free from his hand. He clenched his fingers and thrust his fist into the flames. Kye watched them envelop the bare flesh.

'Come,' said Dorn. 'Make your oath.'

They stepped forwards one at a time and thrust their fists into the flames. The smoke of charring skin rose as they spoke their names and the words of the oath. None of them flinched, or showed any sign of pain. Dorn kept his hand in the flame throughout, his features showing nothing, his eyes focused on each of the warriors as they came forwards.

Then Kye felt himself step up, his left gauntlet releasing. He clenched his fingers into a fist and met Rogal Dorn's eyes.

'Do you wish to give me your oath now, Kye?' asked the primarch. For answer Kye thrust his hand into the flames. There was a fraction of a second, and then heat swallowed every sensation in his fingers.

'I will give you my oath,' he said. He could feel the gaze of the other twenty on him. 'But the name that goes with that oath will not be Kye.'

Silence echoed in the Temple, and he could feel the shock ripple through the other warriors, like the passing of a wave through deep water. Rogal Dorn's expression did not alter, but Kye thought he saw something flicker in the depths of his eyes, a shadow cast by flame-light.

'What are you afraid of?' said Dorn softly.

'That others will die for my weakness. That I will fail,' said Kye. The skin of his hand was peeling away now, the sinew and flesh beneath blistering and charring. The pain had become blades of ice cutting into his finger bones. He kept his hand utterly still and held Dorn's gaze. The moment went on, extending in eternal seconds.

'There is always fear, even if we give it another name,' said Dorn at last.

'I know, lord.'

Dorn held his gaze for a second more. 'What name would you have?'

'Archamus,' he said. 'My oath name will be Archamus.'

'So be it,' said Rogal Dorn. Then he opened his hand, reached through the fire and grasped the charring hand of his son. 'So be it.'

PART TWO
GUARDIANS AT THE GATES

ONE

Arcus orbital plate
Terra

KESTROS LOOKED UP when the door opened, and came to his feet as Captain Katafalque entered. The assault commander looked at him for a long moment, but said nothing. Katafalque's armour was still scratched and gore-stained from the battlefield, and a scabbed wound bisected his left temple. His cold eyes bored into Kestros.

Kestros remained at attention, his eyes fixed on the corner of the cell. Thoughts flicked through his head even as he held them back from showing on his face. He had been ordered to his cell as the company had withdrawn from Damocles Starport. No explanation had been given, just a direct order that brooked no clarification or question. He had seen no one since, save the servitors who had stripped his armour. The cell that he had been taken to was in an unused section of the orbital plate, half a kilometre from his brothers.

'Why am I here, captain?'

'I cannot give you answers,' said Katafalque. Kestros knew it was the closest he would get to an apology, and he wasn't surprised. He had expected none. 'You are being seconded from my command, with immediate effect.'

Kestros blinked. Katafalque watched him carefully. He considered what to say. This seemed like a rebuke, like censure, but if it was then it was for some deed he was not aware of. He disliked indirectness; there was no place for it in the Legion. They were warriors, not courtiers. He felt his annoyance rise in his blood and forced it to cool.

'As you will it, captain,' he said carefully.

'It is not his will, sergeant,' said a deep voice, and another warrior stepped through the door behind Katafalque. The warrior wore lacquered war-plate, and a black cloak topped with white fur hung from his back. Pistons and cables gleamed between the armour plates that partially covered the warrior's right arm and leg. A mace with a black stone head hung at his waist, and he looked at Kestros with dark eyes set above a grey beard. Calm and control breathed off him as he moved.

Kestros blinked and then knelt, fist thumping into his chest as a salute.

'Honoured Master Archamus,' he said, careful to keep his voice devoid of the confusion now rolling through his head. Of all the warriors of the Legion there were many who held high honour: Lord Sigismund, Iapetus, Seneschal Rann; but Archamus was one of the First. One of the twenty warriors who were raised to the Legion by the primarch when he was reunited with the Emperor. With the death of Fleet Master Yonnad in the early days of the war, Archamus was now the last of that brotherhood. For over a century and a half Archamus had served. He had stood at Rogal Dorn's side for the Legion's greatest victories of the Great Crusade. One did not raise one's gaze to such a warrior without being asked to.

He stopped next to Katafalque and nodded to the captain. 'Will he serve?'

'He is my best. A little headstrong, but then you are used to that.' Out of the corner of his eye Kestros saw his captain smile, the gesture as brief as a flash of lightning. Kestros blinked again.

'Enough time and you grow to tolerate anything,' said Archamus, his voice flat and humourless, and though he was not sure, he thought that the smile cut across Katafalque's face again. 'You have my thanks,' continued Archamus. 'I hope he serves me as well as you did.'

For the first time in his years of service, Kestros heard Captain Katafalque laugh.

'I hope he serves you better than that.' Katafalque gave a swift bow to Archamus and then glanced at Kestros. 'Bring us honour in wherever your duty takes you, brother,' he said.

Kestros bowed his head more deeply, but Katafalque had already turned and left the chamber.

'Rise, sergeant,' said Archamus, and Kestros stood. Archamus met his gaze. 'This is not about a stain on your honour, nor that of your company. Nor is it about censure.'

Kestros tried to read the old warrior's face but could not. It was like trying to read the mood of a cliff from the shape of its cracks. He had a likeness of stone, like so many of the Legion. Kestros felt the question come to his lips before he could bite it off.

'What is it about then, lord?'

Archamus gave Kestros a glance that might have held either calculation or amusement.

'Your Legion and primarch have need of your service,' said Archamus.

Kestros felt the words yank the breath out of his lungs.

Archamus half turned towards the door, the machinery of his arm and leg whirring in the quiet of the cell.

'Arm and armour yourself,' Archamus said, and looked at the dark of the corridor beyond the cell door. A long second passed before he continued. 'You have questions, but the answers cannot be given here.'

Kestros blinked. A sensation that he could not understand or process was turning over in his stomach and spreading a shiver over his skin. There had been something in the old warrior's face when he had looked at the dark, as though a thought had passed like a shadow across the inside of his skull. Kestros forced the disquiet from his mind and called for his armourers.

✠ ✠ ✠

Messalina debris drift
Near-Terran void

'WHAT WAS THAT?' hissed Incarnus, twisting in his harness as a deep, metallic clang echoed through the chamber. Myzmadra had been doing her best to rest, but now she was awake, heart beating fast.

'Nothing,' breathed Ashul, from next to the psyker. He had not moved, and still looked as though he were half asleep despite the noise. 'Just stellar debris impacting on the outside. Most likely nothing larger than a seed grain.'

'How do you know?' spat Incarnus.

'Anything larger and it would have ripped a hole. If it were anything really big and fast... well, let's just say we would not be able to indulge in this conversation.'

Incarnus hissed, his eyes swivelling between the walls. Not for the first time Myzmadra thought he resembled a lizard stretched into human shape. Part of her was enjoying the psyker's discomfort, but she could not say that she shared Ashul's apparent disdain for their current situation.

The chamber was not really a chamber, but an airtight cargo slab, twenty metres high and wide, and twice as long. It was of the type used to convey volatile materials by the Jovian Void Clans. Now its only cargo was Myzmadra, Ashul, Incarnus and the five Space Marines.

They had broken Terra's atmosphere and rendezvoused with a small system ship making runs between the void docks. Their shuttle had settled into a sealed bay holding only the container and a cluster of servitors. They had moved to the slab-sided box and been sealed within. An hour later they had been dumped into the void on the edge of a debris drift and left to spin, like the billions of other pieces of stellar refuse clogging the solar void. Myzmadra did not know what they were waiting for; her mission information had long run out by this point.

The five Space Marines treated the situation with total indifference. Most of them remained silent and stood, or sat, mag-locked to the wall. She had begun to notice differences between the five of them now that she had been granted the opportunity to observe them.

Phocron moved without cease, as though he would vanish if he was truly still. Even in the shuttle he had turned his head to take in every detail of his surroundings. His movements were always smooth and precise, though; they just never stopped. He had been stripping and reassembling his weapons continuously since they had entered the container. His equipment and armour was a uniform dull indigo, without mark or adornment, though his primacy was undoubtable. He was tall, though the magnitude of Space Marine physiology made it difficult to judge just how much larger than the rest he was.

The one with the meltagun was called Kalix, and he wrapped stillness around himself like a cloak. He had not moved at all since they had entered the container. A serrated crest ran down the centre of his helm, and his armour plates were lacquered with a subtle pattern of scales. The more she watched Kalix, the more she wanted him to move; his stillness was like a pressure on her eyes.

Orn kept close to Phocron like a shadow. Slightly shorter than the others, his armour still held the dust of the Gobi wastes in its grooves. His face was broad, and his cheeks dotted with fine scars in the shapes of stars. He and Phocron spoke often, but while she heard what Phocron said, Orn never spoke above a whisper.

The last of those she had dug from the dirt was called Hekaron, and was the most unusual of them all. While Phocron and Silonius looked near identical, Hekaron grinned at the world with a face that was a mass of bright green lizards tattooed in luminous dye. Rows of black pearls on silver rings hung above his right ear and eyebrow. He had pulled his helm off as soon as they were out of combat and had not stopped smiling since. His teeth were sharp and gleaming.

Then there was Silonius. The newcomer had talked little and remained on the edge of the others while being one of them. At first she wondered if that was simply because he was a newcomer to a group of bonded warriors, but that was not it. As she had watched them, she had realised that Phocron, Hekaron, Kalix and Orn had no special bond. The Legion had buried them beneath the earth of the Gobi wastes years ago, but if they had known each other before, they gave no sign. They worked smoothly together, but that could be a product of their training, rather than familiarity. Silonius was not an outsider, but he seemed separate, as though he was passing through their company, as though he was waiting for something.

He glanced at her, perhaps sensing her gaze, and she met his eyes for a moment and then looked away. She thought of the item she had brought with her, wrapped in ballistic cloth and carried with her wherever she went, her own fragment of a secret she did not understand.

'Any idea how long we are going to drift here?' said Incarnus. 'There is only so much air we can breathe before this place becomes a very unusual coffin. Of course, that might be the idea...'

'If the Legion wanted you dead, it would already have brought it about,' said Phocron. Incarnus froze. 'All of us are here because we still have a purpose.'

Phocron's perpetual movement had fallen away. All of the legionnaires were now looking at Incarnus, eyes and helmet lenses locked on him.

'Of course,' said Incarnus. Myzmadra could see his throat move under the rubber of his void suit collar as he swallowed. 'Of course.'

Phocron nodded and turned his gaze away. The rest of the legionnaires followed suit a second later. Myzmadra shivered. For a second the differences between the five warriors had vanished. They had been one, a single predator with a united will and intent.

'Silence and patience might be a better approach to making friends,' drawled Ashul. Incarnus looked as though he was going to answer, when the entire container rang and shook. The legionnaires moved in an eye blink, helmets locking in place, weapons readied. A series of clanks shook through the metal walls, and then became a stuttering series of clatters. 'I think the wait is over,' said Ashul. 'Either that or everything is about to come to an abrupt end.'

✠ ✠ ✠

Luna

THE LIGHTER SKIMMED low over the dark side of Luna. Gun turrets tracked it briefly, then heard its clearance signal and went back to covering the void. The lighter banked and descended, hugging the surface. Towers projected from the rims of crater cities. Transport ducts crossed the grey wastes between clusters of buildings. Void shields glittered above the city clusters like blisters of ice. Dead and burned ruins were dotted here and there, the edges of their metal bones catching the weak light. Terra shone as a thin crescent in the black sky, its satellite cities and defences a halo of diamonds glinting in the night.

Within the lighter's small crew compartment, the sight of Luna's surface flickered beneath the static of a pict screen. The lighter was marked as one serving in the Terran Militia bonded to one of the orbital defence platforms. Its clearance was from one of the Regent of Terra's vassal organisations. Archamus had obtained the codes without asking either the Regent or his servants.

'Approaching ordained destination,' droned the servitor pilot.

'Proceed,' said Archamus.

'Compliance.'

'This will be delicate,' he murmured. 'The Selenar Matriarch is an individual...'

He looked at Kestros. The sergeant nodded, but said nothing. Archamus looked back to the screen.

'Do you have any questions, sergeant?'

Kestros shook his head. His frown caught the light of the screen, and sharpened the edges of his expression.

'You are troubled,' stated Archamus. 'Speak your mind. You are not here to remain silent.'

The frown deepened and then pinched into something sharper. He let out a short breath and shook his head without meeting Archamus' eye.

'To speak truthfully, my lord, I am not sure why I am here at all.' He leant forwards, before Archamus could reply. 'I am not a warrior of strategy or mysteries. The edge of the blade and the bolt shell are my realm. I understand what we are doing, just not my place in it.'

Archamus gave a brief smile.

'Then we stand at the same place.'

Kestros gave a snort of laughter, and his frown lightened slightly. Then he shook his head again, as though to clear it of thought.

The lighter suddenly slammed level. The frame vibrated as thrusters fired.

'Descending to landing platform,' said the servitor. The screen was suddenly filled with the coal-black cliffs and dots of light racing past in a blur.

'This is still a war,' said Archamus, as the lighter shuddered down through the dark. 'It is just a war with a battlefield that is difficult to recognise. We are the Seventh Legion. We do not flinch and we do not fail. Our strength will serve the primarch and the Emperor now just as it always has before.'

Kestros clamped his helm over his head and then began to glance to either side, to check squad brothers who were not there. His head twitched up towards Archamus.

'What is the root of victory?' he said. 'What is the foundation of strength?'

Archamus smiled as he pulled his own helm over his head.

'Focus,' he said, and heard his own voice boom from his speaker grille, as the whine of the lighter's thrusters became a scream. 'But the key to strength in war is not just focus, but balance. Too much choler and you can be blind, too much caution and you let the enemy strike as they would choose.'

'So my purpose is to bring balance, then – that is why I am here?'

Archamus said nothing. He thought he could almost feel the young warrior's anger pressing out from behind the faceplate of his armour. He could understand why. He had told Kestros about the attack within the bounds of Terra, and that they had the task of hunting down the Alpha Legion within the system. With every additional detail he had seen Kestros' face harden. This was not an honour; it was a dark and bitter duty that had taken him away from other, purer battles. Neither the highness of the calling, nor Archamus' renown, seemed to dim the core of his dissatisfaction. Secrecy, shadows and deeds done for necessity were not the duty he had hoped to perform for his primarch.

The lighter rocked as it landed. The engines began to cycle down immediately. Kestros came out of his harness instantly, moving towards the rear doors. Archamus followed, bionics whirring as he moved. The doors opened, and the air within the cabin vented into the darkness outside.

Archamus stepped out onto the landing platform. A canyon was extended above him, towers and bastions jutting from its face, each dotted with lights. A set of silver doors sat in the face of the cliff at the opposite end of the platform. The crescent of Terra shone down on them with a cold light.

Kestros was silent as they walked towards the doors, their boots mag-locking to the deck as they took each step. The doors opened and figures leapt out from the darkness within. Kestros had his weapon in his hand before the first of them had made five metres from the door. Archamus' hand snapped out and slammed the barrel down just as the bolt pistol flared. The round hit the edge of the platform and exploded. Kestros tensed to resist, then stilled at a shake of Archamus' head.

More figures bounded onto the platform, forming a wide circle around them. Each of the figures was humanoid but very tall. Segmented black carapace encased their torsos. Enclosed helmets covered their faces, and blue light shone from slits that ran across their visors. Three sprung silver struts extended from their feet and clamped to the deck as they moved. Each of them carried a volkite charger. The charge rings of the weapons glowed as they levelled them at Archamus and Kestros.

'The last time the Seventh Legion came to Luna uninvited and unannounced it ended badly,' said a voice across the vox. A figure moved onto the platform. She did not walk, but floated. A gloss black coating hid her skin, as though she were wearing a layer of oil. Her feet hung beneath her body, the flesh withered on her elongated bones. Her arms extended to either side. Silver tubes arched across her shoulders and burrowed through the black coating into the flesh beneath. She wore a silver mask shaped to resemble a serene face with closed eyes. Spills of silver gauze formed a halo around her, billowing slowly in the thin gravity. She halted halfway between Archamus and the open doors.

'Badly for whom?' asked Archamus, tilting his head to one side.

'Given the current flow of history, a case could be made for all parties, don't you think?'

Kestros glanced at Archamus, but he held his gaze on the figure.

'It is a pleasure to make your acquaintance, Matriarch Heliosa,' said Archamus, with the smallest nod. 'I am sorry if this visit comes as a surprise.'

A laugh bubbled across the vox in reply. Archamus repressed the instinct to wonder how she had latched into their communication channels.

'Not at all. It's always a pleasure to receive Rogal's gene-breed.' Kestros tensed at the casual mention of the primarch, but Archamus stilled him with a gesture. Matriarch Heliosa had pivoted in place and drifted towards the open doors, then stopped when they did not follow. 'You have come this far, are you afraid to go a little further?'

'You know what we are here for,' said Archamus, his voice a low rumble of authority. 'Give it to us, and we will be gone.'

'You make it sound like you don't want to be here.'

'Carry out your orders, and give us what we came for,' growled Kestros.

Heliosa pivoted towards Kestros. The silver-masked head tilted to the side.

'No,' she said. 'Not now. Not without you giving me the brief pleasure of your company and conversation.'

'You would defy the will of the Praetorian?' snapped Kestros.

'I would demand that you do as I request, so that I don't have to defy him.' She turned back to the door. 'Come – are a few more steps and a few words too high a price to ask?'

Archamus watched the Matriarch for a second. He had never met her before, but there was something unsettling about her – an air of familiarity, as if she were someone who knew him, but who he could not remember. He looked at Kestros, noticing that the sergeant's hands were hovering close to his weapons. He gave a small but obvious shake of his head and looked back to Heliosa.

'You are most gracious, honoured Matriarch.'

'Yes, I am,' she said. 'Welcome to the last Fane of the Selenar, sons of Dorn.'

Scavenger vessel Wealth of Kings
Messalina debris drift, near-Terran void

THE MEMORY CAME so fast it felt like being shot.

In one instant Silonius was standing in the cargo container, the clang of magnetic clamps fastening to the outside fading in his ears. And the next...

He was falling from the light of the world, falling down through the blank pit of his own memory, falling with the sound of names from forgotten myths following him down.

Orpheus...

Eurydice...

Hades...

And then a voice...

'Will you serve the Legion in this way?'

'Of course,' said a voice that he knew was his.

'There is not one mission parameter in play. There are several. We are also using assets that were put in place a long time ago. They have slept under the earth of Terra for a decade. The mission parameters they will follow initially will serve our ends, but they are not specific to the current need. You will provide that specificity.'

'Yes, of course, lord,' said Silonius, and now the memory gifted him sight.

He was standing in a long chamber. Columns of light marched away from him through the gloom. Within each pillar the dome of a stasis field buzzed. He could see the shapes of small objects: a near-human skull with canine teeth like knife blades, a silver pendant in the shape of a winged sword, a vial of pale green liquid. A figure stood before him. No, not a figure – a very specific individual. Alpharius looked at Silonius, his eyes still, his face blank of emotion.

'There are security matters that must be accounted for,' Alpharius said. 'This operation's importance cannot be overstated. The future of the Legion and the outcome of this war rest on it.'

Silonius nodded.

'I understand,' he said.

'No, you do not. But you will. You are carrying the key to this operation, and it must remain secret. But you are going to carry these secrets to Terra, and there you do not need to speak a secret to have it taken. Even ignoring the powers of Malcador, or my father, there are others who might see the truth in your thoughts, and once they have seen that truth then it is not your own silence that will matter, but theirs. The only way to truly keep a secret is to keep it from yourself.'

Silonius had nodded, and made himself hold his primarch's gaze.

'Psychic reconstruction,' he stated, and Alpharius nodded.

Two figures slid from behind the columns of light. Both were armoured, their identical faces uncovered. Silver wires and blue crystals gleamed on their bare scalps.

'What is needed will be given back to you when it is required.'

The two psykers watched him without blinking as they moved to stand either side of him. The Emperor had forbidden the use of psykers within His Legions, but the Alpha Legion always followed their own will rather than the rules of others.

'How will recall be triggered?'

Alpharius smiled and shook his head.

'That will remain buried far below your consciousness, but trust that when it is needed, you will know.'

Silonius glanced at the two psykers. They had become perfectly still. Strands of pale energy gathered around their heads. Their eyes had become utterly black.

'What will they take from me?' he asked.

'Everything,' said Alpharius.

And he was falling upwards through darkness, the sounds of the memory vanishing into an echo, and the names followed him like a chanted curse.

Orpheus...

Eurydice...

Hades...

'Brother?'

Silonius turned his head.

He had not moved. He had lost awareness for an instant, but it had been enough for Phocron to notice. The Headhunter Prime was looking at him, turning his head slowly as though to examine Silonius from slightly different angles.

'Is all well, brother?' asked Phocron. Silonius noted the rune blinking at the edge of his helmet display. They were talking over a private channel.

'Yes,' he replied. 'Everything is as it should be.'

Fane of the Selenar
Luna

'I CANNOT HELP you.' Matriarch Heliosa's voice came from all around the chamber, echoing from the walls as though the substance of Luna itself were speaking.

Kestros bit back his instinct to growl at the Matriarch's arrogance. Beside him Archamus did not move or say anything; Kestros could feel the control in that silence, the power.

The floor of the chamber was small. Kestros could have crossed it, corner-to-corner, in ten strides, but the walls went up and up, beyond the range of his helmet sensors. A crescent moon of pale crystal occupied the centre of the granite floor. Six circular pools of water encircled the crescent, the surface of each a black mirror perfectly level with the floor. Lines of inlaid silver spread across the floor from the pools. A circle of symbols marked wherever two or more lines intersected. There were only four symbols, but Kestros could not see the same sequence repeated across the entire chamber.

He did not like it. He did not like it at all.

They had walked across the rock of the moon to get here, passing through black crystal and crossing canyons on silver bridges. Once he had looked down as he crossed a bridge, and seen the reflection of his own face staring back at him from the surface of still, black water. There must have been ways that branched from theirs, but he never saw a doorway or junction along their path. Dust and damage marked much of what they passed: rust bled from bolts, and tarnish crawled over the silver crescents and discs set into the floor. With every step he had felt as though he were walking back into some half-forgotten mystery that was waiting to die.

'This place should not exist,' said Archamus at last, turning and stepping towards the nearest of the six pools. 'The ways of your cult were proscribed when you joined the Imperium.'

'Joined?' said Heliosa. 'That's a kind way to put it.'

'You had a choice,' said Archamus flatly.

'Extinction or service, the choice offered by all conquerors and tyrants.'

Kestros felt the anger pour through him. It beat at the inside of his skull, and screamed at him to draw his pistol and put a shell through the Matriarch's head.

Yet beside him Archamus did not move.

'But you did choose, and because of that I will indulge your words, this time, Matriarch.'

'And if you did not *indulge* them, what then? Would the Seventh Legion come here again to finish the work they left undone two centuries past? That threat lost its teeth long ago. We are dying already.

With every year we are fewer in number. I might even take up your offer of execution. It would be swift at least.'

She is lying, thought Kestros. He could hear it in her voice, in the uncontrolled vibrations at the edge of the words. *She wants more than anything to survive.*

'I have no interest in you, Matriarch, nor the fact that you are lying,' said Archamus. 'I am here only for what you have been ordered to give us.'

'I cannot help you,' hissed Heliosa.

'Then we will see if the Imperium still has mercy in its heart for you,' said Archamus, as he turned and took a step towards the entranceway.

'No!' The word rang clear from the walls. Ripples spread across the surface of the six pools.

Archamus turned back slowly, his head tilted in question.

'I said that I cannot help, not that I refused to.'

'Why can you not help?' said Archamus, his voice as flat and unfeeling as ice.

'Because *she* refuses to obey me,' said Heliosa.

'Bring her here,' said Archamus. 'I would talk to her myself.'

'As you wish,' she said.

'I ALREADY SAID that I have no interest in whatever you want of me,' said the girl in the grey robes. She looked up at Archamus and gave a bored shrug. 'There is nothing else that needs to be clarified further.' Then she sat down on the floor and began to glance around the room, as though looking for something that was more interesting than the two Imperial Fists standing above her.

Her face was thin and pale, and marked only by a single bright red circle just beneath her left eye. Braids of silver wire hung from her scalp in place of hair. She was tall for a mortal, but in that stretched willow-thin way of one born and raised in low gravity. Her eyes were green. The robes were plain, dust-grey. She looked young, but there was a way that she watched the world that seemed knowing beyond her years. Her name was Andromeda-17. That meant, in the traditions of the Luna gene-cults, that she was the seventeenth resurrection of a single gene-identical individual.

Archamus watched her for a second.

'Matriarch Heliosa, please give us a moment,' he said without moving his eyes.

The Matriarch shifted position slightly, and Archamus thought she was going to object, but then she glided to the arched door without a word.

'She will still hear what you say, you know,' said Andromeda. Archamus ignored the words.

'The Imperium has need of you,' he said.

'The Imperium can go and need something else,' said Andromeda with a shrug. Kestros started forwards, hands clenched. Archamus put a hand on his chest before he could take a step. Amusement danced in Andromeda's eyes as she looked at Kestros. 'A level of psychological imbalance in regard to temperament. You know, I have never met one of your kind before.' She turned her gaze back to Archamus and jerked her chin at Kestros. 'Is this one primarily here for intimidation, or because you find him reassuringly straightforward?'

Kestros did not move, but Archamus could sense the sergeant tense with anger.

'Peace, brother,' said Archamus. 'I am sure that she did not mean to imply an insult.'

'Oh no,' said Andromeda, silver teeth flashing in her mouth as she smiled. 'I did not intend to imply an insult. I intended to say that you are stupid.'

Archamus ignored the words. There was something calculating behind the amusement in her eyes, something that was probing, assessing, judging.

'I have come for you,' he said, his voice low and controlled, 'at the will of my lord, who is the guardian of the Throneworld, and the Emperor's Praetorian.'

'Irrelevant,' snapped Andromeda. 'All you can do is kill me, or subject me to pain, though the latter is unlikely given your Legion's psychological pattern. This means you need to persuade me, and you are not going to succeed in doing that.'

'Your Matriarch seems to be equally resistant,' he said.

Andromeda laughed.

'Your kind really are built along straight lines, aren't they? She isn't resistant. She is terrified. She pleaded and threatened me for hours when your message arrived, and she was as successful as you are being now.'

'Terrified?' he asked.

'We are dying, Space Marine,' said Andromeda slowly, as though extending her patience to breaking point. 'We began dying when you first brought us to compliance. Our work for the Emperor bought us some time, but if I am not the last generation of my kind, then the next will be. The Matriarch does not want to see that fact. *She* still hopes that we might rise again. She will do everything and anything to preserve what remains.' She opened and spread her hands, a cold grin on her face. 'I, selfish child that I am, will not.'

Archamus waited a heartbeat, then gave a single, curt nod.

'Very well,' he said. He straightened and began to move towards the door. Kestros moved to follow.

'Is that it?' called Andromeda.

Archamus half turned and offered her a shrug of his own.

'You might think us simple, but we are built to judge strength and weakness, and to know when a fight can be won and when it cannot. So, yes, that is it. There will be no retribution for your defiance.' He turned and took a step towards the archway. 'I am surprised, though.'

'Surprised?'

'I have never met one of your kind before,' he said, throwing her own words back at her as he walked away. 'Impressive in a way, to find that you do not even wish to know what would bring us here.'

'A mundane matter of bullets and blood, I imagine,' she muttered.

'No,' he said, pausing on the threshold. 'I am hunting an enemy and a secret.'

'What enemy?'

'Not one I could tell you of, as you have not agreed to serve.'

Her eyes narrowed. The air of boredom had vanished from her.

'It's something you do not understand, isn't it? Something that is opposite to your nature, something that you need me to understand...'

He allowed a breath of laughter past his lips and took another step towards the door. 'Good fortune in whatever your life here brings.'

'Wait,' she called, and Archamus paused again. 'You are manipulating me. It won't work. I am in control of my nature. Though I must admit that was a good try.'

He walked slowly back towards the seated girl. When he was a pace from her, he squatted down so that his face was almost on a level with her own. His bionics clicked as they braced his weight. He looked into her eyes.

'You must be mistaken,' he said carefully. 'Manipulation is something my kind are far too straightforward to attempt.'

She smiled.

'Whatever it is...' She shook her head again, silver teeth biting her lip. He waited. 'It is something extraordinary, isn't it?'

'Would we have gone to the trouble of coming here otherwise?' said Kestros from by the arched doorway.

'Please don't try to flatter me,' snapped Andromeda. 'Your master is barely competent at interacting with something that does not have a trigger, but at least he has identified that my weakness is curiosity rather than ego.'

Archamus ignored the rattle of words.

'Well?' he said, looking at Andromeda without blinking. 'Will you serve?'

She shook her head and clamped her eyes shut, forehead creasing as though in sudden pain.

'Yes,' she said, and opened her eyes. 'Yes. I will.'

Archamus stood up and walked from the chamber. Behind him Andromeda stayed seated on the floor, eyes now fixed on the black water of one of the pools.

'Follow,' he said, without turning.

'That means you follow,' said Kestros, after a moment's pause. 'There is nothing else that needs to be clarified further.'

TWO

Qokang Oasis
The Imperial Palace, Terra

THE MIST FROM the falling water touched Armina Fel's face, and she breathed in the smell of it. The sound of the torrent falling through the turbine sluices wrapped her, making her nearly as deaf as she was blind. She was not blind, though, not really, and while the crash of water smothered other sounds, she could still hear.

Her mind saw the world around her as though she were looking at a painting. The brush was the flow of the warp, ever-present and ever-changing under physical reality, and the inks were the resonance of thoughts and emotion. The stone balustrade she leant on was made real by the echoed emotions of everyone that had ever touched it. A man had stood here and thought of leaping to his death. He had left with the deed undone, but an imprint of his despair remained where his hands had gripped the stone. A trio of young serfs had sat here last night, their feet swinging in the air, their excitement at the risk they were taking bright and sharp. Long ago the being called the Emperor had stood just as she did now. The ghost of that presence was like heat still lingering in a banked fire. And beneath that–

'You have news, mistress?' Rogal Dorn's voice reached her even through the roar of water. She turned, and his presence filled her mind's eye, a diamond shining with the reflected light of the sun. Armina Fel shook herself. Her body ached from her scalp to the soles of her feet. She was weak, and getting weaker by the day. And she could not afford to be weak.

'A report from Phaeton, lord. Do you wish the direct linguistic rendering or the divined meaning?'

His presence drew closer. His Huscarl bodyguards remained distant, their minds tiny echoes of their primarch's.

'The meaning will suffice,' he said, coming to a stop two paces from her. She bit her lip and let the tiny spike of pain trigger her eidetic recall. The words that came from her mouth were a dull drone of precise recollection.

'All is silence. No ships come. No news comes. All is silence.' Her voice stopped as the last syllables of the divination spooled out of her. She shivered as the memory faded.

'That is all?' asked Dorn after a second.

'Yes, lord.'

'And how current is the message?'

'It is hard to say, but my feeling is that it is recent, sent in the close past or near future.'

'And the other worlds, have they replied?'

'No lord, but–'

'They may not have received the message,' Dorn completed her reply, 'or we may not have heard the replies.'

'Just so, lord.'

Dorn lapsed into silence. Armina Fel swallowed carefully. She could not see within the primarch's thoughts, but the surface of his mind resonated in the warp like the sun radiating heat into the void. He was frustrated, she could tell, but more than that he was worried. There was a reason for his worry too, lingering in his thoughts just beyond her senses.

'My apologies, mistress,' said Dorn. 'I must thank you for your service again.'

She forced what straightness she could into her spine and turned her face up to him.

'We are all warriors in this war, lord. I give what I can.'

'Well said.'

She thought she saw a glimmer of what might have been admiration in the crystal edges of his thoughts. She bowed her head. What moved within the mind of such a being? Rogal Dorn was not human. He was not even transhuman, as his gene-sons were. He was a different order of being, a being who moved and spoke like a man, but only shared those qualities with humans in the same way that fish and men both had blood and bones. He did think and feel, and those thoughts and feelings shared something of the shape of the human equivalent. They flowed and crackled and burned over the surface of his mind, their depth fathomless, and their subtlety impossible for her to grasp. But they were there: anger, sorrow, pain and hope, each of them a thunderbolt to the spark of a human's emotion.

In many ways he was closer to a human than he was to the warriors of his Legion. They shared his blood, but their minds had been cut to their purpose, instincts sliced away, emotions selected, discarded and the remainder reshaped. They were limited creatures. Dorn was not; he was humanity expressed in grand and terrifying transcendence.

She had reflected that perhaps she alone of all mortals was in a position to understand that. She saw not with her eyes, but with her mind, and no others of her kind had stood so close, through so much, as she had to Dorn in the last years of darkness. Sometimes she wondered if it was the same for his brothers. If she looked at them, would she see the same power circling their souls like a crown?

She was about to speak when her mind froze.

She gasped.

There was someone there, reaching into her mind; someone whose own mind burned like a star, so bright that it stole her sight.

'Mistress?' said Dorn, but his voice sounded distant. Her mouth moved, and she felt the spit freezing on her lips as she spoke.

'My apologies,' she said, and inside her tumbling thoughts she heard an echo of the words. 'You have been difficult to reach in recent days, and I am not able to come to find you in person.'

'Release her, Sigillite,' growled Dorn.

'I will, but not yet. We must talk.'

'There is nothing to discuss.'

'No? An exploding ship burns the polar orbits, the planet comes to near full alert, Damocles Starport is a slaughterhouse waiting to be repopulated, there are riots still smouldering in the drift camps, and the Investiary is bare of all but the marks of battle. That seems worthy of more than silence, surely?'

'It is in hand.'

'I do not doubt that.'

'Then there is *nothing* to discuss.'

'The Alpha Legion, Rogal. Here on the soil of Terra, and here still if I understand matters correctly.' Through the grey fog and fire pouring into her, Armina felt the primarch's psyche shift subtly. The voice coming from her mouth seemed to soften on her tongue. 'Do not be concerned, your veil of secrecy over their involvement is prudent and remains unbreached.'

'Except by you.'

'That is my duty, Rogal. This is a war with many battlefields. I fight the same war as you in ways and places that you cannot.'

'And you believe this is your battle, not mine. A war of shadows and silence.'

'Yes. At its simplest, that is exactly what this is.'

Dorn was silent, and after a moment Armina Fel felt her mouth and tongue move again.

'I hear reports that worlds across the domain of Terra are becoming silent. The land beyond our walls is becoming dark. Our enemies draw closer. That should weigh on your thoughts more than this matter.'

'You presume that the two are not intertwined,' said Dorn.

'That is a dangerous way to think. He has got you, Rogal. Alpharius has offended your pride and raised your anger. He wants you to dance with him into the dark, and that is not a place you should let him lead you, my friend.'

'You are wrong. I know my brother and his Legion. Lies within lies and secrets hidden by secrets. This is not a simple incursion into our defences.'

'It is something more? Something grander and greater? Listen to those words. He has you already, even if you have attempted to pass your burden to Archamus. The greatest danger here is to let the Alpha Legion lead us down the path that they have chosen for us. Have you considered that their target is you? Not your life, but your control, your judgement?'

'I have considered it,' said Dorn. 'You might know the shadows, but you do not know *him*. And this is not what *you* believe it to be.'

Armina felt the pause form in her mind. There was now frost over every inch of her skin. She could taste smoke in her mouth.

'I hope you are right, my friend,' said Malcador. 'For all our sakes, I hope you are right.'

The presence vanished from Armina Fel's body and mind. She had a single instant of blankness, and then she was falling to the ground, and pain and nausea were spinning through her, the sound of falling water the only thing in her world.

Warship Lachrymae
Trans-Plutonian region

SIGISMUND PULLED THE helm from his head, and folded it into the crook of his arm. The bridge's blast shields were open, and the light of stars and warship engines filled the dark beyond the viewports. The *Lachrymae*'s sister ships, the *Ophelia* and *Persephone*, were close enough that he could see the gleam of their golden prows. Roboute Guilliman had given all three as a gift to Rogal Dorn as a sign of brotherhood. The three frigates always fought together, a trio of blades cutting fire in the dark. There were larger ships under Sigismund's command, but few faster. The bloated shape of a supply barge hung beside them now, pouring fresh fuel and ammunition into them via vast umbilical bundles and docking gantries. Normally such tasks would occur in dock, but that was not a possibility on the outer wall of Terra's defences.

'You are tired,' came a growling voice from behind Sigismund. He did not need to look to know who it was. That voice had become so familiar it might have been the voice of his thoughts. Fafnir Rann, captain of the assault cadre, halted beside Sigismund. There were fresh cuts on his scarred face, and his black hair was plaited and coiled against the base of his skull. Yellow lacquer clung to his armour amidst a sea of dented and grey ceramite. He had shed his helmet and shield, but his paired axes still hung from his waist. A reek of blood, sweat and gunfire hung about him.

'Two hours and we will be back to full readiness,' said Sigismund, taking a data-slate from a deck officer.

'Two hours to resupply a ship, to scrape the blood and soot from armour and thread rounds back into magazines... And then?'

Sigismund raised his eyes to Rann, careful to keep his face still.

'Something troubles you, brother?'

Rann shook his head.

'Five years,' he said quietly. 'Five years of battle without victory. This is not true war, brother. They come without cease, but this is not and never has been battle. It is winnowing.'

'This is our duty. My duty. And I will see it done.'

'This is not work for the likes of you,' said Rann, and then gave a grin. 'For a dog like me perhaps. Hacking through corridors and feeling the rounds ring on the plate, that is my life. But not yours. You should be at the primarch's side. You should speak with him. Your presence out here is not the optimal use of resources. Hacking through madmen and chasing down rogue ships? Indulge my candour, but that is work for an axe, not a sword.'

Sigismund felt cold rope knot in his guts. He gave a single shake of his head.

'It is as it must be.' He looked back at the data-slate and ignored Rann's stare. That the assault captain was right was irrelevant. 'My father has put me here, and here I will stand until he wills it otherwise.'

Rann watched him for a second and then shrugged.

'Of course.' He nodded and began to turn away. 'As you will it, Lord Castellan.'

Battle-barge Alpha
The interstellar gulf beyond the light of Sol

THE MASTER OF the *Alpha* woke the first hundred of the serpent's children. They had waited for him, long lines of armoured figures lining lightless holds. They were the Lernaeans, Terminator-executioners of the Legion. They were destroyers of civilisations, the Legion's killing edge, and now they were returning to the light of the Solar System. They had not passed the months in stasis – only he had that honour. For them it had been the coma of sus-an hibernation. It took twelve hours from when he triggered the resurrection equipment to the moment when the first warrior shivered awake and spoke.

'How close are we, lord?' he asked, bowing his head.

'Close, and so far undetected.'

The Lernaean nodded and gave another shiver. His Terminator plate growled.

'I am yours to command, lord.'

'Wake the others,' he replied, and left the lightless hold.

He climbed back up through the silence of the ship and took his command throne again. He keyed a series of commands into the few controls with power, and a murmur of information passed to the signal arrays on the outside of the hull. Short-range signals whispered to the other ships tumbling beside the *Alpha*. On each of them, a handful of awakened crew replied, and began to wake their brothers from the dark.

THREE

THE HATCH IN the cargo container was a metre thick and hinged outwards. Myzmadra had felt the pull of gravity return after the walls had stopped ringing. A minute later a series of blows had rung on the hatch. To reach through the metal the impacts must have been powerful enough to dent a tank. Phocron had looked at Incarnus, and the psyker had nodded.

'One person in near vicinity. Human, tense but controlled. No thoughts of storming through the hatch, or luring us out into a gun-line.'

Phocron nodded, and Orn had moved to open the hatch. All of them had kept their weapons ready. Air hissed out as the hatch released. A cone of bright light shone through the opening.

'It's clear,' came a voice from the open hatch. 'Just me out here.'

'By what word are you bound?' asked Phocron.

'Orpheus,' came the reply.

'Your name?'

'Sork. Ship's Captain Sork, if you like formalities. Scavenger King Sork, if you want to flatter.'

'Approach,' called Phocron. A shadow filled the opening, and then became the shape of a hunched man. Augmetic braces circled his body with struts and pistons. A clattering power pack sat on his back. His limbs were gone thin, and the flesh of his face hung in sagging folds beneath violet eyes.

Ashul glanced at Myzmadra and raised an eyebrow. She shook her head and looked back at Sork. He looked more like a refuse sifter than an Alpha Legion operative, but that was the point; nothing ever should be what it seemed.

Sork moved closer, the augmetic braces shortening and lengthening with a clatter of gears. He stopped a metre away from Phocron and raised a hand. The fingers opened with agonising slowness. An electoo of an alpha symbol spread across his palm.

'It has been a long time,' said Sork, his voice a rasping lilt. 'Thought the Legion would never actually come back for me.'

'Report,' said Phocron, as though he had not heard the man's words.

'I pulled this,' the man flicked his eyes around the walls of the container, 'from the drift, right where the instructions said it would be. We are in my main loading hangar now. Don't worry. The whole thing is empty. No one is coming in here but me.'

'On a ship?' asked Incarnus.

The man looked at him slowly.

'Would be difficult to come out to this patch of nothing without one, and it would be hard for me to be a ship's captain without a ship,' replied Sork. 'She's called the *Wealth of Kings*.' He grinned, and Myzmadra saw in that smile that he was not afraid or even intimidated. A rare soul. Just how the Legion liked them. 'The name's a little joke, you see.'

'A scavenger vessel?' asked Ashul from the other side of the container.

'Yes, that's right,' said Sork.

It made sense, thought Myzmadra. The Praetorian kept space around Terra tight, and Mars... Well, no one who was not a special kind of insane would go close to the Red Planet. But the Solar System was a big place, crowded with emptiness and secrets from millennia of civilisation and catastrophe. The Emperor had made it His, but parasites still lived in the cracks of civilisation. Parasites like Sork.

'I have this for you,' he said, unhooking a brass data-slab from his waist and holding it up to Phocron. The casing was dented and scratched through to the plasteel beneath the paint. The Space Marine took it, turned it over and then tossed it to Incarnus.

'Did you look at what it contains?'

'Wouldn't know how to find out,' said Sork, watching as Incarnus turned the slab over in his hands. 'It was in the drop on the Canticle station as per mission parameters. Never saw who left it.'

Incarnus began pulling cables and machinery out of packs, and plugging them into the slab slots.

'He does not look like one of the Martian priests,' said Sork.

'That's because I am not,' said Incarnus without looking up.

'Do what you need to,' said Phocron. 'There will be two more data drops, and they will all need to be sifted.' Phocron turned back to Sork, missing the look from Incarnus that said that he knew his task in the next part of the mission as well as the Headhunter Prime. That, reflected Myzmadra, put him at a distinct advantage; she had no idea what task waited for them, or her place in it. She did not like that – following was not in her nature.

'Where are we headed?' asked Sork. 'The Fists are locking things down tight. The void beyond the sphere of Mars is crawling with monitor craft. If we are going that way it's going to be slow and careful.'

Phocron shook his head and detached from a pouch what looked like a pierced brass coin etched with numerals. He held it out to Sork. 'This will take us to our destination,' he said. 'Take us sunwards.'

Terran Militia shuttle,
en route to Imperial Fists frigate Unbreakable Truth
Terran orbit

'YOU ARE WONDERING why I'm here,' said the girl called Andromeda. Across the compartment of the shuttle Kestros blinked. Beside him

Archamus turned his head to look at them both but said nothing. 'You are though, aren't you?'

'The reason for your presence is a question I do not need an answer to,' said Kestros. 'I only need to know my own purpose.'

'And what is that exactly?'

Kestros looked as though he was about to spit another reply.

Archamus pulled his own thoughts back from where they circled memories.

'You are both here because to see anything clearly you must look at it from two angles,' said Archamus. 'You are here to help me see true.'

'The enemy you are hunting,' said Andromeda. 'It is one of the Alpha Legion, isn't it? That is why you came for me.'

Archamus held her gaze, seeing the spite and intellect and humour dancing in her eyes.

'Yes,' he said.

'There are few who would think to come to the Selenar for insight into the Legions,' she said. 'Few who would know, and few who would remember.'

'Only the old,' he said.

'And those wise or foolish.'

Archamus nodded once to her, slowly. Beside him he could sense Kestros' silence crackling like bottled lightning. He looked at the sergeant and then back to Andromeda.

'Tell him,' he said.

Andromeda smirked and then bowed her head, the movement an exaggerated copy of his own gesture. Then she looked at Kestros, and the humour had vanished from it to leave her face cold, her eyes hard.

'It was not only the Priests of Mars that the Emperor made bargains with to build His empire. In the early days of His rise there were others. Many others. My kind were one of those who He brought to heel and used. The Luna gene-cults had something that He needed, just as the Saturnine Ordo did, and the Jovian Void Clans, and the Mechanicum. The others made weapons and armour and ships, and supplied armies. We, though, helped Him create the means to conquer not just the Solar System but the galaxy. He created the warriors of the Legions, but the means to increase their numbers were limited. In time He would have built gene-forges with greater capacity, but He did not have the patience. So He looked for those to help Him. He looked to us.'

'And you refused,' said Kestros.

'Refused and paid the price for our defiance. Your kind came and taught us the Emperor's capacity for mercy. Once that was done, we took the only choice that remained to us. We helped Him build His dream of war. We took His mysteries and all of the hardy half-feral stock He could drag from the hell-holes of Terra and the ruins of His wars, and made warriors to conquer more worlds in turn. We bought survival by making the weapons by which He would kill others. We turned your kind from armies into Legions.'

Archamus heard the words and thought of the banners honouring the Luna pacification that still hung in the halls of the *Phalanx*.

'The Seventh were amongst the first to grow strong from that bargain we made.' Another cold smile. 'To the conquerors go the spoils, as they say. The Seventh, the Thirteenth and the Seventeenth, all the high and great Legions of later years – the most favoured, the largest and the most honoured... If other Legions had come to conquer us then perhaps they would have been the ones who others envied.'

Kestros' eyes glittered.

'That is–'

'Irrelevant,' said Archamus. They both looked at him. 'Tell him the rest, mistress.'

She shot Kestros a sour look, but carried on.

'We had a hand in all of the Legions. Not their creation, you understand, but their growth. We are not their father, but we raised them up, created and refined the means of their multiplication. We were allowed to divine the effects of the twenty strains of gene-seed, and helped match it to stock that would allow it to bear greatest fruit. We helped to speed the processes that took you from human to legionary.

And we brought millions of you into being. We know you all, because we were there when you were all infants still searching for identity. In a sense we are your surrogate mother.'

'But the Twentieth Legion was not expanded in the early years of the Crusade. Their full foundation was decades later,' said Kestros. 'You cannot know their nature, because you did not help in their growth.'

Andromeda's smile did not shift.

'If you say so,' she said.

'Thank you, mistress,' said Archamus softly, and both of them looked at him. 'You are correct. We are hunting the Alpha Legion, here in the Solar System. We do not know what they intend, how many of them there are, or how to find them. That is why you are both here, for insight and for strength.'

Andromeda smiled.

'Tell me everything.'

Foothills of the Aska mountain range
Terra

ALPHARIUS WAITED FOR night to fall before he began to climb the mountains. He was armoured, but that was as much of a risk as an advantage. By day he would rest out of sight, and the armour would cycle down to shroud both his body heat and the energy signature of its power plant. That was one advantage. The other concerned the weight he needed to carry. His weaponry was both bulky and heavy, and the suspensor web had only enough power for a few hours. The armour made the weight and bulk manageable. The disadvantage was that the armour made manifest fact of his nature to any who saw him clearly. That meant that he had to ensure that no one did.

He travelled at night, keeping to the deserted margins of the great population sinks. At a distance, anyone who caught a glimpse of him would see only a broken, pixelated swirl that dissolved into the gloom.

Even infra-sight would only detect a wash of residual heat. The field projector that created this effect was alien and rare enough that he had never come across it until he woke to this task.

The chances of surviving his mission were low, but then he would not have been entrusted with the mission if that fact had bothered him. Personal survival was a constraint, a luxury that others clung to. He had no constraints. He was Alpha Legion.

After the attack on the tower he had broken off from Phocron's Head-hunter team. No one had questioned it. All of them knew that any or all of them might have different mission parameters. When Phocron had asked him his name, he had given the old, ritual answer and that had been enough of an explanation.

'I am Alpharius,' he had said, and the implication had been understood; he was a blank cipher, a ghost that existed to do the will of the Legion. One amongst many.

An objective waited for this Alpharius in the future, and it had to be accomplished before another day passed.

As the light slid from the sky, he began to move again, blending with the darkness like smoke.

Imperial Fists frigate Unbreakable Truth
Terran orbit

'It does not need to make sense,' Andromeda said, and shook her head.

'It must make sense,' growled Kestros.

Andromeda shrugged, but did not speak.

Archamus waited, but Andromeda was frowning at the glowing data spread across the surface of the table before her.

They were on the frigate *Unbreakable Truth* in orbit around Terra. Archamus had commandeered it, and the rest of Kestros' strike force, in the hours after accepting his duty from Rogal Dorn.

In the hours since they had returned from Luna, he, Kestros and

Andromeda had remained in one of the *Unbreakable Truth*'s planning chambers. A long table of granite sat at the centre of the room beneath a barrel-vaulted roof. Light flickered across the smoothly dressed stone from glow-globes mounted in wrought-iron brackets. The table had no chairs; that was the Inwit way – warriors stood when they came together. Andromeda had disregarded this sentiment by pulling an equipment crate across the tiled floor and sitting on it, legs crossed, back straight, like a queen making a stool a throne. It had taken an hour for Archamus to tell Andromeda what had happened on Terra. Since then, they had circled through hours of argument alternating with silence.

Archamus breathed in and allowed himself to shut his eyes for an instant. The smell of the stone walls filled his nose.

Sandstone, he thought. Pulled from quarries of Ancarin, second world of the Inwit Cluster. In the light of the glow-globes it had the colour of smoke, but under sunlight it would shine grey. Strong, yet more suitable for monuments than fortifications: a stone of subtle grace, rather than rude might.

He let out the breath and felt calm run through him, and opened his eyes.

Andromeda was shaking her head again and looked like she was going to say something, but Kestros spoke before she could.

'Destroying statues. A starport sent into a killing rage. Thirty-five craft destroyed but no forces present to capitalise on the damage. There must be another angle, a way that we are not seeing, on why they have done what they have done.'

'The primarch said it was about pride,' said Archamus.

'Perceptive,' Andromeda said, and bit her upper lip. 'But then perceptiveness is the least that you can expect from a creature like a primarch.' Kestros' hand clenched by his side at the word 'creature'. Archamus kept his own flare of anger smothered. Andromeda carried on as though she either did not notice, or did not care. 'Yes, pride is certainly a factor, but what the Alpha Legion have done is more than saying "I am better than you". They are shouting – "I am better and cleverer than you, and I am so clever and dangerous that I can tell you I am here". This is not just pride. It is validation.'

Kestros shook his head and snorted.

'Oh, you don't think that is what drives them?' said Andromeda, her lip curling around the words.

Archamus held himself still, eyes moving carefully between both of them.

'It is a waste,' said the sergeant with a shrug. 'A pointless and empty gesture. No warrior of worth would take such actions to make such a shallow point. We are missing something, we must be.'

Andromeda smiled, and her eyes glittered.

'The inefficiency and arrogance of it needles, doesn't it?' she asked. 'It would. Your Legion is practical, so aggressively straightforward that you wear your humility like a crown and don't see the irony in that fact.'

Kestros leant forwards, hands resting on the tabletop. Luminous data shifted and swirled under his touch.

'It is still a waste of time and energy for any attacker to do this, Alpha Legion or no. The tactics of the fifth column, of assassins and saboteurs – these have tactical value. What value is there in taking away the advantage of secrecy?'

'It depends on what your objective is.'

'Victory,' growled Kestros.

'But whose victory?' asked Andromeda, coldly. 'Horus' victory? The victory of traitors over their betrayed father and brothers? Or the Alpha Legion's victory?'

'Are you saying that they act on their own whim?'

'Whim? No, but they have never played well with others.' She gave Kestros a broad smile. 'You have that in common with them as well.'

Kestros' lips peeled back from his teeth.

'Enough,' said Archamus softly, and the sergeant froze. 'We have a quarry and must act. The only question that matters at this moment is how.'

'Lock everything down,' said Kestros. 'Everything from here to the system edge. Search every ship. Secure all traffic passing out from Terra. Prioritise those making passage towards Terra. There is the possibility of them linking up with other infiltration forces, or even trying to breach the sphere around Mars. Either way their most likely behaviour is stealth and evasion. We throw a cordon around them and wait for them to come to us.'

Andromeda shook her head.

'No. Yes, that is exactly what should be done, but you will not catch even one of them that way. At least not through anything other than blind luck.' She gestured at the data from the attacks laid out on the table. 'They have had a long time to prepare whatever they are doing – years, decades. And they will expect a lockdown. They will expect you to do what you have just, so predictably, suggested.'

'If they have predicted it they will have taken account of it and planned to bypass a lockdown. They may be off Terra already,' said Archamus. He could see something of the structure of logic that Andromeda was building. 'They may even wish to effect a security lockdown because it plays to their advantage.'

'Exactly,' said Andromeda.

'So why did you say that is exactly what we should do?' growled Kestros. 'Why give them the advantage they want?'

'Because we don't want them to alter their plans,' said Andromeda. 'We want them to keep going. We want them to believe that they have won. Pride... It is about pride, as your primarch said. So we take that weakness and use it to blind them.'

Kestros smiled.

'You said *we,* not you. Was that an accident?'

'How observant,' sighed Andromeda.

'So we order the lockdown, just as we would have done,' said Archamus, before Kestros could respond. 'And then what?'

Andromeda bent over the table and began manipulating data.

A hololith of a pict-capture sprung into being above them. It was of a corpse, its lower lip and neck tattooed with bond-marks. Archamus recognised them – the Hysen Cartel, one of the great trade houses of Terra.

Kestros breathed out.

'The enemy at Damocles Starport bore the markings of the Hysen Cartel, and they used its clearance codes and vehicles. But those must have been covers.'

'All covers have to come from somewhere,' said Andromeda. 'If they used genuine clearance codes, who obtained them? If they had a vehicle, where did it come from? Conspiracies are like cloth, dozens of threads woven together to make the whole. The more elaborate the design, the more threads, and the more subtle the weave. But even the finest cloth can be unravelled.'

'So we pull a thread,' breathed Kestros.

Archamus looked at Andromeda and gave a single nod.

'We pull a thread,' he echoed.

FOUR

The Aska mountain range
Terra

THE TRIO OF gunships chased the sun as it fell over the mountain tops. Air vibrated in their wake. Beneath them the stacked hab-archipelagos glimmered with pinprick illuminations. The yellow of the gunships' hulls was lost in the low light. In the cockpit of the lead craft the pilot blink-clicked a marker rune.

'Waypoint seven reached,' said the pilot into the vox. 'Turning on my mark, all weapons live, launch ready.'

A second later the trio banked as one. In the lead gunship, Archamus checked the weaponry clamped to his armour. Kestros and the two assault squads mirrored him. The side hatch slid open. Air rushed through the cabin space. Andromeda sat next to the door, legs crossed, chrome hair braided and coiled on her head. She wore an armoured body glove under her ragged grey robes, which billowed in the rushing air. A rebreather mask hid the lower part of her face, but Archamus was sure she was smiling.

She glanced up at him and jerked her head towards the ground turning beneath them.

'Is it always like this?' she called, voice loud across the vox.

'Like what?' asked Archamus.

She laughed in reply, just as she had laughed when he had said that she should not be with the strike force. He had no idea why either incident was humorous.

It had taken them only a few hours to identify their lead. The atrocity at Damocles Starport had been committed by a cell of infiltrators posing as trade haulers. The cargo vehicle that had carried the hallucinogen had borne the Hysen Cartel's markings, and the human operatives had worn Hysen colours. Such things were simply costume, easily engineered and faked given time. What was not so easily faked were the shipment and clearance codes used to pass within Damocles' cargo lock. Those markers were the means by which each of the houses maintained its power, each a token of old pacts between trader and port. The hauler had the correct code, and its arrival had been scheduled in the cartel's ledgers.

That was a mark of complicity, as clear as a brand on a thief's face. It was too obvious, though. It had taken Andromeda, Kestros and Archamus twenty minutes to conclude that the Hysen had been betrayed and used. It had taken them another twenty-seven minutes to find the trail of their true quarry.

Dowager-son Hyrakro was not really one of the Hysen. Within Terra's trade dynasties blood was everything. The line on consanguinity bound the great houses. Members of the family held all positions of power or potential with direct blood ties to one another. A hireling might be very useful to a dynasty, and even win lavish reward, but they could never hope to inherit true authority or a stake in the dynasty's concerns. Only those of the blood could do that. It was a system that had served the Hysen, and their peers, for centuries.

There was, however, one other role that an outsider could fulfil. Marriages brought a level of status close to that of a full-blooded family member. Creating children who bore the blood of the dynasty strengthened that bond. They became honorary family members, afforded privileges and even a measure of responsibility. If their full-blooded spouses died, they became dowager-sons or daughters of the clan. Their blood ties broken, they were relegated to luxurious exile. That was what Hyrakro was, and it had been he who had arranged the clearance for the cargo-crawler containing thousands of litres of hallucinogen gas to enter Damocles Starport.

The gunships' flight flattened out. The slopes of the mountains had risen up to meet them, so that now they were skimming low above the roofs of buildings that marched up the mountainside in crowded tiers. Vast water pipes snaked between the buildings, climbing to the towers that marched across the summits. The sky on the other side of the mountain was still bright, but they were riding in twilight. Walled compounds capped the highest peaks, breaking the line of reservoir towers. The compounds had been the estates of the Lord Aquarians, but their power was lost to the Emperor along with their water, and others now lived behind the walls they had built.

'Closing on target,' came the pilot's voice. 'Ninety seconds.'

Archamus glanced at Kestros and nodded. They stood. Mag-locks thumped free of armour. The hatches at the front and rear of the compartment opened.

'Auspex reads slaved weapons and sensors.'

Archamus could feel the weight of Oathword in his grasp. He glanced to the building tops flashing by beyond the open hatches.

'Entering defence weapon range. Weapons locked and ready to fire.'

'For the Imperium,' called Kestros over the vox. 'For Terra!'

And the night vanished in a flash and roar of launching rockets.

ALPHARIUS CROUCHED AS the first rocket went overhead. It hit a turret tower on the curtain wall above him and blew it to shrapnel. Lascannon blasts cut through the dark, slamming into targets deeper in the complex. He had missed the sound of the approaching gunships, but he could hear them now. They roared overhead, accelerating as they turned above the mountaintop compound. Three of them, one Fire

Raptor and two Storm Eagles. The trio of aircraft rose into the rays of the setting sun. They were coming around, fast. The Fire Raptor's flank cannons hurled shells down into the space beyond the curtain wall. Alpharius could hear the rounds slamming into stone slabs.

An alarm was blaring. As he watched, the Storm Eagles broke away, turning, thrusters flaring as they spun lower and lower. He could see their open assault ramps. He had to move fast. His mission was never going to be clean, but now there was a real chance of its failure.

He ran up the scree slope between him and the curtain wall, and pulled the explosive charge free from his back.

The Storm Eagle was right overhead now, and he could see a figure on the rear ramp, light glinting off its yellow armour.

That was not optimal.

The gunship circled above the roof of the compound's main building. The figure at the rear assault ramp jumped.

Alpharius reached the wall and slammed the charge into the smooth stone. He dived aside. Above him the Fire Raptor's guns went silent. The charge detonated. The blast wave thumped out. Stone dust and flame licked across Alpharius' armour as he rose and spun through the breach, weapon in hand.

KESTROS LEAPT AFTER Archamus. The stone of the roof cracked beneath them as they landed. Kestros was up and moving a second before Archamus. Las-fire bit the cracked floor beside him and splashed across his shoulder. The Storm Eagle slid across the air above them, thrusters churning the smoke. His squad brothers were dropping from the doors and ramps, scattering across the compound. Some were already firing.

Kestros saw the first guard come out of the smoke in a blur of dull silver plates and blades. It was bigger than Kestros, a hulking mass of abhuman flesh coated in armour. A mask covered its lump of a head, white and featureless apart from two eye slots. A red blaze ran diagonally between the eyes. Its right fist was a spool of chromed chains, its left a churning mass of blades.

Gene-bonded stock, he thought. *Tough, and loyal to the last.*

Kestros brought his bolt pistol around. The abhuman swung faster. Kestros flinched aside, but not fast enough. A length of chain whipped free of the abhuman's fist and wrapped around Kestros' arm. The bolt pistol fired. The abhuman yanked him towards its grasp. Kestros' fore-arm crashed into the blank mask as he cannoned forwards. White ceramite shattered. The abhuman's head flinched and then crashed back into Kestros' faceplate. His eyepieces shattered. Armour crumpled. Air vented into his face. The chain around his arm was tightening, pulling him into the abhuman's bulk. He heard the motor driving the creature's blade fist gun to life.

'Left!' growled Archamus' voice across the vox. Kestros yanked left with all his strength. The abhuman pulled back, muscles bunching beneath armour, chain biting.

Archamus' mace struck the abhuman's right knee. Armour and flesh exploded in a ball of lightning. The armoured brute fell, its pain boom-ing from its throat. The chain loosened. Kestros rammed the pistol muzzle against the abhuman's arm and fired. The burst of shells sawed the limb from the body in a spray of meat and bone. He shook the chain from his arm and ripped his ruined helm from his head. The air stank of blood and smoke.

A ragged hole lay open in the roof in front of them. A rocket had struck, and punched a hole through metal and stone. Smoke and screams rose up from within. Archamus was at its edge bracing to fire down into the ruin beneath.

Kestros heard the distant boom of an explosive charge detonating as he dropped through the hole.

THE SPACE BEYOND the curtain wall was a charnel house. Chunks of flesh and pulped meat painted the shattered stone. Alpharius could pick out scraps of fabric amongst the remains. White and red, the colours of the man who owned the estate. The household guard had poured out of the manse to man their positions when the first rocket had hit. The Fire

Raptor's cannons had caught them in the open, and turned them to red slime and tatters. There were still some alive in the compound and keep, though. Gunfire boomed and echoed through the smoke and dust.

One of the Imperial Fists came around the corner, chainsword spinning. If the warrior was shocked at the sight of Alpharius, he did not pause. His bolt pistol roared. The round punched Alpharius off his feet. He felt bones and carapace break. Shards of his chest-plate stabbed into him. The fall saved him.

The second shell passed over his head. He hit the ground. The bulk of his weaponry slowed him as he instinctively tried to roll to his feet. The Imperial Fist was advancing on him. Alpharius drew and fired his volkite serpenta pistol. Circles of red energy radiated from the barrel an instant before the main beam ignited. It struck the warrior in the chest. The armour plate blistered. Then the beam cut through to the flesh beneath, in a flash of ash and heat.

Alpharius pulled himself up and ran forwards, clamping the serpenta to his thigh and pulling the missile launcher from his back. It was an exotic variant, designed to fire from the hip rather than the shoulder. He triggered the launcher's suspensor web, and its weight vanished. The wall of the compound's main keep loomed out of the smoke. Gunfire flashed in the high windows. Above him the gunships circled like vultures above a dying animal. Alpharius steadied himself and aimed the launcher upwards. Targeting runes and distance calculations aligned in his eyes. The silhouette of a gunship was clear against the darkening sky.

Confusion, that was always the key – no weapon had slain more heroes, nor brought so many of the mighty low. He smiled at that simple truth and keyed the firing stud.

ARCHAMUS LANDED IN the ruin of a dining hall. Splinters of polished wood and painted porcelain covered the floor. Threat runes lit red at the edge of his sight. He fired as he rose. One round into each of the three uniformed guards, and then he was up and moving. A stream of data filled his ears and eyes.

'*Outer zones clear,*' came the voice of one of the squad leaders who had taken the curtain wall. '*No sign of primary target. Resistance heavy.*'

It had been twenty seconds since they had dropped into the compound, ninety-eight since the first rocket strikes.

He reached a set of wooden doors and went through them. A pair of guards in white, black and red armour were running down the corridor beyond. Archamus' bolt took the first. A shot over his shoulder the second.

'*Do you have him?*' came Andromeda's voice in his ear. She was on one of the Storm Eagles circling above the compound. The roar of the gunship's engines spilled over the link.

'No,' shouted Kestros, before Archamus could reply.

The passage curled before them. Cobweb-veiled faces of stone watched them pass from niches, and dust shook from the arches above.

'*He will be running,*' she replied, as though she had not heard.

'There's nowhere for him to run to,' called Kestros.

'*There will be a passage, a hidden way.*'

A clanking sound filled the air as metal shutters began to drop across the passage in front of them. A hatch opened in the ceiling above, and an autocannon swung down into the passage. The barrel turned towards them, targeting beams red lines in the smoke. Archamus fired. The cannon detonated. Secondary explosions rolled fire across the ceiling. He felt the blast of heat through his eyepieces, and blinked.

'They seem in the mood to fight rather than run,' shouted Kestros.

'*Not Hyrakro,*' said Andromeda's voice. '*He is a coward. The only reason they are fighting is so that he can get away.*'

'Why are you sure?' cut in Archamus before Kestros could answer.

'*I understand the nature of his weakness,*' was all she said.

The first shutter was almost at the ground when he reached it. Archamus brought *Oathword* down on the closing barrier. The head of the mace ripped through to the plasteel, and he rammed his way through the breach.

'Where would such a tunnel be?' Archamus grunted, as he shouldered through the splintered metal. Rounds exploded across his shoulders and chest. Lead stub rounds mashed themselves to flat discs on the ceramite.

'*Wherever he sleeps,*' answered Andromeda.

'Why–' began Kestros.

'*Humans like to feel safe when they sleep. The chance of escape is comfort.*'

Archamus did not understand the answer, but he did not have time to question it. They were burning time, and every second gave Dowager-son Hyrakro more chance of escaping.

'Squad Tancred, hold perimeter,' called Archamus across the command vox. 'Squad Sotaro, converge on my location, maximum speed.'

'*Archamus!*' Andromeda's shout filled his ears. All humour and laughter had gone from it. Now there was just urgency bordering on panic. '*Archamus, there is someone else in the compo–*'

'Lord,' said the voice of one of the Storm Eagles' pilots. '*There is–*'

The first breath of an explosion blew across the vox, and then there was just the roar of static.

THE LIGHT OF the fireball flashed across the sky. Alpharius had not watched the missile strike home. He was already moving towards the main block of the compound. He twisted as he ran, the trio of blind grenades looping high from his hand. The missile launcher bounced against his hip, almost weightless in its suspensor harness. He switched missile type. Behind him the blind grenades exploded. Clouds of dead, grey fog stole the light of falling fire. He put a krak missile into a doorway in the building wall. The armoured door ripped from its frame and spun into the space beyond. Alpharius was through it, already selecting a third type of missile.

A hulking figure loomed out of the pall of dust and smoke. Alpharius had an instant to see a mask of red and white set atop a muscle and armour-bloated torso. He fired without slowing down. The missile exploded in the abhuman's chest. There was a dull boom, and a rush of indigo steam stained the smoke as the bio-acid in the warhead reacted with the abhuman's blood. Alpharius ran on, the scream of agony draining into a wet, gurgling whimper behind him.

KESTROS FLINCHED AS the vox cut out.

'What...' he began, but Archamus was sprinting to the next shutter barring their path. Lightning wreathed the mace in his hand. Two blows and he was through. The vox was a skidding mass of static and scraps of voices.

'Someone else is here,' called Archamus. The pistons in his bionics were thumping as he ran. Kestros was following, but the whirl of events was closing around him. It felt strange, vile, like being tossed into a sudden squall at sea. Like being out of control.

He glanced around as he ran. The walls were curving tighter. The floor was on a slight tilt. The details matched the plans he had memorised before the attack. They were curving down towards the portion of the building set directly on the tips of the mountain's peak.

'We should hold for Sotaro,' he called, but Archamus did not answer.

The walls suddenly flared out into a broad space before a set of double jade doors.

'Hold close,' Archamus shouted, and struck the door. Jade and plasteel shattered in a storm of lightning and surging armour plates. Kestros uttered an oath and followed.

A chamber ballooned around them, hung with tattered tapestries. A circular pool of soft cushions sat at the far end, surrounded by a forest of jugs, chalices and bottles. The room smelt of perfume and dusk, and dark wine was spreading across the floor in a bruised lake. A dozen guards in white carapace were crouched behind pillars to either side. On the far side, Kestros could see seven more guards clustered around a squat man wrapped in thick red fabric. Dowager-son Hyrakro looked back at Archamus with wide eyes set in a quivering face.

Las-fire fell on them as Kestros came through the door beside Archamus. Shards of marble exploded from the impacts of their strides as they ran. Kestros felt a burning slap as a las-bolt skimmed his scalp.

His armour was singed from the heat of countless impacts. Archamus struck the first guard he reached with a blow that turned body to vapour. Kestros turned the other way, lacing bolts into the guards on the other side of the chamber.

He was about to turn his fire onto the other side of the room when a section of wall exploded inwards.

ALPHARIUS CAME THROUGH the hole blown in the wall of Dowager-son Hyrakro's private chamber a heartbeat after the missile hit. His visor fuzzed for an instant, and then it was alive with threat runes. He fired into the centre of the room. Another missile kicked free of the launcher. Las-fire strobed in the murk. The missile hit the wall, and a fresh bloom of blind fog blended with the spreading dust from his entry.

He was as blind as his enemy now, but he had the advantage. His mind and perceptions had narrowed, principles of war and strategy shrunk to tactics and choices made in the blink of an eye. He had to complete the kill. He had to confirm it.

Anything else meant failure. And he would not, could not fail.

He was Alpharius. He was Legion.

ARCHAMUS HAD ALMOST been in reach of the cluster of guards around Hyrakro when the wall blew in behind him. The blast caught him in mid stride. The guards around Hyrakro were eleven paces away. He could see the wobble of the man's jowls, see the stain of wine on his greying beard and the pupils blooming wide in his eyes. If he had had to kill the human, he could have done it then. He could have put a bolt through the man's skull before the man realised he was dead. That was not an option, though. Hyrakro had to live.

A blind missile detonated against the wall. Dull white-grey fog poured through the room. One instant he could see and the next, whiteness was pressing against his eyes.

Time slowed for him. His mind sharpened to a few simple thoughts and instincts.

A new enemy had entered the situation. It did not matter who it was. They were irrelevant. All that mattered was that he did not fail.

In part of Archamus' mind – a part that he was aware of but not listening to – he knew that it must be the Alpha Legion. That they had shot his gunships from the sky, and that they would make sure Hyrakro died before speaking his secrets. He knew all this and listened to none of it. Purpose needed no reason.

He stopped. Armour, bionics and muscles locked steady. His bolter replaced the mace and pistol in his hands without a thought. He did not need to look at Kestros to know that the sergeant was standing at his back, facing outwards, bolter in hand. Their thoughts in that instant were a mirror, fused by the blood in their veins and the way of war they were both forged in: If in doubt, hold ground. If in confusion, wait for the enemy to show their hand. Old truths that were as much a part of him as his blood and breath.

They waited as the instants slid into seconds.

ALPHARIUS COULD HEAR the buzzing purr of power armour thrumming through the fog, and the shallow breaths of the humans trying to control their fear. The fog stole all but the most basic sense of direction, but it was enough. He swung the barrel of the missile launcher up, selected a frag missile and fired.

The explosion pulsed through the fog, staining it black and red for a second. He ducked to the side. Las-fire buzzed out, wild and undirected. He could hear screaming. Enough to guide his aim again, though. He thumbed the launcher's selector to the last of his bio-acid missiles.

A burst of bolt-rounds ripped through the fog. Explosive shells tore the chamber floor in front of him. Stone splinters spun into the smoke. A round exploded beside his foot and pitched him sidewise. The bolter fire switched tone, as a second gun picked up after the first without a missed beat. It sprayed high.

Alpharius began to move forwards again. Too late he realised his mistake.

Another burst, waist height, shells buzzing as they cut the air. The blind fog was thinning. Light flashed through the murk, sounds became sharper. His advantage was dissipating. He pulled his serpenta free and began to fire, pulsing the beam though the fog, feathering it at random. Then he was up and running.

ARCHAMUS STOPPED SHOOTING. Kestros laced fire into the smoke without missing a beat. The magazine fell from Archamus' bolter as he snapped a fresh one into place.

'Back, five metres,' he called.

Kestros' fire hammered out as they pivoted and stepped in unison.

Volkite beams scattered past.

Archamus opened the vents in his helm. He could smell spilled alcohol on the air. Glass and crystal crunched beneath their feet. The blind fog was thinning, his sight pushing further out by the second. The pool of silk cushions was next to them, folds of fabric stained by wine and scattered with rock dust.

The volkite fire ceased. He heard the noise of heavy strides and buzzing power armour at the same instant that the thinning fog parted before him. Hyrakro was there, his cluster of guards ringing him, guns raised, heads and eyes twitching. They saw Archamus and the gun muzzles turned.

He heard a shout of alarm from behind him and turned his head in time to see an armoured figure loom into sight. Fog clung to the indigo-blue armour, scattering light from green eyes in a blank helm. The bulk of a hip-slung missile launcher hung in its hands.

Kestros swung his gun around. Archamus surged towards the ring of guards.

ALPHARIUS' TARGETING RUNES locked on to the man ringed by guards. Hyrakro, dowager-son of the Hysen Cartel, looked up, his face painted red by the converging crosshairs. Alpharius' thumb tensed on the trigger stud.

One of the Imperial Fists leapt forwards, and the target vanished from view. He switched missile instantly and fired. The krak missile kicked free of the launcher as a second legionary burst from the remaining fog. He began to turn but the warrior cannoned into him. He staggered. The Imperial Fist was bare-headed and snarling, face marked with dried blood and soot. Alpharius pivoted, caught his balance and kicked out, stamping into the warrior's chest.

The son of Dorn was faster. The bolter in his hands roared, ripping through the missile launcher and shredding the front of Alpharius' armour. Alarms screamed in his ears. He could feel numbness washing through him as his body hid the damage from his awareness. Instinct snapped in. The Imperial Fist had dropped his spent bolter and pulled a chainsword from his waist. The blade spun to life and rose as Alpharius drew and fired his serpenta. The beam hit the legionary in the side of the chest and blew the ceramite to dust. Flesh flashed and cooked beneath. The chainsword blow crashed into Alpharius' shoulder guard. Sparks churned into the air as the blade skidded across ceramite.

He lashed out, hammering a knee into the wound in the Imperial Fist's torso, and forcing the warrior back. Alpharius pistoned his knee into the wound again and again. Burned blood and scraps of flesh stuck to his knee plate. Ribs and carapace cracked. Shards of bone punched into soft meat, and blood speckled the ground. The legionary tried to grip him, but Alpharius shifted his weight and ripped the warrior from the ground, sending him skidding back towards the door. He did not rise. Alpharius turned, his blood splattering from his wound.

The other Imperial Fist was almost amongst the bodyguards surrounding the target, blocking a clear shot. The dissipating blind smoke was a haze in the air. He aimed and fired. The head of one of the bodyguards exploded, fragments of skull and flesh hitting the human's comrades and ripping into their exposed flesh. Alpharius moved forwards, pain screaming from his dying flesh.

ARCHAMUS STRUCK THE surviving bodyguards. *Oathword*'s power field was deactivated, but the first human it struck broke and fell like a sodden rag. He felt the blow as a tremble through the servos of his bionic arm. He reversed the blow and crushed the head of another guard, and stamped another to red ruin. Dowager-son Hyrakro was screaming now, keening like a wounded animal. Blood flecked his face as he scrabbled away from Archamus, half falling, bare feet skidding on blood. Archamus knew that the Alpha Legionnaire was closing behind him.

He did not need to look. He dropped his bolter and lunged across the last metres. His hand closed on Hyrakro's arm. The volkite beam struck his back as he enfolded the screaming human. Energy burned through the casing of his power plant. His armour screamed. Servos and fibre bundles fired and locked, spasming like the muscles of a dying man. Cooling fluid vented. Sparks sprang from the exposed power stacks.

Archamus could feel the skin of his back burning. The smell of cooking flesh and muscle filled his mouth and nose. But his grip on the human did not slacken. He began to stand, muscles straining against the weight of his dying armour. *Oathword* was still in his hand, the bronzed digits of his machine hand wrapped around the haft of the mace.

ALPHARIUS FIRED AGAIN, but the beam skidded wide. His world was greying at the edges, the numbness spreading inwards from his skin. The legionary who had shielded the target was rising, straining with effort. They were almost close enough to touch, but the bulk of the warrior hid the human. Alpharius shifted angle. He might live to fire one more shot.

A bolt shell hit him in the back of the hip and punched him forwards onto the floor. He fell, twisting. Blood scattered from the ripped join between hip and thigh. As he landed, he saw the other Imperial Fist, lying on the floor where he had fallen, bolt pistol gripped and aimed. The other warrior – the one who had grabbed and shielded the target – loomed above him, the human clutched in one arm, the mace in the other.

Alpharius tried to bring his serpenta up. The legionary swung the mace down. Alpharius heard his hand shatter, and a fresh pool of blankness was added to the numbness of his body. The mace crashed into his head and sent him sprawling on the floor, face down.

'You have failed, traitor,' growled the Imperial Fist.

Alpharius heard the words, but felt nothing. He opened his mouth. He could feel fresh blood on his lips.

'We...' he said, his voice rasping from the speaker grille of his helm. 'We are many, son of Dorn, and we... we know you. We know you all...'

The numbness and greyness flowed in from the edge of his sight, and then nothing.

ARCHAMUS LOOKED DOWN at the legionnaire at his feet. At the other end of the room, Sergeant Sotaro and nine warriors came through the doors, and spread into the chamber. The human hanging from Archamus' arm whimpered; his gaze did not waver from the body at his feet. The front of the indigo-blue armour had been ripped open from crotch to mid chest. The explosive impact of multiple bolt shells looked like a swarm of creatures had taken bites out of the ceramite. A wound in the warrior's thigh leaked a spreading pool of blood onto the floor. It would have taken focus and resolve for the warrior to keep moving, let alone fight.

'My lord,' said Sotaro as he came to Archamus' side.

'Remove his helm,' he said, still not looking up. Sotaro hesitated for a second, then bent down and snapped the helm free from the dead legionnaire. The face underneath was hairless – the features strong, but blandly forgettable. The eyes were still open, staring up at Archamus without life. Blood had flowed down the chin from the mouth.

Archamus held his dead enemy's gaze.

'Bring in the gunships,' he said to Sotaro.

'The Fire Raptor was lost, and one of the others caught a haywire blast, but it is functioning.'

Archamus assimilated the information without pause. He would think about the losses and failures of the mission later.

'Call them in,' he said. 'Then strip this place. Rip the walls apart. Find everything – data-stores, parchment, everything. It goes back to the *Unbreakable Truth.* You have one hour. Then this place becomes ashes and rubble. No traces. No one sees anything that comes from this place.'

Sotaro brought his hand to his heart in salute and then nodded at the corpse that Archamus was still staring at. 'And that?'

'Take it. Put it into stasis and forget that you have seen it.'

'Lord,' said Sotaro and bowed his head.

He looked into the dead Alpha Legionnaire's eyes for an instant more, and then turned and began to walk towards the doors. His armour clanked as it moved. The flesh of his back had passed from numbness to crawling agony. One of Sotaro's warriors was helping Kestros from the floor. Archamus met the young sergeant's eye and gave a single nod. Sotaro had already begun calling orders into the vox and marshalling his squad. Two of them fell in beside Archamus as he walked through the manse.

Night had still not claimed the last of the light when he emerged into a courtyard beside the curtain wall. From the moment that the rockets had launched from the gunships less than ten minutes had passed. His mind was sifting back through every detail of the engagement, analysing it for errors, both personal and tactical.

Dowager-son Hyrakro hung unmoving from his shoulder, perhaps finally succumbing to unconsciousness.

'You have him,' said a voice from the shadows beside the curtain wall. He looked around as Andromeda stepped into sight.

'You were ordered to stay out of the battle area.'

'The battle seems to have passed,' she said, moving next to him but looking at the slumped form of Hyrakro. She matched his pace and reached up, pulling the man's hair so that she could look at his unconscious face. 'Hello, little thread,' she purred. 'Let's see where you lead.'

FIVE

The battleship Lion of the Last Kingdom
Jupiter orbit

THE SILENCE OF the chamber roared at Armina Fel. Without eyes, her mind sat in a swell of stray thoughts and feelings. Fully half of the senior commanders of Terra's Third Sphere of defences stood before her beneath the banners of the dead, and under the gaze of stone warriors. The ghost thoughts of the gathered war leaders washed over her: Solar Auxilia officers, Jovian commodore princes, tech-priests, Ghost Shoal privateers and Callistan militia generals – all were waiting, thinking, worrying.

Armina Fel felt the apprehension of the gathering shiver over the inside of her skin. Questions, doubts and fears splashed colours across her mind's eye. The tech-priests stood out amongst the swell, their minds geometric shapes drawn in static. Lord Castellan Effried and his entourage stood to her right, their minds stars of control. But, no matter who they were, every mind focused on the burning presence of Rogal Dorn.

Armina Fel stood three paces behind him, flanked by her Black Sentinel guardians. At this distance the primarch's presence was like standing beneath a desert sun at noon. She felt it pull at her, rolling her in strength, burning away doubt.

'For the Emperor,' Dorn said, and brought his hand to his chest in the old salute of unity. The chamber echoed as hundreds of hands mirrored the movement and echoed the words. The blossoms of uncertainty faded amongst the gathering. 'Your duty to the Imperium is about to change.' The words cut through the crowd like a thrown boulder. Dorn waited for a second and then continued. 'You have been the leaders of the Third Sphere of defence, its builders, its maintainers, the eyes on its walls and the hands on its weapons. You will have noticed that many of your comrades in arms are not here. That is because they will continue the duties that have been yours. The Emperor has another task for you.'

Surprise, cold and sharp, slid through the ranks. Armina Fel tasted the acid tang of fear, present in all but the minds of the tech-priests and the Imperial Fists. In the most disciplined minds the fear was just a pulse at the edge of control, for others it was a black cloud seeping through their surface thoughts. They had all heard rumours of the forces taken back to Terra, or to Mars. Many were never seen again; some seemed simply to cease to exist. Was that now to be their fate?

'Lord Castellan Effried and his captains will brief you all in the next twenty-four hours, but before then you will prepare the troops under your command for battle, and for warp passage.'

Now shock rose from every mind in the chamber. Even the Imperial Fists pulsed with surprise for an instant. Warp passage meant going out beyond the bounds of the Solar System; it meant leaving the defences of Terra.

Dorn paused again, and Armina Fel swayed as the control radiating from him grew. The silence in the chamber seemed to deepen.

'Our purpose is to defend Terra, but to wait for the enemy to come to you is to invite defeat. The enemy is coming. They are encircling us, waiting and growing in strength while picking how and when they will attack. We will not allow them that luxury. Terra stands.'

There was a moment of silence and swirled emotion, and then a hundred voices filled the air.

'Terra stands!'

Pride and aggression exploded across Armina's senses. She felt it pull her, rolling her own emotions over and over like beach stones caught in an ocean wave.

Dorn bowed his head briefly and then strode from the chamber. Armina Fel followed, flanked by her Black Sentinels and trailed by Lord Castellan Effried. They passed down through the ship in silence, blast doors parting before them, the Huscarls marching in front to cover every step before they took it. She found herself thinking of Archamus as she watched the bodyguards move. The old war architect's absence suddenly seemed palpable, a hole punched in the present situation, a pillar pulled from beneath an arch. Why had Dorn sent him from his side?

They walked down and down past walls plated in copper and bronze, over floors of smooth stone. At last they arrived at a chamber lit only by an array of stab lights hung above granite worktables. Dorn nodded to the Huscarls, and they peeled away to stand beside the door and line the passage outside. Armina's Black Sentinels took their places beside the cloaked Imperial Fists, as she followed Dorn and Effried within.

The doors hissed shut.

'A pre-emptive attack, lord?' asked Effried, as the doors locked with a pneumatic thump. Armina breathed, trying to catch her breath from the walk while her mind focused on Effried. Now they were away from hundreds of minds all clamouring at once, she could see the subtle creases to the Lord Castellan's aura.

'It is a necessity,' said Dorn.

'And you intend to lead it?'

'I would not ask another to take that responsibility for me.'

Effried breathed out, and Armina heard his fingers scratching though his beard as he rubbed his chin. She could tell that he wanted to question the necessity, to understand how and what could move his gene-father to contemplate leading a force away from Terra.

'Your will is mine,' he said, voice rolling like gravel on stone. Armina watched as control and instinct to trust and obey contained the questions pushing to the surface.

'It is not a decision I am contemplating without cause,' said Dorn.

'My lord, I would never think–'

'Your concerns are not without basis,' said Dorn. Armina felt the hard edges of his presence blur, soften and reshape. 'You wonder why I would take strength from our defences and throw them out into the dark? If you have such doubts then others will. You will have to be able to answer them. You must understand the cause.'

Dorn turned to look at Armina Fel. She could not see the movement, but the focus of his intent was like the heat from an open furnace door.

'Mistress,' he said, his voice soft and controlled. 'If I may ask you to share the message from the Esteban System?'

She bobbed her head in answer and began the steps of recall. She pressed the first knuckle of the index finger of her left hand against her thumb and inhaled a single breath in perfect time with the beat of her heart. The keystone memory of the scent of smoke from her father's cooking fire filled her senses...

Her mind flattened. Thoughts dropped away. The impression of the astropathic message rose into sight. It crackled in her mind's eye – a pillar made of broken shards, held together by mist. She let its meaning fill her.

The means by which she, and her fellow astropaths, defied the physical limits of communication were simple to express, but almost impossible to understand. The astropaths sent messages by using their telepathic abilities augmented by the gift given to them when they were bound in soul to the Emperor, throwing meaning into the beyond. To receive a message they cast their minds into the warp and caught it from the aether, as though they were pulling fish from the sea in nets. On thousands of worlds, ships and space stations, choirs of men and women circulated the information that the Imperium, and now its civil war, needed to exist. That was what most knew of astropaths – and it was wrong.

Dreams and metaphor wrapped in the soul screams of humans who burned with fire from within, thrown and falling through a storm of nightmare and paradox, to be heard by minds wandering through ghost realms of thought, in fragments of sensation, sight and emotion. That was the picture of her craft that she had once painted for a mundane human who had wanted to know the truth. And even that was a lie.

The truth was inexpressible to those who lacked the ability to walk those dark places. So when she folded her mind back into the precise recall, she did not remember words; she was possessed by a universe of sensation, inference and symbolism. She was the fire of meaning, and the cold words that came from her mouth were a shadow cast through a pinhole by a hidden inferno.

'Outer system defences have fallen,' she said in the silence, and she felt her will holding back the pressure that was trying to push out from within her. 'Ships from the dark. They are here. They have come. We will hold to the last.'

The words ended. The fire of meaning drained back into her memory, and she was as she had been before: an old woman bent with time, shivering as though she had been doused in ice water.

Rogal Dorn reached out and rested his hand on her shoulder.

'Thank you, mistress,' he said, and she felt the tremble in her muscles lessen. She straightened.

'Do you wish me to recall the others, lord?'

'No,' said Dorn. 'That is sufficient.'

She felt the small, sad smile, even though she could not see his face.

'As you will it, lord,' she said.

He turned back to Effried.

'That message was received two days ago,' he said. 'The time of sending cannot be certain. It could have been sent on the same day as we received it, or weeks before. We cannot know. But its meaning is clear.'

'Esteban has fallen, or is close to falling,' said Effried.

Dorn must have nodded, but in Armina's mind the shape of his aura did not change.

'There are other messages,' said Dorn. 'Most are fragments, echoes of cries for help or warning. Nisos, Mons Galita, Hentaron. But the messages say less than the silences. The number of worlds from whom we have had no word, grows.'

'Phaeton...' said Effried, speaking the name of the great forge world that lay within the dominion of Terra.

'Not just Phaeton. There are many more. They may still stand, and it may be that the storms in the warp have covered them, or that something has happened to the astropathic relay stations. But even those possibilities suggest that the enemy is moving.'

'A systematic attack across that volume could mean–'

'It could mean many things, but cannot go unanswered. The enemy will come, and we will not stand here while the night falls, and the fires of their advance light the sky. We have a chance to break them before they can reach our walls, before they expect to face us.'

'So we go out into the dark,' stated Effried, and Armina thought she heard an edge of relish in his words, 'to face the unknown.'

'That, my son, is what we were made for.'

Garrison Station Creto
Jupiter orbit

GENERAL HESIO ARGENTOS was silent on the shuttle journey back from the *Lion of the Last Kingdom*. Fifteen other officers sat with him as the frame of the shuttle rattled around them. The green of their dress uniforms looked black in the yellow-tinted dark, the silver frogging reduced to the colour of tarnished brass. The officers said nothing to each other, and only a few exchanged glances. He knew why, of course.

He was old enough that at the outbreak of the war within the Imperium he had been a decade past his last field service. A largely honorary position in the Jovian levies had been his to enjoy, as had the indulgence of a mild addiction to spiced liquor. He had had little to do except wither in body and grow in spite. He would have been far down the list for a return to active command, but he had too much experience, and there was too much to do. So they had given him a new uniform, rank, and thirty thousand men and women to command.

It was not a change of situation that improved his demeanour. The niceties he might have affected in his younger days had long fled. His silences seldom meant anything good, and often were just the shadow cast by a storm of temper. He was a difficult man, and his officers hated him. He knew this about them, and about himself. What would have surprised them most was that he did not hate them back.

'Yes?' he said, catching a glance from Astrid Kellan, the youngest of the senior officers under his command. 'Is there a question you wish to ask me, colonel?' He let the words roll with scorn. To her credit the young colonel did not flinch.

'Are there fresh orders, sir? From the Praetorian?'

'As a matter of fact there are,' he said, sighing. 'I was going to save the surprise, but as you are so keen to get on with it... All units are to come to full fighting status. Armour, weapons, everything and everyone prepared and readied to move for transport and/or deployment, within twelve hours from the moment we reach the garrison station.'

'Everyone, sir?' asked another officer, a brigadier called Sutarn. A hard man, efficient and quiet.

'That is correct.'

'Where are we deploying to, sir?' asked Colonel Kellan, and again Argentos noticed that she had the courage to ask what all the others did not. He would have to watch her.

He grinned, pulling his lips all the way back from his spice-blackened teeth.

'That is not something that the honoured Praetorian – greatest of the last loyal sons of the Emperor, who is the lord and master of all that bleeds and breathes from here to the edge of the unknown – graced me with the authority to tell you.' He smiled a cold and broad smile. 'When that state of affairs changes, you will be the first to be apprised, colonel.'

'It is bad then?'

She really *is brave,* he thought.

'That depends if your definition of bad includes bringing closer the possibility of dying or having something shot or hacked off you.'

Kellan did not ask another question, and the rest of the journey passed in uneasy silence.

HOURS LATER, ALONE in the dark of his quarters with a thick measure of spice liquor, he ran the situation around his mind. A strategic shift of this magnitude, commanded by Rogal Dorn himself... It was significant. Useful? Potentially, but it was difficult to be certain. But even though he did not know what the Praetorian was intending, he was certain that it was something big. Half the forces from Terra's Third Sphere of defences... That was considerable battle strength. Moving them from their current position alone would mean that the configuration of the system's defences would change profoundly. And... and if other forces were being called on then... then... Yes, his first instinct had been correct. He could not ignore this.

He put the crystal tumbler down, checked his quarters and made sure that the deadlocks were engaged on each of the doors. When he was satisfied that he was alone, he took the ceremonial dagger from his belt. The silver tiger head with its emerald eyes looked at him from the pommel. The inscription 'Sutarais' ran across the narrow cross-guard. It had been given to him by a praetor of the Legiones Astartes at the close of his last campaign during the Great Crusade, no less. He often told his officers that, though he never said from which Legion it had come. He always carried it, and anyone who knew him expected it to be with him whether he was in dress greens or in field greys. It was as constant a feature of his persona as the acidic temper.

He pulled the dagger free, looked at it and broke it into pieces. A series of fast, precise movements, and the dagger was a series of fragments. From within the pommel he took the cipher device. From the centre of the blade came the length of silver wire, and the lens reader from under the face of the tiger.

It took him several minutes to assemble the components and read the wire. Rows of tiny letters, finer than a hair, ran down the strand of silver. He did not need all the information the wire contained, just the transmission procedure for a flash message of high importance. He found what he needed, memorised it, and then began to encipher his message.

Half Third Sphere force on alert for warp transit by Rogal Dorn's personal command. Possible extra-system strike planned. Target and timing unknown.

The cipher device took the words, and compressed and folded them in random noise. What had been words was now a cough of static. Then he reassembled the dagger, leaving only the cipher device out. It lay on the wood of his desk, next to the glass of liquor. He looked at it for a long while.

It had been ten years since he had last served the Legion, and since then the possibility that he would again had grown smaller and smaller in his mind. Even with the coming of war it had seemed remote. But now the moment had come, just as they had said it would.

From here it would not be difficult. All he needed to do was record an innocent message – a request for supplies, a clarification of orders, or something else equally mundane – and send the blurt of static at the same time. The frequency inscribed on the silver wire was one of several hundred existing Imperial channels. Some of them were channels his communications officers used every day. That was the beauty of the Alpha Legion; it was everywhere, woven into the fabric of the Imperium. That was part of the reason he had accepted their offer of service all those years ago – the elegance and audacity of what they did. Being part of something so superior had seemed the highest form of validation he could be granted.

But now he was not so sure if that reason held, not in the face of what was happening to the Imperium.

This act would make him a traitor.

He looked at the device, just a narrow tube of machinery given to him by a warrior who he had respected. The words on it were few, the details vague, but what might they mean in the hands of the Legion? He had seen them destroy civilisations with weapons spun from nothing. What might they do with those scraps of information?

Despite the mask he wore, he was neither a cruel, nor a spiteful man. He had just learned long ago the value of wearing a different face. The Legion had noticed that about him. They had complimented both his wisdom and his skill at deception when they asked him to serve. Yes, flattery had played its part, but that was not enough for this. He was a liar, but he also believed in loyalty. But which loyalty?

He shook his head at last and stood. He pulled on his dress coat and dropped the cipher device into the pocket. He paused, blinked, and then he picked up the glass and drank the liquor in a single movement. He walked to the door, letting the mask drop across his face as he exited his quarters. The communications watch would be changing soon, and he wanted to arrive just before that happened. He had a message to send.

Battle-barge Alpha
The interstellar gulf beyond the light of Sol

'BEGIN THE BURN now,' he said from the command throne.

'Compliance,' replied a servitor.

A brief clatter of cogwork sounded, and then cut out, leaving him alone with the hum of his armour. He sat back in the throne. Two minutes later the servitor jerked in its niche.

'Message received, by all vessels, order is being executed.'

He nodded to himself, and then leant back, eyes closed. In his mind the consequence of his order painted the image that the blast shutters hid from him.

The war fleet turned over and over, cold and dark, spinning towards a speck of light that shone fractionally brighter than the others that dotted the void. Fire kindled in the engines of one ship, and for an instant its rotation became a wild spiral. Then the fire grew, caught the ship's momentum and pushed it into a smooth arc. The ship would be one of the damaged ones, perhaps a macro transporter, its outer plating torn away, or a light cruiser with its gun-decks gutted by meteor impacts. Like the rest of those who would reach the outer defences first, it would look like one of the ragged vessels that had been clawing at Terra for the last years. It would push free from the cloud of spinning ships. More would follow, their engines lighting one after another, until close to a hundred had broken free of the main fleet. Once free they would turn their prows towards the distant point of light that was their destination. And the hundreds of other ships in the cloud would tumble on in cold silence.

LORD OF CONQUEST

865.M30

One hundred and forty years before the Betrayal at Isstvan III

I

THE WIND WAS rising across the plain beneath the unfinished fortress. Archamus watched as the air caught the dust from the tops of the water levees and pulled them up into spinning columns. Dust devils, that was the Terran phrase for them. Katafalque, raised in the Gobi wastes, had used the phrase, and it had stuck in Archamus' mind. Devil, as though there were a malignancy in the movement of particles and air. A strange phrase.

He watched as the dust devils spun across the flat, green fields of crops. Banks of dry earth bounded each of the fields, and water chuckled at the bottom of the deep ditches that divided them. Further off, the wide channel of the river curved around the foot of a range of hills. Above the valley floor, every inch of the hillsides was brown. Insects sang amongst a covering of tinder-dry grass and scrub. The heat of the sun beat down from the blue sky, unrelenting and merciless. None of the human inhabitants would emerge from their houses for many hours. Apart from the time spanning dawn and dusk, the land was left to the dust and wind.

Archamus looked back to the eyepiece of the theodolite. A blur of grey stone filled his view. He turned a dial and the sighting stake atop the half-built wall snapped into focus. He looked down at the numbers on the polished brass plates. He smiled. The estimate he had made by sight matched the measurement. He unhooked the wax tablet from his waist, and scored the values into the surface.

'A rather archaic method,' said Voss from behind him. Archamus heard the emissary drop onto the top of the wall.

'The people of ancient times raised structures which stood for millennia using such tools.'

'And by the sweat and blood of millions of slaves, but I doubt that you would advocate reinstating those practices.'

Voss came and stood beside him, eyes narrowed against the glare. He had a broad, strong face, with a neat black beard. A ponytail hung down his back. He wore a long coat of layered brown and deep purple despite the heat, and a broad-brimmed hat. Rings glittered on the thumbs and fingers of each hand. He was tall, for a human, but moved with a forceful grace that spoke of muscle under the layers of clothes. His skin had tanned fast since his arrival on the planet, deepening in colour with every cycle of the sun.

He had been with the expedition for only six months, but Archamus had already spoken to him many times. An emissary of some nebulous authority, he had attached himself to the compliance force left on Rennimar, and had been asking questions and watching Archamus and the other Imperial Fists ever since. The man had a habit of appearing when no one else was around, as though summoned by solitude.

'May I, sergeant?' asked Voss, as he moved next to the theodolite. He put his eye to the viewing scope and touched the dials on the side before Archamus could reply. Archamus felt his face and fingers twitch before he could suppress the reaction.

'Do you always do it this way?' asked Voss, still looking through the scope.

'What are you referring to?'

Voss looked up from the scope.

'Measure lengths and angles yourself, by hand?'

'I learned to quarry stone with pick, hammer and wedge. I carved my first stone by hand and drew my first plans with soot ink on parchment. That is the way we learn, from first principles.' He paused and looked out across the plain. He could see the servitor gangs already at work in the quarries they had cut in the foothills ten miles away. 'I do not always use those ways, but when I can, I do.'

'Ha!' snorted Voss.

'Something amuses?'

'Nothing,' Voss chuckled, and then shrugged under Archamus' silent gaze. 'You don't see a contradiction in that? I mean you are a warrior created by mysteries of science, serving an Emperor whose aim is to unite mankind and illuminate it with truth and knowledge.' He spread his arms wide, as though to encompass the land, sky and galaxy beyond. 'We are all in the business of progress. But here is a warrior clad in technology, who could crush my head in his hand and can read a data-slate at a glance, using geometry and a wax tablet to set the walls of a fortress on an already conquered world.'

'It is important to understand the basis of things,' said Archamus carefully, then moved past Voss and began to fold up the theodolite. He had all the measurements he needed. The labour gangs would bring stone up in an hour and fifty-six minutes, once the day's heat had begun to cool. He had two minor adjustments to make to this fortress' plans, but he also needed to check the measurements from the other site across the river.

He lifted the collapsed theodolite in one hand and looked at Voss. The human was frowning.

'Is there something that I can help you with, emissary?'

'No... I mean, yes, but not really.'

'Then I would advise you to get into shade, and drink water.'

Archamus took a step along the wall foundation.

'It's just not what I thought it would be,' said Voss, before Archamus could take a second step. He turned and looked at the human. 'I mean I thought I would see...'

'More killing,' said Archamus.

'Yes!' said Voss. 'This is a crusade, after all, isn't it? You are winning an empire by blood. That is what you are, crusaders. But here you are using equipment old before Old Night to build fortresses on a world which you took in a few hours.'

Archamus nodded. He understood Voss' puzzlement now.

'What is conquest?' he asked.

'The taking of land, the expanding of a domain. That is obvious, but–'

'How does a realm remain conquered?'

'Through the compliance of the people who live there, and through the ability to hold it if they or someone else tries to take it back. That is obvious, and I understand that is why fortresses and strongholds are raised on places like this, but–'

'Others could do it. Others could position this chain of fortresses, could raise them up and set warriors on their walls. Others could do that duty, and on worlds taken by other Legions they do,' Archamus said, and paused. Voss had gone still, listening with total focus. 'We come with blood and fire, we come from the void and from the sky, and we break any who would deny the destiny of mankind. But that is not enough. This world is the Emperor's now, and will be long after we have left it. This world is the Imperium, these people are the Imperium, and they will remain as such. That is our duty, and we do our duty with our own hands, no matter if the deed is great or small. Every deed of war carries a burden. This is ours, and we bear it because it is right for us to do so.' Archamus went silent. He realised that it was the single longest utterance he had made in a long time.

The man was still staring at him, a strange look in his eyes.

After a second Archamus turned his own gaze out to where the heat haze rippled the view of the mountains.

'This world will hold no matter what,' he said, as much to himself as Voss. 'They will all hold. They are the foundation.'

Voss smiled and nodded, and Archamus noticed something in the

man's air that he had not noticed before, something knowing and
without the usual naïvety.

'There is a beauty to that, you realise...' began Voss.

Archamus blinked. Something had changed in the tone of the light.
He felt his skin prickle inside his armour. Voss was still talking, something about how he had seen the Imperial Fists at war in the Solar
System decades ago, something about ideals and change, but Archamus
was not listening. He was looking up at the sun. His vision dimmed
as his eyes compensated for the blinding light. The sound of insects
had vanished. Voss' voice hesitated, and he looked around, suddenly
aware of the shadow spreading across the ground. Archamus could see
it now. A ragged bite was missing from the sun. A vast shape loomed
across the sky, growing as it blotted out the light. Shapes glittered in
the air beneath it. They glowed brighter and brighter.

'What...?' began Voss.

Archamus lifted the man from his feet and began to run. Voss grunted
as the air left his lungs. Archamus took two strides and dropped over
the inside edge of the wall. They landed in the dust at its base. Archamus let go of Voss and pulled his helmet on.

A sheet of light ripped across the sky. Voss was gasping. The world
roared.

Dust kicked into the air. The ground shook, and then shook again.
The vox was a sea of static. Voss was screaming, holding his ears, eyes
wide. Archamus had his bolter in his hands as the blast wave struck.

II

THE ORK ROSE out of the ditch. Water and slime poured off its muscle.
Its blunt head hung low between its shoulders, its skin the colour of
pond slime. Its mouth split wide beneath red eyes. It roared, bellowing between knife blade tusks. It leapt up the bank, axes swinging.
Archamus put a bolt into its mouth. The explosion ripped its lower

jaw and half of its face off. It kept coming, blood spraying from the ruin of its mouth. Its axes were two lumps of jagged iron. Archamus fired again, sawing the burst down the ork's chest. It faltered, chunks of flesh ripping free. He snapped his aim up and put two shells into the remainder of its head. It jerked, but the axes kept slicing down. Archamus rammed his shoulder into its chest. The impact hammered through him. The ork fell, muscles clenching as it hit the ground. He stamped down, foot mashing into its chest. He glanced into the ditch.

More orks were running down the channel, churning the water to froth. Bolt-rounds were whipping in from across the field. Dust exploded from the top of the banks to either side of Archamus. He could see the stone and earth parapet of the bastion on the other side of the field. Muzzle fire breathed from the walls. Yellow armour glinted in the sunlight. He looked behind him. The fields were churning, the stems and leaves of the crops whipping as the tide of orks surged over the plain. Their calls howled through the air, rising and falling like the boom of a storm tide.

It had been twenty-five minutes since the first impact. He had covered the seven kilometres from the unfinished fortress in that time. The orks had moved just as fast. A single open field now lay between Archamus and Voss, and the bastion they were heading for. Fifty strides. Fifty strides that they would not get to take if they waited longer.

'Move!' shouted Archamus at Voss.

The man was on the ground at the base of a tree, hands clamped over his ears, his face and clothes covered in dust and mud. Blood ran from a gash across his forehead. His eyes were wide in the staring mask of his face. He flinched at Archamus' shout, but did not move.

Orks were scrambling up the side of the water ditches. Bolt and auto-cannon rounds from the distant bastion smacked into them as the Imperial Fists on the parapet fired again. Chunks of flesh and blood puffed into the air. More orks surged from the ditch to replace the dead.

'Move! Now!' Archamus roared. The words pulled Voss to his feet, and he staggered forwards. Archamus pulled a grenade from his waist and tossed it into the cluster of orks coming out of a ditch. He caught Voss and yanked him with him. The explosion blew mud and limbs into the air. Bolt-rounds were buzzing beside and above them. The stalks and leaves of crops were whipped past them as they ran.

Forty strides.

Something whistled in the air behind him.

Thirty-five strides.

Lobbed explosive, he thought.

Thirty-one strides.

The bomb landed to his left. He twisted, shielding Voss from the blast, and kept running.

Thirty strides.

Earth and pulped vegetation fountained up. The bellows of rage rose, closer and louder than he would have believed possible. A gun opened up behind him, something kinetic and heavy. Rounds bit into the earth and smacked into the bastion parapet in front of them.

Twenty-five strides.

More guns behind. A round slammed into his shoulder and gouged a furrow in the ceramite. He saw the line of bare earth just in front of him.

Fifteen.

He blinked his vox. Static screeched in his ears.

Nine.

His bionics hissed and thumped with each step. An Imperial Fist rose on the parapet. He recognised Katafalque's black-striped helm, as his Legion brother pointed at Archamus and gestured at the strip of bare ground beneath the wall. Archamus saw, understood, and leapt over the strip of earth and mangled crops.

Five.

Voss gave a strangled cry as they landed just in front of the parapet. Archamus twisted over in time to look back across the field. A wall of surging muscle and wide, roaring mouths was flowing towards them.

The orks in the lead were bounding over the ground, axes and cleavers rising like the crest of a wave.

The mines laid at the field edge detonated. The orks vanished in a wall of fire and shrapnel. The sound rolled up and out, racing the dust cloud to the sky. Shreds of skin and flesh pattered against Archamus' armour. The guns on the parapet opened up an instant after the explosion.

Archamus looked up as Katafalque reached down from the parapet. He gripped his hand and pulled himself and Voss up and over, and dropped onto the firing step beyond. Katafalque looked down at him.

'Just you, sergeant?'

'And the emissary,' he replied, as he came to his feet. Voss was a ball of limbs crumpled against the inside of the parapet. 'Where is Seneschal Calev?'

'He was en route to the northern cities. We have had no contact from him or his cadre.'

Archamus absorbed the possibility that he was now likely to be the senior Imperial officer on a planet that was subject to a major xenos invasion. 'What is our strength?' he asked.

'Twenty-six in this bastion.'

'The rest?'

'Nothing confirmed. The vox is disrupted, both surface and trans-atmospheric.'

Out beyond the parapet the smoke of the mines was clearing. Hulking shapes were already running through it, blades in hand. He glanced to his left and right, and saw warriors brace their heavy bolters and start firing. The falling dust cloud churned with exploding rounds. Behind him on the bastion's other walls, more fire teams opened up as a fresh wave of orks came from the murk.

'Mining party is ready to go out,' said Katafalque.

'Good,' said Archamus, stepping up to join the fire team. 'Proceed.'

At the edge of his eyes he saw a cluster of five legionaries move up behind the parapet. Each of the five held slab-like shields two-thirds their height. Their bolters jutted from firing slots cut into the shields. Each of them carried a thick coil of metallic cord on their backs, one side black, the other dull brown. Explosives ran down the core of the cord. The black side was plasteel weave and ceramite scales to channel and shape the blast. The other half was a layer of metal spheres. Detonated on, or beneath, the ground, the cord sent a cloud of shrapnel upwards. The Imperial Army units that Archamus had encountered had an accurate, if flamboyant, name for it: shredder-vine they called it. He had always liked the sentiment.

'Sortie ready!' called the sergeant of the shield-armed squad. Archamus, and the squad on the firing step, opened fire, spraying the field beyond with cannon and bolter rounds. The squad carrying the shredder-vine dropped over the parapet and formed a shield-wall.

'Sortie advancing!' shouted Archamus, as the shield-wall began to step forwards. Hard rounds whipped out of the smoke-covered field and rang against the tower shields. The sound was like the buzzing of wasps. He and the rest of the squad on the parapet angled their fire up and out so that it marched ahead of the advancing sortie. The shield bearers reached the torn ground where the first mines had detonated. A ragged wave of orks came at them, shedding blood from wounds, grunting with rage. The shield bearers fired, slamming the charging orks back with a synchronised volley.

The warrior on the right-hand end peeled off and moved behind his brothers, uncoiling his shredder-vine behind the shield-wall. He reached the left-hand end, locked his shield next to his brother's and joined his bolt-fire with the squad. The shield-wall moved left, as each of the squad broke off, laid their portion of the charge and rejoined the line at the other end. Then they were pulling back, firing as they moved.

A wave of orks came across the field. Every gun on the parapet, and in the shield-wall, opened up. Rounds ripped flesh and limbs apart, and for a minute the ground in front of the wall was a churning blur of falling bodies and misted blood. The sortie squad reached the parapet and vaulted over. The guns of the Imperial Fists went quiet. Behind him, Archamus heard a last volley echo from the other walls.

Quiet fell suddenly, blowing across the fields of the river plain with the smoke and dust. Above them the shadow of the ork hulk was dropping down towards a darkening horizon. Archamus reloaded his bolter and looked down at where Voss was panting and shaking against the parapet. His eyes were wide as he looked up at Archamus. It had been less than three minutes since they had reached the bastion wall.

'Is this what you thought it would be like?' asked Archamus.

III

THE ORKS FLOODED Rennimar. Vast rocks fell from the sky as their space hulk base turned through the planet's sky. Each rock was a hollowed asteroid, studded in crude boosters and armour. They glowed orange with heat as they punched through the atmosphere. Many did not survive their descent. Some fell into the oceans, sending pillars of steam into the air before sinking to the bottom. Others struck mountain ranges and shattered into burning chunks of stone and metal. But others thumped into the soft soil of river deltas and coastal plateaus. Even in those that landed whole, the casualties were huge. The impact force crushed hundreds of orks, and hundreds more burned in the heat of re-entry, or scattered into the atmosphere as parts of the rocks broke apart during the fall. But for every one that perished there were a hundred that emerged alive to bellow at the sky.

They swarmed from the rocks. While the first of them had simply charged across the land in search of slaughter, the larger hordes moved with more purpose. Thousands of hands pulled the grounded asteroids apart. Metal was torn and reshaped into armour plating, cleavers, axes and tusked helms. From the core of the rocks came machines. Black engine fumes breathed into the air. Vast cannons swallowed shells into their breeches. Trios of copper orbs began to spin around the barrels of exotic energy weapons. Green-and-blue lightning crackled through the air, and the stink of ozone and static blended with the reek of oil and ork flesh.

Archamus watched the horde grow in the eyepiece of his scope. The mountain air was cold on the skin of his face. The temperature in the valleys was scorching, but up in the peaks the altitude lent the wind a razor chill. He was crouched on the top of a rock crag above a wide dip between snow-capped mountain peaks. Bare slopes descended from the pass, running into foothills scattered with thorn trees. At his back the river plain, which had been the site of their first engagement with the orks, stretched down to the distant sea. This point was the only pass across the mountains for hundreds of kilometres.

He breathed in, feeling the cold fill his lungs, and lowered the scope from his eyes.

'If the orks decide not to come this way I assume it will be less than good,' said Katafalque. The young warrior was crouched beside Archamus, eyes watching the slopes beneath them. The blue of his left gauntlet marked him as one of the intake from the Gobi Rust Hives, and he was a child of the dune clans through and through, from the tones of his Low Gothic voice to the wry humour in his words. He had joined Archamus' squad just before they had come to Rennimar. He was blooded but untested by the full heat of a great battle, but he still walked, moved and spoke as though succeeding was inevitable. Archamus liked him.

'They will come this way,' said Archamus. 'Twenty hours, forty-one at the most, but they will come.'

He had locked the scope back onto his thigh plate, and was scratching figures and lines into the face of his wax tablet. The geology left much to be desired. The schist would fragment and slide under bombardment. That could of course be an advantage, but for fortification building it was not ideal. There were deposits of sedimentary rock further down the slope, but they did not have the manpower to move and site more than a few hundred tonnes. That meant that they were looking at using the natural features of the land to create the basis of their defence.

He closed the cover on the tablet.

'One need drives the orks – destruction,' he said. 'They want to fight us. They want to kill us. They will come this way because what they want is on the other side of the mountains. Like water they will find the most direct route. So they will come this way.'

'And we will defeat them,' said Katafalque.

Archamus looked at the horde gathering beneath the mountains. In the two days since the first assault all the surviving forces they could contact had pulled back into the river plain. Archamus had consolidated most of them in the bastion that he had reached with Voss the day before. They had seeded the surrounding ground with mines, and reshaped irrigation ditches and banks to create a killing maze under the watch of firing positions. The bastion wall had grown upwards and outwards, swallowing a fresh water spring. Water channels had been diverted to carry waste out of the compound. Several hundred civilians now sheltered in the bastion, and those who could laboured alongside the Imperial Army and Archamus' brothers. And it was not complete.

Every hour without significant attack meant a new layer of defences and improvement. It was far from the chain of fortresses they had been raising, an ugly child of necessity, but it would grow and harden with every second that the orks gave them. They had held it against six attacks while they built. Most of the orks on that side of the pass had come in small and smaller waves as their numbers dwindled. They were still dangerous, though. They had lost five hundred and two Imperial Army auxiliaries and eleven battle-brothers since the invasion had begun.

How much longer they could hold in the valley was uncertain, but Archamus had no intention of making it his only line of defence. When the orks tried to cross the pass over the mountains they would find it barred.

'We will stand,' he said, and turned away from the sight of the gathering horde. 'We will stand.'

IV

THE BUBBLE OF energy struck the earth rampart beneath Archamus and burst. Waves of pressure ripped out. Splinters of shattered stone rang on his armour. The ground shook and then crumbled. He jumped aside as a section of palisade slumped down the slope. Hard rounds smacked into the gap. Chips from the collapsed blocks pinged into the air. Archamus pushed himself up to the parapet. He was on the lowest of the five palisades they had built across the slopes beneath the pass.

A vista of destruction opened before him as he looked down. The orks were surging up the hill, scrambling over the debris and the dead. Behind them the foothills were a rising sea of bodies and machines. Some of the orks were huge, towering slab creatures bloated by war. They clanked as they moved. Limbs sheathed in battered iron, faces covered by tusked and horned helms. The very biggest were twice the height of a Space Marine, their bodies daubed in blood and dusted in rust. Some carried guns that crackled and spat arcs of oily energy. The air itched with static around them. The sound was shocking, a continual beating river of noise flowing up from the guns and mouths of the orks.

The rock of the parapet beneath Archamus was singing with ricocheting rounds. Even as he looked, one of the orks' machine-mounted guns opened up. A fork of green lightning spat up the hill and struck the palisade on his left. A patch of rock exploded into molten spray. The orks surged for the damaged section of the palisade.

'Fire,' he said into the vox. From the tiered palisades above him, thirty of his brothers and three hundred auxiliaries opened fire. Las-fire and bolt-rounds sheeted downwards. The surge of orks vanished in a blaze of impacts. The volleys began a beat, switching between each of the palisades in turn. Archamus could almost see his brothers locking fresh hoppers to the sides of heavy bolters and rotor cannons, the humans pulling smoking charge packs from laslocks.

The orks replied in kind. Fire gushed up the slope. Beams, spheres and cones of energy smacked into the palisades. Plasteel and rock shattered, melted and blew into the air in fountains of white-hot liquid. In his helm Archamus saw the life markers of three of his brothers blink out.

The ork tide surged towards the defences. One of them made the half-collapsed breach in the lowest palisade. Blocks of armour covered its front, and it dragged a spike-headed mace in each fist. Las-bolts splashed off its armour as it made the wall and leapt up the slope of rubble.

Behind the parapet Archamus remained still. A squad of five of his brothers waited with him. Everything now was timing. The design and disposition of the defences was a simple fact, as solid and immovable as the earth itself. He could not remake the ground he had to fight on. All that remained was to choose when to deliver his blows.

More orks scrambled up the rubble after the first. The fire from the higher palisades intensified. Archamus heard the scream of a charging melta weapon, and one ork vanished as a white-hot beam struck it in the chest. Another took its place, and the rest were suddenly through the breach. They poured into the space beyond.

It took a second for one of the orks to notice the Space Marines crouched on the inside of the firing step. Archamus watched the creature's head turn. The red of its eyes glimmered from inside the slot holes in its faceplate.

'Detonate now,' he said, and shot the ork through the eye.

The ground outside the first palisade exploded. A wall of dust and fire shot into the air. The orks fighting to reach the breach were torn apart. The shock wave from the explosion spilled down the slope, ripping orks from their feet and tossing them down the mountainside.

'Close the breach,' Archamus shouted, and leapt down onto the rubble slope. His brothers came with him. All had tower shields. They spread into two lines across the breach, one facing outwards, one inwards. Archamus felt Katafalque's shoulder and shield thump into his own. They were a line strung across the gap in the wall between the orks who had breached the palisade and the green tide flowing up the mountain.

A second after the shield-wall formed, an ork was on him, swinging a buzz-saw tipped mace. He took the blow. His bionic arm vibrated as the force shook through it. Sparks fountained from the shield face as the ork struck again and again.

Timing. It was always timing.

'Fire to clear,' he said into his vox, and pulled the trigger of his bolter. His squad and the troops on the tier directly above fired at the same moment. Their volleys tore the orks caught between the palisades apart. One managed to reach the shield-wall and cannoned into it.

Archamus staggered as it hit. His shield tipped back, and suddenly the ork was in front of him, streaming blood, faceplate shining with bullet gouges. Archamus rammed his weight forwards. His bionics shrieked, and he felt muscles tear down his back. The ork stumbled.

It was enough. Archamus brought his shield up, felt it touch those to either side, and fired the rest of his clip as the ork lunged at him. It fell, and he saw that the space beyond was a mass of steaming corpses, torn meat and blood-slicked armour. The sky was pulsing with light as the palisades above sent torrents of fire down into the orks and received a reply in kind.

'We cannot hold this indefinitely, sergeant,' said Katafalque over the vox.

'Agreed,' replied Archamus. 'Pull back to the second wall.' The shield-wall began to move as the words left his lips. The orks battered against it, and tried to lap around its edges. They found no weakness. The squad changed formation as it moved, shields and warriors locking into a triangle. They fired without pause. Cables dropped over the parapet of the next palisade when they reached it. Archamus was the last to climb up. He fired his last round and pulled himself over, as the orks poured in and over the palisade that he had been standing on minutes before. He could hear the victory in their cries.

Timing, he thought.

'Promethium?' asked Katafalque from beside him, as he dropped onto the parapet.

'Yes,' he said. Behind and beneath them, in the space inside the foot of the palisade, a platoon of auxiliaries in breath masks spun the wheel valves on pipes that plunged down into the ground and out under the palisade wall. The pipes thumped with pressure, and then the reek of promethium was swallowing the smell of gunfire as it sprayed from the nozzles buried in the ground between the first and second palisades. Katafalque stood and fired a burst of bolt-rounds into the orks pressed into the fuel-soaked space.

Flames ripped across the ground and climbed into the air. Heat blasted across Archamus. His armour chimed a warning. The orks were screaming, bellowing as they cooked. The gunfire seemed to fade as the world became orange heat and black smoke.

After ten seconds, Archamus gestured and the auxiliaries cut the flow. The flames drained to nothing. Black mounds of flesh lay on the ground beneath the wall, cooked meat hissing and popping. Beyond the pall of smoke the orks had retreated down the slope.

'That worked,' said Katafalque.

Archamus nodded. 'Yes, but how much promethium do we have left now?'

'Tanks are two-thirds depleted.'

Archamus nodded to the carpet of bodies flowing towards the pass.

'We will not be able to play that hand again,' he said. 'Get the mining teams out. The approaches need to be reseeded before the next assault.'

'By your will,' said Katafalque, and he began to turn to issue the orders. But then he stopped and his head jerked up, his face turning to the sky. 'What was that?'

Archamus looked up, and frowned as his eye caught something swift and bright in the sky behind the mountain peaks above them. Clouds of smoke hazed the sky above. Lights flashed beyond the grey layer.

'The orks are dropping into the river valley,' said Katafalque. 'We should alert the bastion to be ready for a surge.'

Archamus said nothing. There was something about the flash of light in the atmosphere. He scanned the sky looking for the shadow of the ork's hulk, but could not find it. If they were dropping from orbit then they must be...

The trio of strike fighters came over the mountain peaks with a roar of engines. Archamus caught the flash of yellow-and-black wings as the sonic boom echoed down the slope. Katafalque stared and then gave a bark of joy. Cheers rose from the palisades as the three aircraft swept down the slopes.

Missiles launched from their wings, and fresh fire washed through the press of orks. The fighters banked hard, flicking up into the air as bursts of energy and flurries of rockets rose from the ork horde. Archamus saw the clenched fist insignia on the aircraft's tails, and the black eagle feathers painted on their wings. The cheering rose louder behind him, but he was silent, his mind turning over.

The Accipitridae, he thought, *the Huscarl squadron, escorts to the Lord Primarch, but...*

Three more aircraft came over the mountains, their hulls almost scraping the summits. They were gunships, two Storm Eagles, their hulls yellow, guns tracking the ground. And between them, black and golden hulled, was a sight that halted the breath in his throat.

The *Aetos Dios* banked above them, thrusters roaring as it halted in the air and began to drop towards the ground. Its assault ramps opened when it was three metres above the earth. Yellow-armoured figures dropped to the ground and spread out. Above them the two Storm Eagles had opened up. Rockets and heavy bolters punched into orks advancing back up the hill, holding them back. The strike fighters wheeled and circled in the smoke-stained sky above.

Rogal Dorn dropped from the gunship and landed beside his

Huscarls. The downwash of the thrusters caught his cloak and spilled it behind him as he rose to look down the slope at the ebbing tide of orks. The Storm Eagles swooped low and more warriors dropped onto the scorched ground.

And then all the gunships were rising, and Dorn was striding up to the walls of Archamus' ragged fortress. The dimming light caught his armour and blazed from the burnished plates. Archamus had not seen his lord since he had given Dorn his oath. Nearly three decades of war had passed since then, but while Archamus knew that he himself had changed, time seemed to have left Dorn untouched. Control and strength flowed and echoed from every glance and movement. His features were those Archamus had looked at through the flames, as he had gripped Dorn's hand all those years ago: harsh as iron, as set as carven stone.

The Huscarls ringed their lord until he was at the intact second wall, but the orks did not advance up the hill. Whether it was the strikes from the aircraft, or some other, subtle instinct that kept them at bay, Archamus could not tell.

Dorn reached the palisade and vaulted over the parapet. The warriors on the wall began to kneel, but Dorn gestured and they froze.

'Attend to your guns,' he said. A strange quiet had stolen over the fortress. The sounds of the orks seemed distant, and Archamus was aware of the beat of blood in his veins, and the hiss of wind pulling smoke from the charred ork bodies. Dorn looked up at the tiered palisades, eyes passing over them for a second before turning to Archamus, who knelt, despite Dorn's command. The sound of his bionics seemed loud in the sudden quiet.

'Ten hours construction,' said Dorn, nodding at the palisades above them. 'Given time and materials, near perfect.'

'Yes, my lord,' Archamus said, and he saw Dorn's mouth twitch.

'Calev's design?'

'Calev is dead, lord.'

Dorn's gaze hardened for a second.

'Your work then.'

'Yes, lord.'

Dorn looked around. The Huscarls were moving up through the hold, taking position amongst the garrison at the points where it was thinnest. They moved with silent precision, merging with Archamus' forces seamlessly and without word. Archamus felt a flare of admiration; many marked the Templars of the First Company as the greatest warriors of their Legion, but the Huscarls were something else. Trusted and disciplined beyond the point that most would think possible.

Dorn gave a final glance at the dead orks cooling in the killing ground beneath the palisade.

'Well done, sergeant,' said the primarch.

'I am Archamus, lord,' he said, before he was sure why.

Dorn gave him a long look, eyes seeming black in the unmoving mask of his face.

'I remember who you are,' he said.

V

Archamus followed his primarch into the tunnels behind the stronghold. The walls were smooth and glassy from the touch of the melta-torches that had cut the passages into the cliffs only a day before. Supplies stood stacked in side chambers that were enlarged natural caves. Heavy curtains of blast fabric hung across the doorways to other side chambers where ammunition crates sat like reservoirs waiting for the thirsty to drink. Some of the civilians from the valley were here too, attending to simple set tasks with nervous focus. If there had been more time, Archamus would have liked to have extended the tunnels back and down to concealed entrances on the flanks of the mountain, from which his forces could have sallied out. There had not been time, though, so the small network sunk into the rocks either side of the pass had had to suffice.

Dorn glanced around occasionally as they passed deeper into the warren, but did not speak. Archamus followed behind, flanked by Katafalque and followed by two of the Huscarls. The primarch moved as though he knew the tunnels' layout as well as he did the command deck of the *Phalanx*.

Finally they came to one of the last chambers. The two Huscarls took position to either side of the door as Dorn pushed the curtain aside and stepped in. The light of the glow-globes showed a wide chamber with irregular walls. A table stood at its centre. Neat scrolls of parchment lay on the table. Drafting and drawing instruments sat beside them on squares of soft, black fabric.

On the far side of the room, squatting on the floor, with a loose sheaf of parchment spread on his lap and a brass quill in one hand, was Solomon Voss. The emissary was rubbing his eyes with ink-stained fingers when they entered. He looked up, blinked, and then a smile split his face.

'Rogal!' he cried, and stood up, dumping the parchment on the central table. Archamus flinched at the familiarity of the greeting, but Rogal Dorn was stepping forwards, the stone of his face cracking into a smile.

'I see that you are alive,' said Dorn.

'Barely,' said Voss, still smiling. 'But that is the point, isn't it? To look at the truth of things so closely that you can feel its breath?'

'Too close for someone whose greatest weapon is his words.'

'The Great Crusade must have a memory, my friend. The past defines the future. Without knowing the past, how can we shape what is to come?'

Dorn laughed, the sound like a gunshot in the confined space.

'An argument for another time.'

Voss shrugged.

'An argument I know I have already won, at least with you – or else of all the battlefields of all the Legions, why would I have been allowed to come here?'

'Perhaps to keep you where the great lords of the Imperium will not be able to hear you?'

Voss snorted and then picked up his parchments.

'One day there will be many of us, Rogal. A legion of memory.'

'Then I will have more than one inconvenient civilian to worry about. But at least there is the hope that it would be a burden borne equally by my brothers.'

'Is that why you are here, to get this inconvenient human out of the way of your war?'

'Hardly,' said Dorn.

'Another matter then?' asked Voss, raising an eyebrow above a sharp eye. 'A strategic matter?'

'That is the matter I must now discuss with my officers,' said Dorn.

'Of course,' said Voss, and he made for the doorway. 'We will talk again, though?'

'Of course,' said Dorn, 'when there is time.'

Voss moved to the door and lifted the curtain to leave. He stopped and looked back.

'I have learned much from your son,' he said to Dorn, and nodded in Archamus' direction. 'He has your soul.'

Dorn gave a brief nod. The blast curtain fell back into place after Voss. Archamus blinked, not certain what to make of the conversation he had just witnessed. He flicked a glance at Katafalque, who was still standing to rigid attention at the side of the room.

'Go with Voss,' he said. Katafalque saluted and followed the human out.

Dorn turned back to Archamus.

'Voss is a curious man,' he said, as though answering the question that Archamus could not frame.

'I had wondered why he was here, lord. He is an emissary, but he is not a warrior, a diplomat or specialist.'

'He is a genius, though,' said Dorn, moving to the table. He picked up Voss' untidy stack of parchment, his eyes scanning a few of the scrawled lines. 'He is a wordsmith, a distiller of ideas and images into a language which makes what he thinks and sees live in the minds of those who have never seen or dreamed of anything beyond their own lives.' He placed the papers down. 'But that is not the true core of his quality. He sees a future of truth and illumination, and reaches to create it with his every deed. The Imperium we are fighting to create will be held together by the words and ideas of people like Solomon Voss.'

Dorn's eyes moved to the neatly arranged scrolls, and he picked one up and spread it out on the table. Inked plans for buildings and structures crossed the parchment in black lines. Columns of notes and figures marched down the margins. Dorn examined each of the scrolls in turn, replacing them precisely where they had been. Archamus felt apprehension clench in his guts as his own pen work slid under Dorn's eyes.

'These plans, they are not for fortifications on this world,' said Dorn, spreading the last plan on the table. A soaring structure of high pillars and curved crystal lay across the sheet, dissected and rendered in black ink. 'Unless I have lost the ability to read an ink plan, this is not a fortification at all.'

'Merely an exercise in craft, lord,' said Archamus, unsure if he was facing a rebuke. The plans that Dorn was examining were some that he had been working on before the attack. 'Theoretical works, that is all.'

'They are excellent,' said Dorn. 'Though you have overcompensated for the weight of the dome structures in the thickness of the main pillar.'

'The compression tolerance of most metamorphic limestone seemed to necessitate it, lord.'

'The stone of the Pendelikon quarries has a higher tolerance, and a half degree added to the taper of the secondary pillars will balance the weight transfer, and correct the imperfection in the proportions when seen from the ground.'

Archamus stared at Dorn, not knowing what to say. The primarch smiled.

'You have both ability and eyes that see further than the task in front of you.'

'Seneschal Calev taught me well.'

'You learned well too.' Dorn put the plans back down on the table.

The ceiling shook, and a trail of dust fell from the evening sky. They both looked up.

'They come again,' said Archamus.

'You have built a good dam to hold them back,' said Dorn. 'But it will fall in twelve hours.'

Archamus struggled to control his shock.

'But with you here, lord – now we can hold. They will beat themselves to nothing against us.'

Dorn's smile slid into something more tired and knowing.

'I thank you for your faith, Archamus, but I did not say that it would fall because they would break us. It will fall because we will let it fall.'

Archamus felt the blood pull from the skin of his face. His mind turned over and over, and the question he had not asked now came to his lips.

'Why are you here, lord?'

All traces of the smile had gone from Dorn's face. His gaze was hard and cold.

'The right question. I am here to defeat the orks that have come to this world, to crush them utterly and leave none alive to blight the stars.' He turned back to the table and gestured to a stack of unused parchment, and Archamus' draughtsman's tools. 'May I?'

'Of course, lord. They are yours.'

Dorn picked up a stick of graphite. In his hand it seemed like a grey pin. He began to draw. Archamus stared as circles and lines appeared, and then depth and relation formed in subtle shading. Not once did Dorn pause, and the trace of each line was perfect. Planets, moons and the drift of nebulae appeared. Then marks, runes and zones cut through the impression, marking it with locations, strengths of forces and lines of attack.

Dorn put the drawing aside and took a second sheet, and the surface of Rennimar grew on the blank leaf. Mountains and vast seas spread as though Dorn's hand were scraping the grime from a window that looked down on them from orbit. The positions of the river valley, the mountains and the fortress they now stood in came into being. Dorn paused for the first time, but Archamus sensed that it was for emphasis rather than time to consider. Then other fortifications, large and small, began to appear, dotting the sides of the river plain beyond the mountain-line.

Dorn put the stick of graphite down. Archamus stared at what was before his eyes.

'You were waiting for them...' he breathed.

'Yes,' said Dorn. 'This horde is a shard of the forces of the Over-Tyrant of Grel. When the Sixth and Fourteenth Legions broke the core of the beast's domain, they did not destroy all of the orks. Armies scattered, perhaps to create their own realms of war, perhaps to burn whatever they could find. They do not have the numbers of the Over-Tyrant's horde, but they have more than enough strength to put worlds to the torch. If left unchecked, who knows how that danger might grow and multiply? But while we knew that they had fled, where they went was far from clear.'

'So you waited for them to come to a world.'

'And now we know where they are, they can be killed. I have brought ten thousand of the Legion to this world, no more, and with that we will do this bloody deed and then build a new world on the ashes. A bloodied and scarred world, but a world that will know truth and grow strong.'

'It has suffered much already, lord. The cities to the north of here...'

'Strength and truth shall be its future, but for now it will serve us as a place of slaughter. And this will be a slaughter, Archamus. That is the price of that future.'

Archamus looked down at the plans that Dorn had drawn and the future they outlined. It was breathtaking.

'Why did we not know? Why did you not tell us of what might come for us?'

'I did not know on which world the blow would fall. There are twenty-one worlds with garrisons just like yours scattered before the path we thought the orks might take. And would the preparations that you made have been any less diligent if you had known? Would the forces at your disposal have been stronger from knowing, or weaker from expecting a blow that might not come? What if another threat had come to this place while you were expecting the orks?'

'Ignorance is armour?' said Archamus. 'I... I cannot believe that, lord.'

'Not always, but sometimes it is. But I do not trust in ignorance. I trust in the strength of my Legion, and the weakness of the enemy.' The chamber shook again, and Dorn looked up, then back to Archamus. 'Come. We have a slaughter to bring into being.'

VI

THE LAST WALL guarding the pass fell twelve hours after Rogal Dorn set foot on Rennimar.

The last defenders fired as the orks flowed across the broken palisades. The wall the Imperial Fists stood on spanned the mouth of a gulley between two crags. A towering face of smooth rock and rockcrete, it seemed as immovable as the mountain itself. The orks did not falter. The largest of their breed had come for this last slaughter. Each twice as tall as a Space Marine, they came in a clanking wave. They reached the wall and began to climb. Hooked axes bit into the stone and rockcrete. Jets of flame poured down from the Imperial Fists on the firing step. Some of the orks fell, but the rest kept climbing, liquid fire clinging to them. Smaller orks began to scale the cliffs and crags to either side of the wall. Mines embedded in the rock shredded them. Bolt and las-fire raked the cliffs. Blood showered down to wet the hides of those beneath. But they kept climbing, the living taking the place of the dead as the rounds drained from the defenders' guns.

Archamus stood on the wall, bolter clamped in the metal of his right fist as he fired. In the distance the black sky was brightening with the light of a new day.

'Is it time?' asked Katafalque, from behind him. Archamus traced a burst of fire across the face of the wall and watched as a burning brute of an ork fell, its arms shredded stumps. The orks were almost at the top of the wall – another surge and they would be amongst the defenders.

'All units, pull back,' called Archamus. There were only Imperial Fists on the wall, and they moved instantly. One moment the parapet was manned and bright with muzzle flashes, and the next it was empty. Archamus dropped down on the inside of the wall and sprinted across the mouth of the pass. The ork tide spilled across the wall. Roars of triumph echoed from the mountain tops. They flowed on and on, down through the pass like a river through a breached dam.

Gunfire whipped around Archamus as he ran, hard rounds and chips of stone ringing on his armour. His warriors were at his side, the last twenty who had stood on the wall with him, all sprinting from the enemy they had fought against for days. That reality echoed in his mind, bitter and burning.

The black-and-gold gunship came over the side of the mountain, just above the tops of the trees and outcrops. It slammed to a halt with a shudder of thrusters and turned as it dropped. Its doors were open. Archamus kept running. He could see the open ramp in the craft's chin. A figure in burnished golden armour stood in the opening.

A round slammed into the back of his helm. He staggered, eyes blurring, bionics clicking as his nerves struggled to know how to balance. The ramp of the gunship was just in front of him. He could see script etched into the gilt eagle head beneath the cockpit, which read *The only strength is honour*. His warriors were leaping up to the open hatches; wild bursts of fire were whipping down the mountainside. He took a step and leapt. His foot found the ramp, as the gunship rose with a scream of engines. His balance wavered.

An armoured fist gripped his hand. Rogal Dorn pulled him up.

'It is done, lord,' said Archamus.

Dorn nodded.

'Take us up,' he said into the vox.

'By your will,' came the pilot's reply.

The gunship climbed, banking across the mountainside. Air rushed through the open doors. Beneath them the river glinted under the rising sun. An avalanche of orks was pouring from the pass down the side of the mountain. In the sky above, the shape of the ork hulk was rising from the horizon, like a dark, jagged sun. Archamus could see the shapes of the primary bastion sitting near the base of the valley floor, like a child's sandcastle waiting on the shoreline for the sea. The mountainside was a dark carpet kilometres wide and deep, a sea of countless bodies, all running, all shouting for the joy of destruction. They were almost at the base of the valley.

'Cut the pass,' said Dorn.

Archamus took the detonator from his belt, armed it and depressed the first switch.

There was a second of delay and then twin flashes on the mountain tops. A plume of dust shot into the sky. A resonating boom shook the air as the rock faces above the pass dissolved. Thousands of tonnes of rock sheared from the peaks and buried the orks still pouring across the pass into the river valley. The mass of orks nearest the explosion stumbled as they turned back.

Archamus triggered the next switch. Charges under the ground on the slopes beneath the pass detonated in sequence. A sheet of stone cleaved from the mountain top and slid down, rolling and roaring as it gathered speed, enveloping the orks in a wave of boulders. Those already filling the valley bottom charged on, blind to or uncaring of what had happened to those behind them.

The guns on the bastion on the valley floor opened up for the first time. A lattice of blazing lines scored through the air and cut into the green tide. The synchronised bark of bolters rose to Archamus' ears. Carronades shot volkite beams into the mass. Orks exploded in clouds of boiling blood and burning flesh. The orks surged on towards the bastion like insects drawn towards a flame.

Dorn looked down from the gunship door as the green tide encircled the bastion's walls. Beside him, Archamus could see the yellow-armoured warriors on the walls, shooting jets of flame over the parapet, throwing grenades and hacking down at the orks trying to scale the palisades. Human auxiliaries moved amongst mortar batteries. They acted without flaw or hesitation, but Archamus could read the progression of battle at a glance. The orks would overwhelm the lone bastion within minutes.

'Give the strike orders to the warships,' said Dorn, his voice carrying clear over the sound of the gunship's engines and the roar of the wind.

Archamus looked up. The ork hulk was a looming blot on the sky. As he watched he saw four shapes slide above the horizon, shining bright as they streaked across the lightening vault of fading night. For a second they seemed serene, a silent ornament to the heavens. White light burst around the ork ship as nova shells exploded in its outer mass. Archamus' display blinked black. The light strobed across the sky.

The melta torpedoes hit next. Orange flames flashed over the ork hulk. Chunks of it broke off and fell, trailing burning claw marks.

Inside the gunship, one of Dorn's Huscarls turned towards the primarch. The warrior's helm was a swollen mass of sensor and signal equipment.

'The strike forces are within the ork hulk and advancing on reactor locations,' said the Huscarl signal master. Simple words, but Archamus knew that above them a thousand of his Legion brothers would be hacking, burning and battering through the corridors of the xenos craft.

Dorn nodded acknowledgement.

'Close the fist,' he said.

Beneath them, the valley roared.

Twelve hours had seen nine thousand Imperial Fists drop from orbit. They had come in Stormbirds, flying from beyond the horizon, and from the moment they had landed they had worked to change the river valley into a killing ground. They had sunk trenches into the slopes near the valley bottom. Firing points capped every piece of high ground. These were not the sculpted defences of great fortresses, but piled stone and earth braced between ballistic fabric and plasteel plates, and set by fast-hardening rockcrete.

Camouflage nets covered their more obvious features. The concealment was minimal. An army with any caution would have realised that they were there, and the danger they represented. But the orks had no caution. Driven by their hunger for battle, their ferocity had built with every hour they had battered against the defences across the mountain pass. They were no longer reckless – they were blind. And as they had poured into the valley, Dorn had trapped them in the centre of a fist that now closed with a sound like the end of worlds.

Nine thousand warriors fired within a heartbeat of each other. Within a second over thirty thousand bolts had hit the enemy. A second later the shells lobbed from a hundred dug-in mortar platforms landed in the heart of the horde. The mortar crews had zeroed the impacts in during the night, based on Dorn's prediction of the horde's movement. The mortars struck true. The blasts stuttered outwards, unfolding like a flower of fire and blood.

The second bolter volleys struck, ripping the sides of the horde, chewing into it, biting chunks from its bulk. The mortar platforms had already adjusted their aim, and now a second chain of explosions marched up the valley floor. Other heavy weapons joined the torrent. Conversion beamers drew lines of exploding flesh and armour through the ork horde. The stuttered voice of heavy bolters rose to join the cacophony. Archamus watched ork bodies dance as rounds and shrapnel hit them from every direction.

The orks began to respond. They had lost thousands, and perhaps any other creatures would have broken in those first moments. But the orks were born to thrive in the roar of battle. They charged into the fire, bellowing and leaping over the dead as they fell. Towering brutes shoved their way forwards, bolt-rounds and shrapnel ringing off their armour. Some reached the Imperial Fists' lines and began to batter their way down the trenches. Corridors of howling energy ripped from huge guns.

Archamus could read the flow of battle beneath him. The initial ambush had been devastating to the orks, but they were striking back with the raw instinct and ferocity of a trapped beast that could feel the blood leaking from a mortal wound. In those moments the scales of battle could tip. He had heard that the warriors of the XIII Legion had a name for such a point of balance, just as they did for so many of the details of war. 'The rise of the blade' they called it, for the moment when the victor raised his weapon for a killing blow, and could be killed in turn before it fell. They did not have a name for it but the VII Legion knew that truth all too well. In other battles, this would have been a moment for the armour of the Legion to sally out and drive a killing blow into the enemy's heart. On this day there were no tanks. There had been no time to bring them in alongside the material for the fortifications, but their absence had been planned for.

Dorn took his bolter from one of the Huscarls, checked it and clamped it to his armour. Another came forwards with the primarch's chainsword. Two-thirds as tall as Archamus, its name was *Storm's Teeth*, and each of those teeth glinted sharply. Dorn gripped its hilt and turned towards the open assault ramp. Archamus' squad and the Huscarls tensed, weapons steady as the gunship turned high. The trio of interceptors had joined them, holding close formation above and beneath them. Other gunships moved into the formation, rising from the valley floor below.

The interceptors dived first, dagger shapes stabbing downwards, dawn light glinting from their canopies. Rockets and streams of lascannon fire reached from beneath their wings. The primarch's gunship dived after them. Air roared in through the open hatches. Smoke and ash from the battle blurred the sight of the ground. Missiles streaked free of weapon pods. Blisters of fire burst across the mass of orks. The gunship plunged into the rising heat, then slammed level just above the ground. Smoke swallowed the view beyond the hatch.

Dorn looked over his shoulder at the warriors waiting behind him. 'For the Imperium,' he said, and stepped from the ramp.

Archamus followed. Hot air slammed into him. He hit the ground. Armour and bionics screeched. He rolled and came up into the face of an ork with a fanged faceplate. He fired a trio of bolts into its head. It reeled, and he pulled the seax from the scabbard at his waist. The broad blade punched up under the lip of the ork's helm as it came back at him. Blood gushed over Archamus' machine hand. The ork juddered and shook. Archamus ripped the seax out, and turned. Katafalque and his squad were there, cutting a ring into the orks they had landed amongst. And there beside them was Dorn.

The orks crowding close to the primarch were the largest Archamus had seen, towering, muscle-bloated things, clanking with metal plates and weaponry. For a second Dorn seemed frozen, a still figure amongst a churning sea of wild ferocity. The orks were swinging, raw muscle and weight uncoiling. Archamus could see their mouths, wide beneath the edges of their faceplates, strings of phlegm falling from yellow tusks. The teeth of their buzz-saws slid through the smoke-heavy air, so fast they seemed shadows, and there was no way that anything could stand beneath those blows and live.

Then Dorn swung. It was a simple movement: a step forwards and to the side, *Storm's Teeth* rising, the nearest ork's blow passing just in front of Dorn's chest. So simple. So seamless, and utterly destructive.

Storm's Teeth struck the ork's shoulder and ripped through its torso. Petals of armour plating and scraps of flesh sprayed out as the chainsword ripped free, and the next ork was already striking even as the body of the first hit the floor. The notched edge of its cleaver whistled as it cut. The blow was too close for Dorn to avoid. It struck home, just under the primarch's left arm... and went no further. The ork froze in surprise. Dorn looped his left arm over the ork's weapon as he battered the pommel of his sword into the creature's head. Metal and bone shattered. Blood gushed over the ork's shoulders. Dorn pivoted and threw the corpse into the blades of its kin. And then he was moving, shape blurring, striking and striking, each blow from a different angle. *Storm's Teeth* was a bloody arc drawn in the air around him, and the orks were falling. Archamus felt himself shouting for his brothers to follow as he leapt beside his primarch.

They drove forwards, a wedge of golden-yellow armour with a lord of war as its cutting edge. The world was a blur of movement, of shooting and stabbing, and feeling that he was just one part of a creature of many heads and one will; that he was part of a force greater than any single warrior: indomitable, wrathful, remorseless.

The battle lasted two more hours. The end came suddenly. One second he was pulling his seax free from the neck of an ork, and the next there was nothing in front of them except smoke climbing into the sky above a plain of corpses. Gunfire chattered from one of the trench-lines and then fell silent. Archamus stood for a second, eyes and mind searching for the next threat. Tactical runes resolved in his helmet display, cooling from amber to blue.

He looked around. Katafalque was at his shoulder, eyes scanning the ground. Ork blood and scraps of meat lacquered his armour, hiding the yellow beneath red. A jagged tear ran across the warrior's helm from above his left eye to beneath his chin, and Archamus could see the clotted swelling of one socket through the cut. He looked down at himself, remembering blows that had struck him as they drove through the orks. There was blood inside his battleplate, and he could feel the cold numbness of suppressed pain. His bionics ground through caked gore and dust as he turned the other way, and looked at Dorn.

The primarch's armour was daubed in filth. Tatters of skin hung from *Storm's Teeth*. He was still again, as though the figure who had strode through slaughter only a moment before had retreated behind a wall of control and calm.

'Give orders for the fleet to come into close orbit,' he said, looking down at Archamus. 'Bring in heavy equipment and burner units. Make this plain a pyre. All other units are to rearm and prepare to disperse over the surface. No trace of the orks is to remain. You have twenty

hours to see it done. After that I will see your plans for the fortification and garrisoning of this planet.'

'It will be done, my lord,' said Archamus, bringing his fist to his
chest in salute.

Dorn gave a curt nod and began to walk to where the *Aetos Dios* was
settling onto the battlefield. The Huscarls went with him, their blood-
stained cloaks hanging stiff from their shoulders. Archamus had stood
and was about to turn to issue the first of a litany of orders, when
Dorn turned back.

'The future is not won in battle, but in the moments before battle
begins and the time after battle is done. Remember that, and remember this day. This is the Imperium's victory, but it is also yours, *captain.'*

Archamus knelt, hearing the clogged gears of his bionics squeal.
Beside him Katafalque and the rest of his squad followed suit, and
then across the battlefield every legionary and human auxiliary was
kneeling. Then Katafalque shouted the call that a second later echoed
up through the drifting smoke like a promise made to unborn futures.

'Imperium victor!'

'Imperium victor!'

'Imperium victor!'

PART THREE
THE FIRST AXIOM

ONE

SILONIUS KEYED THE shutters to open. They clanked upwards from the viewport, and the light travelled up his chest until he could feel it on his face. He closed his eyes before the sunlight touched them. He waited and then opened his eyelids slowly. The sun sat beyond a circle of gold-tinted crystal. Its light was so bright that it seemed to be pushing out towards him, pulling him in, filling him up as he looked at it. His eyes adapted to the light, reducing the glare to a flat circle of brilliance.

He could not remember the sun under which he had been born. He could remember snatches of the past now, pieces of a life lived in war, but the picture was incomplete and before a certain point... empty.

Psychic reconstruction. He had spoken those words to Alpharius. He was what remained from that process. That knowledge had not been a kind revelation. If anything it left him feeling empty, a body waiting for blood to live. But that was just a fact, a consequence of what he needed to do, what he needed to be.

One of the shard blades spun in his fingers as he looked at the sun.

He had brought both blades with him from his hiding place beneath the Imperial Palace, and kept them even after he had shed most of his equipment from that phase of the mission. Like the habit he had developed in the last few days of coming to look at the sun from this deserted tower, the blades had remained with him.

He blinked slowly at the sun, his mind calculating where they must be from its brightness and position, and that of the distant stars. The *Wealth of Kings* did not follow a course, so much as weave through the void between Terra and Sol. They had made a brief rendezvous with three other vessels and stopped at a scavenger station built into a scooped-out asteroid. On each occasion, the ship had lingered for only the briefest exchange, and every time Sork had come to Phocron with a new data-slate or archive device. Silonius knew what each of the devices contained, and he knew why they were important. That had been one of the gifts of his slowly assembling memory. He was not supposed to know; or rather Phocron did not know that he knew.

He went suddenly still, the blade motionless in his fingers.

He heard heartbeats, a paired rhythm.

Transhuman.

Then he heard a hiss of breath and the near-silent glide of movements so fluid that they merged into the rumble of the ship, and the pulse of air from the vents.

He knew who it was before the legionnaire spoke.

'We are supposed to confine ourselves to the hangar decks,' said Phocron. Silonius turned. The Headhunter Prime was standing a pace away, hands clasped casually behind his back. Like Silonius he had shed his armour and wound himself in a tattered grey shift. A trailing length of fabric covered his head and the lower half of his face. Phocron stepped closer and looked through the viewport.

'The day the Legion confines itself to anything is the day we die,' said Silonius. Phocron gave a dry snort and then turned to look directly at Silonius.

'We must talk, brother,' he said.

Silonius shrugged. He knew that this encounter would have to happen sooner or later. The Legion trained its warriors to never rely on any weapon or structure that could be changed or destroyed. In training and in battle they changed function, formation and even rank constantly. The fact that Silonius had joined Phocron's team in mid operation should have meant nothing. But as with so much theory, and even practice, it failed in the face of realities.

'If you think so, brother,' Silonius said, and waited for a rebuke or challenge. Had he made a mistake? Had he allowed Phocron to realise more than he needed to?

'Can you believe that it has come to this? That we are here, fighting this war?' asked Phocron, nodding at the image of the sun beyond the porthole. Silonius kept the surprise from his face and began to reply, but Phocron spoke before he could. 'When I was sent to sleep beneath Terra's soil, the galaxy was a different shape. This future was unborn – all the wars that might be were theory and contingency. Now they are reality.'

Silonius met the stare and thought of all the mission parameters that must still exist in the mind behind those eyes, all the other shapes of war that a different word could have unlocked.

Orpheus...

Eurydice...

Hades...

'It was inevitable, brother,' he said. 'It was always going to come to this. A galaxy crowded with sons of war building a realm from dust, each different, yet each the same. How else could it have ended?'

Phocron let out a breath.

'Were you sent here before it began?' he asked.

Silonius paused, considering how to answer. He could sense the trap in the question. He had no doubt that Phocron was sincere in his struggle to assimilate the current context of his mission, but he was also using it as a cloak. Should he answer with part of the truth, or an outright lie?

'No,' he said. 'I was placed on Terra only a year ago.'

'We must have expended a lot of assets to achieve that.'

'No doubt.'

'I will be honest, brother. My original mission parameter did not include an addition to my team.'

'The mission had to be augmented,' replied Silonius. 'The human operatives gave you that information at your waking.'

'Their orders were updated with the rendezvous location by an emergency method hours before they came to wake us.'

'Are you asking me why I am here?'

Phocron nodded. 'If you wish to frame it that way.'

'I do not know. I knew what I had to do once I woke. Now I follow you.'

They stared at each other in silence.

'We cannot help it, can we?' said Phocron after a long moment. 'Nothing we do is drawn in straight lines. Nothing can be simple. No truth allowed to stand free.'

'The simple is easy to subvert, brother. Look at what we have done here already and see that truth. The heart of the Imperium defended by the Seventh Legion should be inviolable, indomitable, but here we are.'

'Yes, we are.' Phocron shook his head. 'Sometimes I envy them. The Fists, I mean.'

'Truly?' Silonius did not try and hide the surprise in his voice. Was this another test, another subtle probing of his nature and purpose?

'They were always heaped with more honour than they deserved, rewarded for obviousness and laboured effort, but that is not what I am talking about. They have an identity, a culture. They know who they are, and what they are.' He brought up his hand and pulled down the fabric that framed his face, and turned it fully towards Silonius. It was the image of Alpharius' face, the mirror of Silonius' own. 'What are we? So many masks worn, so many names, so many secrets that the life beneath is forgotten.'

'We are what we need to be,' said Silonius. 'To win, we are what we need to be.' Phocron turned to look at the sun and nodded, as though to himself. Silonius waited and then spoke when no reply came. 'You know what necessity is, brother. Everything is not about what it should be, but what it needs to be.'

'You have nothing for me then? No extra orders, no clarification, no word?'

'No,' said Silonius.

Phocron gave a slow nod. For several seconds neither of them moved. Then Phocron turned from the viewport so that his back was to it. His eyes began to flick across the shadow of the tower chamber. Silonius realised that while Phocron had spoken his habitual movements had stilled. Now that ceaseless movement was back, as though a switch had been flicked.

'Your secrets are yours to keep, brother. They are not why I am here. I came to find you because the next component of the mission is ready to proceed. We need to prepare.'

'What is it?' asked Silonius.

'There is a signal relay station, in the outer Mercurial Reaches. We will hit it and destroy it.'

Silonius shook his head.

'There are dozens of primary relay stations in the inner system reaches alone. Unless we are going to hit them all–'

'Destruction is only a secondary effect, the confusion it will cause tertiary.'

'What is the primary objective?' asked Silonius, even as the answer whispered at the edge of his memory.

'We need to light the beacon. A Harrowing is coming, and we are its heralds.'

'WHAT DOES "HARROWING" mean?' asked Incarnus. Myzmadra paused what she was doing and looked at the psyker. Silence and stillness formed as an answer.

They were in a small chamber on the *Wealth of Kings'* lower decks.

Rust mottled its walls, and slowly rotating fans stirred the thick air. Hatches hung open in the three doorways leading off. Myzmadra had come there after the mission briefing, mainly to think, but also to strip and clean all of her gear. Pistols and ammunition lay on the top of an upturned crate, oiled components shining from repeated cleansing.

There was a lot to think about. She had intended to be alone, but after a few moments had looked up to find that she had been joined in her solitude. What had surprised her was who it was. Hekaron – stripped of armour, tattooed and branded torso bare above a loose pair of black trews – sat on a crate opposite her. He had nodded at her, grinned and begun to disassemble his bolter. She had nodded back in acknowledgement. They had sat, the quiet broken only by the click, snap and slide of weapons coming apart.

Then Incarnus had joined them. She had known it was him without looking up. There was just something in the sound of how he moved. He had sat down on a pile of chains against the wall. When neither she nor Hekaron spoke, Incarnus coughed and licked his lips. She felt her teeth clamp shut. Then he had asked the question.

'Harrowing? You do not know the term?' Hekaron said, glancing up from the piece of firing mechanism he was oiling with a cloth. There was a sneer to his grin. He shook his head. 'Where did we find you?'

Incarnus stiffened.

'In the same place you find all the people of rare talent who are willing to fight the Emperor,' snapped the psyker. 'I know the *meaning* of the word harrowing. But unless our mission is to turn the ground with a plough, the connotations of despoilment and destruction are just vague enough that I find myself at a loss.'

Hekaron laughed, the sound booming around the chamber. His bare shoulders shook, the tangled tattoos writhing across muscle.

'You have courage, human, I will give you that. I almost like you enough to answer.' He shrugged, placed a piece of the bolter down on the black sheet at his feet, picked up another and began to clean it.

'But almost is not enough. You have a good grasp of the word. You have operated for the Legion, so you have seen how we do what we do. Use that *rare talent* to put the pieces together.'

'Perhaps I should,' hissed Incarnus, and Myzmadra felt heat spike the air. Frost formed around Incarnus' eyes. Hekaron grunted. The piece of gun mechanism pinged out of his fingers. Myzmadra felt static wash up her arms, and she began to rise, reaching for her only assembled gun. Hekaron was trying to stand. She could see a flash of red at the edge of his ear. Incarnus was grinning, eyes black boreholes in thin circles of ice, as he wrapped his mind around Hekaron.

A blur passed her, moving faster than she could track. Incarnus spun into the air, a yell of pain ripping out of his mouth. Her ears popped as a shock wave passed over her. She tasted burned sugar on her teeth. Hands caught Incarnus as he fell, spun him over and slammed him into the deck. Hekaron gasped from where he had struggled to rise, half fell and then launched himself across the room.

'Peace, brother,' said Silonius, his voice low and utterly calm. He was standing above the whimpering form of Incarnus, a foot on the psyker's chest. He was looking at Hekaron, hand raised. Myzmadra had not seen him enter the room. He was just there, as though blinked into being.

'He was in my mind!' growled Hekaron, a clotting drop of blood running down his right ear. 'I could feel him.'

'He is an asset, brother,' said Silonius. 'An imperfect tool, but one that we need.'

Orn appeared at the door, drawn by the noise. Myzmadra saw him look from Incarnus, to Hekaron, and then to Silonius. She caught the briefest flicker of eyes, and Orn remained where he was. It was only then that she noticed the gun in Orn's hands, held so casually it had somehow seemed less threatening than its bearer.

Silonius tilted his head, focusing on Hekaron. The vein in the warrior's neck was beating beneath the inked scales.

'We need him,' said Silonius, carefully. Hekaron clenched his teeth, silver glinting. Then he nodded and turned away.

Silonius waited a second, then reached down and pulled Incarnus to his feet. He held him by the throat, casually, as though he were holding a bundle of rags, rather than a man. Myzmadra could see his fingers were relaxed, but that they were resting over vertebrae, arteries and trachea. Incarnus was whimpering, blood flowing from broken teeth and nose in a thick flow down his chin and cheeks. Silonius' fingers did not seem to move, but the psyker suddenly became completely still. His pupils were wide in his iris-less eyes. Silonius brought Incarnus close, the movement almost gentle.

She stared. It was the most delicately violent thing she had ever seen.

'Do not do that again,' said Silonius quietly to the psyker. He dropped Incarnus to the floor, without waiting for a response, and walked to where Orn stood. The two left, leaving Myzmadra the only person to hear Incarnus' breath bubbling between his broken teeth.

Signal Relay Station 189-56
Trans-Mercury debris shoal

THE LAST THING Silonius saw before the memory took him was the pulse of the compartment lights from the shuttlecraft. The shapes of the rest of the team blinked in his eye, and then the past yanked him away.

'Come with me, brother.'

The summons had come as such things always did, without warning. He had been resting, allowing the healing flesh of his body to ache while his mind focused on the movements of stripping his weaponry down to the smallest parts. He sat in the centre of an explosion of components arranged in a series of circles. The deck beneath him was still and quiet, the tremor of the Sigma's engines absent. The grand cruiser was at anchor in the gas clouds off Shedim. Four hundred warriors of the Legion and five thousand oathbound mortals were aboard the ship, rearming and waiting for their next call to war. Yet despite those numbers the Sigma was near silent. Silonius had not fought the quiet, but let it settle into him.

And then, just when the quiet was deepest, he had heard the words like a breath on the back of his neck.

His hands had frozen as he heard them. His fingers curled slowly around the firing rod he had been cleaning. With casual unconcern, he had reached beneath a rumpled cloth. His hand and the bolt pistol had come up and around in a single movement... and met the gaze of a green eye slit above the vented faceplate of a Crusade-era helm. A warrior stood above him, a boltgun aimed casually at the deck. The warrior's armour seemed black, the crocodilian-scaled blue visible only where the light fell fully upon it.

Silonius felt a tingle of admiration and doubt run through his nerves. To approach this close in still air, with active power armour... That was a feat of worrying skill. He knew every legionnaire on the ship well enough to identify them from gesture or posture. The warrior who stood before him was none that he knew.

'Come with me,' repeated the warrior.

'Who are you?' asked Silonius, not lowering the pistol.

'You are summoned, brother,' the warrior said, and half turned towards the distant chamber door.

'By whose will?' asked Silonius, though he knew the answer. There could only be one answer to how warriors had come aboard his ship without his knowing.

'Your primarch's will.'

Silonius lowered the pistol and rose.

'Follow me,' the warrior said.

Silonius blinked and found Incarnus staring at him. The psyker flinched then put his pale stare elsewhere. The memory was still fresh in Silonius' mind, smudging his perception. He felt fresh understanding and information ache at the edge of his thoughts. The shape of his immediate future altered.

'Coming up on the relay now, stand ready,' said Ashul from the pilot's chair. The doors to the cockpit hung open on rust-jammed hinges. Readings flashed across the controls of the lighter. In the crew compartment, five figures in power armour rose as one.

'Have they seen us?' asked Incarnus. The psyker was still seated, gangling limbs hidden by the bulk of his void suit, his head a bubble of silvered glass.

'Almost certainly,' replied Ashul from the cockpit, 'but we have to hope that they see too much debris around us to pay much attention.'

'Comforting,' muttered Incarnus.

Hekaron growled across the compartment, and Incarnus flinched. Of the human operatives, only Incarnus and Ashul were needed for this mission, and only Incarnus would be going with the strike team once they reached the signal. The rest remained back on the *Wealth of Kings* as the scavenger ship drifted through the debris shoal far behind them.

'Here we go,' said Ashul. 'Let's hope those codes are good.' A second passed then another, and another. A flat block of pitted metal grew in the view beyond the misted canopy. Signal antennae projected from its upper surface and clustered around a single large dish array. Hangar bay doors opened as they came closer.

'We are clear to dock,' said Ashul.

'Stand ready,' called Phocron, and a wave of movement passed through the strike team as mag-harnesses released and weapons were armed.

'What is the garrison strength, again?' asked Incarnus.

'Unknown,' answered Phocron, without pausing in his last weapon checks.

'And that's not a problem.'

'It is a fact,' said Phocron. 'Its relevance is limited.'

'Oh, yes... Of course...'

'Ten seconds,' called Ashul. They pivoted towards the hatch.

The compartment light cut out. There was a hiss and then a thump as the lighter settled onto a deck.

A ripple of subtle movement passed through the compartment as the four other Space Marines tensed. Silonius was second in line. Behind his right shoulder, Hekaron activated the charge coils on his culverin. The buzz rang through Silonius' teeth and into his ears. His bolter sat in his hands, his finger on the trigger. He raised it up, muzzle angled just to the right of Phocron's right shoulder to his front.

The lighter's hatch hissed open.

The crewman on the other side looked up. A bolt shell struck him in the throat and blew his head and shoulders into mist. Phocron charged out of the door. Silonius went with him. Target runes lit in his sight. He fired, switched target and fired again, the roar of the shell merging with the boom of impact. They were in a small hangar. Gantries marched up plasteel walls. Beyond the closing blast doors he could see the glare of sunlight and the glint of stars.

There were guards, human shapes with guns and armour. He killed four before he had taken two paces. The rest of the team followed close behind him, fanning out and firing, the roaring hiss of weapons a wall of noise. He pivoted, scanning up. A guard in a dun uniform levelled a laslock. Silonius' shot hit the guard in the hand, punched through the gun and exploded in the stomach beyond. The guard's body ripped in two. A pulped tangle of flesh fell to the deck.

And then there was silence. The five Space Marines remained still for a second, weapons and eyes fixed on the edge of the chamber, waiting.

'Clear,' called Phocron. Silonius dropped his aim and looked back at the lighter. Its engines were still turning. Incarnus was crouched just inside the door.

'Out,' Silonius called, and gestured. The psyker did not move, but glanced around him like a startled dog. Something had happened to him since he got into the shuttle, something that had spooked him. Silonius felt a cold stillness form in his gut and spread out to his skin. Had the psyker seen something in his mind? He cut the thought loose. There was no time. 'Move, now!' he snarled, and Incarnus jumped as though whipped.

'We have seconds before the alarm goes,' growled Hekaron. 'Maybe a minute before they send a distress call.'

'By the time anyone hears it we will be gone,' said Phocron, flicking a hand signal to Kalix. The melta-armed warrior moved forwards. The

gun screamed and the nearest hatchway blasted into a scatter of molten
metal. They moved, striding, then running. The alarm began to scream
as the last of them cleared the glowing breach. Silonius kept Incarnus
in front of him, shoving the human on. Phocron and Orn took the
lead, running shoulder to shoulder as the corridor broadened. A pair
of guards came through a door in front of them, and were dead before
they could raise their weapons.

'How close is the transmission cluster?' called Phocron, as he put a
burst of bolt shells into a gun mount that folded out of a wall.

'I don't know!' shouted Incarnus, panting, his feet struggling to carry
him, as Silonius pushed him on. 'Somewhere near the core.'

Beside Phocron, Orn's hand went to the side of his helm.

'Signal from the *Wealth of Kings*. There is a monitor craft coming into
close signal range.'

'A patrol?' asked Phocron, and Silonius could hear the unspoken
second half of the question ring in his mind. *Or do they know we are
here? Are they coming for us?*

'Uncertain,' said Orn.

A squall of fire came down the passage to their rear, shot-cannon
rounds ringing off the walls. Hekaron grunted, stumbled and turned,
dropping to one knee, aiming his culverin as shots rang off his battleplate. The volkite beam speared down the corridor.

'Go,' he called. 'I have this.'

Silonius was sure he heard a grin in the words.

Phocron nodded, and the squad ran on. Incarnus was whimpering
now, and Silonius could feel static crawling up his fingers from where
his hand held the psyker's shoulder. The corridor was curving around to
the left, and a set of blast doors loomed above them. Yellow-and-black
hazard stripes covered the doors' metal. Phocron slowed and flicked
a sequence of signals out. Orn peeled away, dropping to the side of
the passage to cover both directions. Kalix stepped towards the blast
door, each movement as unhurried and precise as the movement of
an ancient timepiece. The melta lit and stabbed a beam at the door.

The metal rippled and began dripping as heat spread from the beam's focal point. The sound of gunfire from down the corridor beat against the whine of the meltagun.

'The *Wealth of Kings* says that the monitor is closing,' Orn hissed over the vox. 'It is still out of weapon range, but not for long.'

'Faster,' said Phocron. Kalix did not answer, but began to pan the melta beam across the door, gouging a glowing slash in the plasteel. One cut, two cuts, then the beam was gone.

'Explosives,' said Orn, detaching a cluster of krak grenades from his waist and throwing them to Phocron, who caught them and clamped them to the door beside the yellow-hot wounds.

'Detonate,' he called.

A metallic roar filled the corridor. The half-molten and scored doors blew inwards with a sound like an avalanche of metal. Silonius went through the breach and into the space beyond. Droplets of cooling metal pinged from his armour. Pillars of machinery circled the chamber within. Sparks tracked up and down their sides, and he felt static pull at his skin. A tech-priest with a face of lenses and brass turned from a column of wires, screens and key interfaces. He had a pistol in his hand.

Silonius' shot ripped the tech-priest's gun arm off at the shoulder. He shoved Incarnus forwards. The psyker stumbled, caught himself and staggered towards the central column. The tech-priest thrashed on the deck, reaching up for Incarnus with its remaining arm. Incarnus lashed a kick into the priest's face, then another, shattering the crystal lenses.

'Attend to your task,' growled Phocron at Incarnus, unlocking a canister from his waist and tossing it to the psyker. The human caught it, and began to strip the metal casing from the mass of wires and metal blocks within. He turned to the console and began to move around it, tracing clusters of cable with his fingers, muttering as he gulped breaths. His hands began to dance over keys and switches.

'They got a warning signal out,' said Incarnus. 'That monitor craft will know something is wrong, and soon so will everyone else.'

'Irrelevant,' said Phocron. 'Are you ready to transmit?'

'Ready,' said Incarnus.

'Transmit.'

Incarnus' movements became a spider dance, his breathing hard. The pillars of machinery pulsed. Coils of fresh sparks rolled up their sides. The air crackled.

'Transmitting,' said Incarnus.

Phocron turned to Kalix.

'Join Hekaron. Make sure the route back to the shuttle is clear.'

Kalix went to the wreckage of the door and ducked through. Incarnus had begun connecting cables to the mass of wires and metal blocks. Phocron turned to Silonius and nodded. 'Set the charges.'

Silonius unfastened a bandolier from his back and began to move around the chamber, clamping charges in place.

'The monitor craft is approaching weapon range,' came Orn's voice across the vox. 'If we do not get clear within the next three hundred and seventy seconds, we are not getting clear at all.'

Phocron began to reply, as a roar of gunfire rolled from the corridor.

'We are taking fire from both directions,' said Orn. 'This place has a larger garrison than we thought, and they seem to be of above average competence.'

'Hold,' said Phocron. 'We are coming.' He looked at Incarnus and Silonius.

The human spoke before being asked.

'Not ready yet. If you want this signal burst to reach its target I need more time.'

'Three more charges,' said Silonius, as he moved to the next charge.

'Twenty seconds,' said Phocron, moving towards the door, bolter ready.

Silonius paused over the charges he had already set. Incarnus finished connecting the device to the console, and began keying controls and flicking switches. Silonius moved closer, but the human did not seem to notice. The machine columns pulsed, and the central control gave a clatter of cogs. Out on the hull of the station, dishes rotated and aimed at the darkness. Incarnus pressed a last series of controls.

'It's loose,' Incarnus said, and only then seemed to notice Silonius standing above him. He hesitated, a note of uncertainty in his voice. 'We must...'

'Swing the array,' said Silonius. 'Inner-system transmission, broad focus.'

'But...'

'Now!'

Incarnus flinched back and began to work the consoles, swaying with every movement.

Silonius pulled the blade that had been with him since he woke up beneath the Palace. He held it up. The light of the sparks spread over its edge. He saw the symbols, hidden in the patina of the metal, etched into hair-thin scratches: codes, directions, frequencies. He pulled Incarnus aside. The human fell with a cry. Silonius' hands moved across the controls, faster and faster.

'What...?' yelped Incarnus, the words dying on his lips.

Silonius keyed the final command, turned and pulled the human to his feet. The machines sparked and whined as a third signal loosed from the signal array.

'Move!'

Incarnus shuddered and began to limp forwards.

'We are withdrawing,' came Phocron's voice across the vox.

Silonius grabbed the psyker's arm, lifted him from his feet and began to run.

Phocron was in the corridor outside, firing bursts into the dark. Explosions burst in the distance and las-fire scattered past them. He glanced at Silonius, fired a last burst, stood and began to run as well.

Silonius triggered the charges after twenty-five paces. There was an instant in which nothing happened, and then a series of rumbles rocked the floor and shivered through the air, drowning the sound of gunfire.

'Was the second signal sent?' called Phocron.

'It was sent,' said Silonius. Incarnus gave a small whimper.

They ran on, joining with Kalix and Hekaron, and charging back along the route to the hangar.

In the hangar, Ashul had the lighter hovering off the deck, engines pulsing with restrained power. Orn dropped from a gantry. Phocron was the last on board, vaulting onto the ramp as the lighter pivoted about. The engines shrieked, and the lighter punched into the void.

'The *Wealth of Kings* is on an interception course to pick us up,' said Ashul from the cockpit. 'We should be out of range of the monitor craft, unless it's a lot faster than it looks.'

'Did they get close enough to identify the *Wealth of Kings*?' asked Phocron.

'Difficult to know,' Ashul replied. 'It's possible.'

Phocron said nothing more.

From where he lay panting on the compartment floor, Incarnus looked up at Silonius for a second and then looked away. Silonius sat in silence, fresh purpose and secrets turning over in his head.

TWO

Imperial Fists frigate Unbreakable Truth,
docked with the Phalanx, *Terran orbit*

'HE IS WEAK and a coward,' said Archamus. Before him the pict-feed from within the cell showed Dowager-son Hyrakro lying on the floor, curled into a foetal ball. Behind the screens a speaker hissed with static and the sound of low weeping. The man they had taken from the mountaintop compound had done little but sob since he had gained full consciousness. They had returned to the *Unbreakable Truth*. The frigate was docked with the *Phalanx* in high orbit above Terra, like a pilot fish attached to a whale.

'Yes, he is both a coward and weak,' said Andromeda, looking up at him from the screen. 'Why does that worry you?'

Archamus paused, blinking. He had not been aware that his voice had carried any of the doubts that rolled through his mind. The healing skin on his back itched beneath his black robe. The hand of his bionic arm squeezed shut with a hiss and then snapped open.

'Why would the Alpha Legion use such flawed tools? Why would they trust him with anything of value?'

'They may not have had a choice. Even the most elaborate and finely

balanced plans must sometimes include weak links. The world outside
the Legions is not built uniformly.'

'Even within the Legions it is not,' said Archamus. Andromeda raised
an eyebrow, waiting for him to elaborate. He remained silent.

'They tried to kill him,' said Andromeda, at last. 'That suggests that
they both knew his weakness and needed to ensure his silence.'

'Perhaps,' said Archamus.

Andromeda's mouth opened and then closed.

'You don't want to know what he knows?' she said, and her voice
was cold.

'Want?' he asked, and could feel the edge in his voice. He looked at
her and saw her flinch. He shook his head, feeling the muscle tense
in his jaw. 'Just get it,' he said. On the screen Hyrakro twitched, and a
moan came from the speaker. 'All of it.'

He turned away and left the chamber.

ARMINA FEL WAS waiting for Archamus as he left the cell observation
chamber. Two warriors from Sotaro's squad stood guard to either side
of the door. They had orders to let no one enter, and to ensure that
anyone who entered the detention complex was moved on without
delay. But one did not question the Praetorian's personal astropath.
That she had boarded the *Unbreakable Truth* from the *Phalanx* without
asking permission was also unsurprising. There were few other beings
under the light of Sol who touched as many secrets as the woman who
stood in front of him, leaning on a black-and-silver staff.

'Lady,' he said, and bowed his head.

'Master of Huscarls,' she said, her voice cracking with age and fatigue.
She turned her head towards him, the white mane of hair shifting as
though rising on a breath of air that was not there. 'You requested audience with the primarch. I am here to take you to him.'

'Aboard the *Phalanx*?'

She nodded and began to walk down the corridor, back bent forwards,
staff tapping a slow rhythm on the deck. They climbed up through the

frigate's decks and crossed the docking limb to the *Phalanx*. An hour of travel saw them pass through chambers hung with hundreds of victory banners, and pass under the stone gaze of long-dead heroes. Archamus knew them all. Many of them he had known in life. Some he had seen die. He had the sudden feeling that he was alone, a relic of an age that belonged to the dead who now were stone.

'You are over a century older than me,' said Armina. It was the first thing she had said in hours, and it surprised him enough that he could only blink, as she continued. 'When I was born you were already a warrior, already a leader of armies. When you bore your Legion's banner I was a girl playing in the dust of what was once the Achaemenid Empire. When the Emperor took my sight I was still a girl, and you had served the Imperium for over a century. Yet here we are – the aged warrior and the crone.'

'You are looking in my mind,' he growled.

'Yes,' she said. 'The surface at least.'

'Why?'

'If your eyes are open they see the world around them,' she said, and sucked in a wheezing breath.

'Did your observation have a point?' he asked.

'Age is not time. It is the mark of service.'

'As you say,' he replied.

They walked on in silence, their steps marked by the tap of Armina Fel's cane.

Dorn waited for them in a small planning chamber close to the main strategium. Archamus noted that the Huscarls guarding the corridors and entrance to the chamber waited for the astropath to speak, rather than him, before admitting them.

I am not one of them, he realised, and felt something cold pass over the burned skin of his back. It was as it should be, but it felt like something else. Like a judgement.

The primarch did not look up as Archamus entered. Parchment and data-slates lay on the circular table, arranged in neat islands. Dorn wore armour, but had stripped the gauntlets from his hands. A set of multi-legged callipers lay under the fingers of the right, a brass stylus in the left. When he spoke it was to Armina Fel rather than Archamus.

'Phaeton?' he said, as though posing the next question in a discussion that Archamus' arrival had cut into. Armina Fel shook her head.

'No word. Though that could mean nothing.'

'Every silence means something.'

'Our communication with Phaeton has been facilitated by the relay station at Ashela. If there has been a problem with the station...'

'Whether we have lost a forge world, or if the enemy have taken Ashela station to blind us, it is becoming difficult not to presume the worst.'

'We will renew our efforts, lord,' said Fel, then dipped her head and shuffled out of the chamber. Dorn turned his eyes back to the parchments beneath his stylus. Archamus waited, feeling the moments pass with the scratching of lines and figures.

'How many did you lose?' said Dorn at last, looking up at Archamus.

'Four,' said Archamus. He did not need to ask what his primarch was referring to. The mission to the Hyrakro manse was hours old, but there was nothing in the actions of his Legion that was beyond Dorn's sight. 'Three brothers in the gunship that was lost, one on the ground.'

'A heavy price for one man.'

'It was a flawed mission in both planning and execution, too rushed and without contingency for wider possibilities.'

'And the target of the raid?' asked Dorn, his voice cold and emotionless, as his stylus continued its path across the parchment.

'Is in chains on the *Unbreakable Truth*. The... He is being put to the question now.'

'Has he given you answers?'

'Not yet, my lord, but...' Archamus felt the words drain out of his mouth.

Dorn's stylus stopped in its movement over the parchment. The primarch looked up. 'Why are you here then?'

'This task, lord. It... is not what we are. It is... not the war we were made for, nor the war we should be fighting.'

Dorn put the stylus down and straightened.

'Necessity,' he said.

'It is not what we were made for. We are conquerors, we are build-ers, we–'

'We are the last line against the darkness. Darkness, Archamus, not defeat but the swallowing of all that was and might be. We cannot fail.'

'And the necessities we face...'

'Are vile. Are terrible,' Dorn put the callipers down, and for a sec-ond Archamus thought he saw a flicker of weariness in his primarch's eyes. 'Are inevitable.'

'Lord, is that not what the Alpha Legion might say? That victory mat-ters more than how that victory is won? So much of this war happens in the dark. We hear its echoes, or see its fires on the horizon, but never know what might have been won or lost already. All unknown, all weights on the balance of disaster or survival. But that victory if won will be won here, and rest in our hands. The Imperium will stand, but only if the choices we make are pure.'

Dorn looked at Archamus, dark eyes boring into him, his face utterly still.

He remembered the Alpha Legionnaire's dead eyes looking up at him. *We know you. We know you all...*

Archamus shook his head.

'Why are we doing this? Of all the threats that might come against us, this is not one that demands such attention, let alone such secrecy. The more I think of it, the more I consider what has happened, the less sense it makes. A unit of Alpha Legion, ten units, a hundred. What could they truly do? And for what threat they do pose, the hunter cad-res of Malcador's Chosen are more skilled in hunting such foes.'

'Because I trust you,' said Dorn. 'And understanding is not required.'

Archamus blinked and bowed his head.

'By your will,' he said, and half turned to leave, but then stopped and the old question, asked of him decades before, rose to his lips. 'What are you afraid of, my lord?'

Dorn was silent for a second, and Archamus felt as though he could feel the tremor of vast thoughts turning behind the face of his primarch. Archamus held himself still, eyes steady, even as the instinct to kneel and ask forgiveness pulled at his old flesh.

'What will it cost?' said Dorn at last. 'We will have victory, because I will not allow us to fail. But what will that victory cost? Because, at the last, whatever that cost, it must be paid.'

'And what of the future we were to build, lord. Will it be built in the ashes of our honour?'

Dorn was silent, and for a moment Archamus thought he saw other faces in the shadow lines of his lord's face: Mortarion, Corax, Curze.

'That,' said Dorn at last. 'That is what I am afraid of.'

Archamus bowed his head, unable to hold his primarch's gaze any longer.

'I will follow your will and this duty to the end,' he said, and brought his hand to his chest in salute. 'I will not fail you.'

'No, you will not,' said Dorn.

ARMINA FEL WATCHED Archamus leave. The glow of his thoughts was like fire embers, brightness and heat crackling under cold layers of ash. She stepped back into Dorn's chamber. The primarch's mind was briefly a flame that shrank to darkness, hidden by force of will.

'What are your orders, lord?'

'It is time. Once Archamus' ship is loose, the *Phalanx* will move to the rendezvous with the fleet off Neptune. You are prepared?'

'Everything has been arranged between the other principal astropaths and me.'

Dorn nodded once in acknowledgement, and Armina knew that the gesture was both acknowledgement and dismissal. She did not move.

'Master Archamus... You did not tell him, lord?'

Dorn's mind flickered, but remained closed and dark.

'No,' he said. 'He has his duty, and I have mine.'

'Should he not–'

'Make what preparations you need to, mistress. We leave within the hour.'

'Of course, lord,' she said, and bowed her head.

KESTROS WAS WATCHING the monitor when the door opened. He did not look up. It was Andromeda. He could tell from the rhythm of her steps on the stone floor, light and smooth, like the movement of a feline predator. She stopped just beyond his arm's reach and looked at him for a second.

'I thought you were having your chest split open and sewn back together,' she said.

He said nothing. They had closed him up an hour before. The right-hand side of his chest was a layer of grafted flesh over a frame of plasteel and ceramite bolted to his bones. The pain was a storm still crackling through him, and he could taste blood with every breath.

When he neither moved nor answered, she turned to look at the monitors.

There were nine screens, each hung with cables and showing a different angle of the same image: the slumped form of Dowager-son Hyrakro. Chains led from loops on the wall to manacles locked around his wrists and ankles. He wore a plain shift of off-white, stained by sweat.

'He has been here for almost thirteen hours. The temperature in the cell will mean that he must soon begin to suffer adverse physiological effects.' Kestros paused, breathed, blood and pain bright on the edge of everything. 'I also notice that he has no water.'

Andromeda nodded. 'As it should be.'

He felt the muscles in his jaw tighten, his eyes still on the screen. As he watched, the man shook his head as though trying to shake himself awake. A low moan came from a vox speaker hung in the dark behind the screens.

'I am not going to kill him or tear him apart,' she snorted, and shook her head. 'You really are a creature of paradox. You will wade through blood and kill without mercy, but a thirsty man in chains brings out your righteous side.'

'You claim to know us so well...' he began.

'Better than you know yourselves,' she spat. 'My kind are numbered for our lives. I am Andromeda-17, but Andromeda-15 died by the hands of the Emperor's warriors. By your hands. You think that a veneer of honour is enough, that ideals wash blood from you?'

Kestros looked at her. The pain was there, holding his anger in a cage of sharp edges. She was staring at him, eyes dark and glittering, the slightest hint of teeth showing between her lips.

'You hate us,' he said, speaking the realisation as it came to him. She let out a breath and glanced away.

'How much love do you think winning an empire by slaughter buys?'

'We are the necessity of greater futures,' he said.

She laughed. 'You still think that? Blindness really is the greatest comfort.'

He let the questions go unanswered and the silence deepen. On the screen Hyrakro shuddered and stilled. The clinking of chains came from the speakers. Her words rolled around his thoughts, blurring with the lightning crackle of pain. She was trying to goad him. He knew that, but still there was the problem that she was here, and the will of both Archamus and the primarch had placed her there. Why would that be if everything she said was wrong?

'Why did you agree?' he asked. 'Why did you agree to serve the Emperor at the side of those you hate?'

Her expression shifted. Anger? Scorn? Surprise? Then she shrugged.

'It intrigues me,' she said, nodding at the screen, 'and I can't say that I like the alternatives offered by being on the other side.' She shivered. 'I am going to get on with this.' When she reached the door, she glanced back and jerked her chin at the screens. 'Feel free to stay and watch if you like.'

✠ ✠ ✠

THE AIR IN the cell was a thickening soup flavoured with sweat and the smell of machine oil.

Dowager-son Hyrakro could feel the moisture covering his body like a liquid second skin. He had been there for... He was not sure how long he had been there. He was trying to think of what was happening, and what might help get him out of the chains and heat, but his thoughts kept circling back to water.

Water. Cold and vast.

Water held in oceans and falling from the sky.

Water roaring down the pipes to fill deep pools.

Water sliding over the lip of a silver jug into a crystal glass.

Water–

The door to the cell opened. He blinked. His eyes had begun to close, pressed down over his eyes by heat and–

The slosh of liquid against metal.

He came to his feet, eyes staring at the silver jug and crystal cup. He lunged forwards, sweat scattering from him. The chains snapped taut, and the manacles yanked into his wrists and throat.

'It is warm in here, isn't it?'

He noticed the figure carrying the cup and ewer. A woman. No, a girl. A girl in ragged grey with a thin pale face and chromed hair. She took another step, and the sound of water sloshing in the silver jug was like the crash of ocean waves. He reached again, the noise of the chains rattling taut lost under the silken sound of water.

'Warm enough to give you a thirst,' said the girl as she sat down on the floor. She put the jug and cup down in front of her. Hyrakro could see that there were beads of moisture on the outside of the jug. As he watched, a drop slid down the metal.

'Please...' he moaned.

'Of course,' the girl said, and filled the cup to the brim. He watched the water splash into the crystal and rise up the sides. The girl put the jug down and slid it over the floor towards him. Water sloshed over the rim of the cup, and he whimpered. 'Go on,' said the girl, and he glanced up. She nodded at him. 'Go on, drink.'

He reached out, hand a blur, chain rattling... and stopped. His hand was a finger's breadth from the cup. He stretched, but could not reach it. He collapsed back, his mind throwing up thoughts through the haze of his thirst.

He was in trouble, he knew that, something to do with the war, something that had brought the Angels of Death to him. They had brought him here, and that meant that the girl was with them. She wanted something from him. That made sense to Hyrakro; everyone wanted something.

He starred at the cup of water. His tongue was too dry to lick his lips.

'Drink, honoured dowager-son,' said the girl, and he looked at her.

Dark eyes glittered above her thin smile.

'I...' he said, the words hissing across his tongue. 'I... don't have anything you want.'

'You should drink, then we can talk about what I want.' She reached out, dipped a finger into the brimming cup and licked the water from it. 'Just water – no neurotoxins, no pain enhancers, just an end to thirst.' She nudged the cup forwards so that it was just in reach.

He hesitated.

And then the cup was in his hand, and the water was pouring into his mouth and down his throat, so cool that it seemed sweet. He could feel it running over his chin and spattering down his front, and the cup was empty and he was gasping with relief.

'Thank you,' he said, still breathing hard, and put the cup down. 'But I don't have anything that you want.'

'You are a member of a trading dynasty controlling one-tenth of the trade on a planet that rules the galaxy. I think there is a great deal that you have that I might want.'

He laughed, the sound bubbling up from the euphoria of quenching his thirst.

'You should check your facts, girl. You called me dowager-son, so perhaps you should know that my only link to the Hysen is that title. I married in, you see, and then my delightful bride died, and the cartel don't entrust anything to someone without a living blood tie. No blood, no stake.'

He licked his lips and looked at the jug of water. The wetness in his mouth was fading, and the heat was pressing his skin again, squeezing sweat from his pores.

He picked up the cup.

'No, no, no,' the girl tutted. 'You see everything is situational – strength, respect, value. In this room, right now, this water is everything to you, or will be by the time the cup you just drank sweats out of your skin. Yesterday when you were sitting, sipping something rare and expensive it would have meant nothing to you. Circumstances change, and everything changes with them.'

He blinked.

'I... I don't understand what you–'

'Come on, Hyrakro. You are weak, but not entirely stupid. You might not be of the blood of the Hysen, they might not trust you or give you positions of real responsibility, but you still have privileges, knowledge of how they work, all those little connections and seams in trade operations, all those gaps and grey areas which exist.'

'I don't know what you are talking–'

'Don't! Just don't even try to be *that* stupid!' The girl was shouting, the sound so sudden that it struck him like a whip. She was on her feet, looming above him, breathing into his face as she spat out words. 'I know already. I don't need you to confess to know that you do favours, the right credentials for trans-atmospheric shipments, small loads added to cargos, veneers of respectability over layers of excrement. All while you take favours and coin in return, enjoying the sensation of tainting the business of the family who would not let you really be one of them.'

She straightened, the anger and intensity gone as quickly as it had come. She bent down, picked up the cup and drank a mouthful, made a face and spat it out. 'In my world those facts are valueless.' She upended the cup carelessly onto the floor, walked back to the place where she had sat before and resumed her cross-legged position.

Hyrakro looked at the cup and the water spreading across the floor.

'Who are you?' he asked, and heard the thinness in his own voice.

'A representative of the master of your world.' She saw a shiver run through his face despite the heat. 'Did you think the Space Marines were just for show?'

He shook his head. Part of him wanted to be angry, to shout and bluster that they could not do this, that he would not stand for it. But another part of him thought that the girl would just laugh at him.

He licked his lips, nodded and looked at the cup.

'Please?' he asked again.

She gave a tiny shake of her head.

'I don't want your capitulation, Hyrakro. That was a given as soon as we started to talk. What is of value to me is your cooperation, your complicity in helping undo what you have helped bring about.'

'I...'

'I know you don't know what I am talking about. Be thankful for that. So let's start with what you do know. The little off-the-book favours and manipulations, in whose world did they have value? Who paid you for those?'

The heat was inside his skin again, pressing in and rubbing dust into his tongue. He bit his lip and looked at the cup.

'Later,' she said, moving the cup closer to her. 'Now you talk.'

So he did. He told her about how he grafted secret consignments into Hysen shipments, used their good name and charter to move people and goods between Terra's hives, starports and orbital stations, to help people who wanted to keep their business discreet and unrecorded.

The girl listened and asked questions, and he talked and talked all the way down from the generalities to the first deal he had cut with the Venusian smugglers five decades ago. He told her all of it, until his lips had cracked.

'That's it,' he said at last, blinking at the grey haze that was creeping into his sight. 'I don't know what else I can say.' He looked at the girl and the water jug, and felt a twinge of disgust at the pleading he could feel on his face.

She looked at him for a long moment and then poured. The water rang as it sloshed into the cup. She picked up the cup, as though to pass it to him.

'One thing,' she said, and hesitated.

He looked at her, teeth gritting as he tried not to whimper. He wasn't feeling the heat much now, just the dull grey haze that was flowing from his eyes down his nerves. He nodded and shivered.

'Ask,' he said.

'You helped someone get a shipment into Damocles Starport,' said the girl. 'A big shipment, one needing clearance codes for a macro transporter, identification seals for a crew, maybe even a bit of dynastic regalia to dress the whole thing up.'

He nodded. He remembered it: a big deal, expensive for the other party, worthwhile for him.

'Yes...'

'For whom did you do that little favour?'

He blinked. His thoughts were moving, but not connecting properly. The heat...

'Hyrakro...' said the girl gently. 'These truths have no value for you any more. Not in the world you now live in.' She raised the cup in front of him again, half a taunt, half a promise.

'The Venusians,' he said. 'One of the smuggler concerns. Not a big outfit.'

'But not a small one either,' she added.

He nodded.

'One of your older associations?' she asked.

Another nod. Words felt like pins holding his tongue down.

'The oldest?' she asked.

Nod. He was floating free...

Grey all around him, and a feeling like he was floating in water...
Water...

He barely felt the fingers tilt his chin upwards, or the first drops fall into his mouth, then it was pouring into him.

She was right. The Venusians were his oldest clients, the first in fact. Without that first approach and suggestion that he might be able to help them, he would probably have never begun.

The water stopped, and he felt the cup being put into his hands. His vision was a little clearer.

The girl put the jug down beside him.

'Do you have a way of contacting them?' she asked.

Nod. He was trying to get enough control back in his hands to put the cup down next to the jug.

'How?'

The jug was wobbling in his hands.

'A signal...' he said, managing to get the word past his teeth. 'Don't know how they pick it up, but they do.'

'What signal?'

He told her. He tilted the jug towards the cup.

'Codes, phrases, protocols?'

He winced as he listed the details.

He managed to pour the water. The first splash of water missed the cup, but then it was bubbling and churning down, and then into his throat, and he could not remember pouring or filling, just the sensation of it filling him, and knowing that it was everything.

When at last he looked around, the girl was gone and the jug was empty.

'TOO BARBARIC FOR you?'

Kestros looked up as Andromeda stepped back into the observation room. The grainy light of the monitors washed her features, but there was a gleam and sparkle to both her eyes and smile.

'He barely resisted,' he growled. 'Are you sure he told you the truth?'

'As he understands it, yes. He told me everything. It was inevitable given human weakness, and he is very human and very weak.'

'It's not a trick by the Alpha Legion?'

'No,' she said. 'Or if it is, then it's more subtle than I am.' She paused, frowned, then shook herself.

'Is that your personification?' he asked, and saw her blink in surprise. 'You are bred for subtlety?'

She blinked again and then laughed.

'Not quite, but close. It's a matter with more facets than that, and we don't talk about it outside our own kind. Not in detail at least. Think of it more as a focusing of familiar things into one person.'

'Does that focus have a name?'

She shook her head, the gesture small but not precise.

'I understand human weakness very well, and I like to win, let's leave it at that.'

'What use would a gene-cult have for such qualities?'

'The same use that any culture has for things that are sharp and nasty. And who said my existence was about usefulness? You and your kind were made to be used, but not everyone is the same.'

She grinned again, and he had to fight the feeling that the expression was there to confuse him. He frowned and was about to ask a question when the chamber door opened.

Kestros saluted. Archamus nodded as he entered. He looked worn, the darkness around his eyes deeper, the lines on his face drawn tighter.

'What did you get from him?' he asked, and Kestros caught an edge in the old warrior's voice, a weary sharpness.

Andromeda told him. When she was done, Archamus grunted, then lapsed into silence. Kestros waited. The pain in his torso rose to fill his awareness as the silence grew.

'Send a signal to the Venusian smugglers,' said Archamus at last. 'Use the frequencies and protocols he gave us.'

'What should it say?' asked Andromeda, and Kestros noticed that her voice held none of the acid he had come to expect, as though something in Archamus had stilled her to caution.

'That someone has come for Dowager-son Hyrakro. That he is fleeing Terra on course for Venus and wants help.' He looked at Kestros. 'Pick a location in the Grave belt, somewhere quiet and dark. Add the location coordinates as a rendezvous.'

Kestros nodded.

'A direct approach...' began Andromeda carefully.

Archamus looked at her.

'Yes,' he said.

'They might not come for him,' she said, meeting his gaze.

'They tried to kill him. He is alive. They will come.'

'And then?' she asked.

Kestros felt the old warrior stiffen, control rolling off him like a blast of heat from a fire. He felt the hairs prickle up his neck.

'We surround them, capture them and use them to lead us to whatever else is out there.'

'Not destroy them?'

'If we destroy them we may leave the greater threat intact.'

Kestros shook his head. 'This is not a war we–'

'It is the war we are fighting,' said Archamus, his voice cold. 'Follow my orders, sergeant. Ready the squads and prepare plans for the engagement once the ambush site is determined.'

Kestros felt the blood run cold under the skin of his face.

'By your will,' he said.

'MASTER?'

The armoury servitor droned the question. Archamus clamped his teeth shut. The servitor tilted its iron-masked face, its calliper fingers holding the back plate of armour in place. The connections between his bionics and the healing flesh of his back sparked fresh pain up his nerves. He held himself still, his gaze fixed forwards. The cluster of servitors waited, frozen in mid movement, the pieces of his armour and weapons held still. He felt his connection to the pain dim.

'Continue,' he said.

'Compliance,' the servitors said, and began to lock the pieces of armour over his limbs. The pain rose again, and he let it dissolve into the cold of his thoughts.

'Lord,' came the voice from beyond the light of the servitors' arc torches.

'Approach, sergeant,' he said. Kestros stepped closer and saluted.

'The squads are ready, honoured master.' The sergeant kept his head bowed, but his posture was tense, the set of his face an ill-fitting mask.

'Good,' Archamus said, and was about to dismiss Kestros, when the words faded from his tongue. For the first time in many lifetimes he felt tired: tired and worn. He breathed out and the sound made Kestros look up, a frown on the younger warrior's face.

'Honoured master...' he said carefully. 'Did you know I was called a master when I was only a captain? Not because of the warriors I commanded or the wars I had fought, but because of what I had built. Stone and steel, fortresses and cities. I have raised hundreds into being. I was a master builder before I was anything else.'

'Are you not still that?'

Archamus was silent. As the question turned over, the last of his armour plates settled into place on his form. He had helped his lord in the fortification of Terra, and the building of the orbital battlements around Saturn and Pluto. But that was not creation – there was no beauty or truth or hope to it. Only necessity.

'No. I am not,' he said at last.

Kestros' mask of control was still in place, but the anger behind it had slid into something else, something that echoed in his eyes as he stared at Archamus. 'But you could be again. Once this war is done.'

'What will be left to build on? What things will such an age need to be built?'

'What will you do then?'

'Things change,' said Archamus. 'People change. That is the judgement of time. Of all things it is one of the few that we cannot defy.'

'You sound as though you were different once.'

The servitors stood back, cables snapped free of power connections.
Archamus felt the weight of the armour hang briefly on his limbs,
and then the fibre bundles meshed with his nerves, and the strength
of the armour and his body were one. He stepped forwards, and for a
moment the weariness within dimmed.

'Everything was different once,' he said.

THREE

THEY ALL LOOKED at Phocron as Sork finished speaking. The Headhunter Prime held his gaze steady on the scavenger captain. Myzmadra felt the silence run through the chamber and begin to settle. Each of the Space Marines was still. Even Phocron's continual flow of movement had paused.

'It is certain that it is him?' asked Phocron.

'The signal coding and key phrases are correct. It's him.'

Phocron nodded, not blinking.

'How easily could what this merchant knows be used against us?' asked Silonius. The hulking warrior stood against one of the walls, armoured but face bared.

'We are only at one stage removed from the smuggler clans. If our opponents find them then they get Sork's associates in the Venusian collectives, then they get the name of this ship, then they cut away until they find where it has been, and from there...' Phocron left the word hanging.

'A low probability of events unfolding like that,' said Orn softly. He sat closest to Myzmadra, and she could see the slight raising of an eyebrow that turned the statement into a question. He was running his bare palms over each other.

'Yes,' said Phocron, 'but we are moving in a volatile section of the operation. Small chances could now have a disproportionate effect on the outcome if we are not careful.'

Orn shrugged and looked at his hands, continuing to run them slowly over each other, palm to palm. Myzmadra found her eyes pulled to the movement. In someone as precisely still as Orn, it was like a scream.

Not for the first time she wondered at the minds of these warriors. They had just learned that Sork's contacts in the Venusian smugglers had received a signal. The signal was from a man called Hyrakro, a dowager-son of the Hysen Cartel and one of the assets the Legion had used in the opening stages of its current operation. The man was supposed to have died, along with two other assets whose continued existence held more risk than opportunity. The warrior they had left on Terra, the one who had taken the honorific Alpharius, was supposed to have eliminated Hyrakro. The news from Sork's contacts meant that mission had failed.

The fact that it also must mean that the enemy were on their trail, and their Legion brother was most likely dead, had not even been remarked on. All that mattered now was how they responded. Did they eliminate Hyrakro themselves or get a proxy to do it for them?

Their discomfort at that choice was what shouted from Orn's fidgeting, Phocron's stillness and Hekaron's silence. They did not like having to respond to circumstance. They created circumstance and marshalled confusion. For all of their obsession with the fluidity of war, they were used to control.

'He dies,' said Phocron at last. 'That is my decision. No loose ends, not at this stage.' He looked at Sork. The scavenger captain gave a small flinch, but then controlled himself. 'Get your contacts to confirm the rendezvous and then make best speed for it. We are going to do this with our own hands.'

Sork nodded and turned to go. The man looked shaken, but he was good at hiding it.

Phocron looked around the assembled team.

'The ship will hold at a distance. An execution element will go to the rendezvous in a lighter, confirm the kill and withdraw. We exchange signals every five minutes – two missed and the ship runs.'

Myzmadra nodded.

'The execution element?' she asked.

'I will go myself, and you,' Phocron said, nodding at Myzmadra. 'He will be expecting smugglers so you will be our human face. We must confirm identity before termination.'

'I should go too,' said a thin voice, and they all looked around. Incarnus met their stares and shrugged. 'The smugglers would never come alone, and if you want to be certain that this Hyrakro has not already been compromised, you need me to have a peek in his brain before you turn it to mist.' The psyker bit his upper lip as silence answered his words, but he did not drop his eyes.

Phocron nodded at last.

'You are right. You come.'

'You need a back-up,' said Silonius, and Phocron looked around. 'If this is not what it seems, or if there is a problem, you will need cover.'

Phocron looked at Silonius and nodded again.

'Agreed,' said Phocron.

Silonius looked up and his eyes met Myzmadra's. She felt a cold surge in her skin. There was something about Silonius that she could not identify, something that she had noticed more in the time since the strike on the signal station. It was as though there were something else watching her from inside the warrior's eyes.

Artefact 9-Kappa-Mu
The solar void

THE VOID ARTEFACT had turned around the sun since before the earliest charts of the Solar System existed. The Red Priests of Mars had given it what passed for its name. They had labelled it Artefact 9-Kappa-Mu, but while the dry collection of symbols and letters implied something easily classified and indexed, the truth was that neither the tech-priests, nor any of the other organisations that had endured from the Dark Age of Technology, knew what it was.

A geodesic sphere of black metal, thirty kilometres in diameter, the artefact looked to the eye like a dark moon in search of a parent planet. Beneath its outer layer, passages threaded between a honeycomb of vast spaces open to the void. Huge, ragged holes sat open on its surface, and a pall of debris hung around it like a cloak. The debris, just like the artefact, had always been there, resisting the natural forces that should have pulled it into the great drifts long ago. The greatest mystery, though, was that it was invisible to anything but touch or natural sight. Auspexes looked straight through it, and its substance defied both technology and scholarship.

There had been expeditions, analysis, sifting of the records compiled by the scholars of the Conservatory, but all attempts to discover its origin or purpose had failed. There had been attempts to destroy it, to clear it from the reaches between Terra and Venus. Those attempts, like the attempts to understand its nature, had failed. Melta, seismic and graviton charges had not scratched its main structure. So it remained, bearing its prosaic title and surrounded by satellites which broadcast warnings to any vessels that came close.

Of all the corners of the Solar System, there were few darker.

Silonius reflected upon this as he hugged the shadow at the edge of the chamber. The location for the rendezvous was in a part of the tunnel network that had been the base for one of the Mechanicum's attempts to discover the artefact's secrets. The structure defied all attempts to bond anything to it, so the tech-priests had threaded plasteel passages and chambers through the black metal tunnels. Smugglers had used it and abandoned it since, but there was still air inside the tunnels. There was no gravity so they had advanced to the chamber with the thump-thump of boots mag-locking to the floor. They were not going deep into the artefact, but even the scant few hundred metres felt like they were walking past an invisible barrier into the unknown.

Silonius blink-cycled from infra-sight to dark-vision as he moved. The corridors shifted between total black, hazed green and the stark colours of hot and cold. Myzmadra and Incarnus were ahead of him, grey shapes brought alive by the orange of their body heat.

'Nothing on the auspex,' said Phocron across the vox. The Headhunter Prime was twenty paces behind them. 'Though this place...'

'I do not like it,' said Silonius, echoing Phocron's unvoiced thought. 'A better sight for a counter-ambush you could not find. There could be anything out there, and we would not see it until it was on top of us.' Tactical runes fizzed with static in his helmet display as he spoke. The substance of the artefact made them doubly blind.

'Indeed, but that applies to our quarry as much as to us,' said Phocron.

Ahead of them, Myzmadra went still and folded into the side of the corridor. Incarnus followed her a second later. Silonius saw the humans' movement and halted, pivoting and dropping to one knee to cover the passage behind them.

'This looks like the place,' whispered Myzmadra. 'No sign of anything.'

'Move into position and wait,' said Phocron.

'Going firm,' said Silonius, shifting his position to behind a block of cold machinery, locked to one side of the passage. He flicked a glance over his shoulder to make sure that his sightlines extended cleanly in both directions. He could see Myzmadra and Incarnus crouched next to an opening into a larger chamber beyond. Both were orange-yellow blurs in cold blue. Phocron had vanished, the heat from his armour a smudge in the air.

Silonius steadied his heartbeats, cycling them down to a low pulse of utter calm. He did not like this. He did not like the fact that they had been drawn here. He understood Phocron's reasoning and could not fault its logic, but...

He blinked. The passage in front of him fizzed in its shades of blue and black. A sharp tingle ran up his arms. His fingers suddenly felt like they were locked in ice. He fought not to let out a gasp. Something vast and cold was rising from within him, clawing up the base of his spine until...

He was moving through the Sigma, the warrior who had come to escort him walking in front of him.

They passed through the ship, winding through corridors he had not trodden in years, descending bit by bit into the deep regions, where the air tasted of stagnant water and electric charge. There were few lights here; those who tended the machine heart of the ship needed no light to see. Red furnace-light glowed from around corners, and the hammer pulse of reactors trembled through the floor and walls. The route they followed was winding, but not cryptic. He wondered about that even as he memorised each detail. He had a feeling that they were going to somewhere he had never been before, somewhere hidden on the ship he knew so well. That did not surprise him; it was the Legion's way. What made him wonder was that there was no attempt to conceal the route. That openness held... possibilities.

He almost missed the moment when they reached their destination. His escort simply opened a hatchway, as he had done twenty-one times already, and they both stepped through. But no corridor waited on the other side. Vastness struck and enfolded him as the hatch clanged shut behind. The sound of magnetic bolts thudding into place rolled through the dark. He turned fast, but his escort was already facing him, bolter raised and steady.

'What is this?' said Silonius.

'An audience,' said the warrior.

Silonius held still. At his back he could feel the space booming against his senses. The air was cool. The smell of dust and weapon oil hung on the edge of every breath. His escort stared at him, the glow of his eyepieces a slash of green in the dark. The hum of active armour pulsed against the sound of his own hearts. Nothing else moved in the chamber.

'Who called me here?' Silonius growled. 'Who are you?'

'I am Alpharius,' said the warrior.

MYZMADRA GLANCED AT Incarnus and moved forwards into the chamber. The blackness rolled back in front of her dark-vision goggles. She could see the nearest wall and the floor sketched in granular blue. Incarnus edged forwards slowly, head twitching as he glanced around. Like her he was wearing a patched void suit. He had a shot-pistol strapped to his thigh, but he kept his hands empty. His gloved fingers opened and closed as he moved, like the feelers of an anemone waving in ocean water.

She hefted the volkite charger she had brought as she glanced around again. The weapon was big, heavy and could reduce a body to ash in a single shot. She liked it a lot. She didn't like this mission, though, and she liked the inside of the artefact even less. She could not shake the feeling that she was inside a cage. She wanted to be in cover, to be out of sight, but her job was to be obvious.

Somewhere off in the dark, Phocron and Silonius would be waiting. Where, she did not know. Like so much about the Legion there was strength in ignorance, even in the smallest things. If there was a problem, then she could not accidentally betray their positions. The element of surprise, supreme in war, would be maintained. She had learned that lesson before she had been recruited. She had always wondered if it was that quality which the Alpha Legion had seen in her. She hoped so. It was a better quality than a willingness to work against the system that had created her.

'Someone is coming,' Incarnus whispered over the vox.

She felt her muscles tense and forced them to relax.

'How many?' she asked.

'Just one, at least I think so.'

'You don't *know* so?'

'This place, it–'

'Quiet!' she hissed, because off in the dark a dot of light had appeared. She flicked the arming switch on her charger. The gun began to buzz with readiness. The dot of light was bobbing in the dark, growing larger. 'Shine a light,' she said, quietly. 'Give them something to come to.'

Incarnus pulled a flare from a pouch on his suit. It lit with a burst of pink light. He tossed it onto the floor in front of them. Myzmadra's goggles blanked as they flooded with light and then gave the world back to her. The chamber was bigger now, stretching up to a flat high ceiling. Gantries and hoists sat in the centre of the space, like a forest of metal struts, hung with creepers of chain. A short, fat figure was walking towards them. It had a glow-globe clutched in one hand and was moving with the staggering steps of someone not used to exertion.

'Is it him?' she asked.

'Can't tell.'

'Why–'

'He is thinking about the light, and how much he wants to sit down, and...'

'Yes?'

'Water,' said Incarnus, puzzlement edging in his voice. 'He isn't thirsty, but for some reason he is thinking about water.'

'Try harder.'

'I am, but without letting him know what I am doing, that's not as easy as you might think.'

She went silent and waited, focusing on keeping her heartbeat level.

The figure stopped twenty paces from them.

'I...' said a male voice, that even through a speaker was vibrating with nerves. 'I am a wanderer in... in... a lost kingdom.'

She paused, her finger on the trigger of her gun.

The code phrase was the one given in the signal setting up the rendezvous, but that did not mean that this was Hyrakro. If she shot now, and he was watching from further back... She needed to be sure. She glanced at Incarnus, but for some reason the psyker had moved closer to the figure.

'Did you come on a lighter?' asked Incarnus suddenly. The fat figure with the glow-globe flinched.

'I... I... I am a wanderer in a lost kingdom.'

'I heard you,' snapped Incarnus, 'but how did you get here? Where is your shuttle?'

'I...'

'Incarnus, what are you doing?' she said into the vox.

'Have you confirmed the target's identity?' Phocron's voice broke into the vox.

'Where is your shuttle?'

The man was backing away from Incarnus. The globe was shaking in his grip. He glanced behind him.

Cold snapped through Myzmadra's nerves. In her mind the man turned to look back into the dark behind him in exquisite and terrifying slowness. Her finger tensed on the trigger of her charger.

'Have you confirmed the identity–'

Myzmadra spoke the answer to the code phrase, the words echoing loud in the dark emptiness. 'I am a guardian of a forgotten city. You stand at the gates, traveller.'

The man with the glow-globe froze in place. She could see his eyes wide and dark behind his void suit visor. His mouth began to open to reply.

'No!' shouted Incarnus, and suddenly the psyker was leaping forwards. Myzmadra began to bring her gun up, but the psyker was fast, faster than she had ever seen him move before. And suddenly her muscles were lead, and there was frost exploding across her visor, as she felt Incarnus' will clamping over her own.

'They are going to kill you,' Incarnus was shouting. 'Get us to your shuttle. Run! Now!'

Then blinding light stole the world from her eyes.

'I am Alpharius,' said the warrior in the dream.

Silonius laughed, the sound booming in the dark of the chamber. The warrior in front of him lowered his weapon and reached up to release his helm.

The light in the eyepiece vanished. The helmet came free. Silonius met the eyes beneath and knelt, head bowed.

'Lord,' said Silonius, and now it was Alpharius' laughter that echoed in the empty air.

'Rise,' said the primarch. 'My method of summoning you rather undermines the need for formality, do you not think?'

Silonius rose and met Alpharius' eyes, dark in a still face. A spark of doubt filled his mind. There were many within the Legion who bore the deliberate likeness of the primarch, some of them so exact in their appearance that only prolonged observation might reveal the deception. Silonius himself was one such individual, but there were hundreds of others. Then there was the fact that Alpharius was only one face of a coin with two sides, though few outsiders knew it. Lord Omegon was not just the same in looks as his twin, but identical in his superhuman nature. Added to this was the fact that both primarchs and their legionnaires often bore the name Alpharius as a form of grim jest combined with a method of sowing confusion. True, he had felt a twinge of command the moment he looked on his summoner's face, but did that mean this was truly his primarch?

He forced the doubts down.

'How may I serve?' Silonius asked Alpharius. Around him the vast darkness of the chamber trembled as some distant machine woke and sent a shudder through the Sigma's *hull. The beat of his hearts seemed to rise to the distant sound, as the doubt needled in his mind, persistent and shrill.*

Is this a lie?

Alpharius was silent for a second, then stepped past Silonius into the space beyond. Shafts of light appeared in the dark, marching away into the far reaches of the chamber.

Silonius saw objects sitting on plinths in each pool of light. A set of four rings sat on top of an obsidian pillar at the centre of the nearest shaft. Branching marks ran between green gems circling each ring. In another sat a pauldron, the rearing hydra of the Legion worked in bronze on a field of enamelled blue scales. Further off he could see more fragments of armour and weapons, each glimmering and brilliant.

'You doubt it is truly me, when before you were so certain,' Alpharius said, and smiled, but his eyes were still and unblinking. 'An understandable reaction. Do you know what this is?' He gestured at the object in one of the pillars of light. It was a spear, as tall as a mortal man, both ends capped with blades whose edges glinted sharply. Serpentine bodies wound across the black of the shaft in golden inlay. Silonius knew what it was, and if he had

any doubts as to the truth of Alpharius' presence, they should have vanished at that moment. But the doubts lingered.

'It is the Sarrisanata, the Pale Spear,' he said, 'symbol of our mastery of war, the hydra's tooth, the weapon of our true heart.' He looked at Alpharius. 'Your weapon.'

The primarch reached into the shaft of light and plucked the spear from its stand. He spun it as he stepped back, the gesture so smooth and fast that it made no sound. He held the spear up with one hand. The tip of one of the blades was a finger's width from Silonius' face. The primarch looked at Silonius from the other end of the spear.

Neither moved.

Then the spear spun back. Alpharius held it up again, this time with both hands gripping the haft. He twisted, and a series of clicks sounded, like the murmur of a dozen tiny locks all turning at once. He twisted again, hands a brief blur. The clicks rippled on, and then there was a single, loud crack. The blades unlocked from the shafts broke into shards, each a razor sliver that gave no hint of the whole it had once been part of. The spear shaft split, once, twice, three times. Alpharius placed each piece on the empty stand as it came free. The whole process had taken only three seconds.

'And now?' asked Alpharius. 'What is it now?'

'It is still the spear,' replied Silonius, without hesitation.

Alpharius gave a small nod and then picked up one of the blade shards, and handed it to Silonius.

'And now?'

'It is still the spear. No matter how many times it is broken, it is still the spear.'

Alpharius nodded. It was an old lesson explained in many ways, and put into practice in many more.

'A whole of many parts, a weapon of many parts, but which can come together. The many that are one.'

For a moment, Silonius thought the primarch was going to emphasise the point by rebuilding the spear, but he picked up another splinter of the blade. Alpharius lifted the sliver in his right hand and flexed his left. The *gauntlet peeled back from the flesh beneath with a series of soft clicks. Silo-nius watched in silence, wondering what was happening. Alpharius looked at the bare flesh, then sliced the shard across the tip of one finger. A bead of blood formed in the instant before the wound closed. Alpharius scraped the blood from his fingertip with the blade shard and held it out to Silonius, a red pearl balanced on gold.*

'We wear lies as our armour, but the greater the deception the more we must trust one another.'

Silonius looked at the tiny sphere of blood and understood. He reached out and took the shard. It felt like a feather in his hand. He brought it to his lips. Alpharius' eyes were steady on his. He touched the blood drop to his tongue and swallowed.

He gasped, reeling, fighting to breathe. Partial memories exploded in his mind: the image of a long stone hall and three figures turning to look at him, a man shouting one word at him the second before a bolt ripped him apart, and then the glowing explosion that might have been pain, or birth, or revelation. And on and on in a rush of glimpses and sensations. The moment passed, and Silonius found himself on his hands and knees. The deck of the ship twisted one last time beneath him and then was still. He looked up, breathing hard.

'I do not think that separating truth from seeming was what my father intended when He implanted His Legions with the ability to glimpse the minds of others by tasting their blood.' Alpharius smiled, and this time his eyes glittered with cold amusement. 'But it is a useful side effect.'

'Lord...' began Silonius, but Alpharius cut him off by reaching down and pulling him to his feet.

'It has been a while, Harrowmaster,' said the primarch. 'Your suspicion does you more credit than credulity would have.'

Silonius felt pride and caution surge and retreat in his hearts.

'Why am I here, lord? Why did you summon me?'

And the answer fell away into the present with a roar of gunfire.

Stark, white light was pouring down the passage from the direction of the rendezvous chamber. Silonius' mind was rolling with scraps of sight and sound.

'I am Alpharius.'

'How may I serve?'

Silonius ran down the passage and the ghosts of the past followed him.

MYZMADRA FELT INCARNUS' hold on her will break, and she dived to her right. A burst of bolter fire ripped through where she had been standing. She rolled and came up. Frost still covered her visor, shining white in brilliant light. She hit the helmet release and yanked it free. Beams of light sliced across the chamber. She could see figures pouring out of doors at the other end, figures in power armour. Yellow armour, laurels and black lightning haloing the emblem of clenched fists. The sons of Rogal Dorn had found them.

Incarnus was fifteen paces away, clutching Hyrakro and shouting something that she could not hear. She brought her charger up and fired. The beam flashed wide. One of the Imperial Fists turned to look at her, boltgun rising at the same moment. Her augmented reflexes snapped her aside as the bolt exploded where she had been. She dived for a coil of chains at the base of a gantry as the burst of fire followed her. She came up behind the cover and snapped a shot off.

'Phocron!' she shouted into the vox. 'Silonius!'

Static washed back at her as a bolt-round hit the heap of chains. Broken links showered into the air. She ducked low as another round hit, and then another. An Imperial Fists legionary moved into sight on her left. She fired. The beam hit the Space Marine's chest. Ceramite flashed to red. She feathered the trigger, raking the beam across his torso. Blackened chunks of armour exploded from the impact.

'Phocron!' she shouted, but there was no answer, and part of her already knew there would be none. She had served the Legion for fifteen years, all the way back to the 670th expeditionary fleet. There had been disasters in those years, huge and echoing disasters that she had come through with death breathing down her back. But she had survived, and never doubted that she would. Now she was certain that it would end here, not in a grand failure, but in a simple ambush that they had walked straight into.

Another legionary came into her line of sight, gun up and aimed at her.

She did not see where Phocron came from. One second the Imperial Fist was there, and the next there was just an expanding sphere of plasma. She gasped, clamping her eyes shut as neon bruises swam across her vision. She forced them open in time to see Phocron sprint from an opening in the chamber wall. He threw another grenade as he moved, and another ball of plasma bloomed into being. She could see the shapes of Imperial Fists crumpling within the burning sphere.

'Do you have the target in sight?' said Phocron's voice over the vox. He was firing as he moved, raking bolt shells across the opposite side of the chamber, moving without pause, a blur of armour and gunfire.

Myzmadra glanced around her cover, found that she was clear for another five paces and sprinted to the base of another gantry. She could see Incarnus still struggling with Hyrakro. She raised her weapon sight, finger poised on the trigger.

'I have him, but Incarnus is in the shot.'

'Take them,' said Phocron, 'both of them.'

She fired without hesitation. The volkite beam hit true. Hyrakro, dowager-son of the Hysen Cartel, came apart in an explosion of embers and sparks. Incarnus dived aside as she pulled the trigger again. The beam caught his left hand, and he hit the floor shrieking as his arm burned into ash. She switched aim, and...

A huge figure in golden-yellow armour stepped across her sight. She had an instant to note the black cloak and the bronzed bionics of his right arm and leg before the warrior levelled his bolter at her.

SILONIUS DID NOT see the ambush force until it was nearly too late. His senses were ringing with voices from raw memories, eyes blurring with the after-image of Alpharius standing in front of him in the past.

The first Imperial Fist came from a corridor to his right, hacking down with a sword that glowed with lightning as it cut. It was a good cut, back-handed, fluid and fast. It was meant to hit Silonius on the right of his neck and slice down across his chest.

The blow never landed.

Silonius caught the Imperial Fist's wrist, and turned it with a snap of bone and ceramite. He crushed the fingers into the sword grip, turned the still-active blade inwards and sliced it across the warrior's neck. Silonius had the sword in his hand as the dead legionary struck the floor.

The passage was narrow, a battleground pressed between two walls. Another Imperial Fist was directly in front of him. The firing pin inside the warrior's bolter kissed the back of a bolt casing. Silonius cut the bolter in two as the shell ran down the barrel.

It exploded.

The Imperial Fist staggered, blood streaming from torn armour. Silonius stepped in and cannoned his foot into the warrior's chest. The legionary flew backwards, chest cracked, shards of bone and armour crumpling into his hearts. Silonius had the grenade free and flying through the air as the dying warrior struck his squad brothers in the passage behind. The grenade detonated. Shrapnel and fire ripped through the corridor.

Silonius' bolter was in his hand, and he was pivoting and firing into the space behind him where more Imperial Fists were already moving. A wall of three overlapping shields faced him, gun-barrels jutting from firing slots. He saw the Imperial Fists brace to fire an instant before the volley hammered up the passage at him. He pivoted against the wall, pulling a plasma grenade and frag grenade from his waist as he moved. He threw the frag grenade high, looping the throw so that the grenade struck the ceiling plates, bounced down and hit the floor just in front of the shield-wall. It detonated. Shrapnel rang against the wall of plasteel. The Imperial Fists did not pause, but surged forwards, firing as they came.

Silonius ran from them, bolter in one hand and the stolen power sword in the other. He felt a bolt hit his side. The shock of the explosion split his armour. The Imperial Fists came on, feet ringing on the deck. None of them noticed the plasma grenade wedged into the corner of the floor.

Star-bright heat filled the corridor with a scream of expanding air and distorting metal. The shield-wall vanished. Silonius felt the wash of heat from the blast, but had made it past the lethal radius with one pace to spare. He strode back into the wreckage. He could feel the heat of the guttering plasma through his armour. The passage walls were glowing. Rivets had popped out of joints between metal plates. The dark material of the artefact's true substance showed through in places. Air hissed through the glowing tears.

A single Imperial Fist tried to rise from amongst the molten sludge of his comrades. The blast had vaporised the back of his body. Scorched liquid ran from his torso. His legs did not exist beyond the knee. Yet still Silonius saw yellow fingers trying to grip the butt of a bolter. He stopped, looked down at the warrior, aimed and put a bolt shell through the green eyepiece that looked back at him.

He paused for a second and then turned. The light of another battle was rippling down the corridor from the rendezvous chamber.

Memories slammed into him as he began to run.

Alpharius rose from the dark inside his skull. For an instant he could see the primarch's mouth moving, but could not hear the words. Then they came too, cutting in as though at the press of a switch.

'Who am I?'

'You are Alpharius.'

'Are we not all Alpharius?'

THE MUZZLE OF the bolter loomed in Myzmadra's sight. She felt the instant slow. Every detail of the Imperial Fist aiming at her was sharp. She could see the grey smudges running through the white fur that topped his black cloak. The laurel leaves running around the crown of his helm were green enamel. The word *Rennimar* was etched into the edge of the left pauldron.

A *Huscarl*, she thought. *One of the companions of Rogal Dorn.* She felt her own muscles moving, the nerve grafts and fibre bulk firing fast, but still too slow.

A cluster of bolts hit the Huscarl on the shoulder as he fired. Bolts sprayed across the deck as the bolter kicked wide. Phocron strode into sight, firing as he moved. Myzmadra squeezed the trigger of her volkite. The beam snapped out, but the shot went wide. The Huscarl was not down, not by a long way. He cannoned forwards, right hand tugging a mace free from his waist. Lightning wreathed its head as he swung. Behind him more Imperial Fists were flowing into the room, boarding shields locking together. She could not even see Incarnus any more.

'Withdraw,' said Phocron. 'Get back to the ship. Now!'

She pushed up and ran for the doorway they had entered from. The Huscarl struck Phocron as she took her second stride. The blow was huge, driven by raw power and momentum. It looked simple, the kind of blow that would break whatever it touched, but which would never land. Phocron swayed back, bolter ready to fire into the Huscarl's face as the blow passed.

The blow did not pass. The Huscarl flicked the mace over as it fell, and swept it up into Phocron's midriff. It was an impossible blow, a blow designed to deceive and then kill. Phocron lifted from the floor, lightning crawling over the crater in his chest.

SILONIUS CAME THROUGH the door in time to see Phocron fall. An Imperial Fists Huscarl was standing above the Headhunter Prime, mace still swinging high in his hand. Blood was falling through the air and burning as it passed through the mace's power field. Stark white light bathed the chamber. Gunfire leapt at Silonius. Bolts burst on his armour. More damage, more blood inside his armour. His eyes flowed across the advancing squads of Imperial Fists, and his mind assessed the situation before he had taken a step. He saw the body of Phocron on the floor, limbs scrabbling in spreading blood.

He ducked back into the mouth of a corridor. Myzmadra was

sprinting towards him, a shield-wall of Imperial Fists closing on her from behind. He fired at them. The first bolt struck a warrior whose eyes were a fraction above the shield-line. The bolt smashed through his left lens and turned his skull into a bloody pulp inside his helm. The warrior dropped.

Myzmadra twisted to fire back into the closing enemy.

'Keep moving!' he shouted.

His eye found cracks running down the face of one of the Imperial Fists' shields. Two shells shattered the shield and a third took the warrior in the throat.

A volley of fire lashed across the chamber. Myzmadra dived. Explosions burst amongst the gantries and hanging chains.

Myzmadra was past him and into the passage beyond. He fired a last burst and followed. The passage was thick with smoke and flame from plasma grenade detonations. Five strides from the door, Silonius paused and pulled a last grenade from his belt. It was heavy, and locked to the metal wall with a magnetic thump. A red light flashed on its casing as it armed. Silonius turned and ran after Myzmadra. She was leaping over the molten remains of the dead Imperial Fists.

'Cut-off unit?' she shouted over her shoulder.

'There may be others,' he said. Behind him the krak grenade exploded, pulling the walls and ceiling of the passage down. The shock wave slammed into Silonius' back, but he ran on without stumbling.

'This way,' he said, as they came to a junction.

'The lighter...' said Myzmadra, breathing hard.

'The sons of Dorn are not fools. The lighter will have become wreckage the second they closed the trap.'

'Then...?' she said, as they turned down a passage that led them away from where they had left the lighter.

'There is a contingency,' he said.

As he spoke he heard the buzz of activating power armour as a second Imperial Fist cut-off unit stepped from the side of the corridor and locked shields. They had been waiting, five of them immobile in the dark passages, armour shut down and silent. Twenty paces separated them from him. Possible responses and tactics blurred through the edge of his awareness, and became a simple, direct necessity.

He charged.

The Imperial Fists fired. Bolts slammed into him. Armour cracked and blood scattered in his wake. He did not stop. He struck the shield-wall and felt the impact shudder through him. The servos in his armour screeched. Damage alarms rose in his ears. The shield-wall bent backwards, and then his momentum was pushing him into the opening gap. The power sword was in his hand, lightning running down its edge as he rammed its point into the gut of a warrior and ripped it upwards. Ceramite split. Blood and bowel fluid sprayed across him as he pulled the blade free and turned, hacking down into the leg of another warrior. The legionary fell to the floor, firing into the air as his finger pulled the trigger of his boltgun. Silonius kicked out. The warrior's head snapped back, armour servos and bone breaking. He was side by side with the enemy, armour scraping against theirs as they turned to try and engage him. He did not give them the chance.

His hand snapped out, gripped the top of a shield, yanked it down and sawed his sword across the face of the Imperial Fist behind. The warrior began to fall. Silonius pivoted, still holding onto the shield top, power snapping through him as he threw the dying Imperial Fist into his two remaining comrades. They brought their shields around, fast. A volkite beam speared out of the dark and hit one on the shoulder. The shield dipped, and Silonius rammed the tip of his sword into the warrior's faceplate, dragging it sideways before the dead weight could pull the blade down. The blade edge burst from the side of the helm and sliced into the last Imperial Fist's pauldron. The sword's power field failed.

The Imperial Fist lurched back, blade embedded in the meat and ceramite of his right shoulder. Silonius' bolter was back in his hands as he stepped close, pressed the barrel against the warrior's gut and emptied the remainder of the clip. The Imperial Fist staggered back, a bloody crater bored in his stomach. Silonius let the warrior sag down the wall, reloaded and put a final shell into the corpse's left eye.

It had been only a matter of seconds since the Imperial Fists had appeared. He looked around. Myzmadra advanced towards him, her volkite levelled at him. He could read the hesitation in her stance. She had had time to aim and fire once in the course of the encounter. He looked at her, then turned towards the waiting dark of the passage beyond the fallen Imperial Fists.

'Come,' he said. 'We are close.'

She did not move, or lower her gun. 'What... What are you?'

He felt images and echoes of thoughts fizz at the edge of his mind.

'I am a warrior of the Legion,' he said, looking at her. 'We must move.'

She lowered the gun after a long moment, and they began to run.

The second lighter was waiting in a dark space on the edge of the artefact, powered down and silent. Ashul looked up as they climbed aboard. He activated controls, and the craft's frame began to purr with power.

'Are we waiting?' he asked.

'No,' said Silonius. Ashul glanced at Myzmadra who nodded.

The lighter broke free of the artefact and ran into open space at full burn.

In the vibrating dark of the compartment Silonius breathed out and let a cold blackness overwhelm his thoughts.

From across the compartment Myzmadra watched him, eyes dark inside the shell of her visor.

'There is something I need to say to you,' she said carefully. 'I had instructions, for if Phocron was lost.'

He blinked, she reached into a pouch in her void suit and pulled out a small object wrapped in black fabric. She held it out to him.

'Hades,' she said.

And the dreams uncoiled through him.

ARCHAMUS TOOK IN the wreckage choking the passage the Alpha Legion warrior and operative had vanished through – it would take at least

twenty minutes to clear with melta-torches and lascutters. Twenty minutes was far, far too long in this situation. The ambush had closed
almost perfectly. Twenty of them had waited in the dark for the Alpha
Legion. Utterly still, their armour soundless and unmoving, they had
become part of the artefact's silence. When the enemy had reached
the rendezvous chamber they had closed the circle. Everything up to
that point had proceeded as it should, but now he felt that there was
something at work that they had not accounted for.

'Clear it,' he said pointing at the blocked door. Three warriors came
forwards. Two of them carried lascutters and began to slice into the
debris. Archamus turned and strode back across the chamber, his warriors falling into formation around him as he made for the entrance
on the other side of the chamber.

'Their lighter was located and destroyed,' said Kestros, 'and the cut-off
unit is in place to block them. Either way they are trapped.'

'Never a wise assumption to make with the Alpha Legion,' Archamus
said, and gave the younger warrior a hard look. He halted beside what
remained of Dowager-son Hyrakro. Steaming liquid and ash was seeping from the scraps of the man's void suit.

Another figure lay nearby, with a Legion Apothecary knelt beside
him. The man's right arm had been blown to ash below the elbow.
Archamus' bionic hand twitched instinctively at the sight of the smoking stump. The human began to convulse as Archamus looked at him,
black pupils contracting in white, iris-less eyes.

'I... I can...' gasped the figure, limbs thrashing against the floor.

The Apothecary keyed the controls to the narthecium on his wrist.
A silver needle snapped out of its casing, and he stabbed it into the
human's chest. The man's convulsions weakened. His head lolled,
eyes unfocused.

'Will he survive?' asked Archamus.

'He will,' said the Apothecary.

'I can...' said the man, the words falling slowly from his lips. 'I can
help you. I know... I know...'

His eyes flickered half shut, and he let out a slow breath as the drugs took hold of him and pulled him down into quiet. Archamus watched as the man's eyelids slid completely closed.

I know...

'They broke through the cut-off squad.' Kestros' voice cut into his thoughts.

'Broke through?'

'Slaughtered them all. Sotaro's dead. There must have been more than the lone warrior and human we saw. The *Unbreakable Truth* is coming in fast, but it is saying that a lighter launched into the void and is making for the sunward dust clouds.'

'They had a contingency,' snarled Archamus.

'Always a fair assumption to make with the Alpha Legion,' said Kestros, and Archamus felt a rebuke rising to his lips, before he bit it off.

'Bring the ship in,' he growled. 'Full speed to cut off the lighter.'

'They are already moving, but they say that it is unlikely that they will be able to intercept the target. They are detecting engine flare from the edge of the dust cloud the lighter is making for. A ship, small but fast.'

They had needed to withdraw the *Unbreakable Truth* to a distance where it would be out of range of enemy vessels bringing their quarry to the artefact. That necessity also meant that the vessel was now too far out to run down a fast ship. He had known this was a risk when he had planned the ambush, but there were always risks.

He looked down at the human at his feet, now slumped in a drug-induced coma.

I know...

'Tell them to pursue as far as they can,' he said. 'But tell the Luna witch that we have another thread for her to unravel.' Kestros saluted. Archamus acknowledged it with a nod, and then stared at the unconscious man's pale eyelids, now closed over eyes that had fastened on Archamus with something like hope. 'We may not need to chase them down to end this hunt,' he said, as much to himself as anyone else.

FOUR

Memory

Alpharius watched Silonius in silence.

'Why are you here?' the primarch said at last, and gave a smile that had no echo in his eyes. 'You are here because we have a duty for you, a very particular duty. We were preparing for this war before it began. We have moved within the circles of conflict, sowing our own seeds and shaping the victory that will come.' He stopped. 'But things have changed. We are the masters of confusion, but now we reach a tipping point.' Alpharius paused and reached out to place the sliver of blade in his hand back with the rest of the broken spear on the plinth beneath the light.

'We are in the last stages of this war,' he continued. 'All the blood scattered on the ground, all the battles won and lost for advantage will soon become the past. Horus is going to move to take Terra. The day long promised is waiting just beyond the present.' *Silonius blinked, unsure whether he was more shocked to hear the Warmaster's name used with familial ease, or the revelation that the final gambit of the war was so close.* 'His road has been long, but he is coming, and he will not be stopped. That possibility has long passed.'

'What does that mean for the Legion, lord?'

'It means that we have a choice. We can either stand aside, or we can act.'

Silonius frowned. 'I sense that the choice might also have passed.'

Alpharius looked at him for a long moment and then nodded.

'We have begun. The domains of Terra already burn, and the darkness grows around Rogal in his fortress. He will have noticed, I am sure, but he will be thinking in terms of grand assaults, of millions coming from the stars to break against his wall.' Alpharius smiled again, and the cold stillness was in his eyes once more. 'Too simple in vision, too burdened by duty, too strong without understanding strength – those were always his weaknesses. He could stand against whatever horde the others could throw at him, and fight and win even as he was drowned in blood. But there are other ways and other weapons.' Alpharius paused, his eyes going back to the deconstructed spear. 'His defences are flawed, and he does not even see how.'

'We are going to Terra,' said Silonius. It was a statement, not a question, and fell from his lips with flat certainty.

Alpharius shook his head.

'We are already on Terra. We are in the Solar System. We always have been. But there is more, much more. We are going to wound Dorn and his honoured sons. We are going to humble them and strip the ground of certainty from beneath their feet.'

'And then, lord? What then?'

'I offer my brother a choice,' Alpharius said, and turned away.

'And what is the victory we seek?'

Alpharius shot him a sharp look. 'We have already won, Silonius. We won years ago. It is merely a question of the shape of that victory.'

Silence followed those words. Silonius spoke at last.

'And my part in this, lord?'

'Someone needs to be there,' said Alpharius. 'Someone needs to go to Terra to begin this. And to see it end.'

✠ ✠ ✠

Imperial Fists frigate Unbreakable Truth
The solar void

'HE SHOULD BE awake now.'

Incarnus heard the voice from behind a grey fog. Everything was warm, soft, numb. He tried to reach out with his mind, but recoiled as a sharp spike of pain flashed through the fog like a fork of black lightning.

'Oh, no, no, no...' said the voice. 'You really shouldn't do that. Not if you don't want the pain to split your skull. Open your eyes, if you can.'

The pain still clinging to the inside of his skull, Incarnus willed his eyes open. They moved sluggishly, and the world became a watery blur of shapes. He could feel cold metal circling his neck, wrist and shins. The burned stump of his arm was strapped across his chest.

'Hold still,' said the voice, and he blinked rapidly as jets of liquid washed his eyes. After a second he found that his sight had cleared. 'There,' said the voice, and he saw that it belonged to a young human female with a pale face framed by braided chrome hair. He noted the red circle tattooed under her left eye and blinked again in surprise. 'Now at least you should be able to appreciate your circumstances,' she said, and stepped back. Behind her stood two Space Marines in the gold-and-black heraldry of the Imperial Fists. Both had their helmets on and were staring at him with unmoving glowing green eyes. He saw that one was the same warrior he had seen before... before he had fallen into nothing.

He swallowed.

The girl smiled.

'I am advised that the device attached to your skull can detect if you attempt to use your witch gift, and will reward any such attempt with an excess of pain. Unless that is something you desire, I suggest you keep your thoughts inside your skull.'

'You...' he said, feeling his tongue move sluggishly. 'You are one of the Selenar.'

The girl's smile did not falter.

'Well done. And you... I had thought that none of your kind remained.'

'We... I found a way to survive,' he replied, the words rasping from his lips.

'By agreeing to serve the Alpha Legion in return for protection, yes?'

'At least...' he hissed. 'At least we didn't sell ourselves to barbarians and worshippers of ignorance.'

'No, you chose traitors and deceivers instead.'

The Imperial Fist who bore the marks of a sergeant shifted, and the girl flicked a glance at him.

'He is a Crimson Walker,' she said. 'One of the last in all likelihood.'

'I know of them,' said the cloaked warrior without looking away from Incarnus. 'They were witch-breed, gene-mutilators and techno mystics. The warlords and monarchs of Old Night used them as viziers and advisers, and they returned the favour by creating machines and monsters for them. They were exterminated decades ago.'

'But extermination is rarely perfect,' the girl said, and looked directly at Incarnus.

'I want...' said Incarnus. 'I want sanctuary.'

'Why?' she asked.

'I am afraid...'

'Begin telling us something that will help us,' said the girl.

'They are...' he breathed. 'The attacks on Terra... were not without purpose.'

'To cloud our minds with doubt and shadows, to seed fear in the ranks of the loyal,' said the cloaked Imperial Fist. 'That was their purpose, and in that they have failed.'

'Have they?' Incarnus asked, and licked his lips. The numbness in his mind and body was fading. A ghost throb in his vaporised arm was replacing the pain of the psy-clamp. Things had not gone as he had planned. He had hoped to flee back into the diaspora of lawlessness that existed in the voids of the Solar System and vanish from sight. Now he was in the hands of the Imperium, and facing their judgement for both his nature and his alliance to the Legion. There was a chance of survival, though, a slim desperate hope. He had to give everything he knew and hope that it would buy mercy. The Selenar girl knew that, he could tell.

'The Legion does not operate with simple objectives,' he said. 'It has parameters, volumes of possibility in which there are many potential victories and outcomes. The erosion of your spirit was only one of the possible objectives of the strikes on Terra. It was not the primary objective.'

He paused. In his mind he saw the face of Silonius, its features the mirror of Phocron's face.

'What was the objective?' asked the girl.

'Information,' he said. 'You have traitors in your midst, eyes and ears which watch and listen for the Legion. They have been there for a long time.'

'The agents of the Sigillite have eliminated–' the sergeant began.

'Have found the *chaff* sent by Horus' other allies. The Legion is neither clumsy, nor amateurish, and they have had longer to prepare than you suspect. This thing they are doing, it is... It is beautiful.'

'You admire those you claim to want to betray out of fear?' said the girl. 'How thoroughly paradoxical of you.'

'I hate and fear them,' he said, 'but you have to admire their abilities, don't you?' None of them replied. He licked his lips, feeling his tongue moving more easily with every word. 'The Legion's agents are not deluded sympathisers, or naïve ideologues. They are not new converts to rebellion. They have been in place for years. Some of them do not even know who they serve.'

'Who are these traitors?' asked the sergeant.

'I do not know, and anyway their identities do not matter – only their existence matters. You see, alone, each of them has only a narrow view of events. But if focused on a single event, those eyes and ears form an image.'

'And that is what they created,' said the Imperial Fist in the cloak.

'A single point of focus.' Incarnus thought he heard an edge of bitter realisation in the warrior's voice.

'We attacked, and they watched. They watched which forces moved and those that did not. They saw how you controlled information, they watched how you isolated a threat. They saw your soul, praetorians.'

'And the information from all of those sources?' asked the girl. Her eyes had a hard, intense focus to them.

'Collected, compiled.'

'Where is it?' asked the girl.

'Gone,' he replied. 'Sent out into the darkness.'

'To Horus,' said the uncloaked Imperial Fist.

'No,' he said. 'That is what I thought at first, but they are jealous creatures. Information is a weapon, and they intend to use that weapon themselves.'

'What...' began the girl, but Incarnus cut through her with the word that he had been readying since he had started talking.

'A Harrowing,' he said.

The girl blinked, eyes briefly flaring wide.

'What does that mean?' asked the sergeant.

'It is not theirs,' said the cloaked Imperial Fist. 'It was a term that came out of the wars of Unity, long before they made it their own. Then it meant an attack with overwhelming force, delivered after a time in which the enemy's ability to respond has been undermined, its defences eroded and its strengths neutralised. Destruction in detail.'

Incarnus forced himself to nod. The bolts of the psy-clamp dug into his scalp as he moved.

'Yes, that is what it means, and it is coming.'

'That is ludicrous,' said the sergeant. 'This is the Solar System. Even the full strength of the Alpha Legion...'

'Does more than one Legion stand beside you?' spat Incarnus. He needed them to believe. He needed them to see the truth of what he was telling them. 'Are you so strong that a thousand of you could stand against ten thousand? And what makes you believe they will give you that luxury? You are masters of defence, but they have assayed those defences. They have planned a counter to each one of your advantages.'

'He is right,' breathed the girl. 'Remember they do not account victory in the way you do, or even most do. They do not have to take Terra. The Solar System is already at war. How long will it stand against Horus if its outer spheres are in enemy hands, or half of its guardians slaughtered?'

'What is the shape of this Harrowing?' asked the cloaked Imperial Fist, taking a step closer. Incarnus felt his skin prickle, and the moisture seemed to dry on his tongue. Control and brutality seemed to seep from the warrior.

'I do not know,' said Incarnus, carefully. 'I do not think that the team I was a part of knew. That is the way of the Legion – secrets and lies are the air they breathe, and they hide things even from themselves.'

The Imperial Fist did not move, and Incarnus suddenly thought of the figure of Silonius staring back at him from the dark.

'Part of it will come from outside of the Solar System, and soon,' he said quickly. 'The signal they sent, it was aimed into the outer dark, and if it was to be received and acted on, then the receiver would have to be close.'

'What other preparations have they made?'

'I do not know,' he said. 'But there was another signal. I do not know what it was, but it was sent within the Solar System, and the one who sent it hid it from all of the rest.'

'They hide things even from themselves...' the sergeant said, and glanced at the other Imperial Fist. Incarnus licked his lips. He had them, and he could feel that his chance of survival was close. He just had to make them understand the last thing he had to tell them, the most difficult thing, and the thing that had frightened him enough to make him start to think about finding a way out.

'The one who sent that extra signal...' he said, the words forming slowly in his mouth. 'He joined us on Terra. He seemed to just slide into the fabric of the team, like he was not there, but he was always there, on the edge of things, and... I looked into his mind, just the surface, but that was... incomplete, as though most of it was asleep.'

'Asleep?' asked the girl, raising an eyebrow.

'Asleep, suppressed, hidden from itself,' he said.

She nodded slowly.

'Psychic reconstruction,' she said.

'Yes,' he said. 'Exactly that.'

The girl looked at the Imperial Fists as though hearing a question that had not yet been asked.

'A mind can be reshaped, parts of it suppressed and cut off from consciousness,' she said. 'In Old Night, warlords would use what they called sorcery to implant an assassin's soul into the mind of someone close to their enemies. It also serves as a very effective means of preserving a secret.'

'What purpose beside paranoia would that serve?' asked the sergeant.

'If this legionnaire knew something valuable then they would want it protected from discovery, either accidental or by that mind being violated.' She gestured at Incarnus. 'Given the current circumstances, their paranoia had grounds.'

'What could be so vital that they would go to those lengths?' asked the sergeant.

'What was his name?' asked the cloaked Imperial Fist. 'The legionnaire whose mind had been... altered, what was his name?'

'He was called Silonius,' Incarnus said, and felt cold run over his skin as he spoke the words. 'He believed that was his name. But that is it... That belief... I think that belief was a lie.'

Battle-barge Alpha
The interstellar gulf beyond the light of Sol

THE SIGNAL HAD passed out of the Solar System with the light of the system's star. Out in the gulf between stars, it touched the signal array high on the spine of the battle-barge *Alpha* and began to pour its mean-ing into the ship's systems. On the bridge, the figure on the throne was brought to full wakefulness by the clatter of machines. The trio of Lernaean Terminators at the throne's foot did not move from their position.

The figure waited, listening to the signal servitors clatter and buzz. Once they were silent, he spoke.

'Show it to me,' he said. The servitors heard, and twitched as they complied with the command.

Cones of projected light sprang from holo-projectors suspended above the throne. Images moved before the enthroned warrior, plan-ets and ships, and streams of information in words and symbol systems that none outside of the Alpha Legion would understand. There were words too, voices scratching with signal degradation and decryption distortion. They spoke as the images moved, and he watched as the Solar System's defences responded to the first attacks on Terra. It was all there – the Praetorian's defences not only visible, but moving, respond-ing to threat. There were holes of course, areas where agents or data siphons had not been able to gather intelligence, or only a partial impression. But it was still a beautiful and terrible thing to behold.

'Truly, the doom of empires is not in the strength of warriors, but in their weakness,' he whispered to himself, and then raised his voice. 'Bring the commanders to full waking, and signal the rest of the fleet to connect for conclave within the hour.' The Lernaeans heard and obeyed.

An hour later a hundred figures filled the dark space before the command throne. Many were present in body, but many others were holo-projections of those who stood in the strategiums and on the bridges of the other ships tumbling through the void beside the *Alpha*. The cold light of the ghost images gleamed off the armour plate of their brothers. They all watched and listened in silence as the intelli-gence from within the Solar System unfolded before them.

It was Ingo Pech who broke the silence. The hulking First Captain raised an eyebrow and looked around at his brothers.

'Dorn took the bait,' he breathed.

'And had the courtesy to show us his hand before quitting the field,' said Herzog from his side.

'Was there any doubt of either?' asked Pech.

'The Praetorian is no fool,' said Herzog. 'This was a delicate operation...'

'It still is a delicate operation,' said the warrior, from his place on the command throne. The eyes of those assembled went to him, and silence fell instantly. The Legion was a fluid beast, mutable and filled with paradoxes of structure and authority, but one quality allowed them that freedom: discipline. Cold and sharp.

And so now every one of the senior commanders assembled beneath him waited to hear his will and obey his command.

'Rogal Dorn has left the Solar System. But his sons still remain. The ground is prepared for the Harrowing, but we still need to lay the blade to it. You have all seen the detail of the battlefield. Current projections put us on intercept within Pluto's orbit as planned. Within one hour you will give your tactical assessments and mission parameters for the forces under your command.' He paused and felt a smile form on his face, a face that was the mirror of many that looked up at him.

'The hydra wakes,' he said.

The assembled commanders bowed their heads briefly as the words echoed from their mouths. They dispersed, only Pech and Herzog remaining. They were the most senior officers of the Legion present, and much of the detail of the attack would be created by them. That was as it should be, and he had no doubt that they would perform those duties with perfection. That they did not have overall command was of no consequence – rank and command were separate in the Legion, and they had wielded the power of the full Legion many times before. This time, though, he did wonder if they felt any jealousy that he rather than they had been given the honour of being master of this greatest of Harrowings. If they did, they did not show it as they looked up at him.

Pech spoke first.

'What is your will, Silonius?' he asked.

Imperial Fists frigate Unbreakable Truth
The solar void

THE FACE OF Effried resolved in a haze of static fog. The bridge of the *Unbreakable Truth* was almost silent, the murmur of the servitors and the distant noise of the engines rolling through the air like the growling of a far-off sea. The frigate was cutting through the void in the wake of the fleeing scavenger vessel as it dived into the reef of debris off Io. Archamus stood before the holo-projection of Effried.

'*Master Huscarl,*' said Effried, voice hissing and popping as he looked out at Archamus.

'The primarch,' said Archamus, his voice snapping out. 'Brother, I need you to get a message to the primarch.'

There was a pause as the signals flowed out through the void, connected and passed back. They were close to Jupiter and its moons, but even so the time slid on and on, as Archamus waited for Effried to respond. He did not know where Dorn would be, and so the fastest way of getting a message to him was via an astropath. Effried was Castellan of the Third Sphere, the closest commander to Archamus and the fastest way of reaching Dorn.

'*He is gone, brother,*' said Effried. Archamus heard the words, and the blood in his veins seemed to freeze. His flesh and body seemed to vanish.

Gone? The question echoed in the sudden silence behind his eyes. *Where could he have gone? Why would he have gone?* And his own thoughts answered, pulling him back through the weeks before the attack: the fading contact with nearby worlds, the questions Dorn had asked Armina Fel when he was there, and the words he had spoken over the bodies of the Alpha Legion warriors.

Effried's image spoke again after another delay.

'*He has taken half of the strength of the Second, Third and Fifth Spheres. He strikes at the enemy at Esteban.*' A pause, a hollow, numbing pause that stretched in static, and the rising roar of the ship's engines. '*I presumed that you knew his plans.*'

Archamus shook his head. 'No. I was not aware.'

And he knew that Dorn had not told him, had kept him ignorant.

Because I chose to follow this quarry, he thought. *Because once I entered the cradle of lies I was set apart.* The numb chill was his world now, as the logic turned over in his thoughts. Lies within lies, misdirection within misdirection. Dorn had thought the attack on Terra a feint, a distraction to pull him away from the truth of the war, and so he had cut himself away from the possibility of knowing, and focused on the truth not the distraction.

But... but the truth was not the truth, and whatever had happened to Phaeton and Esteban, it was nothing but a feint to draw the eye from what was, in truth, a death blow.

'*What is it, brother?*' asked Effried. '*What is wrong?*'

I have failed, thought Archamus.

What are you afraid of?

My brother was cradled in lies.

I have failed him...

Begin to think about what he is doing and you are already giving him his greatest weapon.

... and others will pay the price of my failure.

'Send the invasion signals, brother,' said Archamus. His voice sounded separate from him: cold, controlled, other. 'Alert all forces. Full alert throughout the system.'

The long pause, the fizz and click of static.

'*You are certain?*' asked Effried. '*The enemy are coming?*'

Archamus shook his head.

'They are already here.'

Memory

'*Will you serve the Legion in this way?*' Alpharius asked Silonius.

'*Of course,*' said a voice that he knew was his.

'There is not one mission parameter at play. There are several. We are also using assets that have been put in place a long time ago. They have slept under the earth of Terra for a decade, and the details of the war they wake to were not known to us then. The mission parameters they will follow initially will serve our ends, but they are not specific to the current need. You will provide that specificity.'

'Yes, of course, lord,' said Silonius. He glanced around at the columns of light marching away from him through the gloom. He could see the shapes of small objects resting in the light: a near-human skull with canine teeth like knife blades, a silver pendant in the shape of a winged sword, a vial of pale green liquid.

He looked back at his primarch.

Alpharius looked back at him, his eyes still, his face blank of emotion.

'There are security matters that must be accounted for,' Alpharius said. 'The importance of this operation cannot be overstated. The future of the Legion, and the outcome of this war, rest on it.'

Silonius nodded.

'I understand,' he had said.

'No, you do not. But you will. You are carrying the heart of this operation, and it must remain secret. But you are going to carry these secrets to Terra, and there you do not need to speak a secret to have it taken. Without even the powers of Malcador, or my father, there are others who might see the truth in your thoughts, or touch its edges, and once they have seen that truth then it is not your own silence that will matter, but theirs. The only way to truly keep a secret is to keep it from yourself.'

Silonius nodded, and made himself hold his primarch's gaze.

'Psychic reconstruction,' he stated, and Alpharius nodded.

Two figures slid from behind the columns of light. Both were armoured, their identical faces uncovered. Silver wires and blue crystals gleamed on their bare scalps.

'What is needed will be given back to you when it is required.'

The two psykers watched him without blinking as they moved to stand either side of him. The Emperor had forbidden the use of psykers within His Legions, but the Alpha Legion had always followed their own will in all things.

'What is the process for the recall to be triggered?'

Alpharius smiled and shook his head.

'That will remain buried far below your consciousness, but trust that when it is needed, you will know.'

Silonius glanced at the two psykers. They had become perfectly still, but strands of pale energy were gathering around their heads. Their eyes had become utterly black.

'What will they take from me?' he asked.

'Everything,' said Alpharius.

Cords of lightning leapt from the psykers' eyes and coiled around him. Pain lanced through Silonius, sharp and bright. He felt his mind crack, thoughts peeling back like flower petals to reveal the bloody mass of emotions and beliefs and personality beneath. Invisible hands reached in and down into the wet meat of his soul.

And pulled him apart.

Thoughts ripped free of meaning. Memories dissolved in fire. Sensation compressed to a single razor line drawn onto a black horizon.

...and then he was watching as though his eyes were holes cut in a screen, as the psykers turned their gaze on Alpharius, and the lightning wreathed the primarch.

...and he opened his eyes inside another skull, and for a second he was looking back at himself, at Silonius stood in front of him, as though he had stepped into the reflection of a mirror.

Scavenger vessel Wealth of Kings
The solar void

He opened his eyes. The light seemed different: brighter, shapes sharper, shadows deeper.

Has the light changed, or do I see it with different eyes?

He could feel the others looking at him, the humans, Hekaron, Orn, Kalix. They were all there, standing back at the other end of the hangar chamber. They hung back, watching him uncertainly. Myzmadra had not said anything to them and stood at the back of the circle of watchers. He ignored them. The ship was roaring as its engines pushed it out beyond the range and sight of the Imperial Fists.

He sat on a crate at the centre of the chamber. The shard blades lay at his feet. They had been his only weapons when he woke beneath the Imperial Palace, slivers of sharpness cast in silver. The velvet-wrapped bundle that Myzmadra had given him unfolded in his hand. Another shard lay there on the smooth blackness. Then there were the other pieces that had been given to him in the Palace. He took them all, pulling them from the shells that had concealed them. Leaves of metal, splinters of glittering matter and black cylinders. It took seconds, his hands following a will that reached from behind the thinning veil in his thoughts.

'Phocron is gone,' he said as he placed the last piece down on the deck at his feet. He sat at the centre of the halo of components.

'Who has mission command?' asked Orn, his voice soft and cold.

'I do,' he said.

'What is our mission parameter, then?' asked Hekaron.

He looked at the exploded components.

'Hades,' he said.

'I am not aware of that parameter,' said Orn. His voice and face were blank, but his eyes were skating across the shining pieces on the floor.

'You are not yet, but you will be aware,' he said. 'That, amongst many reasons, is why I am here. The hydra has slept in the light of the sun for long enough. Now the hydra wakes.' He bent down and picked up one of the pieces of metal on the floor, and then another and another, each one snapping together, his hands moving with fluid speed.

'Who are you?' asked Ashul, the human operative's voice calm, but layered with sudden doubt and fear and wonder.

The last piece snapped into place, and he stood. The double-bladed spear rested in his hand, light slithering across it.

'I am Alpharius,' he said.

BROTHERS OF WAR

999.M30
Six years before the Betrayal at Isstvan III

I

THE BANNERS LAY broken at the foot of the iron mountain. The dead lay with them, still heaped over the trenches, their flesh slowly fuming into the cold air. There had not been time for the flies and insects to come and begin their feast. They would, though. Even within the ice reaches the processes of death still moved, albeit at a delayed rate. Above the dead, the hive rose up to the pale blue sky, its spire pointing at the ships hanging above like the accusing finger of a corpse.

Archamus watched as the procession approached. Every figure looked tattered and bloody, but they had made their best effort to hold on to some dignity. A block of infantry came first, their silver-and-red brocade coats buttoned to their necks, laslocks held at port. They marched with precision, but Archamus could see the stains on the fabric. Bandages wound over the face of a soldier, fresh blood bright beside the ochre of dried pus. The jaw of a trooper in the front rank was bound shut, and her head had the asymmetric slumped look of a fractured skull.

Behind the infantry came their officers and commanders, each of them raised above the ranks on sprung calliper boots. Their faces were grim and their eyes hard, but there was something broken behind the

defiance of their expressions. Last of all came the World-Prince, thin as
a bare branch, silvered robes flowing down to spill over the edge of his
palanquin. Twelve slaves in blank masks and bare torsos bore the dais
chair forwards, sweat glistening on their muscles. Behind them scribes,
advisers and courtiers followed in a loose gaggle. All of them had the
blank-eyed look of people who had just had everything they knew
and relied on vanish. Of all of the procession, only the World-Prince
himself did not wear surrender on his face. He stared out at the battlefields, eyes never even turning towards those waiting for him, anger
screaming from him in silent waves.

Rogal Dorn waited with his commanders on top of a low hill just
beyond the trench-lines encircling the hive. Ten thousand Imperial
Fists stood on the field around him, and beyond them half a million
soldiers of the Imperial Army stood at attention. Tens of thousands of
tanks and war machines sat between the ranked figures. A trio of Titans
stood above them, their vast pennants shifting slowly in the breeze. It
was a spectacle of might and power that would have brought some to
their knees, but not the ruler of this newly conquered land.

'Still defiant,' said Yonnad from just in front of Archamus. The fleet
master was bare-headed, and the cold air stirred the dark hair above
his hawk face. His eyes were hard black chips embedded in the rust
of his skin. 'His kingdom is in ruin, his armies broken, but he is still
fighting us in his heart.'

'That is not defiance,' said Sigismund, without looking around. 'That
is disdain. This man does not have the grace to know that he has been
granted the chance to be part of something greater. So instead he chooses
to pretend that he has won a victory. Was there ever greater folly?'

'It is human to want to cling to the past,' said Rogal Dorn, his voice
low. 'Always remember that, my sons.'

'Lord,' said the commanders, bowing their heads as they spoke.
Archamus alone did not move. Above him the Legion banner rippled
in the wind, the silver lightning bolts and sable fist stirring on their
field of gold. He felt the standard pole tug at his grasp in the gusting

air, but he remained unmoving. Beside him and the primarch, twenty Huscarls stood in double rank, black cloaks hanging from their backs, bolters held across their chests. Beside them twenty of the Templar Brethren stood with drawn swords. On Rogal Dorn's left the towering bulk of Alexis Polux stood beside Yonnad. The fleet master's apprentice in void warfare was as stone-faced as always, his eyes cold. On Dorn's right was Sigismund in the black-and-white heraldry of his office, his sword in his hand. Armed and armoured, Rogal Dorn stood like a burnished statue between them.

'Did the...' began Yonnad, and then stopped, his mouth open as though he did not wish to bite down on his next words. 'Did the *other* Legion not wish to be present for this?'

'Clearly not,' said Sigismund.

Silence fell again as the procession crossed the last metres of ground. The World-Prince on his palanquin came to a halt. His guard came to attention with a snap of taut muscle and poised weapons. Archamus noted a bead of blood slowly running from under the edge of a bandage swathing the face of one of the soldiers. She did not move from attention as it ran down her face. He felt admiration touch his thoughts and made note to find these warriors once this was done. The Imperium needed those with such strength.

'Imperium victor,' called Archamus, his voice echoing from the grille of his helm. In sequence each of the Imperial Fists and human soldiers heard the words and echoed them. The cry rose and rose until the air seemed to be made of sound. Archamus raised the Imperial Fists banner high, and the entire force came to attention, the movement rippling outwards from Rogal Dorn. Archamus saw some of the defeated officers flinch at the sound and movement. The World-Prince looked at Dorn at last, and his eyes glittered with rage. When he spoke, his voice shook with control.

'My son, my nephews, my father, my brothers, my cousins... Make no mistake that you have bought this world with their blood. And we *shall* remember.'

Rogal Dorn met the man's shaking gaze.

'I stand before you and offer what was offered before, that you may become part of the Imperium of Mankind, that you may know the truth of Illumination and live without fear of the dark. For this the Emperor demands that you give Him loyalty, and follow His wisdom, and the rule of those to whom He has given authority.'

The World-Prince looked back, lips twisting over his teeth, hands flexing on the arms of his chair.

'As ruler of this domain,' he said at last, chewing off each word and spitting it out, 'and master of its people, I... I yield to you, and offer fealty to the... to the *Emperor.*'

Silence followed as Rogal Dorn continued to look at the man.

'When you speak those words,' he said at last, his voice low and cold, 'you kneel.'

The World-Prince blinked, and for a moment Archamus thought he was about to say something. Then the man lowered his gaze and gestured at his palanquin bearers. Slowly the muscle-brutes lowered the weight from their shoulders. The World-Prince did not stand, but slumped forwards from his chair to his knees, as though the strength to stand had fled from him. Behind him, the procession that had followed the prince out to meet their conquerors knelt and pressed their foreheads into the dust of their world.

Rogal Dorn bowed his head in acknowledgement.

'In the name of the Emperor of Mankind I accept your fealty,' said Dorn, and though he did not raise his voice, his words seemed to roll to the horizon.

II

IT WAS NIGHT when they came to the Spire Palace. The one-time seat of a royal cousin, it now served a different purpose, its servants and slaves replaced by command officers and military serfs. Since the world's surrender the mechanisms of Imperial conquest had ground into motion, and were already breaking and remaking the defeated society. Surveyor forces were sweeping the population, cataloguing resources and assessing existing social structures. Military forces were being evaluated and plans drawn up to redistribute the most able into Crusade forces. The first battalions from the conquered world would join a Crusade force within twelve weeks to help conquer others. Iterators had been at work within the masses, and the world's compliance shaped into a narrative that would let the population come to see their new situation with pride.

Rogal Dorn had moved between each facet of the operation, hearing the plans of generals and meeting with the humans who would shepherd the world into its new future. He had not stopped, and he had weighed each decision, both great and small, as though it were of equal importance to all the others. Archamus had once heard the great Iterator Evander Tobias describe it as 'a total lack of toleration of anything but complete precision or competence', and the description was as adequate a portrait of the primarch's focus as Archamus could think of. But – like so many pithy epithets – it fell short of the truth.

Archamus had watched Dorn at work for over a century, and never once had he seen his path waver or deviate from its course. He did not simply wage war; he was changing the world he moved through by force of will. That had caused trouble in the past, the kind of conflict that came when such a drive met an equally great force on a different course. And it was going to cause trouble now. Archamus had known it as soon as he learned what other force was to share this victory with them.

They reached the space in front of the palace's throne room. Guards from the Seventh Outremar Elite stood to either side of the silver-and-jade doors, power spears held at attention.

Dorn turned and met the eyes of his commanders.

'You have done well, my sons,' he said, and Archamus knew that this would be the only word that Dorn would give on the conduct of his warriors. There was no need to say anything more. Each of them bowed their heads. Dorn nodded. 'You have your duties, see to them. We will speak at the fifth hour.' Yonnad, Polux and Sigismund moved away. Archamus remained. That was his purpose – to be his lord's shadow and protector. He had once heard a human officer wonder aloud why a being like a primarch needed a personal guard. There were many reasons, of course, and only some of them had to do with the threat of harm. But the core of why Dorn had a bodyguard was simple: to guard against hubris.

Dorn gestured to the squad of Huscarls behind Archamus.

'Disperse,' he said. The warriors moved away, folding into the edges of the corridor. Archamus waited. Dorn did not normally issue orders directly to the Huscarls. They were trained to move around him as though they were not there, their actions calibrated to never intrude on his actions or awareness. The order he had just given said that something was different.

Archamus' awareness sharpened, his mind filtering through the details of the situation and surroundings. His memory pulled details of the Spire Palace's layout before his mind's eye. He looked slowly at the doors that led into the audience chamber. A crowned figure looked back at him from the sculpted silver, its hands holding a sceptre and a crescent moon.

'Do you intend to enter the throne room, lord?' he asked.

'Yes,' said Dorn, carefully.

'I presume you are aware that the security protocols have been manipulated. There has been no security sweep of the throne room in the last hour, and there are no guards within.'

'I am aware of that. Do you wish to advise caution?'

'I am going to assume that I have already, and that you have said that you will proceed as you intended.'

Dorn smiled, the expression fading as quickly as it rose. 'A good set of assumptions.'

'I must insist that I come with you, lord.'

'Insist?' growled Dorn.

'I am oathed not only to your service but your protection.'

Dorn looked at him for a long moment.

'Very well.' The primarch gave a single nod. 'Very well. Do you know what waits for us inside?'

'I think I do, my lord.'

Dorn's mouth twitched into a fleeting smile. 'There are many battles in this Crusade – some costly, some bitter, some that it would be better not to fight.' He put his hand on the door. 'Question everything you see,' he said, and pushed the doors wide.

III

THE THRONE ROOM was dark. Light spilled from behind Archamus and Dorn as they stepped through the door. The walls were sheets of beaten copper, curved and riveted so that they looked like the rippled fabric of curtains. Tiny beast heads carved in jet capped each rivet head. The floor was an oval expanse of brushed steel. An oval table sat at the centre of the floor. The ceiling soared up and up, tapering to a shadowed point far above. At the far end of the room, on a plinth of raw iron, was a throne spun from carbon and gold wire.

A figure sat on the throne, hands resting on the chair's arms, the light from the door gleaming off his armour's silver trim. Scales covered the curved plates, and a crest of bronze serpents rose from the crown of his helm. The throne would have been huge for a human, made to amplify the power of those who sat on it. The armoured figure fitted it perfectly, his size and presence making it seem not a throne but a mundane chair. The emerald hydra on the figure's chest winked reflected light as he inclined his head in greeting.

Dorn met the green glow of its eyes.

'Close the doors,' he said to Archamus softly.

Archamus turned and pushed the doors shut. The light vanished, and the gloom became true darkness.

'A little too dark for such a meeting,' said a voice from the throne.

Pale light kindled within the folded surface of the walls. The metals gleamed, shifting between colours of ice and moonlight. Dorn stepped forwards, eyes fixed. The sound of his steps rang softly on the floor. He stopped in the centre of the room, next to the table. Archamus stayed next to the door, his hands still beside his weapons.

Dorn looked at the figure on the throne for a long second and then turned away.

'Dispense with the theatrics,' he said.

A second figure in armour stepped from a fold in the chamber's walls. His armour was also the indigo-blue of the Alpha Legion, but plain and adorned only by an alpha symbol on one pauldron, and a crocodilian head snarling in silver on the other. To Archamus' eye the figure was fractionally shorter and less bulky than the figure on the throne.

'An attempt to impress?' said Dorn to the second figure, his voice level and cold. 'Or a test?'

'My apologies,' said the second figure. 'A habit, that is all.'

'No,' said Dorn, 'a choice.'

Archamus stepped away from the door, eyes moving from the two figures to his surroundings. He blinked briefly through infra-sight, dark-vision and images formed from sonic and electro-field distortion. Then he blinked the augmented views away and looked with his eyes alone.

'My lord,' he said, 'there is another one, to the right of the throne, armour cycled down to minimal power.'

Dorn nodded.

'Thank you, Archamus. I was just waiting to see if my brother was going to reveal his presence now, or whether he was going to continue this charade.'

Dorn turned as a third figure stepped forwards, armour purring to life as he moved. This one was also smaller than the figure on the throne, and wore armour that spoke perhaps of a line captain or battalion commander. A crest of stiff, white-and-black striped horsehair haloed the top of his helm, and a green cloak hung from his shoulders. His right hand rested on the pommel of a sheathed sword.

Dorn kept his eyes on this newest figure. At a glance Archamus could tell that all three of them were shorter than Dorn, but taller than himself – very large for legionaries, but within a blurred zone of size that made it difficult to judge whether they were legionary or primarch. There were differences, though: tiny variations in stance and posture that would have been lost to a normal human eye. The one on the throne was the largest, and his armour and demeanour screamed that this was a lord of the Alpha Legion... But there was something too blunt about that picture. Archamus had had a fleeting impression of a slight restriction in the way he moved, as though the figure were as much armour and machine as flesh.

As for the other two, the one in the plain armour would not have been out of place standing in a rank of a hundred Legion warriors. The most recent one to appear had size and moved as though used to command, but both qualities were expected in a ranking Space Marine.

'Again, my apologies,' said the same deep and smooth voice as had spoken before, but this time it came from the helms of all three figures.

'An apology only has meaning if it is rooted in regret,' said Dorn. 'Your words are meaningless.'

No reply came, but the third figure reached up and unlocked his helm, as the figure in the throne rose, stepped down to the floor and took his own off. The warrior in the plain armour followed suit.

Three near-identical faces looked up at Dorn. All were olive-skinned and clean-shaven, their skulls hairless. Archamus could see echoes of both Dorn's features and those of the other primarchs, but somehow no one feature dominated – as though the face were a blend of all the others. The three faces were very similar, though there were minute differences in bone structure and subcutaneous musculature. But no two sets of differences were the same. Each of them seemed to wear a mask that was deliberately the same, but also different enough that anyone trying to sort one from another would become lost in differences. And of course, he realised, that was exactly the intention.

Dorn's eyes had not moved from the figure who had worn the plumed helm.

'Alpharius,' said Dorn, as he stepped forwards, eyes hard. The other two warriors began to bow, yielding their pretence as Dorn went to greet his brother primarch.

Dorn turned suddenly, his hand flashing out to the figure who had stepped from the throne. The blow never landed. The figure twisted aside from Dorn's fist, the speed of the movement the mirror of Dorn's attack. Archamus' bolter was in his hand even as the two Alpha Legion warriors drew their weapons.

'Hold!' roared Dorn, and the room froze. The sound of the word folded and echoed off the walls.

He lowered his fist, and the figure he had tried to strike straightened.

'Try my patience again, and I will not stay my hand,' said Dorn.

Alpharius – for Alpharius it must have been – raised an eyebrow. The other two warriors stepped next to him, and for a moment it was as though Archamus were looking at three paintings of the same subject to different themes: lord, warrior, son.

'When did you know?' said Alpharius, and Archamus recognised the voice as the same that had spoken throughout.

'Before I stepped through the door,' said Dorn. Alpharius breathed a cold chuckle.

'These are my senior commanders in this warzone–'

'Compliance,' said Dorn. 'The war is over.'

Alpharius gave the smallest of shrugs.

'We will see,' he said, and gestured to the legionnaire with the cloak and crested helm of a centurion, and the giant in the plain armour. 'This is Ingo Pech, and Kel Silonius.'

'I know of them,' said Dorn.

Alpharius looked at Archamus. 'You can lower the weapon, Master Huscarl. With both my brother and myself here there are few places in the galaxy safer than this room.'

Archamus kept his bolter steady. Dorn glanced at him and gave a small nod. Archamus lowered the weapon and clamped it to his thigh.

'We can speak alone if you wish,' said Dorn.

Alpharius shook his head. 'I do not keep things from my commanders.'

'That is a lie,' said Dorn calmly.

Alpharius smiled. 'Do you really wish us to be at cross-purposes, brother?'

'We are at cross-purposes, and honesty is a quality I value.'

'And I do not? Is that the point you are trying to make?'

'You did not declare that you were operating on this world. Not until you had to.'

'Our ways are not the same, but you cannot question their effectiveness.'

'You did not have to kill them!' Dorn's voice shook the air like a roll of thunder. Archamus looked at his primarch, but Dorn's face was as fixed and emotionless as ever. Only in the dark glitter of the eyes did the rage leak out. When he spoke again, his voice was low and controlled. 'You did not need to kill them.'

A heartbeat of silence followed the words. Archamus watched Alpharius and his two warriors. All of them were as unmoving and expressionless as statues.

Everyone in the chamber knew what Dorn was referring to. The world they stood on had resisted initial overtures of compliance. A so-called World-Prince and a web of blood-tied nobility saw the world as theirs, and theirs alone. Their pride would not let them bow to any other, no matter how mighty. But the billions living within the planet's hives, and the potential contribution those hives could make to the Great Crusade, could not be allowed to remain outside the dominion of the Emperor. Mankind had endured more than enough fracture and folly to allow such defiance to pass. Dorn himself had taken the task of bringing the world to compliance at the head of his Imperial Fists. They had been winning, hive by hive, battle by battle. And then the Alpha Legion had arrived.

They had announced themselves by taking one of the smaller hives, set to be the focus of the Imperial Fists' next offensive. The hive's leadership surrendered suddenly following a coup. A signal for Rogal Dorn's personal attention saying that the hive would fall had been received six hours before it surrendered. The signal had used the Imperial forces' highest level of clearance and had signed off by saying that Lord Alpharius and the XX Legion were honoured to be joining the VII Legion in bringing the planet to compliance. There had been attempts to meet with Alpharius and his warriors, but if they heard those calls, they had remained silent.

Alpha Legion forces had been sighted in the weeks that followed; a wing of armour had swept out of the ash wastes, to lend their aid to the assault on a primary surface hub of the planet's subterranean tunnel network. Scattered reports had placed warriors in variations of Alpha Legion colours in multiple battle-zones. Dorn had pressed on, and hive by hive the world had continued to fall. But a core of resistant hives remained, centred around the seat of the World-Prince.

On the eve of a renewed assault to take the last hives, the World-Prince had sent a signal surrendering. In the course of a single hour all of his direct blood relatives had been killed. The assassin in each case had been someone trusted and close to the slain. At the end of that hour the World-Prince had given his world to the Imperium, and four hundred and one members of the planet's ruling nobility were dead.

Alpharius shrugged, the enamelled scales of his armour shimmering with the gesture's movement.

'We did not need to kill them. That is true. We could have waited for you to grind your way through their troops, step by tedious step.'

'The future cannot be won by a war waged in shadows.'

'It will not be won any other way.'

'Then that future will be dead before it can begin.'

'Do not moralise at me, brother!' spat Alpharius, and now it was his turn to flick from control to anger. 'Would the deaths of all those you would have killed been acceptable because they died in open battle?'

'Yes,' said Dorn.

Alpharius held Dorn's gaze.

'I think we see the universe very differently, Rogal.'

'No. I do not think we see the same universe at all.'

They looked at each other, both of their faces set, so similar for all their differences.

'The end matters,' said Alpharius at last. 'Victory matters. Everything else is just delusion. With victory we can build dreams, but without victory they remain just dreams.'

'And how would you salvage a dream from your *victory*? Here and now, on this world. We cannot trust the World-Prince to rule for us, and you have removed those who could have taken his place. Even a defeated people prefer rule on their own. You have won this battle, but you have done it by seeding the ground with resentment and bitterness.'

'Some would call what I did gentle compared to the ways of our other brothers. Curze, Mortarion, Angron, even the Khan and feted Horus – would you call what they would have done preferable?'

'They–' began Dorn.

'You are certain that you are right,' said Alpharius, 'but if you disdain me, then why not my maker? Why not *our* father? He created us all. Or do you think my nature accident, or Him ignorant of what I do for Him? What any of us do for Him?'

'You think He approves of your methods?'

'He created us all, moulded the mysteries in our blood, put us to use as He needs, sees what we do and yet chooses to do nothing. What does that tell you?'

'That He expects us to see our own flaws and overcome them,' said Dorn.

'Yes? And how are you progressing with yours?'

Nothing moved in the chamber. Pech and Silonius glanced at each other, but Alpharius waited, unmoving, eyes unblinking.

'You will withdraw your forces from this world,' said Dorn. 'All of them. The agents and operatives too. I know that you use them, and I know how. I will be looking for them, and if I find any they will not be spared.'

'You will not find any,' said Alpharius.

Dorn shook his head and began to turn towards the doors. Archamus moved with him. He could feel the pressure of his lord's anger aching through the air like cold from a glacier. Dorn stopped at the doors and turned back.

'Your initial strikes were misdirected,' he said to Alpharius. 'You infiltrated one hive, and made it fall by systematic destabilising of authority, but you should have waited. You could have used it as a node from which to disperse your human operatives and agents into the other hives. You managed that to a degree, but you could have forced a total collapse in their defences across the planet, not just surrender by assassination. That move was also mistimed. Another thirty-seven hours and the pressure from our assault would have been eroding their ability to communicate. Secondary psychological fear, doubt and confusion would have been rising to a peak. You could have ridden that, played and controlled its pace, forcing hives to fall or change sides at the exact moment when it would amplify whatever effect you wanted. What you did was effective, but it was not optimally so, by your own criteria.'

Dorn stared at Alpharius, but the Alpha Legion primarch did not reply.

'I know you, brother,' continued Dorn. 'I knew that you were here before I walked through the door. I knew it was you on that throne, but not because you made an error in your masquerade. You made no mistake. Yet I still knew it was you. Think on that, brother. It is not that I do not understand what you are, or what you do. I understand both. We are what we choose to be.'

Dorn turned and walked to the doors. Archamus followed.

'For the Emperor,' said Alpharius as Dorn pushed the chamber doors wide.

Dorn paused, then walked on without looking back.

PART FOUR
HYDRA

ONE

THE MONITOR CRAFT closed swiftly on its target. She was called the *Implacable,* and she was a block of reactors, armour and guns wearing the shape of a chisel's head. She was fast and had enough firepower to hurt a ship many times her size. Her quarry was outmatched in all but speed. A scavenger ship, it was one of the small, fast craft that normally skulked in the dark corners of the system. Now it was in the open void, and its engines were flickering with failing power. Aboard the *Implacable,* auxiliaries ran for boarding craft and airlocks. Orders shook the air as helms locked into place on void suits. Volkites and laslocks activated with a static hum.

The *Implacable* closed in, eating the distance as the scavenger craft's engines flickered and died. The scavenger offered no resistance as boarding gantries locked into place. Signals flickered back and forth between the ships. At last the scavenger opened its airlock and the auxiliaries stormed forwards from their boarding gantries. The first wave came fast, flowing out into the scavenger ship's cargo hold.

Seven figures waited for them: three humans, two clad in body gloves and breathing masks, one in the ragtag finery of a scavenger chieftain. Beside them three Space Marines stood in deep blue. They were still, faces hidden behind their helms. With them was a single figure, also armoured, but somehow seeming greater than the rest.

The auxiliaries slowed as they entered the space. The seven figures at the centre of the room did not move. At last an officer stepped forwards from the circle of soldiers. Like the rest, his void armour was marked with the horned skull of the Saturnyne Rams, but the insignia on his shoulders marked him as a strategos: a senior line officer in the Solar Auxilia. He walked forwards, serpenta pistol drawn. He pushed up his visor, looked at the armoured warriors and then bowed.

'My lord,' he said. 'I respond to the call of Hades.'

Alpharius nodded.

'Is everything progressing as needed, Strategos Morhan?'

'We are three hours out. We have the cargo, and our arrival is logged and cleared with First Sphere command. Hydra station has been expecting a replacement astropath for four weeks, and we made sure that the escort orders were issued to us, rather than us requesting the duty. They will let us in because they have asked us to be there.'

'Hydra station?' said Ashul, a note of surprise and laughter in his voice.

Every eye turned to him.

'It is the First Sphere of defence's primary communications hub, its eyes and its voice,' rasped Kalix.

'I know, I just wondered if we were pushing a point.'

No one said anything.

Ashul bowed his head. 'My apologies, Lord Alpharius.'

Alpharius gave no acknowledgement, but turned to the ragged figure of Sork.

'My thanks, captain. You have your mission parameters. Carry them out. It will have to look good. The Imperial Fists are no fools.'

Sork bowed his head, face grim.

'I understand. It has been an honour, my lord.'

'The greater honour is mine. The hydra wakes,' Alpharius said, and began to walk through the ranks of auxiliaries, his entourage and Strategos Morhan trailing him as he made for the docking gantries and the monitor craft.

'For the Emperor,' called Sork as they left.

Algelth mine
Ariel moon, Uranus orbit

LOADING GANG BOSS Thao 4X56 frowned at the man who was shouting at him.

'What?' he snarled. The man was one of his crew, a sub loader called Unt 6X67. Stripped to the waist, Unt's exo-rig gleamed with oil sheen as he waved his servo-claw next to his head and said something again.

Thao couldn't hear him. Chains and cables were rattling through the pulleys just a metre behind him, and the clank of the loading gang going about its work stole what quiet was left. Unt waved and continued speaking.

'You dumb clank, I can't hear you!' shouted Thao.

Unt shook his head.

Thao stomped over to Unt, gears and pistons doing what his wasted frame couldn't. He had been on Ariel for a decade since his indent, and those years had a cost. A big cost. The Algelth was the oldest mine on Ariel, bored into the moon's flesh over thousands of years. Its central pit was tiered and cut down into the dark. Sub passages snaked off it, and its furthest reaches were so remote that some had not been worked for centuries. Capped by a scab of armoured plasteel ten kilometres wide, it was home to hundreds of thousands. It never slept, the tonne upon tonne of rock, crystal and ore that it sent to Mars and the Jovian orbital docks equalled only by the number of workers it ate. Ten years was a long time in the low gravity and cacophony.

Unt was newer, barely a few months fresh from some Terran sump hive. He still had the muscle mass that his pre-indent life had given him. He also still had better hearing than the rest of Thao's gang.

'What is it?' shouted Thao, his face so close to Unt that their cheeks were almost touching.

'...outing.'

'What?'

'Shouting.'

'You need to shout or I can't hear you, you dumb piec–'

'Can you hear the shouting?' bellowed Unt.

'Only yours.'

Unt shook his head. Behind them a pulley engine started to wind cable around its drum.

'I can hear shouting, or singing.' Unt stuck his arm out, and the exo-rig clattered as it followed the motion. 'From down there.'

Thao frowned. Unt was pointing down at the dark beyond the edge of the loading gantry. Thao stepped closer to the edge. Looking over he could see the lower gantries and crane rigs criss-crossing the gaping void. Pools of light dotted the gloom where work was done.

'I can't hear anything.'

'Turn your rig off,' shouted Unt. Thao hesitated, but something in Unt's manner was making him nervous. He shut his rig down. The drive engine went quiet, and suddenly he was a frozen statue of struts and gears. He listened. The sound of the mine still washed over him: the vibration of hundreds of machines, the clatter of chains and the rumble of deep drills.

Except...

A frown cut the dust-plastered skin of his face.

And he heard it. Low but rising, like a pulse, like...

'Chanting,' he said.

'What?' shouted Unt.

'It's not singing. It's chanting,' shouted Thao, and now he could hear it even without trying. A light appeared in the dark at the bottom of the pit. He realised that the rest of his loading gang had stopped their work, looks of puzzlement on their faces.

The indent penalties for loss of productivity crossed his mind, but his eyes were locked on the light beneath. The chanting rose louder and louder, rumbling like a rock fall, louder than the sound of the machinery. He could see figures on the lower gantries and walkways pause and look down into the dark.

'*Halfar...*' said Thao to himself.

'What?' called Unt from beside him.

'It's what they are chanting – "*Halfar to mag*", or something.'

Unt shook his head. The light was flowing up the tiered sides of the pit now, and he could see it did not have one source but many. Thousands of torches held in thousands of hands, oil flames shredding the dark. And the chanting rose and rose as the torch-bearers flowed up and up, faster and faster.

Cries began to ring out, beating against the rhythm of the chanting. Thao started his exo-rig and turned to see overseer troops in their vulcanised armour running to take up firing positions. Guns mounted on the gantries armed and swung their gaze downwards. There had been riots before, even attacks by bands of mutants. But this...

Thao stomped back towards the pulley rigs. He knew what he had to do, and he didn't need one of the overseers to tell him.

'Shut down the hoists!' he shouted, pointing at the machines spooling cable and chains. Down at the other end of those chains, containers of mined rock and crystal were rising from the depths in cages and cradles.

He could hear the chant, its beat growing and growing. A warning light flicked amber on one of the machines – a hoist was almost at the top. His gang were looking at him, confusion and fear blinking from their wide eyes.

'Shut it down!' Thao shouted again.

'Alpha to omega!' shouted Unt from beside him. The new ganger had followed Thao across the gantry. Thao turned and looked at Unt. Something was wrong. The ganger did not look confused; his dust-caked face seemed calm, almost serene. 'That's what they are chanting. Not halfar to mag. Alpha to omega – beginning to end.'

'What are you saying?' snarled Thao. 'Get moving, and shut down the hoist.'

Unt stepped closer, and Thao noticed the rest of the gang frantically scrabbling at the pulley machines. The cable kept on spooling onto the drum. Out on one of the gantries across the pit, a squad of overseers opened up with tripod-mounted guns. Lines of stubber rounds breathed down into the dark. And now he could hear the words that Unt had spoken boiling up louder than anything he had ever heard.

'*Alpha to omega! Alpha to omega! Alpha to omega!*'

The light on the pulley machines flicked to green. The top of the hoist came level with the gantry. He saw the curve of power armour and the gleam of light on lacquered plate, on huge figures standing on the hoist platform. Glowing green eyes turned to look at him. He saw the dark shine of boltguns, and an impossible name formed in his skull: *Legiones Astartes...*

A clank of pistons came from close behind him, but he could not move. He looked down. Hydraulic fluid was glistening as it ran down his rig. Thao had a second to see Unt's calm face as the ganger gripped him, twisted and flung him over the edge of the gantry.

He fell, tumbling end over end past a streaked blur of gunfire and flame, the words rising to meet him.

'*Alpha to omega! Alpha to omega! Alpha to omega!*'

Satellite munitions fortress Kadal
Jupiter close orbit

Magos Sec-Lo-65 emerged from his subroutine immersion as the warning signals chimed through his control room. A residual flesh instinct to blink became a clicking whir of focusing rings in his eyes. He listened to the warning chime, swallowing and digesting its tonal code. It was a sensor error alarm rather than a full alert. Sec-Lo-65 sighed a stream of imperfect code. The errors in the security system had been occurring for the last few days. Doors and sensors had been giving false returns, or shutting down at random. There was a malady in the machine-spirits, but no matter what he did he had not been able to purge the affliction. That alone was vexing. That the error was occurring in the control system in one of Jupiter's major munitions magazines was a cause of greater disquiet.

The Kadal munitions fortress was one of the primary reserves of fleet ordnance in the system. A lump of ultra-hard ore, it had taken the Mechanicum two decades to excavate, and another decade to graft the fortress structures into its insides. Nova shells, torpedo warheads, macro shells, propellant and explosive precursors, all lay in vibration and temperature-controlled dark at the core of the rock. When a ship needed rearming it would approach and hold anchor away from Kadal. Barges would then shuttle the munitions load out and return. Nothing and no one approached closer than several thousand kilometres; anything that tried to come closer would be greeted by Kadal's formidable defences. When dealing with enough destructive material to crack open a moon, there were no acceptable risks.

Sec-Lo-65 disengaged himself from his data cradle. Cables snapped free of his skull. The bionic tentacles that had taken the place of his legs flexed across the floor, and he glided towards the door. He was going to have to convene a data conclave of all his subordinates. The next days were going to be filled with code dissections and purifications.

He reached the door and murmured his clearance command, and the layers of plasteel peeled back.

He moved forwards, and stopped, eyes spinning as they focused on the figures standing in the corridor.

<Beta-42-8?> he queried in binaric as the junior tech-priest turned, red robes swirling about brass limbs. <I did not issue a summons. What is the reason for your...>

His eyes whirred as they focused on the figure standing behind Beta-42-8. Pattern processors bonded to Sec-Lo-65's brain outran his thoughts, flooding his awareness with details: Legiones Astartes, power armour of the Third Mark, with modifications for heat and energy baffling, deep indigo lacquer, micro impacts consistent with abrasion by interstellar dust. Surprise followed all of these observations, and shock flooded the remainder of his biological components.

<What... How...> he blurted in code.

<Alpha to omega,> replied Beta-42-8, as the Space Marine brought his weapon up and fired.

A tiny scrap of brain material and intellect circuitry was still processing Magos Sec-Lo-65's last thought ten minutes later as his blood and machine oil was pooling on the control room's floor.

<...omega... end... terminus... omega... end...>

He had no senses left to see a lone shuttle break free of a launch bay and boost for the open void.

Ten minutes after his last thought flickered to static and emptiness, the facility exploded with the shock and light of an entire void war compressed into a microsecond.

The Solar System

THE WARNING MESSAGE burned across the Solar System. In the Whispering Tower in the City of Sight, the great choir of astropaths shouted out in a hundred synchronised howls of imagination. The word raced out, travelling at the speed of thought. On hundreds of ships and orbital fortresses, astropaths woke from their trances and spoke their message. But even as the alarm flowed out, it found the Solar System already in chaos.

In the orbits of Mars, contradictory alerts and orders spread through vox-channels. Firing orders were given and countermanded. Auspex failed on a dozen ships. A pair of monitor craft fired on each other, their sensors seeing enemy targets. Fire stained the dark above the Red Planet.

In the sphere of Jupiter, the explosion of munitions fortress Kadal shone brighter than the sun.

In the Sheol Forge Fortress above Saturn, a techno-virus spread through the controls of a thousand automata. The robots tore apart the facility they guarded.

On and on the confusion and strife spread. It spread in the riots that boiled up in the moon colonies of Neptune. It shone in the flames of a dozen ships set ablaze as they mistook each other for enemies. It sang in signals and words and images that told of armies rising from the dark, and fire falling from the skies. It spread in an eye blink, eating the truth and hiding lies in the smoke of its passing.

And with it went the truth that gave every lie power: that the enemy had come at last to the gates of Terra.

TWO

THE SHIPS CAME from the night in a ragged cloud. They were the skeletons and carcasses of warships, their flanks gouged by asteroid impacts, haloed by leaking atmosphere. From Pluto's orbit the fires of their engines appeared one at a time. On the bridge of the *Lachrymae*, Sigismund watched the pict-feed of the approaching fleet and looked at Boreas.

'Signal the fleets into position,' said Sigismund.

Boreas nodded at the data hanging in curtains of holo-light above the command platform.

'It is a large formation,' said Boreas. The Templar champion's pale face was set, the features hardened around his eyes. 'Fifty vessels at least, warships too – damaged but still active. We are reading power in the weapons, but it is difficult to get a clear reading. There is a lot of moving debris out there at the moment.'

Sigismund shrugged, conceding the point. The Solar System was never entirely empty. Shoals of broken rock and ice tumbled though the void on millennia-old journeys. Added to which Pluto dragged belts of refuse with it as it circled Sol: husks of ships and stations that had been dead for hundreds or even thousands of years.

'They could be survivors from a storm,' said Sigismund.

'Or another attack fleet...' said Boreas.

'Indeed so,' said Sigismund without moving his gaze from the pict-feed.

This latest vomiting from the warp was bearing down on Pluto. Between the outer planet and the abyss spun its moons: Charon, Styx, Nix, Kerberos and Hydra. The smaller moons were little larger than the biggest warships. Warrens of tunnels and bunkers cut through their rock and ice.

Hydra sat furthest from Pluto. While her sibling moons were fortresses, she was little more than a shell around a core of reactors. Those reactors powered equally vast signal and sensor arrays. From Hydra the watchers on the Solar System's outer sphere could see far and coordinate the firing and signalling of all the rest. Of those others, Kerberos stood apart in another way. Clad in steel and weapons, she watched over the void with enough firepower to break a battlefleet. The name Kerberos was an echo of a tale which told of a three-headed hound that stood at the gates of death. Sigismund could not think of a more appropriate title. Together, Pluto and its moons were a fortress on the edge of the abyss. One day the last battle of the Imperium would begin, and on that day Pluto would be the first wall against which the attackers broke.

'Do you ever wonder why they come?' Boreas grunted. 'Is it spite, or strategy, or insanity?'

'It does not matter why, only that they do,' said Sigismund.

'This is no longer a war of hope. This is a war of vengeance and obliteration,' murmured Boreas.

Sigismund glanced at the other warrior.

'Strange words, and not your own. Where did you hear them?'

'From a lost friend,' said Boreas, but added nothing more. Sigismund turned away. Something had changed in Boreas in the time since the war had begun.

Have I changed as much? wondered Sigismund. *What will we be by the time we must fight for the last time?*

'What is the battle order?' asked Boreas.

'Move us to within gun reach. Broadcast orders for them to cut their engines and make their weapons cold. Prepare targeting to hit their engines on my command, and only on my command. If they are hostile, Inwit and Sol battle-groups strike the middle and cross. Fire to cripple, and then we board them.'

'How many ships do you wish to hold back on the line?'

'Acre battle-group. The guns of the moons can handle anything that gets through. Take the engines – if they try to push through deeper in system then execute them.' He paused. 'If they are hostile–'

'My lords!' the shout came from the communication pit to the side of the platform. Sigismund looked in the direction of the voice and saw one of the astropathic relay officers rising from his seat. The man's face was pale above his black-and-yellow uniform.

'Speak,' commanded Sigismund.

'The choir has received word from the Third Sphere,' said one of the other officers. 'An attack is in progress...'

Another officer began to speak, hands pressed against the vox connection bonded to her ears.

'The forces of the Fourth Sphere are reporting.'

'Lord Sigismund,' a voice cut through the others. It was the voice of Anasis, the senior amongst the communications officers and the one directly linked to the Astropath Prime on the Hydra moon fortress – if she asked for his attention it took priority even over the dire news coming from within the Solar System. The other communications officers fell silent, as she looked up.

'Fire on the mountains,' she said.

Sigismund blinked once, not needing to question what she had said, or doubt its meaning. Within his mind he saw an old memory of events that had not yet happened: the walls of the Imperial Palace falling in fire, a sky of iron, the dead covering the ground. It had come, at last, as it was always going to.

He looked up at the pict-feed of the ragged swarm of ships closing from the void. And as he looked, the first of them fired. Alarms cut through the air, shouts rose from the auspex pits.

'All ships engage,' called Sigismund. 'Maximum force.'

Boreas was shouting orders a second later. The *Lachrymae* shook as it came to full life. Sigismund pulled his helm from his waist and clamped it over his head. The war was here. The enemy was come at last, and he would be the first to face them.

Docking gantry Gamma-19, Hydra moon fortress
Plutonian orbit

THE DOCKING COLLAR clanged as it locked into place. Myzmadra glanced at Ashul, but he had lowered the visor of his void armour. Around them the auxiliaries stood, faceless behind masks of brushed plasteel. Between them the caskets of the two dead astropaths sat on a tracked trolley. Her volkite charger felt heavy in her hands, its weight familiar in a way that brought old memories to mind. Her pistols were hidden in a pouch at the small of her back. She shifted her weight. Air began to hiss around the door hatch. Strategos Morhan nodded to her, his exposed face as blank as the masks his subordinates wore.

'Alpha to omega,' he said, and the words startled her. She blinked.

'Omega to alpha,' she replied.

Lights in the docking bridge pulsed. Ashul was a still presence at her shoulder, his finger tapping the casing of his gun.

Tap-tap... Tap-tap...

She drew and held a breath. Calm, focused, the next steps clear in her mind.

She could hear the track units humming beneath the casket.

A line of blue light arced around the hatch in front of them as it opened. Warm air billowed in and became mist. She felt her muscles begin to tense in sequence. Figures stood in the grey air beyond the hatch. Armour plates bulked the figures' shoulders. Weapons hung from their hands, pipes and weapon feeds stretching to their backs. Light glinted off gloss crimson-and-white carapace.

Inferallti Hussars, she thought, as her eyes filtered through them. One of the Old Hundred. Elites. Twenty. Heavy weapons. Loaded and readied. Fingers on triggers. Could have been worse. It could have been the Imperial Fists.

Tap-tap... Tap-tap...

She forced stillness into her muscles.

'Your orders?' A voice came from the ranks of the hussars, the words a growl of speaker static.

'We are the escort for the astropaths from the Throneworld. They died en route. We are here to give the bodies to the astropath enclave.'

'What would they want with corpses?' asked the hussar.

Morhan gave a shrug that somehow managed to convey that he thought answering was as beneath him as the questioner.

'That's their matter.' A pause. Morhan gave another shrug, arrogance and disdain rippling through him. 'If you wish to eject the body of an esteemed member of the Telepathica into the void, I am sure it will end well for you in the long run.'

A pause hung in the pulsing of the lights.

'Clearance?' asked the hussar.

'You have it already, or we wouldn't be here. Now either move aside and offer us escort, or start shooting. There are what? Twenty of you red-and-whites... You might even stand a chance.'

Tap-tap... Tap-tap...

Myzmadra clenched her teeth; the sound of Ashul's finger on his gun was like a drum in her ear.

'You may pass within,' said the voice. The hussars parted, stepping in sync to form a corridor between their guns.

Morhan executed a perfect salute. Myzmadra and the rest of the squad came to attention. For an instant she felt like she had stepped sidewise into the life she had left behind. Then they were marching forwards, the astropaths' caskets rolling between them.

They had gone two hundred paces when sirens began to wail. Amber lights blinked, and the deck began to ring with the sound of running feet.

Another squad of Inferallti Hussars ran towards them. Myzmadra tensed. Ashul's finger stilled on the trigger of his gun. Then the hussars were running past them. Morhan turned and called out to the squad's sergeant.

'What is the alert?'

'Fire on the mountains, sir,' called the sergeant, without stopping. 'The invasion has come.'

Then the hussars were gone, but the sirens and lights beat on.

'Double time,' called Morhan and the auxiliaries began to pound down the corridor, the caskets rocking on their track units.

Imperial Fists frigate Unbreakable Truth

Trans-Neptunian region

'COME ON, COME on,' muttered Andromeda.

Archamus ignored her. His eyes were on the pict screens, watching the feed of information from the frigate's auspex systems. They had been following the projected path of the scavenger ship for ten hours. So far they had seen no sign of it.

'Doesn't this thing go any faster?' she hissed, stamping a foot on the deck.

'We are degrading the plasma reactors with our speed,' growled Kestros.

'No, then,' she said.

'Quiet,' said Archamus. His eyes focused on the screens, where amber runes had begun to spin where before there had been only blue. 'There it is. Chayo, what is that?'

'Lord Archamus,' answered Magos Chayo from the column that loomed above the command deck. 'We are detecting the engine output of a ship. It is consistent with the craft we are pursuing. It is losing speed.'

'Why?' asked Archamus.

'Its engine output is fluctuating. Sixty per cent probability of engine or reactor damage. Of this we are in concordant certainty.'

'Good.'

'Our weapons and engines are prepared. What outcome should we facilitate into being?'

Archamus felt his face twitch.

Unlike some warships, the *Unbreakable Truth* was a gift of the Machine Cult to the VII Legion, and crewed almost entirely by tech-priests, servitors and Mechanicum helots. On other ships, officers of different stations would have answered Archamus' commands, but on the *Unbreakable Truth* Chayo alone was the voice of the ship and its crew. It was efficient, but also meant that the Magos referred to both himself and every other part of the ship in the personal plural. It had taken a while for Archamus to not find it disconcerting.

'Maintain intercept course,' he said. 'Run her down.' He glanced at Kestros. 'Boarding assault. Everything within dies. I want visual confirmation that the Alpha Legion are on board. Andromeda, get the prisoner. He comes with us and gives us confirmation of the presence of... of our target.'

'You trust the psyker?' asked Andromeda.

'I trust him not at all, but I will take whatever advantage we can.'

'And if... *he* is aboard?'

'We withdraw by snap teleportation and then blast the ship to atoms.'

'By your will.' Kestros saluted.

'Lord Archamus!' came Chayo's voice. 'Their primary engines have failed. They are firing secondary thrusters to try and turn. We are closing.'

'Why would they turn?' asked Andromeda.

'Evasion,' said Archamus, pointing at the tactical readouts. 'There is a dust drift they could reach, and try to hide in.' He shot a look at Andromeda and Kestros. 'Get to the launch decks.'

They moved to comply, as a notion cut into his thoughts.

'Wait!' he said, looking back to the data on the screens. Kestros and Andromeda froze. 'How long ago did their engines begin to fail?' he called to the tech-priest.

'Just before we made the detection. The engine fluctuations are the reason we saw them.'

'All weapons lock to target,' said Archamus.

'Master?' asked Kestros, but Archamus nodded to the tech-priest.

'Fire.'

'Compliance,' said the tech-priest, and a heartbeat later the ship shook, and shook again.

Macro cannons, plasma annihilators and turbo lasers hurled their fury across the dark between the *Unbreakable Truth* and its quarry. The beams of las-light struck first and carved into the scavenger's hull. The macro shells and plasma streams hit an instant later and split it open in a burst of light.

'What...?' began Andromeda, but Archamus was already calling to Chayo.

'What craft are logged as passing through this volume in the last nine hours?'

'Compiling and accessing,' replied Chayo.

Archamus turned to look at Kestros and Andromeda.

'We should not have been able to catch them. That scavenger craft was faster than this ship.'

'Its engines...' began Kestros.

'Failed and revealed its location. It should have been far beyond this point already, but instead it is here. Why would it have lost time on us?'

Andromeda cursed.

'If they had stopped or slowed to meet with another craft,' said Kestros.

'The monitor craft *Implacable* bearing two astropaths to the outer system defences, with a contingent of the Fifty-Sixth Veletaris Tercio, of the Second Solar Auxilia Cohort, passed through the zone of potential convergence with the recently destroyed vessel. Projected time of potential meeting between the vessels between two and five hours prior to present. Accuracy of projection is sixty-nine per cent.'

'If we had boarded then they could have detonated reactors and removed us in an instant,' breathed Kestros.

Archamus nodded.

'And who would think to track the position of an authorised monitor craft.'

'Where was this ship?' asked Andromeda.

'You are referring to the system monitor designated *Implacable*?' said Chayo.

'Yes, yes,' snapped Andromeda. 'Where was it taking these astropaths?'

'To the communication fortress in the First Sphere,' said Chayo. 'To the Plutonian moon designated Hydra.'

Archamus felt a shiver pass through his bionics. Andromeda's face was fixed in a grin, as though at a joke she had just understood. Kestros met his gaze and completed Archamus' thought.

'They were never fleeing Terra,' he said. 'They were moving towards their strike point.'

'Get us to Hydra,' said Archamus. 'Burn the reactors to slag if you have to, but get us there.'

Astropath Sanctuary, Hydra moon fortress
Plutonian orbit

THEY REACHED THE outer doors of the sanctuary as the sirens rose in pitch. The alert lights began to blink red.

Active battle footing, thought Myzmadra, as they halted before the door. Four Inferallti Hussars stood either side of the entrance. Her eyes flicked over their weapons: two with drum-fitted shot-cannons, two with rotor cannons, ammo feeds looping to their knees from hoppers on their backs. Augmetic bracing struts ran over their shoulders and torsos, as though they were being hugged by metal spiders.

Morhan stepped forwards.

'Sanctuary is on lockdown,' said one of the hussars, a male from the voice.

'No,' snapped Morhan. 'These are two of *their* dead, and you are either going to call one of them out here to take charge of these remains, or I am going to dump them out of an airlock and explain that it was what you suggested we do because you were more worried about a lockdown drill than respecting the custom of the Telepathica.'

'It's not a drill,' the hussar said, and raised the barrel of his shot-cannon. The other three all did the same. 'Back away.' The hussar released the firing catch on the cannon with a deliberate flick of his thumb.

Myzmadra swallowed hard, and the sub-vocal mic pressed against her throat activated. Static popped in her vox-bead.

'Stand by,' she said. She had a throwing blade pressed between her palm and the fore-grip of her gun: a quiet and swift way to kill, and the last thing that the hussars would expect.

'Back away,' repeated the hussar. Morhan nodded and stepped back, shaking his head slightly as though at manifest stupidity. Myzmadra drew breath to speak the kill command.

A metallic clank pealed out through the air. The doors to the sanctuary were opening. Piston bolts disengaged one after another, the layers of plasteel pulling back into the walls. The hussars twitched in surprise, but kept their weapons levelled. Myzmadra held the breath she had drawn. The last leaf of armour parted, and a figure stepped out, flanked by two masked soldiers in coal-coloured armour.

Black Sentinels, she thought, the life-wards of the astropaths within the Solar System. Between them hobbled an astropath wrapped in green velvet and ermine. He carried a silver cane in each hand, and his face was so thin and pale that it seemed like a skull with the skin still clinging to the bone. The astropath stopped and looked up at the corner of the corridor, and Myzmadra saw that the sockets of his eyes had been filled with clusters of rubies. Red light glittered from the jewels as he turned his head from side to side, as though trying to hear something. His tongue flicked to the edge of his lips and then back.

'They said that you have come bearing the body of two of our number,' said the astropath.

'Honoured one,' said the hussar. 'A full lockdown and confinement is in place–'

'Shut up,' the psyker snapped, and banged one of his canes on the floor. The hussar hesitated and then fell silent. The astropath turned his blind gaze back to the twin caskets borne between the two lines of auxiliaries. 'Is this them?' he asked, but stepped forwards without waiting for an answer.

He took both canes in one hand and placed the other on the polished metal of a casket.

'You stupid idiots...' he whispered, close enough for Myzmadra to hear. For an instant she thought he was talking to her, or the hussars, but she saw his fingers tremble on the casket top and realised that he was talking to the corpse within. 'Why did you not stay in the City of Sight? This is a time of war, and... and...'

He looked up, and she felt his blind gaze fall on her for a second. It was like a breath of freezing air. She felt a shiver of sympathetic anguish run through her. So the dead astropaths had been people that this other one cared for. She wondered for a second if that had been deliberate, another little detail put in place by the Legion to use if needed.

'How did...' began the astropath, straightening. 'How did they die?'

'In their sleep,' replied Morhan. 'It was sudden. We don't know more I am afraid.'

The old astropath looked at him.

'In their sleep?' he asked, and Myzmadra felt another shiver of cold on her skin. Beside her Ashul had begun tapping his finger on the case of his gun again.

Tap-tap... Tap-tap...

'Yes,' said Morhan.

'You are lying,' said the astropath simply.

Myzmadra threw her knife in the space that it took Morhan to blink. It hit the nearest hussar in the neck just below the bottom of his visor. He staggered. Ashul fired from behind her. A line of las-light hit one of the Black Sentinels in the head. The soldier fell, and Ashul raked into the other coal-armoured figure. Myzmadra swung her volkite around and fired it point-blank through the face of the astropath. Vaporised skull and flesh exploded around the path of the beam. The man's body was reduced to ash. The beam lanced on into the hussar behind. Fragments of armour, bone and exo-rig ripped out hitting the other hussar as burning shrapnel. One Black Sentinel and one hussar remained between the auxiliaries and the open door of the sanctuary.

'Through the door!' shouted Morhan. The Black Sentinel was fast and was already running back towards the opening. The surviving hussar braced and fired his shot-cannon. Clouds of pellets exploded through the auxiliaries, ringing off armour and ripping through blast fabric. Two went down. The cannon roared as it swallowed shells. Morhan leapt at the hussar, sword pulling free of its scabbard, and sawed the blade up under the soldier's chin. Gloss blood sheeted down the white-and-red plates of armour.

Myzmadra dropped to one knee, aiming her charger at the Black Sentinel. He was ducking and weaving without rhythm or pattern.

Good training, she thought. *Very good.*

Three strides separated him from the open doors. She breathed out and pulled the trigger. The beam hit the running man in the small of the back and exploded through his torso. Myzmadra was up and running before the corpse hit the floor. The auxiliaries were sprinting next to her, now lugging the metal bulk of the two caskets.

They cleared the doorway. Morhan was already at the door controls. The layers of plasteel began to slam shut. The auxiliaries were spreading out, covering the archways leading off the entrance chamber. They had left two wounded outside. There was no helping that; neither time nor circumstance was on their side.

It was suddenly quiet, the blare of alarms and flash of warning lights shut out as the blast doors sealed. Ashul was already snapping the seals around the lid of one of the caskets.

'Atmospheric protocols in force,' she called over the vox. 'Make sure your masks are sealed.'

The lid came off the casket. Beneath it lay the corpse of a man. Dark veins marbled the pale skin of his face, and the green silk of his robes lay over his limbs. Pale mist coiled from inside as the coolant gases within met the warmer air of the chamber. Ashul reached in and yanked the corpse out onto the floor. Four quick movements, and two metal panels snapped free from the bottom of the casket. Beneath them, a dozen cylinders of brushed steel nestled in neat lines. Ashul began pulling out the cylinders, throwing them to Morhan and the auxiliaries.

Myzmadra caught one. It was heavy and cold even through the padding of her gloves. She found the release trigger.

'Stand by to arm and disperse on my order,' she said into the vox.

The Black Sentinels fired without warning. She had not even seen them approach. Las-fire snapped through the air. An auxiliary went down, a hole burned through his faceplate. Another was punched backwards off his feet. Myzmadra was moving and firing before any of the rest, snaking from side to side as she pulsed the volkite beam into the passage opening where the fire was coming from.

'First section, release!' she shouted. 'Release now!'

Silver cylinders flew over her head and crashed down into the passage openings. The hiss of releasing pressure cut through the sound of gunfire. A shot buzzed past her head from behind, so close it blurred her sight. She saw the splash of its impact and a figure slump from beside one of the entrances.

'Nice shot,' she snarled.

'My pleasure,' replied Ashul.

The auxiliaries were firing back. Morhan was shouting at the section forwards.

A fresh squall of las-fire breathed towards her, and she jinked aside. Her blood was singing with reaction enhancers. Her augmented heart was beating out a machine-gun rhythm. The Legion had given her many things, and taken much in return, but the full range of those gifts was something she rarely had the pleasure of using. The first passage opening was in front of her. A Black Sentinel crouched low in the lee of the arch, a carbine pointed dead at her. The face behind the sights was a lacquered mask of a grinning beast, its cheeks painted silver with swirled tears. The Sentinel began to squeeze the trigger. She snapped to the side. The muzzle of the carbine wavered and then flared. Las-bolts spat past her as she kicked from the floor.

The auxiliary armour she wore was bulky, made to weather damage rather than allow the wearer to dodge it: not ideal, but still not a real hindrance. She struck the Black Sentinel in the chest with both feet. His chest-plate cracked beneath the impact. He cannoned into the passage wall as she landed. He rebounded without a pause and brought his gun up to fire. Myzmadra landed and rammed the barrel of her gun into his painted mask. The lacquer split. The man within sucked a breath, struggling to bring his weapon up to fire. The gas that was flooding through the air flowed in through the crack in his mask, and down into his lungs. He slumped to the floor, dead before the muscles of his legs had finished folding.

The auxiliaries were storming into the passage openings. Myzmadra followed them, triggering the release on her canister.

'Second section, release,' she shouted, and threw the gas canister through an unsealed blast hatch.

Five minutes later the gas had flooded the sanctuary. The ten astropaths of the choir lay on the floor of their communion chamber, utterly still, their mouths open in the act of taking their last breath.

Myzmadra checked the last of them and then activated a new channel on her vox.

'The blind are silent,' she said. 'Alpha to omega.'

THREE

Warship Lachrymae
Trans-Plutonian region

THE VII LEGION strike fleet plunged into the ragged ships coming from the dark. The Imperial Fists were few – thirty against over a hundred, but the numbers did not matter. The thirty gold-and-black-armoured warships struck the ragged fleet in a tapered cone. Broadsides battered down the attackers' few active void shields, and lances sliced at their engines. The enemy ships began to tumble, their momentum pushing them forwards even as they spun over and over.

At the tip of the Imperial Fists' formation, three ships cut between the enemy vessels. They were the *Three Sisters of Spite,* and at their head – trailing the fire of her engines like a wound cut across the dark – was the *Lachrymae.* Fire crashed after her and her sisters, cutting the empty void as she plunged deeper and deeper into the cloud of enemy ships. Behind her, her sisters began to loose boarding torpedoes. Schools of silver darts the size of hab spires slid from launch tubes on jets of flame. Each torpedo held a contingent of warriors in the rattling dark of its hollow core.

In the belly of the *Lachrymae,* Sigismund stood in silence at the edge of the launch bay. The words of his oaths threaded through his mind, as he wrapped the links of chain around his wrist and pulled them tighter. The largest of the enemy ships grew in his eye, its shape projected across the eyepiece of his helm. It was vast, an ugly block of metal. Craters pitted one side of its hull, as though it had borne the brunt of a storm of asteroids. It was still a warship, though, no matter how wounded. Macro batteries fired down the vessel's length even as Sigismund looked at it. A moment later he felt the *Lachrymae* tremble as it rode the edge of a blast wave.

He tightened and fastened the last link of chain, and then raised his blade, feeling its balance settle in his grasp.

'Is it secure enough yet that you will not drop it?' growled a voice from behind him. He glanced, and in his clear eye the face of Rann grinned at him. His armour was clean, but the marks and dents of battle still marred the yellow lacquer.

Sigismund nodded at Rann, but did not answer as he rose from where he had knelt on the deck. He looked behind him. A hundred Templars rose as one. Rann's chosen – his head takers – stood in loose order beside them. The air rang as they beat their fists against their battered shields. The air was keening with the rising whine of engines. Servitors and serfs were moving back from the dozen gunships. Fuel lines were snapping free of wings. Heat was shimmering across the deck as thrusters lit.

Sigismund looked at his strike force, moving his eyes across each legionary. Then he raised his sword in salute, turned and strode to the waiting gloom of his gunship. The warriors followed.

'So, this is the day, brother,' growled Rann from his shoulder, as they swung up the gunship's assault ramp. He could hear the snarled grin in the words.

Sigismund gestured, and the hatch began to close. The frame of the gunship began to tremble as it strained against its tethers.

'Launch,' he said into the vox. The sound of engines rose, and then gravity hammered through them as the gunship streaked out into the void.

✠ ✠ ✠

Primary communication array control,
Hydra moon fortress, Plutonian orbit

'ALL SYSTEMS AND connectivity functioning within ordained tolerances.'

Captain Koro of the Imperial Fists acknowledged the Primary Magos' drone with a nod, but did not look up from the tactical displays.

'Ensure that signal priority is given to fire coordination and the link with Lord Sigismund's fleet.'

'It is so commanded and ordained,' clattered the magos from its place in the roof above Koro's head.

Twelve magi oversaw the operation of Hydra's primary communication array. Suspended in webs of cable around the machine column at the centre of the chamber, wrapped in tattered, red shrouds, they resembled chrysalises hanging from the branches of a tree. They did not have individual names, and the designation 'Primary' shifted between them. Together they existed to oversee Hydra's vast communication and sensor systems. Everything from vox communication, to fire-control coordination and auspex readings passed through these twelve. That data, and the systems which created it, were dispersed across the moon, but this was the point through which all data had to flow. Sited beneath the dish of the largest array, it was a quiet place for all of the voices that passed through it.

Koro glanced at his sergeant. Ten of his company elite were with him in the control chamber, silent and watching from the edges of the walls.

'Full lockdown is complete?'

'Yes, captain. One ship docked before the lockdown, a monitor craft bearing astropaths from Terra. But all other traffic has ceased.'

'Good,' Koro said, and moved his gaze to where the dull grey of plas-teel blast shutters closed off the view of the moon's surface.

Jutting out from the crust of structures, the array control had clear sight into the void. Sometimes you could see the light of the fleet engaging if they were close. Koro had watched from here many times as his brothers fought in the void. This time though... he had heard the words of the alert signal.

Fire on the mountains.

He felt his fingers flex without consciously willing them to, and realised he had bared his teeth at the shuttered view.

An alert light blinked at the edge of his sight. He frowned and turned, as one of the servitors wired into the banks of consoles turned its face from side to side, like a dog sniffing the air.

'External sensors detecting movement on surface,' droned the servitor.

'Which zone?' asked Koro.

The servitor twitched, mouth chewing the air, and then spoke.

'This zone. Primary communication array exterior.'

Koro's eyes locked on the blast shutters. Cold slid across his skin. His hearts skipped into a lower rhythm as he drew his weapons. His command squad were already moving, weapons lowered, fanning out across the chamber.

'Give me the status of the exterior auto weapons,' he called.

'Exterior weapons eleven through twenty-four are reading as active, but not responding to direct command.'

'Get me a visual–'

The shutters blew inwards.

Koro's helmet visor dimmed with the flash of the explosion. His world seemed to pause, the blast unfolding before him with all the gradual delicacy of a slowed pict-feed. A point in the centre of a shutter glowed red, then yellow, then white. The glow of heat raced across the grey metal as the centre bulged inwards, and then burst. A hollow cone of blue-hot liquid reached inwards. Servitors and machines ignited beneath its path. A shock wave formed in concentric rings, shimmering as they distorted the air.

Time snapped back into full flow. The blast hit Koro and slammed him backwards. Heat blew through the front layers of his armour. His helmet display became a cascade of red damage runes. Debris and glowing pellets of metal spun through the air. Servitors and blocks of machinery ripped from the floor. Koro hit a pillar, spun to the deck and rose in time to see the first figure come through the breach in the shutters.

Bolt-rounds were spitting across the chamber as the air rushed out into the void. Warriors of his command squad were already firing into the glowing wound. Koro braced to fire.

A shape came through the breach. It moved so fast that Koro saw only a blur of cold, blue armour and a flash of a blade cutting the light of gunfire. The spear struck him below the sternum, punching through armour and up through his left heart. He fell, his sight a blur, his throat filling with his own blood as he tried to rise.

A figure stood above him, holding the spear transfixing his chest. The pressure down the blade was like the weight of a mountain, though the armoured figure seem relaxed, as though he were doing nothing but resting his hand on the weapon's haft. Koro noted the indigo-blue of the armour and the hydra coiling over one shoulder guard.

Alpha... Legion... he thought, his mind struggling to focus as his body fought to stay alive. The figure pulled the spear free and was gone. Gunfire streaked the air above him. He could hear the sound of detonations and the shriek of a meltagun rising above the rush of escaping atmosphere. Then the gunfire slackened, and suddenly the sound of battle ceased. Somehow that sudden quiet was worse than anything else.

He pushed himself up. His remaining heart was still beating, struggling to pump blood even as it poured out of him. His armour was critically damaged, a dead weight on his failing frame. Above him the twelve tech-priests hung in their cocoons of cables. Corpses covered the floor, servitors blasted to shreds of meat and metal, and amongst them figures clad in yellow power armour. Blood sheened them all, pumping free from the stumps of severed limbs and punctured torsos. Four Alpha Legion warriors stood in the ruin, three of them moving amongst the dead, eyes and weapons searching for signs of life. The figure with the spear stood still at the centre of the carnage.

'Remove them,' said the warrior, looking up at the magi suspended from the ceiling. The other Alpha Legion turned and fired into the twelve tech-priests. Bolt shells ripped through cables and red robes. Black oil and blood spilled down, pattering on the metal deck.

Koro had his bolter in his hand. That fact was all that mattered –
not the blood that was filling his lungs, not the shame of failure, not
the shock of the enemy he was facing.

'Find the back-up controls for the array,' said the warrior with the
spear, his voice carrying over the howl of escaping air. 'Send the signal
to the attack fleet that the time has come for us to show our hand.'

'By your will, Lord Alpharius,' said one of the others with a nod.

Alpharius. The thought began then ended as Koro cut it away. All that
mattered was lifting his bolter and squeezing the trigger, just as he had
countless times before.

The gun came up, steady in Koro's bloody hand.

Alpharius turned, moving and spinning the spear. A blur of silver
and blue was the last thing that Koro saw.

Unknown intruder vessel
Trans-Neptunian region

'BREACH!' ROARED RANN, as the melta charge detonated. Droplets of
glowing metal sprayed out as the bulkhead door dissolved. Sigismund
came through into the space beyond. A thick spray of hard rounds
greeted him. He charged. The streaked walls of the passageway were
a blur at the edge of his sight. Figures loomed in his helmet display,
sketched in the monochrome of dark-vision. He saw bloated muscle beneath blank iron masks and machine-braced limbs wrapped
around rotor cannons. The nearest figure dragged the barrel towards
him. Rounds danced across the deck as Sigismund leapt across the distance. He took the masked figure with a back-handed blow that carved
through its mask, and sliced through the skull and brain beneath. The
figure fell backwards, rotor cannon shrieking as its spinning barrels hit
the deck. Sigismund was already past the corpse, turning momentum
from his kill stroke into a rising cut that took the next enemy in the
side, and tore up through its torso.

Rann was beside him, axes hacking and weaving, as they advanced down the corridor. They were already deep within the intruder ship, and there was no doubt that it was hostile. But something was wrong, something that itched down his muscles even as he carved through those who came to face them. There was something dulled, almost clinical about the ship. They had taken hundreds of intruder ships in the last years, and their insides had crawled with the signs of madness. Not this ship, though. Its darkness was cold and empty, as though it were a skin over something unseen.

'Lord Sigismund.' The voice sounded in his helm, laden with static from its journey across the void from the *Lachrymae* and through layers of hull armour.

'Speak,' replied Sigismund, pulling his sword free of a corpse. The corridor was clear, the sound of gunfire and crack of weapons suddenly absent. Darkness and silence stretched ahead of him.

'*Boarding groups across the battlesphere are reporting moderate resistance. But some have found nothing.*'

'Explain,' he commanded.

'*Fifteen of the enemy ships are empty, zero resistance – engines running, but no sign of crew besides servitors.*'

Sigismund paused, suddenly feeling the weight of his sword in his hand. The silence of the passage pressed around him even as his assault team moved up next to him.

'Pull them back,' he said into the vox.

'*My... lord...?*' came the voice of the officer, a burst of static chopping through the words.

'All assault forces, pull them back to our ships, now.'

The static rose again. '*...confirm...*'

Sigismund turned to Rann. 'Pull back to the gunships, immediate full withdrawal.'

Rann nodded, and the vox clicked as though he were about to speak. Static shrieked and boiled across the channel. Sigismund felt his sword rise, pulled up by a cold instinct running under his skin.

Green eyes lit in the dark. The air buzzed as armour activated. Lightning shivered down claws and blades as hulking figures stepped from the dark. Plasma lanced down the corridor. Sigismund was moving, sword already a blur as he ran to meet the enemy. Rann was calling out for a shield-wall, and the dark was gone, as fire and the roar of the ambush tore the silence apart.

Trans-Neptunian region

THE ALPHA LEGION attack fleet spun from the dark. Two hundred warships, each of them falling end over end, like a swirl of dry leaves blowing through the night. In their path Pluto loomed, its face sparkling with the flash of weapons and the streak of engine fires, as warships engaged in battle. If an eye or sensor had looked out from one of the ships in that engagement, they would have seen only the open abyss of the interstellar gulf. The shine and wink of distant stars would have seemed bright and cold. What light there was might have caught a drift of dust, or the edge of a lump of ice-bound rock. Looking deeper it might have seen a glimmer of movement, and noted the thin light snagging on a sharp edge of something jagged and vast, arching slowly closer.

Then the first engine fired, bright and true in the black, and then another and another. And the tumbling mass of ships were no longer falling, but spinning into formation, engines roaring to full life, void shields snapping into place, weapons turning to find targets as a battle-fleet hundreds strong fell out of the dark at the edge of the sun's light.

The Imperial Fists fleet saw them. Already engaged with the intruders who had closed on Pluto, now they were facing a second, and vastly more deadly, enemy. Signals snapped between Sigismund's warships. Snatches of confused shouts and static flooded the vox. Orders barked back and forth. Ships already engaging the intruder fleet began to turn, to meet this new threat.

The battle-barge *Alpha* fired its first volley. A full payload of torpedoes launched from its prow. A mountain range of guns on its back hurled fire across the dark. Bombardment cannons punched shells out, one after another, building-sized breeches ringing as they slammed open to swallow the next shell. The rest of the Alpha Legion fleet spoke a second later. Fire raced ahead of the ships as they bore down on where the Imperial Fists vessels had moved to engage the first wave of intruders, on the edge of Pluto's orbit.

The first ship to die was the *Judgement's Intercession*. It was an old ship, a dark-hulled grand cruiser, with scars from hundreds of battles that had failed to claim it. Macro shells exploded across its void shields. They crumpled, bursting like the skin of a soap bubble. Lance beams stabbed through the clouds of debris and struck the *Intercession* along the length of its gun-decks. Blocks of armour melted. The grand cruiser fired back, half blinded by the cloak of boiling gas wreathing its hull. Batteries howled into the inferno. Shells struck the shields on the oncoming Alpha Legion fleet. Then the second volley hit. The *Judgement's Intercession* exploded, cleaving in two as though struck by a god's axe.

The Alpha Legion fleet fired in concert, ships pouring their volleys together, cutting into the engaged Imperial Fists formation. The defenders of the First Sphere of Sol began to die. Those nearest the newly appeared Alpha Legion fleet vanished as deluges of energy and explosions struck them. Shields and armour crumpled. Reactors breached and spheres of white plasma burst into being, racing out like hungry suns.

Ten Imperial Fists ships were already stains of light and debris when the first salvoes of torpedoes hit. Haywire warheads detonated against the hull of the battle cruiser *Arcadian*, darkening its sensors and shields. Three double-stage warheads hit seconds later, sliding past the *Arcadian*'s silent defence turrets and slamming into its central mass. Melta charges reduced its armour to white-hot liquid an instant before the secondary charges sent the molten metal lancing into the ship's guts. Pressure waves rippled through the corridors, blowing out hatches and crushing crew even as it stole the air from their lungs. The ship slewed sidewise, nose dropping from its path of flight as it burned from its core outwards.

The Imperial Fists ships came around, raking fire at every target within reach of their guns. A battered intruder was caught between the guns of four frigates and torn apart by macro cannon fire. A pair of Alpha Legion gunboats tried to cut into the engine wake of a squadron of light cruisers, and ended in a splash of plasma and hull fragments.

Within the ships that had been boarded, the Imperial Fists made their way back to their gunships. The Alpha Legion emerged from the dark to cut them off. The Imperial Fists fought on, pushing through explosions and gunfire, armour and boarding shields shedding sparks with each step.

Then the twelve fireships hidden amongst the intruders exploded. Hulls packed with munitions and plasma reservoirs became expanding stars of blue-and-white light. Waves of energy engulfed ships, smothering their shields and swallowing their hulls. Heat blasted through cracks in armour. Human crew roasted at their stations. Oil and fuel ignited, and the fires raced on, tearing air from the lungs of the living, blowing through hatches and billowing through vents. Blackened ships emerged from the inferno, weeping burning atmosphere and sloughing armour.

As the bulk of the Imperial Fists ships rolled amongst the blaze, the Acre battle-group thrust from where it had been holding close to Pluto's outer orbit. Held back in case any of the intruder fleet broke through, the ships now kindled their engines to full burn and turned to meet the new enemy coming from the dark.

The battlesphere was now a stretched ellipse, reaching from the edge of Pluto's orbit into the gulf beyond. Nearest to the planet, the bulk of the Imperial Fists fleet was tangled amongst the ships that had first approached, while the Acre battle-group raced to cut off the main Alpha Legion fleet before it could join the fight.

Spreads of torpedoes and nova shells kicked free of the Acre battle-group as it closed with the Alpha Legion fleet. Vast explosions flared as the shells detonated. Waves of energy broke across shields and hulls. The battle-group accelerated into the attack. At the front of the formation were the *Warrior of an Unknown Sky*, *Storm Wrought* and *Victory's Son*. They fired in synchronised volleys. A torrent of shells poured from their gun-decks. Explosions wreathed the *Alpha*, blue, orange and pink curtains billowing out from its side as the volleys slammed into its shields.

High in the command castle of the battle-barge, Silonius watched the confusion created by their assault spread and multiply in sculpted light and glowing markers. The battlesphere was a tangled mess. Hundreds of burning brawls between ships littered the holo-projection.

The Imperial Fists were scattered across the void, some dying, many damaged, the remainder trying to find a target to fire on. Some of them were doing a lot of damage. Even as he watched, a trio of small ships cut across the nose of one of his vessels and broke its back with coordinated gunfire. The battle-group that had moved out to meet the *Alpha* and its sisters were still together, but their target had dissolved before them, scattering into dozens of small squadrons like shrapnel flung from a bomb blast. Wherever the Imperial Fists tried to apply strength the Alpha Legion moved in contradictory directions, lashing out with opportunist blasts of fire. It looked without shape, order or pattern; it looked like slaughter and disaster.

Silonius noted every detail and saw that everything was as it needed to be. He opened the signals channel to Hydra moon communication control.

'Lord Alpharius, secondary phase is complete. Imperial Fists ships are fully engaged. Our own force strength has degraded by twenty per cent. Our numerical advantage is estimated at two hundred per cent. We are approaching range of the moon fortress guns. We await your word.'

'*Proceed*,' said the voice of the primarch.

'By your will.'

Alpha Legion ships turned from their courses and bore down on the orbits of Pluto. Kerberos was their first target. The fortress moon's guns opened up. The blackness of space vanished. Plasma annihilators and turbo lasers drained reactors and breathed star-hot fury at the closing ships. Shields flared and cut out, blinking away one after another. The Alpha Legion held course. They were known as a Legion of stealth and guile, but they were still a Legion, and in that moment they rode into the mouth of the guns like the Angels of Death they were crafted to be.

Building-sized shells slammed into Kerberos, shattering its void shields and toppling gun towers. Dust shook from passage ceilings beneath the moon's crust. Kerberos' fire intensified, and the first Alpha Legion ship died, battered to flakes of metal and pools of gas. A beam of las-fire caught the strike cruiser *Silver Serpent* and carved the weapons and bridge from its back. It pitched over, bleeding into the atmosphere. A rolling volley struck it in mid turn and ripped its spine open.

But the rest of the fleet was close enough.

Boarding torpedoes flew from prow launch tubes. Gunships boosted free of launch bays, spiralling as they danced through the flash and surge of explosions. Teleportation chambers flooded with ghost light, as hundreds of Terminators vanished and hurtled through the warp. The Alpha Legion ships flipped over and burned away from the teeth of Kerberos, as their scattered payload struck home.

The Imperial Fists had prepared for a boarding assault on the fortress moon. They had prepared with a thoroughness that was bred into their nature. Inside Kerberos was a labyrinth of passages, blast doors and kill chambers. Teleport jammers had turned the warp into a jagged tangle of currents. A company of Imperial Fists – the 404th, the Lords of the Long Watch – garrisoned the fortress moon beside thousands of auxiliaries and battle-servitors. All were ready and waiting as the Alpha Legion assault began.

The Lernaean Terminators struck first, appearing in pillars of light, armour breathing warp mist and smoke. Many were out of position. Some materialised within the fabric of the fortress, and shock waves roared out as overlapping matter collapsed in a scream of paradox. But many struck true. Five hundred of the Legion elite, clad in adamantium, they were the brutal edge of a Legion known for subterfuge, but still made for slaughter.

Blizzards of gunfire met them, rattling from their armour, strobing shadow over guns and blades. They fired back. Plasma streams, bolt-rounds, melta-beams, flame and cannon shot ripped through blast shields, poured down corridors and pulped bodies. The Lernaeans advanced, striding in time with the roar of their gunfire. Their targets were the moon's defence turrets. Sections of the defence network blinked out, as servitor and sensor clusters were ripped apart.

The boarding torpedoes slammed into Kerberos. Their snouts exploded, boring holes through the moon's skin as assault hatches unfurled. Warriors charged out, blazing and hacking through anything that moved. Across the moon, death laughed through the passages and outer chambers. In the primary docking trunk a demi-company of Alpha Legion met twenty of the Imperial Fists garrison. Thirty legionaries fell in the first second as heavy weaponry scythed through them. Units placed behind the Alpha Legion force cut them off and crushed them between two gun-lines.

But for every invader who fell, the Alpha Legion's fangs sank deeper into Kerberos.

The squads already inside the station triggered the signal beacons they carried. Out in the void a wave of gunships locked on to the signals and homed in. Stormbirds and Storm Eagles spiralled into captured hangars or wounds blown in the surface. Each of them carried a handful of legionnaires, but their true cargo were Techmarines, forge masters and servitor thralls. They moved with speed, machine cant buzzing between them as they made for captured fire-control centres and key system nodes. All of them had a single purpose and order passed to them by Silonius from the primarch himself.

'Turn the guns of Kerberos. Make them ours.'

FOUR

Imperial Fists frigate Unbreakable Truth
Trans-Neptunian region – Pluto approach

THE FIRES OF battle grew in Archamus' eye as he strode through the machine decks. The projection of Pluto flickered and shone in the left eyepiece of his helm. Behind him Kestros and Andromeda followed, their voices silenced by the command he had just given.

'Do you have any questions?' he asked.

'No, lord,' said Kestros.

'No, no questions,' said Andromeda, her voice surprisingly steady considering she was almost running to keep up with their progress through the ship, as it closed on the orbits of Pluto. 'In the circumstances there are very few options, given that I doubt you would advocate fleeing.'

Kestros growled.

'I thought not,' she said.

'My strike point?' asked Kestros. 'Hydra is a small moon, but still a moon. If this is to work we cannot be hunting through the whole fortress.'

'The central communication centre,' said Andromeda, without

hesitation. 'They will have taken or destroyed the means for our forces to sense or speak to one another. We start there.'

They reached a junction. A squad of warriors armed with boarding shields met them and fell in beside Archamus without a word.

'When you have...' The name he was going to say caught against his teeth. He stopped in his stride and turned to look at Kestros, who had halted as well. 'When you have the target confirmed, send the signal. I will be ready at the core reactor controls.'

'And then you will become the destroyer, praetorian,' said Andromeda, and he saw that the expression on her face had lost all traces of her bite and bile.

'You may remain on board the *Unbreakable Truth*, mistress,' he said, 'for all the safety that may afford you.'

She laughed, the sound high and clear.

'No, I don't think so. Surviving this is unlikely to be the better option of those available. And besides, work undone is a tragedy.'

Archamus nodded once. 'As you will it, daughter of Luna.'

'Thank you, son of Dorn.'

'Will it succeed?' asked Kestros as Archamus began to turn, and he saw that the sergeant's jaw was set, his eyes focused on some distant point before them.

'I do not know,' he said. Around him the ship quivered as it cut through the void. Machine noise buzzed down the passage. The sound of running feet rang on the deck as servitors hurried to their tasks. 'But I do know that it is what we must do. If any in Lord Sigismund's fleet have heard our warning, they cannot reach Hydra in time. We alone know who is here, and are able to strike.'

He held Kestros' gaze for a moment before turning and striding down the corridor, his lone squad following in his wake. Before him the doors to the teleportation chambers clanked open. Kestros and Andromeda remained looking after him for a second, before the doors closed.

✠ ✠ ✠

Storage Vault 278, Hydra moon fortress
Plutonian orbit

RED LIGHT BLINKED across Myzmadra's eyes as she came through the door. The crew serf at the opposite door turned fast and collected a volkite blast in the chest. Flame raced through his body, ash blurring the pulsing light. She was already at the next door. Morhan and the rest of the auxiliary squad were behind her. The hatch in front of her was sealed shut, the keypad stubbornly blinking failure at each attempt to open it. A glance at it told her that she could fire every weapon at it that they had and do no more than distress the surface.

'Primary, this is Rho-Two,' she said into the vox. 'Entry into the vault is deadlocked. I repeat. Entry to target hangar is deadlocked.'

'*Code override is not possible,*' replied a voice across the vox, and she recognised the texture of Hekaron's voice, growling from the communication control centre on the other side of the moon. '*There is an auxiliary squad inside the chamber. Patching you through to vox-hailers inside the hatch. They have had no orders or external contact since the beginning of the mission. Make it sound good.*'

'Confirm,' she said. 'Make the link.'

The vox-bead spat static in her ear.

'This is auxiliary squad Aries,' she shouted, panting breath into the words. Beyond the hatch her voice would be booming from vox speakers, into the hangar bay. 'Open this hatch. Enemy is inside station and closing. We have Senior Astropath Nureen with us. We need access now. The enemy are inside the fortress and closing. I repeat, open this hatch.'

The static boiled up in her ear again, but no reply came. She frowned and began again.

'This is–'

The hatch in front of her trembled, as mag bolts released. She fought down a thrill of surprise as the door hinged outwards. A metre-thick layer of adamantium and plasteel slid outwards, and inwardly she reflected that it would need a turbo laser to bore through it. That, or more time and patience than she had. She braced to push it as a crack appeared around the door. She leapt through the gap. She saw a figure fall in a tangle of limbs, and then she was through, weapon raised and firing as she ran. Her shot hit an auxiliary in the face and burned through his head. Behind her the rest of the squad poured through the hatch, and the other three auxiliaries died before they could fire a shot.

She stopped after ten strides. The chamber extended away from her, echoing and empty. Structural pillars rose from the floor to meet the vaulted ceiling. Scuffed hazard stripes marked the edge of the floor. Pools of dirty light fell from grates set high above and at the edges. Lifter hoists hung from rails overhead, bunches of chain hanging from them.

'Move the homer in. We need to be done and clear of here fast.'

'This is it?' said Ashul as he stepped through the hatch. 'This is a lot of emptiness to have as a key objective.'

'It's a volatile munitions vault,' she said, eyes still scanning the gloom. 'Near impregnable once sealed. Vox can't even get through without a link.'

'I know what it is. It just seems a strange place to set up a teleport homer. We have just spent a long time shutting down the teleport jammers built into this place. I mean, why would we want to shunt troops through the immaterium and then have them appear, very precisely, here?'

'Who says it's for our troops?'

'Oh...'

'Get set up,' she said, looking around as Morhan and another auxiliary lugged the second casket through the door. The dead astropath was long gone from inside, and the panels beneath peeled back to reveal the equipment within. 'We don't have long.'

Plutonian orbit

THE ALPHA LEGION fleet twisted around Pluto and squeezed tight. At the instant that Hydra fell, Silonius' fleet had split into three distinct parts.

In the gulf beyond the system edge, eighty warships had spiralled around the Imperial Fists vessels as they came about and clawed back towards Pluto's orbit. The afterglows from the fireships' detonations were spreading and changing colour, like bruises left on the skin of space. Fire and debris bled from the Imperial Fists ships. Blades of macro fire cut to and from them, latticing the dark.

Closing with the moons of Pluto was the swarm of intruder ships that had drawn the defenders out. The wrecks of their sisters lay in their wake, sacrificed to the Imperial Fists guns.

The main Alpha Legion assault fleet cut through the sphere of orbit. One hundred and fifty-six warships followed the *Alpha* into the curve of Pluto's gravity well. They swept past Hydra, pausing to drop troops into the already stricken station. That task done, the fleet bore down on the next fortress moon in its path. Nix poured munitions into the path of the warships, and fire churned the darkness around the Alpha Legion vessels.

For a moment it looked as though they would have to run the gauntlet of the wall of fire, as they had with Kerberos; but then Kerberos itself emerged from behind the bulk of Pluto and fired on its sibling moon. Ordnance hammered into Nix's surface, burning through its crust and breaking scabs of armour from its bastions. Its own batteries fired back, and the space between the two moons became a bridge of burning light.

If the garrison of Nix had hoped for help from Styx and Charon, their hopes guttered even as Kerberos mauled them. Hydra had poured contradictory firing and target information into the communications network. Commands to treat the attackers as friendly, different firing orders and competing priorities warred for attention. It took the fortress seneschals and tech-priests on Styx, Charon and Nix several minutes to sift the false from the real, and give true firing orders. Not long, but long enough for the Alpha Legion strike fleet to close and launch a wave of assault craft. Kerberos switched fire as the gunships and torpedoes powered towards Nix, and its fleet-breaking firepower began to hammer into the surface of the next fortress moon.

In the outer layers of Nix, the Imperial Fists and their vassals were waiting as the torpedoes crashed through armour and rock. The tips of the torpedoes blew open, blasting molten armour and stone through vaulted chambers and passages. Bolt-rounds hammered out from firing points to greet the warriors who emerged from the torpedoes. They stepped into the light, the deep, iridescent blue of their armour stark in the blinking flare of gunfire. They were the Lernaeans, the teeth of the hydra, and they had come to claim the kill for their Legion. Each squad raised their weapons as one, reaper cannons arming, chargers activating with a buzz like the promise of a lightning strike.

Out in the deep dark of one half-dead enemy vessel, First Captain Sigismund emerged from the mouth of a passage. Blood covered his armour and tabard, daubing him in gloss shades of red and orange.

'Get everything back to the fortress moons,' he shouted as soon as his vox came in range of the *Lachrymae*.

And the reply that stole the feeling from his limbs came from far Hydra, cutting through vox-traffic with a rasp of cold static.

'*Pluto has fallen,*' it said. '*You are broken. You are alone.*'

Imperial Fists frigate Unbreakable Truth
Orbital approach, Hydra

ARCHAMUS WATCHED THE moon grow ever closer. Stitches of light crossed his helmet display. Drifts of burning gas cloaked Hydra's surface. He blinked the display away. Pillars of machinery rose around him, aching with growing power. Static was spidering up his bionic limbs. The teleport chamber seemed to crowd around him, high walls and ceiling pulling close as though both were suddenly nearer than they should be. His squad ringed him, helmeted, shields and weapons ready. His teeth began to ache. A high-pitched whine grew in the air. Neon worms skipped across the metal disc beneath his feet.

'*Strike force gunships ready to launch,*' said Magos Chayo's voice, the vox chopping the words into sharp bursts of noise. *'I have done my best to conceal our approach using the manifold instances of macro destruction and ordnance deployment occurring, but at some point they are going to notice us.'*

'Will we be in range at that point?'

'Very probably. In fact we should be at optimal launch and teleportation displacement location in fifty-six seconds.' Chayo paused. *'Presuming that the ship is not annihilated by enemy fire in that time.'*

'Good,' said Archamus. 'You have my command to activate the tele-porter and launch Kestros' gunships.'

'By your will.'

'And, Chayo...'

'Yes, Honoured Master Huscarl?'

'Thank you.'

'Twenty seconds,' said a machine voice from the dark. The pillars began to glow. Cords of lightning flicked into the air. Archamus' skin felt as though needles were pushing out from beneath its surface.

In other circumstances he would have spoken, would have cast his voice across the vox to his brothers waiting in the dark of the gunships or standing beside him. But now, at this moment, he said nothing. They did not need words, and he had none to give. Not now, not as they all stood on the precipice.

You are old, he thought, *old and worn by war. But I will not fail in this. I will not submit to it.*

A face emerged from memory. The face of a youth who would never grow to be a warrior, the face of the brother in blood, and then it became the tattooed face of a man who had sat in the dark with him in another life that now seemed a dream.

'That is why I chose you, Kye,' said the face in the forgotten dream.

'Approaching launch terminus in three, two, o–'

Brightness. Blue-white.

A lightning strike that swallowed sight and sound.

Cold blood. Dead sound.

Blackness.

And then a flash of colour and shape, and the feeling of falling without moving.

Silence wrapped around him.

He blinked and sight came back. The chamber walls rose above him, steel spreading up to a vaulted ceiling. High banks of machines marched away into the quiet gloom. Lights winked and flickered across a block of machinery on the floor. Antennae rose from its sides, and the air above it shimmered.

'Teleport homer,' said the Techmarine, moving from the rest of the squad. He was called Nucrio. Archamus had brought him to deal with the moon's reactor controls. Now he bent down beside the homer, head tilting to the side as he examined the cluster of machinery. 'Pulled us right onto its beacon. We are a long way off target.'

'Kestros,' Archamus said, triggering the long-range vox. 'Chayo, do you hear me?'

Flat static filled his ear in answer.

'This is a shielded vault,' said Nucrio. 'Signals will not be able to get in or out.'

Spirals of warp smoke rose from the shoulders of his squad as they divided into trios and moved outwards, shields raised, gun muzzles tracking the quiet shadows. Archamus paused by the teleport beacon. The lights blinked on its casing.

Pulse-pulse... Pulse-pulse...

Pulse...

'Disperse,' said Archamus. His skin was still prickling from the teleportation, but underneath that he could feel ice running through his skin. 'Find an exit. Maximum caution.'

Hydra moon fortress
Plutonian orbit

'STAND READY,' SAID Kestros. The gunship's internal lights blinked red, and the assault hatches peeled back. All sound vanished. Harsh white light flared across his sight. His jump pack cycled to life. The surface of Hydra turned beneath him. Grey towers, armoured domes and spires of aerials flicked past as the gunship dived. Three other craft hugged its wings. Explosions burst high overhead, but this close to the moon's skin the defence turrets were silent. The Alpha Legion's taking of Hydra had stolen its ability to defend against a small incursion force, but once they were inside their target it would be very different.

The gunship banked hard, wings trailing a skin of mist through the moon's thin atmosphere. The main communication array loomed above them, the arc of its dish cutting into the fire-streaked black of the sky. At the base of the array sat the primary communication control. Kestros' eyes found the blackened hole blown in the armoured shutters.

'Explosive entry,' he said into the vox. 'It seems you were correct in your assessment of how they took the moon.'

'*Of course,*' came Andromeda's reply.

The gunships spun closer. G-force thumped through the fuselage as they banked tight around the array.

A rune began to pulse amber at the edge of Kestros' helmet display. The array was so close it felt as though he could touch it. The rune snapped to green.

He leapt from the gunship. For a second he spiralled, his momentum pushing him on as the moon's weak gravity caught him. Then he fired his jump pack. Twin tongues of flame breathed from his back and slammed him into a dive. His weapons were in his hands. Behind him, his brothers followed, spiralling in his wake as they dived from the gunships.

The wall of the control centre grew closer, filling his vision. The hole in the blast shutters was a widening mouth into darkness. He triggered the jump pack's maximum thrust. Force crashed through his body. Blood pulled away from his head and chest, even as his second heart fought it. He triggered his chainsword. Vibration trembled up his sword arm. The breach in the blast shutters came up to meet him, and for an instant he felt that he was frozen – balanced on a point between the starlight and the blackness that lay beyond.

He burst through the breach. He had an instant to form an impression of the circular chamber and banked machines. A burst of gunfire reached up and punched him from the air. He fell, hit the deck, and the thrust of his jump pack yanked him into a block of machinery with the force of a Titan's kick. His helmet display flashed red with damage runes. Jagged edges of broken armour cut into his flesh. He cut the jump pack as he rolled and came to his feet.

His eyes found a target, a warrior in scaled armour, and he was sprinting forwards, bolt pistol firing, shells exploding across the warrior's shoulders, shredding silver trim and blue lacquer. The warrior flinched aside, brought his boltgun up and fired. Kestros' chainsword struck as the first bolt shell kicked from the muzzle. The spinning teeth cut through the warrior's wrist joint and ripped down through skin, muscle and bone. The boltgun spun away, tumbling with recoil. The Alpha Legion warrior staggered, but the loss of a hand did not slow him. He rammed the crown of his helm into Kestros' faceplate, and his helmet display cut out. Kestros spun back, instinctively, and felt something sharp slash across his throat.

Blood began to run. Atmosphere hissed from the slit in his neck armour.

His visor display blinked back on. He could taste the air in his helm thinning. The warrior was in front of him, a dagger in his remaining hand. Kestros cut, slashing his chainsword across the legionnaire's face. The warrior swayed back, the chain teeth snarling as they spun through air, then snapped forwards, muscle and momentum focused behind the tip of the dagger. Kestros slammed the muzzle of his bolt pistol into the warrior's throat and pulled the trigger. Bolt shells ripped out, sawing the warrior's head from his body in a shower of detonations. Kestros was already past the corpse as it fell, firing and hacking into the next enemy.

The chamber was a blur of blue and yellow armour, of blades and gunfire. His eyes moved through every detail even as he cut and fired, and the air hissed from his helm. There were only a handful of Alpha

Legion in the control centre. Three or four at most. They were good, but they would not stand against the thirty Imperial Fists facing them. And he could see no sign of their target.

By the breach, Andromeda was climbing down to the floor, her movements slowed by the bulk of her void suit. Dragged behind her was Incarnus, his limbs bound to his sides, floating in a suspensor net.

'Andromeda,' he said, his voice a hiss in the draining air of his helm. 'The target, is he here? Is Alpharius here?'

Andromeda moved closer to Incarnus, and he heard the crackle of static.

'No, he is not, but the turncoat says that he can read something in the surface thoughts of the others.'

'What?'

'He was here, and he knew someone would come for him. They are ready.'

Kestros felt numbness spread through him, even as he ducked aside from a burst of gunfire and raised his pistol to fire a reply.

'Reach Master Archamus,' he said. 'He must–'

'I have tried,' she cut him off. 'There is no reply.'

Storage Vault 278, Hydra moon fortress
Plutonian orbit

ARCHAMUS LET THE static buzz in his ear for a second before cutting it off. The storage vault was still quiet.

'*The exit hatches are sealed, lord,*' said Nucrio. '*The lock mechanisms have been overridden.*'

'Can you break them?'

'*Yes, but not quickly.*'

'Begin.'

'*Lord,*' came the voice of one of the other squad members, '*there is something–*'

A sound like silk rippling flicked through the air. Archamus turned, eyes focusing on the direction the sound had come from, boltgun ready.

'Squad, converge on chamber,' he said into the vox. He heard a blurt of static from the vox and then the sound again. No reply came from the vox. He turned his head slowly, vision cycling between threat displays. Nothing. Just the low hum of active power armour diluting the silence.

Archamus lit *Oathword*'s power field. Lightning wreathed the mace's head. He was perfectly still, his senses stretching into the stillness of the chamber.

There was a blur at the edge of his sight. He began to turn.

The spear struck him in the chest. The blade passed through his armour without a sound.

Coldness whipped through his torso. He felt blood gush into his throat. Black smoke was rising from the wound as armour and flesh dissolved. Alpharius stood in front of him, holding the spear steady in his chest. The primarch's head was bare, his eyes dark and without feeling. Archamus gripped his mace and willed it to rise.

Alpharius ripped the spear blade back. Blood and vapour poured from the wound, and Archamus felt himself fall as numbness spread through his body.

He hit the ground, breath bubbling from between his lips. Alpharius looked down at him.

'Poor Archamus. I wondered which bait my brother would take, but it seems that he has left you to die in his place.'

Primary communication array control,
Hydra moon fortress, Plutonian orbit

'Is HIS VOX active?' Kestros snarled as a burst of gunfire chewed into the machine stack above him. He subconsciously counted the rounds and timing, and rose and fired back as the volley slackened. His squad moved past him, firing their bolt pistols in perfect synchronicity.

Bolt-rounds burst in the open door from one of the entrances to the control room. He saw one warrior reel, the front of his armour shredding, before he was up and running forwards.

The Alpha Legion counter-assault had come within seconds of them taking the control room. Kestros and his brothers were engaging enemies in three directions. He had already lost five of his command in scant moments. That the *Unbreakable Truth* was still active somewhere out in the void, and in vox contact, was a small point of light in a darkening situation.

'Negative,' said Chayo in his ear. *'I have lost all contact with Lord Archamus and his squad. Aetheric sensors detect that the station is alive with teleport jamming and distortion signals. If it seemed plausible I would say that they knew someone would try to teleport aboard and pulled them to an individual location.'*

Kestros let out a breath as he reloaded his bolt pistol. He thought of all of the things that Andromeda and Archamus had said about the Alpha Legion: lies within lies, deception within deception, traps within traps.

He turned and looked at where Andromeda and the captured psyker, Incarnus, sheltered from the gunfire behind a bank of machinery. The psyker was looking at him, the iris-less eyes pale behind the transparent visor of his void suit. Incarnus smiled, pupils dark pinpricks in white.

'This was a trap,' Kestros said across the vox. 'We did not follow them here. They led us.' Andromeda's head jerked up as she heard his words. Then she froze, her face still inside her visor, mouth and eyes open, as though she were a still pict image. Frost spread across her suit.

+Alpha to omega,+ said Incarnus' voice inside Kestros' skull.

Kestros tried to raise his pistol, but frost was climbing his arm, and his limbs wouldn't move. Pain lanced into his skull.

+I was of the Crimson Walkers,+ said a voice inside his skull. +Did you honestly think that a psy-clamp could hold me?+

Kestros felt his gun arm begin to rise, but now it was not his will that moved it. Pain coiled down his arms as invisible cords yanked his muscles into movement. Around him, the rest of his squad were still moving, oblivious as they fought. He poured his will against the presence in his skull. Blood was running from his tear ducts.

+The Luna witch is right. You really are very simple creatures.+

'The Luna witch is also stood close enough to do this,' said Andromeda. Incarnus spun, as Andromeda brought her knife up into his gut. Incarnus gasped, blood splattering the inside of his visor. Kestros felt his limbs unlock and aimed his bolt pistol.

'Get clear!' he shouted. Andromeda ripped the knife free and leapt back. Kestros fired. A bolt hit Incarnus in the chest and ripped his torso into shreds. Scraps of void suit and bone pattered against the banks of machines.

He looked up at Andromeda and tilted his head in question.

'The Alpha Legion are not the only ones with secrets,' she said.

'What–' began Kestros, but Chayo's voice cut him off.

'*Something is happening.*' Static boiled up. '*...fleet...*'

'Repeat,' shouted Kestros. 'What is the strength of the enemy fleet?'

A burst of gunfire hit him from his right as more Alpha Legion warriors came from a passage opening. He gunned his chainsword and leapt towards them. Chayo's voice was a static-cut shout in his ears.

'*...the fleet is...*'

His feet shook the floor. His armour sang with the kiss of shrapnel.

'*The fleet is ours.*'

Blood was iron in his mouth, and he could see the enemy, dark-armoured silhouettes behind the veil of flame.

And then Chayo's voice came again, though what he said seemed utterly impossible.

'*The* Phalanx *is here.*'

Plutonian orbit

THE PHALANX CAME from the trans-Neptunian gulf like a comet. She was the largest ship that had ever served mankind. Others had made warships that tried to rival her size: the *Vengeful Spirit*, the *Furious Abyss* and the *Iron Blood*. None, though, could match the flagship of the Imperial Fists. A fortress set to move amongst the stars, she possessed enough firepower to destroy fleets and break empires. Fortress clusters crowned her bulk, rising in black stone and gilded metal. Vast cannons extended from her spine. Tiers of weapon batteries and launch bays marched down her flanks. Within her heart rode thousands of Imperial Fists, and tens of thousands of mortal soldiers. Alone she was a sight that had brought civilisations to surrender.

But she was not alone.

The *Monarch of Fire* cut through the night. Plumes of plasma trailed from vents on her prow and cage-topped towers. Arcs of blue lightning wreathed her guns as they built charge. Within her hull, reactors – which were a mystery even to the highest initiates of the Machine Cult – poured raw plasma into the cannons that studded her prow. Vast doors peeled back along her flanks. Racks of bombardment launchers slid into the starlight. In any other fleet she would have been a queen of devastation, but in the armada of Rogal Dorn she was the herald to her monarch.

Behind the two great ships an armada followed. Battle-barges, grand cruisers, destroyers, gun barques and frigates cut the night into shreds with the fire of their engines.

All of them had been travelling on momentum from the inner system. Slingshotted through the Solar System's competing gravity wells, they had arrived at the system edge unseen by both Pluto's garrison and the Alpha Legion. Now they lit their engines and fell from the dark like burning arrows.

The *Phalanx* and the *Monarch* fired as one. Three Alpha Legion ships ceased to exist. Spherical explosions blinked into being. Waves of force and energy rippled out. Gunships launched from the *Phalanx*, a cloud of black-and-gold specks, spreading out and out. The ships circling Pluto slid on, frozen in movement, trapped in an instant of shock. And then the *Phalanx* fired again. Void shields collapsed across multiple targets.

Fresh clouds of fire added to those already glowing like bright inks poured into clear water. Guns roared and roared, fire pouring into the dark without pause. Light flared and strobed as hulls tore and reactors poured their life energy into the vacuum.

Kerberos hurled macro shells and las-fire at the *Phalanx*. Its layered shields flared with rainbow colours as they burst. Stone bastions shattered. Stone and corpses spun away from it, burning in the wash of energy. The *Phalanx* bled, but held its fire from Kerberos. Smaller ships darted forwards, turbo lasers reducing the fortress moon's defence batteries to glowing craters. Bombers swarmed Kerberos, spinning around the torrents of fire pouring from the stronghold.

Light blistered Kerberos' face. Its batteries fell silent. Targeting arrays became slag, and guns became blind. The assault craft ran into the gaps in the fortress moon's defences. Storm Eagles flew down canyons gouged in the rock, scattering assault troops from their doors. Breaching pods slammed into the surface, bit through and poured Terminators and breacher units into the warren of tunnels beneath. The Lernaeans met them, and the gloom roared with the scream of chainfists and the howl of volkite beams.

In the gulf beyond Pluto, Sigismund's fleet pulled free of the tangle of Alpha Legion ships as the *Monarch of Fire* plunged into them. The *Three Sisters of Spite* spiralled in the great ship's wake.

And within Pluto's orbit, the *Phalanx* moved with unhurried brutality, an empress of war walking her domain, cloaked in the gold and red of destruction, the light of her guns the glitter of jewels in her crown.

Before her lay Hydra.

FIVE

'YOU ARE ALIVE.'

Archamus heard the voice. There was a taste in his mouth, not iron but ozone. His eyelids trembled...

Pain.

A world of sharpness and brightness, and needles and knives. And though his eyes would not open he knew that the chirurgeon rig would be there above him, holding his ribs open as it lowered another portion of his new self into his flesh.

'One of your hearts is still beating. I can hear it.'

He could feel the pulse, each beat a bladed thread pulling through his veins, each second redder and brighter than the last.

'Survival is unlikely. I am sorry for that. You deserved better. We all deserved better.'

His eyelids moved.

'Kinder to cut your throat, but this is not a kind age.'

Air sucked into his lungs, and he felt his last heart's hammer. The world was a white sphere, holding him, keeping him still, burning him from within and without. He could not go on. It was too much. He was defeated.

'I...' he said, the word surprising him as it came from his lips. 'I... will... not... submit.'

'No, you will not. That was always your Legion's problem. Your flaw, and your virtue. I admire it. I always have.'

Something in the words was not right. His eyes opened, and the present poured in.

Alpharius stood above him, bare-faced, looking down, a double-ended spear in his hand, the edges of the blades seeming like shadows cast in smoke.

'Your secondary assault force is contained and in the process of being slaughtered. Within two hours Pluto and all of its moons will be ours, and no one will know. If any other attempts what you have attempted, they will die here. These are facts.'

'Pride...' hissed Archamus, pulling the word from his throat even as his vision swam. Alpharius tilted his head to one side, as though in question. 'Your flaw, but... not your virtue.'

Alpharius laughed, the sound an echo in the quiet. He looked as though he was about to say something else, but then stopped. Archamus heard the click of the vox in Alpharius' armour activating and realised that the primarch must be connected to a link within the vault. Alpharius listened, his face set.

'Let them get within teleport range,' he said, but his words were for whoever was on the other end of the vox. 'Then turn the jammers on.'

His eyes flicked down to Archamus.

'He is here,' he said, and stepped back next to the machinery of the teleport beacon.

A wind rose in the vault's still air. Drops of Archamus' blood rose from the floor. Bright worms of static ran up the walls. Pressure was building inside Archamus' skull. His skin felt like fire inside his armour. Alpharius raised his head. Shreds of luminous ash formed and fell. Black cracks ran through the air. The pressure in the Huscarl's skull was the beat of a hammer.

Reality split. Lightning-bright lines cut into the air. Starlight burst outwards. Pressure waves ripped through the chamber.

A circle of golden-yellow figures stood above him, the plates of their Terminator armour fuming pale light. Clenched fists of jet sat on their shoulders. Emerald laurels circled the black skulls on their chests, and silver lightning bolts crossed their pauldrons in echo of their warrior ancestors who had unified Terra. Archamus knew each of them, recognised them even through the layers of Indomitus-pattern plate and the blur of his failing sight. They were his brothers, the Huscarls of whom he was master. And at their centre stood the only other being besides the Emperor who could bring them to battle.

Archamus found a breath come to his lips, and the numbness in his limbs and the pain in his chest receded.

'Lord...' he rasped, and the limbs that had refused to move until now, and the flesh that had failed his command, pulled him to his knees, and then to his feet.

Rogal Dorn stood, head bare, flanked by his warrior sons, the gold of his armour luminous with warp smoke, blood rubies glittering in the claws of silver eagles. Black eyes glinted in a face of hard control and harsh shadow.

From across the chamber Alpharius met his brother's gaze.

'There are things that we should talk of, brother,' said Alpharius.

Dorn's face did not move.

'Fire,' he said.

The Huscarls fired. Light and bolt-rounds sheeted out, rattling from barrels. Light flashed through the dark as the gunfire slammed into fields that had snapped into place around Alpharius. Blinding whiteness filled the chamber as the shields flashed under the impacts.

Archamus forced every sensation down, every feeling of weakness, every shred of agony and forced himself forwards. The flaring light met his helmet lenses, and his sight vanished in a blur of stars and static. He reached up and yanked the helmet free. The air reeked of explosions and ozone. There was blood. Blood pouring from him, pooling inside his armour, falling on the deck as he staggered on towards his lord and brothers.

Alpharius was nowhere to be seen. The Huscarls advanced. Archamus could tell from their movements that they were half blind from the light of their shields. The Huscarls kept moving, Dorn at their head, bolters firing as one. The rolling thunder of teleportation blended with the roar of gunfire, as huge figures materialised in the chamber.

Archamus was on his feet. Around him two tides of armour slammed together, golden and blue. Huscarls and Lernaeans crashed into combat, blades shrieking as they bit into armour. Dorn swept forwards, and all Archamus could see was the blurred arc of *Storm's Teeth*, rising and falling, blood and sparks and shredded metal. A Lernaean flew back, a bloody canyon in his chest. Another stepped forwards, and the tip of the chainblade met his faceplate and bored into the skull beneath. Shards of metal and bone sprayed out as Dorn lifted the Terminator from the floor and then ripped the blade free. The next blow was falling before the corpse hit the floor.

The Huscarls moved with him in a wedge, hammer blows falling, false thunder pealing. The Lernaeans tore into them. A chainfist sliced into a Huscarl's chest. Enamelled leaves fell as diamond teeth chewed through the honour laurel and into the armour and flesh beneath. A warrior with a saurian helm of tarnished silver punched the fingers of a lightning claw into a Huscarl and ripped the warrior in half with an explosion of lightning. Sheets of volkite discharge stained the air red.

And suddenly Alpharius was amongst the killing tide, his attacks not following rhythm or pattern. One instant he was in the front rank, the *Pale Spear* orbiting him, its blade a blur of blood and smoke as it cut through armour and limbs – the next he was retreating and lashing out as the Huscarls moved into the space. Then he was pressing close, hacking and stabbing like the butchers of the World Eaters, then piercing a throat with a thrust that was as light as a breath of wind.

Dorn drove into the Lernaeans, red spattering his face, *Storm's Teeth* shedding blood. Then, with a suddenness that halted the shallow breath in Archamus' throat, Alpharius' spear thrust up from the press of ranks. Its tip shimmered, silver reflection fading to mist, and Archamus thought that the sound fled from his ears, as it drove at his lord's chest.

It was a beautiful strike. In all his years of war Archamus had never seen the like, its simplicity like a line drawn by a master artisan on a bare parchment. It was death and ruin, and silence without end...

And *Storm's Teeth* met the spear thrust, and reality shrieked. A sheet of silver sparks exploded from the point at which the two weapons met. Alpharius and Dorn stood before each other, and it was as though the universe made space for this meeting of brothers.

'I came here for you, Rogal,' said Alpharius as he slid back, spear spinning. Dorn was cutting again and again, and each blow churned the air. 'This is about victory. True victory.'

A Lernaean stepped into Dorn's path. *Storm's Teeth* cut up through the torso of the Terminator. Gut fluid and blood gushed out, as the dead flesh and armour fell. The Lernaeans and Huscarls were a shrinking circle around the two primarchs.

'Look at this. Look at what I have done here. This is not a war you can win your way,' called Alpharius. Dorn stood before him, and the spear was suddenly still as his brother loomed above him, a sculpture of vengeance cast in gold. Dorn sliced downwards. Alpharius raised the spear. The weapons clashed, and suddenly the Alpha Legion primarch was spinning close, *Storm's Teeth* arcing past him harmlessly. 'But you are blind to what you are fighting. We are both fighting for the future, Rogal.'

Alpharius lunged. Dorn jerked aside, blink-fast. The spear-tip caught his shoulder and punched through the golden armour. Dorn staggered.

Archamus roared, breath ripping from his lungs as he plunged towards his primarch. A Lernaean slashed at him with lightning-wreathed talons. He brought his pistol up and emptied the clip into the warrior's face and chest. Explosions punched the Terminator back. Archamus dropped the pistol and drew his seax. The wide-bladed sword slid free of its scabbard and rammed into the Lernaean's throat. Archamus wrenched it back, feeling the edge catch on bone as blood gushed over his bionic arm.

'I did this so that you would understand,' shouted Alpharius. 'So that you would see that you cannot win. I am not here to kill you, brother. I am not here for Horus. I am here to give you victory.'

Dorn was a stride in front of Archamus, blood bright and scattering as he wrenched free of Alpharius' spear. The Huscarls fell, their legs cut out beneath them as Alpharius spun wide, spear arcing low like a scythe through long grass. And now Dorn stood alone, blood running down the gold of his armour.

'I know the enemy,' said Alpharius. 'I know your weakness, and theirs. I know the truth.'

Dorn stepped forwards, *Storm's Teeth* slamming down, battering into the spear blade in a blaze of light. Alpharius slipped to the side, and Dorn turned the direction of his cut as it fell. But Alpharius was not where his movement should have taken him. He was behind Dorn's cut, the blade of his spear slicing down.

'I can give you victory, brother,' Alpharius urged him again.

Dorn swayed aside, and the spear blade skimmed his chest. Slivers of gold and silver feathers fell to the deck, and Alpharius was over-extended, and Dorn was turning, his strength flowing into a wide lateral cut that would never land.

It would never land, because in that instant Archamus saw what was about to happen. Alpharius was not overextended; he was exactly where he needed to be to turn past Dorn's blow and make another, last, perfect thrust with his spear.

Archamus felt his blood-drained body try to move faster, try to push itself across the few metres separating him from the lord, whose life and service were the reason he did not fear.

Dorn cut. *Storm's Teeth* blurred. Alpharius swayed back, pivoting and sliding a hair's breadth past the screaming edge.

Archamus lunged to his lord's side, his seax blade reaching for the spear thrust even as it unfolded. His blade caught the haft of Alpharius' spear, and the force of the connection kicked through his metal arm like the kiss of a lightning bolt. Archamus reeled back staggering to the deck.

And the spear struck home. It rammed through Dorn's armour and into the flesh.

And stopped.

Dorn stood, unmoved, the spear embedded in his shoulder where he had stepped in to take the blow. His left hand was locked around the spear's haft. For an instant the two primarchs were an arm's reach apart, eye to eye.

'Brother–' Alpharius began.

And Dorn hacked *Storm's Teeth* through Alpharius' arms above the wrists.

Blood and sparks fell in the flash of gunfire. The world became a slow-sliding tableau of movement.

Dorn's face, cold stone, marked with blood and strobing shadows as he pulled the spear from his shoulder. Alpharius staggering, lashing out with a kick.

Another cut, scything from left to right. *Storm's Teeth* ripping armour like parchment.

Red gloss sheen on indigo-blue, and a demigod falling, his torso an open cave of meat and bone. The only sound the growl of *Storm's Teeth* and the clang as Alpharius struck the deck, and began to rise, strength defying the red ruin of his body. Dorn still had the spear in one hand.

'But... *victory...*' Alpharius gasped.

Dorn rammed the spear through his brother's chest. The tip punched through the power plant on the back of Alpharius' armour. Alpharius' mouth opened, his eyes wide. A great wash of blood poured from between his teeth. Dorn held him on the spear, the two so close that it seemed almost an embrace. The air around them was blurring like a heat haze as the blood struck the floor.

A high wail was rising with a coil of wind, which circled the pair. Alpharius' mouth moved, forming words. Dorn was still for a second, his eyes blank and black in the carved stone of his face. Then he pushed Alpharius away. Snakes of light writhed through the air. The primarch of the Alpha Legion staggered, mouth still moving.

Rogal Dorn brought *Storm's Teeth* around. The blade cut down through Alpharius' skull, and then tore free in a spray of blood and a detonation of light.

SIX

THE LAST PLANET of the Solar System turned in silence.

Explosions flashed.

Ships glittered like snow falling through a winter night.

Lives ended. They ended in small spaces with the air sucked away, in the roar of gunfire pouring through passages, in the spinning blackness where the last sight given to them was the blink of explosions and the light of stars.

And they ended in the heart of a moon, with the blood of a being who had been more than human, but less than a god, pooling on a floor of cold iron.

Rogal Dorn, Praetorian of Terra, looked down at the corpse of his brother. Around him, the world turned. Groups of warriors appeared in fresh flashes of teleportation light. They spread through the vault, as the doors crashed open and Kestros ran in, and saw a sight that none would have believed. A moment that should have stopped the galaxy on its axis. A primarch dead at the hands of his brother, within sight of the world of their creation.

But the Solar System turned without pause, unknowing or uncaring.

✠ ✠ ✠

IN THE LAUNCH bay hangars Myzmadra swung up through the hatch of a lighter, as Ashul kicked the engines to life and the machine lifted from the deck. She glanced back as the hatch began to shut. The entrances to the hangar bay were already glowing hot from where lascutters bored into them from the other side. It was over; she had known that from the moment she heard the warning cries on the vox, and the false thunder of teleportation displacement. The Legion had taught her many things: subtlety, brutality, the kind of courage that existed in silence. And it had taught her that survival was better than death in a failing cause. The lighter turned its nose to the fire-stained dark beyond. The Solar System was a large place, large enough to vanish into like a drop of water into a lightless pool, large enough to give her the sanctuary of shadow while she waited.

'Go,' she said, and the lighter shot out into darkness.

IN THE COMMAND throne of the *Alpha*, Silonius watched the holoscreens and felt the ship shake around him as it took fire. In a dark pit of his being, he felt an emptiness grow.

'Shield failure across ninety-eight per cent of frontal zones,' called one of the senior enginseers. 'Damage to dorsal and prow zones critical.'

'Do we have teleport range to the Hydra moon fortress?'

'Negative.'

The pulsing shake of impacts ran through him, as he watched the cascade of tactical information, force strength depleting across the fleet by the second.

'Signal to all forces,' he said. 'Full withdrawal.'

'By your will.'

'We are legion,' he whispered to himself. 'We are many, and we are one.'

IN THE LAUNCH bays of the *Lachrymae*, Sigismund stared at Rann as the armourers and servitors yanked damaged plates from his armour, and arc-torches sent plumes of sparks into the air as they repaired what damage they could. The damage to his body would be a matter for later; for now there was only this moment of transition.

'They are breaking?' he asked.

Rann nodded.

'Like dogs running from lions. Our ships are pursuing,' Rann grinned, scars cracking the mask of dried blood on his face. 'The slaughter will be great.'

Sigismund shook the armourers free.

'Bring me my sword,' he said.

AND THROUGH ALL the quiet, and the deafening echoes of the past becoming the future, the dead slipped away, one by one, to be forgotten or remembered.

In the dark, Archamus heard the sound of his breath. Short gasps, wet with blood, growing shorter and shorter. Darkness filled his eyes. He must have fallen again, he thought, though he could not remember. He could not move his limbs. There were sounds, close by and loud, but so distant that they seemed like silence.

What are you afraid of?

He felt a presence close by, and hands lifted his head and shoulders off the floor.

'Archamus?' said Rogal Dorn.

'Lord...' he said, and felt himself gasp for breath with the effort. 'You... You were wounded...' The blackness bloomed and rippled around him. 'Alpharius... What... What he said...'

'Lies, nothing more.'

'It... should never have come... come to this... I should have stopped him before it came to this... I failed you.'

'You have never failed me, my son.'

'I am... not your son, my lord... I am your praetorian.'

And then the last slice of the past fell into the future, and the darkness and silence became absolute.

EPILOGUE

Names

OMEGON WOKE.

He had never slept, had never dreamed, or felt the tug of mortal fatigue in all the days of his existence. Yet here he was, waking from black oblivion, the cold deck of the ship beneath him, the darkness of his arming chamber close about him. The pulse of the *Beta*'s engines was a distant rumble on the edge of silence. Coldness poured through his flesh. Moisture beaded his skin. He could taste blood in his mouth, thick and harsh with iron. His hands were numb, the fingers hooked as though grasping something that had vanished. He moved the fingers and then brought them up to his face. Sharp needles of pain prickled beneath his touch.

And then a new feeling came, crushing in its weight, undeniable in its truth even though he could not tell how it had arrived.

He was alone.

Words began to form on his tongue, but the door to the chamber was already opening. Arkos stood in the light from the door, his battle-plate humming as he stepped within.

'Lord Omegon,' Arkos said, bowing his head briefly, then stopping as his eyes fell on the primarch. 'Is there something wrong?'

'No... No. Is there...?' He blinked. Cold spirals of light wormed briefly at the edge of sight.

Alone.

'Is there word from Lord Alpharius?' Omegon asked, still looking at his hands. He could sense Arkos' frown without needing to see it.

'None,' he said. 'But there is something else...'

Omegon looked up, the muscles of his neck cold as they moved.

'Warmaster Horus wishes to consult directly with Lord Alpharius.'

'Do we have any indication of what his concern is?'

'No, lord,' said Arkos. 'Our sources within the Warmaster's court have become... unreliable.'

Omegon nodded, glancing over his shoulder as though he had heard something in the empty dark.

'Prepare the metatron,' he said. 'I will speak with my brother.'

Arkos nodded, his gaze lingering on his primarch for an instant before he left.

Alone.

Omegon armoured himself, the blind servitors bolting the plates of his armour over his flesh as the numbness in his hands and neck became a smouldering pain.

I am alone.

The knowledge rose through the coldness of his thoughts, certain and inescapable, though he could not say how he knew that it was fact not fear. He had never been alone, not truly. Even from the first spark of a thought in his consciousness he had known that he was one of many, a fragment of a greater whole, a piece of a great destiny. And now...

He walked from his armoury, the scaled and crested helm of the primarch of the Alpha Legion under his arm.

Arkos was waiting in the sealed chamber where they kept the metatron. Omegon nodded, and the attendants began to unbolt the mask from the one-time astropath's head. He watched as the famine-thin figure writhed, ghost light and smoke pouring from its mouth to form a shadow in the air above it, a shadow with a face and form. Frost spread across the floor and up his armour. He bowed his head even as the shadow turned to look at him.

What had happened? What was happening? What was he now?

And he realised that the words he was about to say would trap him for the rest of existence, the jest turned into mocking truth.

'I am Alpharius,' he said. 'What is your will, my Warmaster?'

ANDROMEDA LOOKED UP as he entered the cell. She sat on the top of the room's only table, grey robes blending with the low light, chromed hair tinged gold by the grimy light of the glow-globes.

'Are you to release or silence me, Kestros?' she asked, and tilted her head, eyes calm and unblinking. He let out a breath as the door sealed behind him. After a second she shrugged. 'I see you wear the cloak of the Huscarls now.' Her eyes moved deliberately over his armour, pausing on the laurel-wreathed skull, and the black cloak and the ice lion fur covering his shoulders. 'It suits you.'

She reached down to the tabletop beside her, picked up a cup of water that sat there and took a sip.

'Knowledge is a dangerous thing,' she said. 'How far has the purge progressed?'

He shook his head slowly.

'The primarch has ordered a systematic sweep of the system's defences, and reconfiguration of elements which were found wanting.'

'A purge is still a purge. The act itself does not change because you give it a different name. Have you found all of the Alpha Legion warriors and operatives who were embedded within the system?'

He held her gaze.

'Who knows. Some escaped. Many have been engaged and destroyed. A few may have taken refuge in the system.'

'They will have,' she said. 'There is no question of that, and that is presuming that all of the assets they placed here were activated. I would not trust that presumption if I were you.'

'We are being thorough,' he said.

'I am sure you are,' she said, and smiled coldly. 'After all, you are here. One more unfortunate factor to be dealt with. I don't blame you. Knowledge is poison, and I know too much. You can't let the knowledge of the full scope of their operation spread outside of those who have to know. That Alpharius was here in the Solar System, on Terra... Too much, too dangerous a truth, to let live.'

He nodded once.

'It is the primarch's will that no record be made of Alpharius' death, no word spoken of it. Even within the Legion, only he and the Huscarls know.'

'Denying Alpharius even the honour of memory in death...'

'Something like that.'

'And now you have come to me,' she said, and he saw the defiance flash in her eyes. 'Have you considered what they wanted, what they were trying to achieve? Were they a harbinger force, the first stage of an invasion? Or did they simply want to see what you would do? They have that now, even if it cost them their primarch. They have seen your strength and measured it. Knowledge is a weapon, remember.'

He breathed out, and the breath became a sigh of laughter.

'Which is why the primarch does not cast it aside.' She frowned and opened her mouth to speak, but he carried on. 'You are called to serve the Imperium, Andromeda. Lord Dorn has met with the Sigillite, and you can be of further use to us.'

'And suppose that I choose not to be of use?'

It was his turn to shrug.

'You will. It is your nature.'

She held his gaze for a long moment.

'Archamus was right to pick you,' she said.

He turned away and keyed a control beside the door. It clanked open.

'There have been developments,' he said. 'A fleet is approaching the system's outer sphere.'

She slid off the table and took a step towards the door.

'Another attack?'

He shook his head.

'No – the Khan has returned, with a great host of his White Scars. He comes to stand beside the Praetorian,' he said. 'The darkness grows, and the full force of the storm is just beyond the horizon.'

Andromeda smiled.

'You have the echo of a poet within you, Kestros.'

'That is no longer my name,' he said.

She frowned.

'Do you know what an oath name is?' he asked as he stepped through the door.

ABOUT THE AUTHOR

John French has written several Horus Heresy stories including the novels *Praetorian of Dorn* and *Tallarn: Ironclad*, the novellas *Tallarn: Executioner* and *The Crimson Fist*, and the audio dramas *Templar* and *Warmaster*. He is the author of the Ahriman series, which includes the novels *Ahriman: Exile, Ahriman: Sorcerer* and *Ahriman: Unchanged*, plus a number of related short stories collected in *Ahriman: Exodus*, including 'The Dead Oracle' and 'Hand of Dust'. Additionally for the Warhammer 40,000 universe he has written the Space Marine Battles novella Fateweaver, plus many short stories. He lives and works in Nottingham, UK.